VELVET PASSION

Amberlie walked through the damp labyrinth of the cave's corridors. She noticed a torch flickering to her left and headed toward the light. Entering a deeply shadowed rock-hewn room, she bumped into Tedric.

"Do you search for me, my lady?" he asked in a voice that sounded husky and melodious at the same time. He spoke so close to her ear that she felt his breath upon her cheek.

"I — am lost," she answered. In the semi-darkness, she caught his musty male scent.

"I am lost too, my lady, lost beyond all reason," he whispered, and his words slid warmly over her like black velvet. She felt his arms go around her waist, pulling her against him. Suddenly she'd ceased thinking clearly. It seemed the most natural thing in the world to lift her face and encounter Tedric's lips as he claimed hers in a kiss which was sweet and demanding . . .

D0733646

CAPTURE THE GLOW OF
ZEBRA'S *HEARTFIRES!*

CAPTIVE TO HIS KISS   (3788, $4.25/$5.50)
by Paige Brantley

Madeleine de Moncelet was determined to avoid an arranged marriage to the Duke of Burgundy. But the tall, stern-looking knight sent to guard her chamber door may thwart her escape plan!

CHEROKEE BRIDE   (3761, $4.25/$5.50)
by Patricia Werner

Kit Newcomb found politics to be a dead bore, until she met the proud Indian delegate Red Hawk. Only a lifetime of loving could soothe her desperate desire!

MOONLIGHT REBEL   (3707, $4.25/$5.50)
by Marie Ferrarella

Krystyna fled her native Poland only to live in the midst of a revolution in Virginia. Her host may be a spy, but when she looked into his blue eyes she wanted to share her most intimate treasures with him!

PASSION'S CHASE   (3862, $4.25/$5.50)
by Ann Lynn

Rose would never heed her Aunt Stephanie's warning about the unscrupulous Mr. Trent Jordan. She knew what she wanted—a long, lingering kiss bound to arouse the passion of a bold and ardent lover!

RENEGADE'S ANGEL   (3760, $4.25/$5.50)
by Phoebe Fitzjames

Jenny Templeton had sworn to bring Ace Denton to justice for her father's death, but she hadn't reckoned on the tempting heat of the outlaw's lean, hard frame or her surrendering wantonly to his fiery loving!

TEMPTATION'S FIRE   (3786, $4.25/$5.50)
by Millie Criswell

Margaret Parker saw herself as a twenty-six year old spinster. There wasn't much chance for romance in her sleepy town. Nothing could prepare her for the jolt of desire she felt when the new marshal swept her onto the dance floor!

Available wherever paperbacks are sold, or order direct from the Publisher. Send cover price plus 50¢ per copy for mailing and handling to Zebra Books, Dept. 4045, 475 Park Avenue South, New York, N.Y. 10016. Residents of New York and Tennessee must include sales tax. DO NOT SEND CASH. For a free Zebra/ Pinnacle catalog please write to the above address.

LYNETTE VINET

KNIGHT'S CARESS

ZEBRA BOOKS
KENSINGTON PUBLISHING CORP.

ZEBRA BOOKS

are published by

Kensington Publishing Corp.
475 Park Avenue South
New York, NY 10016

Copyright © 1993 by Lynette Vinet

All rights reserved. No part of this book may be repro-
duced in any form or by any means without the prior
written consent of the Publisher, excepting brief quotes
used in reviews.

Zebra, the Z logo, Heartfire Romance, and the Heartfire Romance logo are trademarks of Kensington Publishing Corp.

If you purchased this book without a cover you should
be aware that this book is stolen property. It was re-
ported as "unsold and destroyed" to the Publisher and
neither the Author nor the Publisher has received any
payment for this "stripped book."

First Printing: January, 1993

Printed in the United States of America

To Martin,
My own knight

Chapter One

Woodrose Keep
England, 1067

"I pray for the Lord to send misfortune to the murderer of my son. I pray that Tedric, the barbarian Saxon, knows no peace, that his tongue rots in his mouth—"

"Lady Julianne! Please, that is enough," a flustered Father Ambrose told the middle-aged woman, and nervously wiped the palms of his hands on his coarsely woven brown robe. "You mustn't pray for these things; vengeance is wrong. Look into your heart for forgiveness."

Clearly that was the wrong thing to say, and the priest was immediately quieted when Lady Julianne de Fontaine, a dour vision in black, rose threateningly to her feet. "Forgiveness? *Mon Dieu,* but you're like every fainthearted priest I've ever known, always preaching forgiveness. I forgive nothing and no one." Julianne sent a frosty-eyed glance in the direction of her daughter-in-law, who sat seemingly composed on the window bench. The dark-haired young woman glanced up from where she sat, stitching a linen headdress, aware of the older woman's attention.

No one would guess the depth of emotions within Amberlie de Fontaine at that moment. From earliest childhood, she'd been schooled by her parents to mask her feelings and be obedient to her elders. Neither Father Ambrose nor Julianne was aware that Amberlie's stomach muscles were bunched into knots, or that her mouth hurt from tightly clenching her jaws together for the last half hour, the length of Julianne's tirade. Instead they saw only her calm and pretty demeanor; the turmoil was inside, hidden behind doe-brown eyes.

Each day for the last six months Amberlie had been witness to Julianne's all-encompassing grief for Henri, and to her vindictiveness, directed against Henri's murderer. Amberlie had been forced to listen to the venom and dutifully, quietly agree that the Saxon named Tedric, formerly of Woodrose Keep, who'd lived within the very rooms which they now inhabited, should suffer for his crime. If not for the renegade Saxon, Henri would still be alive to flatter his mother and to impregnate Amberlie with the much-longed-for heir. But Henri was dead, and now Amberlie had done the unforgivable in Julianne's eyes. She had rescued this same Tedric's dim-witted sister from ravishment by one of Julianne's Norman soldiers. Such an action was tantamount to treason in Julianne's eyes, and Amberlie now steeled herself for the woman's expected onslaught.

Julianne pointed an accusatory finger at her. "Even my son's wife has forgotten him, Father. My Henri is dead barely six months, killed by the hand of a barbarian, and what does his widow do but protect his sister. I can not bear such treachery—"

"Maman!" Amberlie burst out in her native French tongue before Julianne had finished speaking, startling herself and Father Ambrose. She was not about to apologize for helping Edytha, the Saxon girl after her capture. "I hate Tedric of Woodrose! I care not for Tedric's sister, nor have I forgotten Henri. But allowing a knight to attack an innocent girl won't avenge my husband's death. Edytha is barely more than a child in years though she has a woman's body, and—and—you must realize her mind has not matured with her body; otherwise, she'd not have returned of her own volition to Woodrose." Amberlie faltered beneath Julianne's contemptuous sneer, wondering where the courage had come from to contradict her mother-in-law openly.

Julianne was a hard, cruel woman who'd never loved anyone but Henri. No matter how earnestly she'd tried, Amberlie hadn't won the woman's affections, and now she didn't wish to try any longer. She disliked Julianne, and always had, but she was under Julianne's authority, and that of Julianne's stepbrother, Guy de Bayonne, until King William could choose a new husband for her.

The hatred congealed on Julianne's face, and Amberlie sensed that the woman would erupt again, so she tried a new tack, one which not even Julianne could fault. " 'Tis our duty, *maman,* to protect this Edytha. She is a captive, and King William would insist she be treated with the fairness due all captives."

As Amberlie had realized, Julianne couldn't argue with such logic since it would never do to incur William's wrath. Too much rested on gaining his good grace; they must do so if Amberlie was to make a favorable marriage after her days of mourning had passed. A favored alliance would certainly bring more lands and heavily filled coffers for Woodrose Keep. If there was one thing which Julianne valued as much as her late son, it was wealth.

Julianne breathed deeply before turning her simmering gaze upon Father Ambrose, forgetting Amberlie. "I will have my revenge, I swear on my son's grave!" she declared, and rushed from the solar with her black bliaut swishing about her.

The priest smiled weakly in Amberlie's direction. "I fear the Lady Julianne spends too much of her time worrying about things she can do naught about. Henri is gone, but alas, 'tis a pity she has no grandchild to worry over."

Amberlie tensed and tightly clutched the mending needle. *"Oui,* a child would have occupied Julianne's time," she conceded softly as a slight flush colored her peach complexion and forced her to drop her dark-eyed gaze to the stone floor. Father Ambrose wasn't being intentionally cruel about her childless state, that she knew, for he was a kind and considerate man. But she was well aware that part of Julianne's dislike of her centered on the very issue of her barren state. God knows how much she'd have welcomed a child, especially now that she was in this strange and barbarous land without Henri and the parents whom she'd adored. She'd been married to Henri for five years before his death, and not once had she conceived. Despite Henri's youth, he'd been lusty in bed, so the fault couldn't have been his. It had to be hers. And this was one point to which Julianne constantly alluded: She hadn't done her duty to Henri and the de Fontaine family by providing an heir; she'd been a poor wife to one of King William's most noble knights. Clearly, she was to blame.

Ambrose gently touched her on the shoulder. "Forgive me, milady. I meant no disrespect to you."

Bestowing a gentle smile upon the priest, Amberlie nodded. "I know, 'tis only that *maman* stretches one's patience."

A laugh lighted up his face before it dissolved into seriousness. "Where is Edytha? I trust she shall come to no harm."

"I've placed her with Magda in the weaving room where she'll be safe. None of the soldiers will bother here there, not with Magda nearby." Magda was a serving woman who'd lived at the keep and served its former masters. She was also a large, formidable woman who'd guard her charge with her life, and Amberlie trusted Magda to keep the girl away from the knights.

"Good, good. The Lord shall bless you for rescuing her, pagan that she is."

Amberlie smiled tightly. "Will He, Father? Somehow I believe that the Lord is punishing me.

11

My parents both succumbed to a fever within days of each other last year, and my husband was brutally murdered before I could conceive a child. If I'm not being punished for something, then He has forgotten me."

"Have faith, milady. The Almighty works in wondrous and strange ways."

"Strange, yes, I agree. But wondrous, no, Father, I don't believe; otherwise, I'd not have been left to Julianne's and Guy's mercy."

"But — but — you aren't," Ambrose objected, clearly puzzled. "I'd thought Woodrose Keep was yours, now that Henri has died. King William gave the castle to him, didn't he, as a favor for joining his forces? The property passed to you upon his death, I'd assumed."

Amberlie laid aside her mending and nodded, "*Oui,* but though I own the keep and the lands surrounding it, I have no power. Julianne controls the coffers and her brother controls the knights. The servants barely listen to me for they're so frightened of Julianne that they obey her without question. I am useful to my family only as a pawn. They hope to persuade William to marry me off to the richest of his noblemen by using my property as the bait. After all, what man would wish to marry a woman known to be barren without such a lucrative inducement?" She lifted a hand to push a dark wisp of hair away from her face. "So you see, I have riches but no value in myself."

Ambrose stroked his chin in thought. "You underestimate yourself, milady. Perhaps it is through your property that you'll find true happiness, and the Lord's plan for you will come to fruition."

Amberlie laughed in amusement and rose to her feet. "My father once said that all clerics were soothsayers. I believe he was right." The priest grimaced, but bowed to her as she headed out of the solar and went to the weaving room to see how Magda was keeping Edytha occupied.

The serving women momentarily ceased their chores, glancing at Amberlie for barely a second longer than was necessary before realizing that the unwelcome intruder wasn't Julianne. Then they continued their work. Amberlie headed toward where Magda sat on a stool, attempting to instruct the very pretty Saxon girl in an intricate embroidery stitch. Edytha knelt beside the old woman, but appeared more interested in a tattered cloth doll she held in her arms than in learning anything about needlework.

"Now, now, Lady Edytha, 'tis important to know how to mend and embroider a garment, for one day you'll marry," Magda softly cajoled, and placed the needle in Edytha's hand. "Your husband will not want his clothes frayed."

Soft waves of blond hair swirled gently around Edytha's shoulders as she shook her head and raised large blue eyes to Magda. She clutched the doll tighter to her breasts. "Nay, 'tis only my Mercy I want to mend."

"And who is Mercy?" Amberlie asked, stopping near them. She smiled at Magda, though she knew the woman wouldn't return the smile. But Edytha sidled away from Amberlie and grasped Magda's hand when Amberlie made a movement toward

13

Edytha's wariness disappointed Amberlie, for she had hoped the girl would begin to trust her and, perhaps, they might be friends — which was a ridiculous notion since Edytha was a prisoner and not quite normal in mind, though she was perfect in body; the young girl was full-breasted and lushly pretty, with masses of pale blond hair hanging past her waist.

" 'Tis her doll," Magda replied without a hint of friendliness in her voice. Amberlie sensed that the portly woman didn't like her or regard her as mistress of Woodrose Keep. Most probably she didn't care for Julianne either, but since Julianne was the one who ran the household staff, and the person who meted out the punishments, no one dared to cross her or be openly hostile. However, none of the servants placed much value in Amberlie's commands, and at times they openly disobeyed her. But she never wished to berate them; cruelty wasn't in her nature. Still, she did regard the Saxons as barbarians and held them responsible for Henri's death. So why did she feel a need to win Edytha's affection when it was the girl's own brother who had murdered Henri?

"Your doll is very nice. I'd like to hold her sometime if you'd let me," Amberlie said pleasantly to Edytha, but gained no response. Apparently Edytha didn't remember that Amberlie had been the one to save her from the knight's unwanted attention.

"Lady Edytha is not a child," Magda stiffly reminded Amberlie. "One day she'll be forced to give up her cloth baby for real ones. I've looked after

14

her from the moment she entered this world. 'Tis my duty to steer her along the right path, now that her family no longer lives here. If not for the doll" — and here Magda shot a disparaging look at Mercy, who was still clutched in Edytha's hands — "then my Lady Edytha would never have wandered back to the keep on her own."

So the doll was the reason that Edytha had returned to Woodrose only to be captured. Amberlie had wondered why the girl had wandered away from her family and wherever it was they were now hiding.

"Is her family far from here?" Amberlie inquired, hoping somehow to break down Magda's silence. "If not, we can return her to them."

"I know not where they are, my lady," was Magda's icy but courteous reply as she turned her attention back to Edytha. Amberlie realized Magda was close-mouthed and much too loyal to the keep's former owners. Seeing that Magda had dismissed her, Amberlie left the weaving room only to encounter Guy outside the doorway. He smiled at her, as if he were genuinely pleased to see her.

A tall man, taller than Henri had been but not as stocky, Guy wore his dark hair, sprinkled with gray, brushed forward in the Norman style, while the back of his head was shaved to ear level. Though this style originated with King William and was worn by William's loyal knights, Amberlie thought Guy looked as if he wore a bowl atop his head. His red tunic covered muscular arms, indicative of his prowess with a sword. Each day Guy

15

practiced in the bailey, easily besting his opponents, each of whom, in his mind's eye, was Tedric the Barbarian.

Amberlie knew that Guy was obsessed with capturing the Saxon and ending his renegade activities. As long as Tedric roamed free, Woodrose Keep wasn't truly safe. Guy had already begun turning the simple stone keep into a more fortified castle with their knights' help.

"Safeguarding our prisoner?" he asked with a leer, standing extremely close to her, though there was enough room in the hallway to keep a distance. She smelled a potent wine on his breath.

"I was only checking on her, to make certain she is safe."

"Thanks to you she is, my dear Amberlie. Your stepping in to soundly trounce Sir Baudelaire with a candlestick was quite brave. 'Twas very naughty of the young man to try to take liberties with a lack-witted girl. Even now, he pays for his crime by being forced to clean the stables of horse droppings — and since the stalls are covered with the smelly mess, he shall be too preoccupied to bother our little Saxon."

"*Oui.* That is all well and good, but would it have been *less* naughty for a man to take liberties with a girl who isn't lack-witted, *mon oncle?*" Amberlie demanded, a fire growing within the depths of her dark eyes.

Guy chuckled and took her hand in his. His skin felt warm and moist and Amberlie suppressed a shiver. She disliked the way Guy looked at her most of the time, almost as if she were a morsel to

16

be served up at a feast. He'd always shown her lusty looks, even when Henri was alive. Since her widowhood, he'd grown bolder. "You're most charming when angered, *cherie,* but leave the discipline of the knights to me, *s'il vous plait.*"

He fastened his gaze upon her lips, letting it linger there a second too long before he heard Julianne shrieking for him below stairs. Grudgingly, he moved away from Amberlie, leaving to see what his sister wanted, for no one kept Julianne de Fontaine waiting.

Amberlie felt unbearably warm suddenly, almost suffocating in her need to get away from Julianne's condemning words, from Guy's lecherous looks. She needed to breathe free, and headed for the one place where she might be alone and collect her thoughts. Since she knew Julianne would object, she decided not to tell her. Instead she'd sneak stealthily away.

Chapter Two

"There she is, my lord. I told you 'twas her, and now I'm certain." A shaggy dark-haired young man nudged his tall companion and pointed to where the object of his attention stood in a crystal-clear pond, innocently washing her stockings. His low whisper had an immediate effect on the other man, whose shoulder-length blond hair was ruffled by a slight breeze. He nodded, and both men dropped to their knees and onto their bellies. The grass stained their coarsely woven leggings and the short cloaks over the tunics each wore, but neither minded. For some time they watched the young woman, hidden from view as they were by undergrowth and bushes that grew wild along the shoreline.

"Are you certain she is the one we seek, Wulfgar?" The blond man spoke quietly, a worried frown deepening the furrows of his brows. "I see no soldiers, no knights offering protection. Mayhaps 'tis a serving wench."

Wulfgar shook his head. "Nay, my lord, 'tis the

Lady Amberlie. I sneaked near the keep one day and old Magda pointed her out to me. Look at the black chemise she wears for proof that she is de Fontaine's widow and is still in mourning."

Tedric of Woodrose Keep looked. He couldn't help himself. He'd been unable to tear his gaze from the beautiful woman in the pond since he'd first laid eyes upon her minutes ago, or was it hours? Time seemed to stand still as he watched the voluptuous beauty bathing in the pond. Despite the ugly, black chemise she wore, Lady Amberlie de Fontaine was incredibly beautiful. He hadn't realized a Norman like her would be so captivatingly lovely.

Long hair, the color of black sable, spilled to her small waist in a riot of soft curls. The afternoon sunshine coated her skin in a peach hue, and somehow, though he was too far away to see, he guessed her eyes were a dusky shade of brown. She was surely possessed of the sort of perfect figure that could drive a man mad with lust. Even now, as she bent to rinse out the stockings, her full breasts strained against the wet chemise, her pouting nipples seeming to beckon for his touch. Tedric imagined how soft her breasts would feel clasped in the palms of his hands, how the nipples would swell against his flesh like dewy rosebuds . . .

"My lord, did you hear me?"

Tedric started, unwillingly drawn from his reverie by Wulfgar, who stared at him with a knowing expression on his face. Tedric flushed, aware that the man had read his thoughts. "Nay, what did you say?" he snapped disagreeably.

"I asked you if we . . . take her now," Wulfgar whispered with some hesitation at his lord's gruff reply. "Our horses are in the glade. Kidnapping her will be a simple feat, as long as the Normans don't realize she's gone. But we don't know for how much longer that will be. If you hope for Edytha's return, then we must act in haste."

Edytha. Aye, Edytha was the reason he was here, the reason he'd prowled the area of the keep since his poor sister's kidnapping by the Normans some two weeks past. Hope filled him that somehow his sister would be freed—and now here was the solution to his problem, thrust into his lap as if by a kind fate. He mustn't allow anything or anyone to distract him. Edytha's return was of the utmost importance, not a Norman wench, no matter how beautiful. Stealing another glance at the lovely Amberlie de Fontaine, Tedric hardened his heart.

His eyes deepened to a cold shade of blue, and he faced Wulfgar with an uncompromising stare. The scar on his left cheek, a reminder of his last skirmish with the Norman knight Guy de Bayonne, looked extremely white. "Aye, Wulfgar, 'tis time we strike at these Norman dogs."

Silently, the two men rose to their feet and headed for the horses.

Chapter Three

Lady Amberlie de Fontaine knew she shouldn't have come to the pond alone. She now wished she'd heeded her mother-in-law's earlier warning about leaving Woodrose Keep unescorted. Times were uncertain and perilous—especially now that Tedric the Saxon might be prowling the area.

But Amberlie hadn't intended to be long absent from Woodrose Keep. And she'd grown tired of spending all of her time indoors, cloistered like a nun from the glorious autumnal hues of gold and orange that blazed in the treetops like small sunbursts. She'd been eager to remove the itchy black mourning garb and allow warm sunshine to clothe her flesh.

At first, she'd reveled in the feel of the pond's cleansing water as the droplets slithered like satin across her skin. It had been so long since she'd committed an openly defiant act, except for helping Edytha, that sneaking away had seemed the greatest of sins, one she'd confess to Father Ambrose at eventide. If her mother-in-law discovered she'd disappeared, she would suffer at her hands as well. But her need to be alone, and away from Guy's treacherous smiles, had won out over her reluctance to challenge Julianne de Fontaine's domineering ways.

More than anything Amberlie needed to pretend that she was still in her native Normandy, that she'd not yet sailed across the Channel to join Henri in England — home to barbarians and their pagan customs, a land filled with murderous renegades — and that she'd not yet found herself newly widowed.

But as she stood in the shallow pond, Amberlie swallowed hard, suddenly sorry that she'd willfully stolen away from the keep and her Norman knights' protection. A cool breeze chilled her black-chemise-clad frame, her earlier pleasure waning as she noticed that the sun had already sunk lower in the western sky and no longer warmed her. Goose flesh rose warningly on her body, for suddenly she sensed she wasn't alone.

She ceased rinsing her woolen stockings. Her dark brown eyes covertly surveyed the densely forested shoreline. Lengthening shadows blended into the dapples of sunshine, somewhat obscuring her view of a solitary fawn, contentedly munching on a bit of shrub.

Listening for a few moments, she heard the guttural cadence of a frog nearby and the melodious song of a meadowlark coming from inside the forest. Instinctively she glanced to her right and left, and twisted around, but no one peered at her from any direction. Still, an uneasiness nagged at her and she knew it was time to return to the keep. Clutching her stockings against the bodice of her wet chemise, she hastily waded to the edge of the pond, to the spot where she'd earlier placed her clothes.

Quickly donning her black bliaut, she sat upon the grass to put on her wet stockings and shoes. In a tight little voice she chided herself in French. *"Mon Dieu,* there's nothing to fear out here, nothing at all. Our knights are nearby for protection. All I must do is scream and surely someone will hear me." But her own reassuring words didn't dispel her fear for she knew that, at this time of day, most of the men would be supping inside the great hall.

She silently blamed Julianne for upsetting her with loose, bitter talk about Saxon barbarians. Guy referred to them as renegades, traitors against the king, men who by their very defiance of Norman law begged to be hung. However, none had been spotted for months, none at all—not even Tedric the Barbarian, an odd occurrence in itself since Edytha was Tedric's sister.

Guy had ordered Woodrose Keep to be constantly guarded. The knights had been restless for battle, expecting Tedric and his renegade force to besiege the keep and rescue the girl. But days and nights had passed without incident. And as the soldiers had finally grown lax in their watch, Amberlie had sneaked away, eager for a bit of freedom. If only Guy and the knights would discover Tedric's hiding place, then she wouldn't have to be afraid to leave her home to bathe in the pond. Another reason to hate the loathsome Tedric.

During the last six months, he'd roamed the area with his renegade army and infuriated Guy, who'd controlled the keep's defenses even when Henri was alive. Guy was obsessed with Tedric's capture, an event to which even Amberlie eagerly looked forward. She longed to see Tedric of Woodrose, the former owner of the keep which now belonged to her, brought to her in chains like the murdering swine he was. She felt certain that Guy and Julianne would devise some sort of torture for him, something so hideous that he'd beg to die. But instead he'd die slowly as they watched—unlike the way Henri had died. But before he closed his eyes in death, Amberlie would make certain that he knew she was the widow of Henri de Fontaine, one of King William's noblest knights, the man he'd murdered in a failed attempt to regain the keep. Tedric would know how much she hated him and what he'd taken from her when he killed her husband.

The sky darkened with the first purple glaze of evening. Amberlie had finished dressing and pulled her mantle about her shoulders. Pushing her dark hair away from her face, she turned in the direction of the keep, her thoughts centered on the unpleasant confrontation with Julianne which she feared would follow upon her return home.

Treading down the forest path which led to the keep, Amberlie startled when suddenly she heard a horse snort, and glancing up, she found her way blocked by the largest black gelding she'd ever laid eyes upon. And upon the horse's back sat a man with shaggy blond locks that hung in disarray to his broad and powerfully built shoulders.

He appeared to be made of stone as he stared at her from his perch above her. Even in the dim twilight she discerned his eyes were hard like twin blue agates. She'd never seen this man before now, but instinctively she knew him. The servants told tales of Tedric the Barbarian, the golden Saxon who refused to surrender. He was known to be fierce and strong, a titan of a man who wasn't easily cowed by Norman authority — as Guy could clearly attest.

The scar on his left cheek stood out upon his bronzed complexion like a pale crescent and caused him to appear fearsome. A cold sweat broke out upon her forehead for all she'd heard was true. And now here he was, no doubt looking for a way to rescue his sister.

Her gaze traced the distance from the path to the keep, which lay beyond the forest. Not a great distance, but right now it seemed as if safety were an eternity away.

Be brave, she told herself, and prayed he didn't sense her fear. Her courage rose a bit when she realized that he probably didn't know who she was. Perhaps she could convince him she was a serving woman and meant him no harm. She looked at him again with a thumping heart, and was surprised when he inclined his head in a mock bow. He haltingly spoke to her in her native language. "Lady Amberlie, I'm pleased to finally meet you."

Her courage failed her, as she'd not expected him to know her identity. Maybe he was only guessing, she decided, and licked her lips. If only he'd move his damned horse out of her path so she could run to the keep! She needed time to persuade him that he was wrong.

"You are mistaken, *monsieur.* I am not the Lady Amberlie."

"No?" He didn't seem to believe her.

"Only a serving woman at the keep, *monsieur.*" Her breath came in tiny gasps her fear was so great.

"Ah, I see. You're a washwoman then?" His eyes glinted with devilish amusement.

For the moment Amberlie forgot her fear in her outrage. How dare this barbarian confuse her with one of the washwomen, who always smelled of lye and would spread their legs for any of the serfs and knights! "I am not a washwoman," was her cold and haughty reply.

"If you're not a washwoman, then what is your position at the keep?"

Amberlie thought quickly. "I serve in the great hall."

"Ah, a most highly sought-after post, but do you know what, *demoiselle?*" The barbarian leaned forward, his blue gaze running over her and causing fear to sweep anew through her like a sudden squall. "Never have I known a serving wench to speak such pretty, refined French or to wear linen of such rare quality. I think you're Lady Amberlie de Fontaine."

"No, no, I am not she." Any further words died in her throat as she quickly understood that he didn't believe her and had known all along who

26

she was. After his dark and dangerous assessment of her, she knew she must escape. She backed away and made a mental inventory of the landscape. To her left was the forest and to her right were brambles, but if she could make it through them, the horse would be unable to follow. Somehow she would stumble onto the path again and would rush to the keep. "I'm—not—she," she squeaked out again.

The golden giant smirked and spoke in his own savage tongue, the whole time moving the horse toward her. "You are Lady Amberlie, and you know who I am too, I think."

Hot anger surged through her for him to appear so sure, so arrogant. This was the man who'd murdered Henri and caused her such grief. Hate contorted her face. "I know who you are, Tedric the Barbarian! Murderer! Savage!" she screamed up at him, and was shocked when he laughed at her. Her hatred turned to numbing fear when he made a swiping gesture and succeeded in grabbing her around the waist. "No, let me go! Let me go!" She kicked out and hit the horse instead, startling the animal. Tedric retained masterful control of the beast and of Amberlie.

"Wulfgar!" Tedric shouted. His cohort appeared from the shadowy woods, and was instantly beside the struggling Amberlie. "Quiet her, man!"

"Aye, my lord." Wulfgar pulled a rag from his waistband and thrust it into Amberlie's mouth. Swiftly, he tied her hands behind her back with a rope, suffering a painful kick to his shin from Amberlie before Tedric hauled her onto the horse to place her in front of him. Wulfgar groaned and grabbed his leg. " 'Tis an ornery witch you've got, my lord."

"Lace her ankles too," Tedric ordered. "Be quick about it. Her screaming may have alerted the soldiers."

"Aye, my lord." Wulfgar quickly tied Amberlie's ankles together, but not without some difficulty. A number of times he was forced to duck or be brained by her feet. When he'd finished, Wulfgar climbed onto his own horse, a small brown mare.

By the time they'd traveled around the pond, night had fallen. Amberlie could see nothing in the gloomy darkness as the horse carried them deeper and deeper into the dense forest. She was aware only of the man who sat behind her and whose right arm encircled her waist like an iron tether. His breath fanned her cheek, and his chest felt like a stone wall behind her. The rag in her mouth made her feel like retching, but he didn't seem to care.

The stories about Tedric were true, she decided, and was unable to stop the shiver of terror which swept through her. He was a barbarian, a savage man who no doubt would beat and torture her—or make her submit to him in ways she cared not to dwell upon. Her body trembled from fear and an anguish unlike anything she'd ever experienced.

He forced her to make eye contact with him when he touched her chin and turned her face to his.

"I'm sorry for the rag, my lady, and that I must keep you bound. But you will obey me. Our time together will pass much more pleasantly if you do everything I demand of you. Do you understand?"

Amberlie glared at him, but her fear dissipated somewhat with his touch. The man had the audacity to believe she'd behave herself when she was a prisoner. But he left her no choice in the matter, having made the decision for her when he'd kidnapped her. Her life depended upon him, and dependence was something she related to very well. All of her life she'd depended upon someone else, first her parents and then later Henri and his family. She'd been raised to be dependent, though she longed to be free and do whatever she liked. But defying the barbarian Saxon at such a time as this would be very unwise. And most certainly, she wasn't stupid.

She made some sort of sound of acquiescence behind her gag, and was only too relieved when he stared away from her, for there was something in his heated gaze which unnerved her more than her fear.

He chuckled mirthlessly. "I think you understand only too well, my lady."

Chapter Four

Moonlight streamed through the leafy overhead branches, casting soft, lacy patterns upon the ground. Night sounds reverberated through the woods like ominous warnings of doom. Amberlie had never felt more alone or frightened. Her entire body trembled with her fear, and her shivering didn't go unnoticed by Tedric, who placed his mantle around her shoulders. This kind gesture surprised her, and she wondered if the man might truly be something other than a barbarian. "I don't wish you to become ill and die before I ransom you," he coldly explained. And that ended her kindly thoughts about Tedric.

It seemed they'd been riding a very long time. Amberlie's backside was sore and her legs were cramped. The ropes dug painfully into her wrists and ankles. The rag in her mouth had nearly choked her, and when they were a good distance away from the keep, her captor had removed it with a warning not to scream. Not that it would do her any good, Amberlie had decided, since her mouth was so dry she could barely utter a word.

Soon the sounds of human activity and voices alerted her, and she made a croaking noise through dry lips in the hope that someone would help her. Tedric laughed ruefully, and his blue eyes glittered. "Shout all you wish, my lady, but we've reached my hiding place." Amberlie's disappointment and embarrassment were obvious. Her fear intensified as the huge black horse came to a halt.

An old man rushed forward with a torch in his hand and quickly glanced at the three riders. " 'Tis our Lord Tedric and Wulfgar!" he shouted in relief to a group of people who waited by the yawning threshold of a cave. He grabbed the horse's mane and looked warily at Amberlie, but bestowed a large smile upon Tedric. "We've been worried, my lord. Your mother has been asking for ye. 'Tis glad we be to see no harm has come to ye."

"I'm fine, Wick. Tell my mother I've arrived safely and will soon speak to her." The old man nodded and headed toward the cave's entrance. Tedric lowered himself from his beast's back and reached for Amberlie. Wulfgar did the same, his fingers going to Amberlie's waist and encountering Tedric's powerful hands. "I can handle this wench," Tedric bit out. Wulfgar flinched at Tedric's stinging tone, but bowed his head.

"Aye, my lord. I meant only to help—"

"I know well what you meant. Keep your

31

hands to yourself!" Tedric ground out quietly from between clenched teeth. "This Norman wench isn't to be touched or trifled with. Make certain the men know she is my captive and that they'll answer to me if my orders are disobeyed."

"Aye, my lord," Wulfgar readily agreed, but his eyes lingered over Amberlie's face and figure as Tedric plucked her from the horse and slung her over his shoulders like a sack of coarse grain.

"Untie me so I may walk," Amberlie pleaded, but there was a note of authority in her voice which wasn't lost on Tedric.

"You give no orders here," he barked back, and walked into the cave, lighted by wall torches, and past a gaping group of his followers.

"I detest you," she hissed under her breath, her eyes level with Tedric's broad back.

"Your kidnapping was not done for love of you, my lady, of that I can assure you."

"And I have no love for you, you accursed barbarian. May you burn in hell!"

"Very likely I will, but for now my soul's salvation is not my chief concern." And with that retort left ringing in her ears, he proceeded to ignore her. People clustered around the tall and powerfully built man and his unwilling prisoner, whose long hair nearly dusted the cave's floor.

"Ah, so you've captured the Lady Amberlie, my lord," a man muttered, and guffaws of approval floated over Amberlie and chilled her with the hatred she heard. Tedric moved to an empty place in a corner and gingerly set her in a sitting position. Through a halo of hair obscuring her face, Amberlie realized she was the center of attention from a motley assortment of people. From what Amberlie could see of their plain dress, they were peasants. At least twenty faces curiously peered at her as if she were a rare pet on a tether.

"With her hair all a-tumble, she's not a fancy-looking lady now," sourly noted a woman whose two front teeth were blackened.

"Aye," agreed old Wick, who appeared from another part of the cave and placed the torch closer so all could get a better look at the haughty Norman lady. "Odd hair and skin coloring, not fair like us. The Devil himself must have spawned her."

"That's enough! Go about your chores!" ordered Tedric, and everyone quickly dispersed as if a king had spoken. He looked down at her with arms akimbo, until Amberlie could no longer stand his unnerving gaze.

"Stop staring at me!" she snapped. "I hate to be looked at in such a manner. I'm not an animal."

"Nay, but you think I am."

"I . . . do . . . not . . ."

"Aye, you do, but I care little what you think of me." Tedric turned and called to Wick, who instantly came at his master's summons. "Guard our prisoner well and see she is given food and drink."

"Aye, my lord."

"Untie her also."

"Aye, my lord." Wick didn't appear too certain about that command.

"I assure you, Wick, that she looks more dangerous than she is." Tedric noted Amberlie's disheveled state with an amused smirk before leaving his disgruntled captive with the wary old man.

Tedric made his way through a labyrinth maze of torchlighted corridors to find his mother. So far, the cave had served his purpose well. He'd known about the place since he was a young boy, having stumbled across it when he'd gone stag-hunting with his father. It was cut deep into the belly of a large boulder, hidden within the lush vegetation of the forest. There had been some evidence of Druidic worship, but for whatever reason the cave had been abandoned for a long time when Tedric remembered it after he and his family had escaped their home a year ago. The cave was now their haven and their home, at least until he could reclaim Woodrose Keep again. And God willing, that would be soon.

"My boy, my son." His mother's pale face brightened the second she saw him. She lifted her head from her pallet and held out her arms to draw him close. Tedric was dismayed at her frailness. Once, his mother had been hearty and smiled a great deal. Since his father's death at the hands of Guy de Bayonne, her grief had caused her to grow thin, and she very seldom smiled — even less since Edytha's disappearance. Yet her

34

eyes contained hope. "You've brought Edytha?"

Sorrowfully, he shook his head. "Nay, Mother."

"The Normans have her." It was a statement, not a question.

"I've been told she wandered near the keep and was captured," he said, forced to admit the truth.

His mother's frail form shook, and her voice broke. "How . . . will we get her back?"

"I've kidnapped Lady Amberlie de Fontaine. I plan to ransom her in exchange for Edytha."

Her chin trembled, her lips grew white. "Oh, Tedric, no—no—Edytha will suffer for this, if she hasn't already. You know she isn't like others . . ."

"Don't worry," he said soothingly, and stroked her graying hair. "All will be well, Mother. I promise you that Edytha shall be safely returned to us."

"But at what cost, son? I trust not these Norman dogs. Your father was killed by Lady Amberlie's family."

"Rest now, Mother," he said, and kissed her forehead, seeing that she was growing more upset. He wished now that he hadn't told her about Amberlie de Fontaine, but he had known word would filter back to her.

A slight movement from a dark corner of the cave alerted him that they weren't alone. A pretty woman with golden blond hair that hung to her waist in a braid came forward from the shadows and placed a light but possessive hand on his shoulder.

"I'll see to your mother, Tedric," Lady Glenna told him.

Tedric glanced appreciatively at the young woman whose comely figure beneath the blue kirtle always brought a smile to his lips. In the days he'd been away, he'd nearly forgotten how pretty Glenna was, how just looking at her brought a familiar heat to his loins. Not only had she taken care of his mother since they'd been forced into hiding, but she'd cared for him in more intimate ways — ways he intended to enjoy this very night. He was weary and worried, and he longed to lay his head upon her soft breasts. Glenna always knew how to ease him. A man would be proud to call her his wife. He knew she wanted him to honor their marriage pledge, but he couldn't marry Glenna now — not until he was lord of his home — not until he'd driven de Bayonne out of the keep.

Tedric gently squeezed her fingers. "Aye, 'tis grateful I am for your care of Mother."

Tears gleamed in Glenna's pale blue eyes. "Lady Mabel is like my own mother since, since . . ." Glenna couldn't go on. Her own mother's death still weighed heavily upon her. Shortly after the Normans had invaded the countryside, Glenna's home had been destroyed. She'd fled to Woodrose Keep with her widowed mother and a few servants. But her mother hadn't been strong enough, and had perished the day before the Normans attacked the keep.

"I know," he said sympathetically, and wished

his mother a good night. He got up and started away, but Glenna moved beside him and clutched at his arm.

"I shall bed with you later?" she whispered, and leaned lewdly into him.

Tedric nodded and lazily traced her sensuous lips with the pad of his thumb. "Aye, I'll be waiting for you."

When he saw Amberlie again, she was eating a piece of mutton. Even as she sat in a cave, her dark hair tumbling around her face in disarray and a fire within the depths of her brown eyes when she saw him, Tedric was struck by her elegant beauty. She wasn't beautiful in the Saxon way. He preferred his women to be blond and fair. But there was a great deal to be said for Amberlie de Fontaine's own peculiar loveliness. Her mane of hair resembled the finest sable, and felt that way too. Strands of her hair had blown against his cheek during the ride to the cave. He'd liked the feel of the soft tresses against his skin, and recalled breathing in the herbal scent from each strand. The fireglow emphasized her clear complexion, which was a shade darker than Glenna's—due no doubt to her French blood. Unwillingly, his gaze traveled down her body as he remembered how it had felt to have his arms around her as he guided the horse earlier. Her waist was tiny, just the span of his two hands. She was small in stature, not as tall as Glenna, but her body was better proportioned and her breasts more voluptuous. Though the ugly black bliaut covered her entirely, Tedric imagined that her breasts would be peach-tinged like her face. His hands ached to cup them, his lips longed to tease the dusky nipples . . .

"What are you staring at, barbarian?"

Her condemning voice brought him up short. Any lustful thoughts he harbored for his captive quickly dissolved. For all of her desirability, she was his prisoner. Her relatives had killed his father, a fact he mustn't and wouldn't forget. Even now Guy de Bayonne held his own sister captive at the keep. And there was no telling what horrors might have befallen his poor, simple sister at that swine's hands.

Tedric suppressed a shudder, but he grinned at Amberlie and came close to her, causing old Wick to back away. This haughty Norman wench needed to be put in her place and to understand she was at his mercy. "I'm staring at you, my lady."

"I do not like to be stared at," she retorted bravely, but found herself retreating toward the cave's wall, wishing she could dissolve into the stone. She didn't care for the way he looked at her, finding his eyes upon her more than disturbing. If this barbarian should take liberties with her, no one would help her for she was the enemy.

Tedric bent down and whispered in her ear, "I was thinking how unlike you are from a Saxon maiden, in dress and appearance."

"Bien, for that I am grateful." She wasn't cer-

tain he meant his words as a compliment, and she didn't care if he was pleased with her face and form. She looked away from him.

"My lady, your sharp tongue wounds me, but there is one thing you mustn't forget as long as you're my prisoner." His hand turned her face, and she found herself looking up into his eyes, which were now an indigo color. Within their depths was a touch of fire, and she didn't know if they burned bright from lust or reflected torchlight. "I will look at you whenever I please; as your captor it is my due. So shrink not away from me, for if I wanted you I would take you."

He stood up and ordered Wick to prepare a sleeping place for her. Amberlie was shaking so much that she could barely move, scarcely breathe. If the barbarian had wished to frighten her, he'd succeeded. She feared for her honor now, more than her life. Nothing prevented him from taking her by force. She was at his mercy, that she knew. But a primitive yearning had surged through her when he'd touched her. And this disturbed her greatly. How could she feel desire for a savage, the murderer of her husband? What was wrong with her? Was she losing her mind? Somehow she must fight her own perverse nature, though until that moment, she hadn't even known she was perverse.

He turned to walk away from her, but she could not allow him to believe he'd bested her. "Barbarian!" she called after him in a cool, clear voice that elicited shocked gasps from his followers. Twisting around, he stared at her with eyes so frosty that Amberlie shivered, but she wasn't about to back down or become an amenable prisoner because he'd touched her. She took off the green mantle he'd laid upon her shoulders earlier and hurled it at him, so that it puddled near his feet. "This belongs to you. I want nothing of yours to warm me!"

He raised an eyebrow in her direction. "Are you certain of that? 'Tis cold at night with autumn's chill upon us."

"I'd rather freeze than wear anything of yours!"

After a few tense moments, he bent down to pick up his cloak. "As you wish, my lady. I want only your happiness while you're among us." He gestured toward Wick and said in a loud voice for all to hear, "Give the Lady Amberlie no covers to warm herself when you prepare her pallet." Wick nodded, and jovial titters followed Tedric as he stiffly headed out of the cave.

"Ye heard Lord Tedric," Wick grumbled, and pushed Amberlie toward the spot in the cave where she was to sleep. "Aye, but you're a contrary woman. My lord didn't have to give ye his cloak to warm ye. But what's one to expect from a Norman but contrariness, I ask ye that." He shook his head as Amberlie sank onto a spot, covered only by rushes.

Glancing around, she noticed that the spot was secluded from where other people began reclining for the night. Wick settled himself about thirty feet away from her, and she wondered if she could escape without being observed. But she quickly realized that escape was impossible. There simply were too many bodies to cross over, and from what she could see, four men guarded the cave's entrance. There was no telling how many men Tedric had posted outside.

She sighed wearily, her fear giving way now to exhaustion as she lay upon the prickly rushes. She envied the soft-looking pallets upon which the others slept, especially the animal furs which Tedric's followers used for covers. Perhaps she shouldn't have goaded Tedric with his cloak. At least it had offered some protection against the chill, but she didn't want to take anything which belonged to her husband's murderer, even his kindness. So now, she had nothing but the clothes on her back to protect her from the cold night air which seeped into her bones, and had to content herself with her lot.

Amberlie was nearly asleep when she heard a woman speaking to Wick about her. Opening her eyes a crack, she saw a golden-haired woman whom Wick addressed as Lady Glenna. "Aye, that's her, my lady. That's the Norman wench Lord Tedric took."

"Norman witch is more like it with that black hair and olive coloring," Glenna jeered through thinly pursed lips, staring hard at her.

"She's a haughty one," Wick put in with a chuckle.

"Hmm, is she? Well, not for long, Wick. I'll

break her of her Norman airs very soon. Tedric has placed her under my control while he waits to ransom her."

"Ah, 'tis good, Lady Glenna, for she's a she-cat. Just ask Wulfgar. He'll tell ye how hard she strikes."

Glenna laughed coldly. "I've no interest in Wulfgar's tales, Wick. My interest is only in Lord Tedric."

Amberlie closed her eyes and feigned sleep, but she knew the Saxon woman intently watched her. Finally, she heard the woman's footsteps retreating away from her. Amberlie groaned silently to herself. Who was Lady Glenna and why did she hate her so much? She'd heard the dripping venom in her voice. Perhaps the woman viewed her as a rival for Tedric the Barbarian? But that was ridiculous. She'd sooner plunge a dagger through his savage, black heart. But suppose Glenna were Tedric's wife. Suddenly her own heart leapt in her chest at the thought of such a thing.

"Silly goose," she groused under her breath at her own wayward musings. She didn't care if the hateful man *was* wed to the icy Lady Glenna. Being wed to such a shrew would be just reward for his villainous deeds. He meant nothing to Amberlie, nothing at all. Yet she started to weep as her true situation struck her. She was a prisoner, a captive of a barbarian. No matter how much she'd hated living with Julianne and Guy, their company was much preferable to that of this motley rabble. She vowed that if she ever was freed from Tedric, she'd have her revenge upon him — somehow, some way. With that comforting thought swirling around in her brain, Amberlie fell into a fitful sleep.

Had he been too hard on her by denying her a coverlet? Tedric pondered this question as he paced outside the cave. The moonlight shone brilliantly, and he stared up at the sky, half-expecting the answer to come from the heavens. He'd learned over the years, though, that answers didn't come from above but from within oneself. And he feared he'd made a mistake with Lady Amberlie de Fontaine.

Kidnapping her had been a necessary evil. In the morning he'd send someone to the keep to arrange for the exchange of prisoners. And he had no doubt that Guy de Bayonne would be eager to have back his nephew's wife in exchange for Edytha. Tedric's spies at the keep had informed him that the treacherous Norman lusted after his beautiful kinswoman. Did Amberlie return the lust? Had she surrendered herself already to de Bayonne? After all, she'd been a widow for some months, and a woman so young and beautiful as Amberlie de Fontaine must have given into her body's cravings by now. She'd been married for some years and was used to physical pleasure.

Disgust roiled inside Tedric at the thought. What bothered him was why it mattered to him. Amberlie de Fontaine was a Norman — a relative

43

of the man who'd coldly murdered his father. Yet there was more to his perplexing feelings concerning her, more even than the fact that she believed he'd killed her husband. *Had* he killed him?

Tedric didn't know. On the morning of the initial attack, he'd called together his men and fought valiantly when Henri de Fontaine and his knights had invaded the keep. Guy de Bayonne had been among them. Tedric remembered de Bayonne, for he'd seen the man coldly and cruelly lance his own ailing father. He'd have killed de Bayonne then and there, but his mother, sister, Glenna, and the servants had already fled to the forests. His father was dead and beyond help. Since he knew what his father would have wished, his duty was clear. He escaped and led his people to the cave and safety until he could build a new army of men.

But he didn't forget Guy de Bayonne's ruthlessness. Tedric had led skirmishes against the keep for some months afterward. During the last one, de Bayonne had come close enough to slash his cheek in battle. Though a lack of arms had prevented him from retaking the keep, Tedric comforted himself with the fact that he'd lanced de Bayonne in the side before he and his men had retreated to their wooded hiding places, which included spots other than the cave. During that skirmish, Tedric had wounded a number of Norman knights, but he didn't remember killing Henri de Fontaine. Yet the man had died. Consequently, Amberlie de Fontaine hated him for it, and now he was feeling guilty for the death of a Norman dog, a man he didn't remember killing. He resented Lady Amberlie for the way he felt, since he knew he shouldn't feel any remorse. After all, he was a warrior.

"Aggravating woman," he mumbled, feeling the nighttime chill sting his flesh. Why couldn't she have been sensible and just kept the damned cloak to warm her? She was evidently too prideful for her own good.

His thoughts veered in another direction when he noticed Glenna coming toward him.

"Tedric, 'tis cold out here," she said.

"Aye, 'tis cold," he agreed, only partially happy to see her.

She put her arms around him and kissed him with such passion that Tedric groaned and pulled her closer against him. It had been so long since he'd lain with Glenna that desire ate away at him. "Can you warm me?" he said, breaking the kiss.

"Aye, come." Taking his hand, she led him into the cave, and they crossed over the sleeping shapes of men, women, and children. Tedric was in a haze of passion until he noticed Amberlie, asleep on the rushes. He saw that she shivered, but he moved on. She was a prisoner, his tender enemy. It wouldn't do for him to take too much notice of her.

But Glenna saw how he looked at Amberlie. "She's not very pretty," she said pettishly. Tedric only grunted, unable to say anything though he found his captive to be extremely beautiful. "May

I assume that she will be in my care on the morrow?" Glenna asked. "I'm certain I can find something for the Norman witch to do to earn her keep while she is here."

"Aye, you have my permission," Tedric tiredly drawled, missing the cruel smile that twisted Glenna's lips.

They walked into a small, secluded section of the cave which had been set aside for Tedric's use. Animal furs were piled upon the floor for comfort and warmth. Glenna smiled provocatively, and began pulling off her kirtle before quickly burrowing beneath the furs like a small golden cub. Tedric removed his clothes and followed suit, the chill in the cave dissipated beneath the furs and with the heat of Glenna's body as she pressed against him.

Her hands massaged his chest while he cupped her small breasts in the palms of his hands. How good it felt to be loved, he thought, to be looked at like a man and not an animal. Amberlie de Fontaine regarded him as an animal. He groaned. Why must he think about her now when Glenna, the woman he would most likely marry, was doing such wonderful things to him? Even now, her hands moved from his chest to his rib cage, and down, down they went to encircle his pulsating shaft. The pleasure was more than he could bear.

Tedric flipped Glenna from her side onto her back. Instantly she parted her legs for him, eager and anxious to feel his first thrusts. "Ah, Tedric, Tedric," she moaned and raked her fingers

46

through his shaggy locks. He poised above her, more than ready to invade her sweet warmth. But a mental picture of Amberlie de Fontaine, shivering on her bed of rushes, flashed through his mind. She'd looked so small and helpless, so unlike a hated enemy.

"Tedric, now! Now!" Glenna's pleading and writhing beneath him brought him back to reality.

He started to penetrate, but found his shaft had suddenly gone limp. Desire for Glenna disappeared, and he moved off her. "What's happened?" she asked, and in the torchlight he could see that her eyes were huge, round, and worried.

Tedric gave a short chuckle. " 'Tis obvious that I'm more fatigued than I thought."

"But this—has never happened before now," Glenna persisted, and Tedric wished she'd be quiet. " 'Tis a bull you are, my lord—usually." She eyed him suspiciously, biting her lower lip in contemplation.

"The bull is tired and needs to sleep."

"But—but—I've not been pleasured yet!" she blurted out. "Shall I seek my pleasure elsewhere, my lord?"

"Are you testing me, Glenna?" This time his eyes narrowed at her. "For if you are, then understand I share my woman with no man. But if you want to belong to someone else . . ."

"Nay, nay, Tedric. Only you." She huddled beside him in a state of misery, fearing that Tedric might not want her any longer. She'd dreamed of

47

a marriage to Tedric all of her life, and one day he'd regain the keep and she'd be mistress there. They'd have been married by now if William the Bastard had only stayed in his native Normandy. Glenna placed a warm kiss on his lips and smiled sensuously at him. "I'd like you to finish with me, my lord."

He knew what the lusty wench wanted, and it was little to ask. For months now Glenna had cared for his mother and sister without complaint — and she'd shared the furs with him whenever he needed a willing bedmate. It wasn't her fault that he couldn't complete their lovemaking, but the fault of that dark-haired Norman wench who'd so completely invaded his thoughts. He must stop dwelling upon a woman whose family had brought his own so much pain.

"Part your legs," he softly coaxed, and Glenna instantly and willingly obeyed. When he slipped his fingers inside of her wet warmth, she arched greedily toward him. So hungry was she that she found her pleasure almost immediately. Tedric had no doubt that Glenna would never be the type of wife to ignore her husband's physical needs. Her own needs were as great — if not greater than any man's.

"I love you, Tedric," she murmured against his chest minutes later.

He patted her arm. "Sleep now, Glenna." For some reason he couldn't tell this woman that he loved her, though it was expected they would marry. Otherwise, he was using her as his leman.

His own mother had asked him when he would marry Glenna. How unfair it was to the girl to bed her without spoken vows between them. She wasn't a common skullery maid to be toyed with at will. The blood of ancient Saxon kings ran in her veins, as well as his own. He knew his mother was right, and he'd eventually do what was expected of him. So far, Glenna hadn't questioned him about marriage, and he was grateful. But he reasoned it was only a matter of time before she did. Most women of quality expected marriage.

The wall torch had nearly been extinguished, leaving the place where they lay in almost total darkness. Glenna had moved away from him during sleep, her low, steady breaths barely audible. Yet Tedric, who'd slept for only a few minutes, was now wide awake and unable to reclaim sleep. He stared at the rock-hewn ceiling, recalling the huddled and shivering figure of Amberlie de Fontaine. He'd dreamt about her too. Damn the woman for intruding into his dreams!

Well, there was only one thing to do if he wanted to sleep. Slipping from beneath the furs, Tedric grabbed a large bear pelt and wrapped it around his waist, to hide his nakedness and to keep him warm. Then he took two sheepskin furs from beneath the pile where he slept, barely disturbing Glenna. Leaving the sleeping chamber, he trudged the distance along the cave's winding corridors to where Amberlie de Fontaine lay on the rushes.

A wall torch illumined his prisoner. She shivered, apparently unaware that during sleep she'd rolled off the rushes and onto the cold ground. Just like the silly woman, Tedric noted with a frown. She couldn't accept anything from him, even in sleep. Tedric threw a fur on top of the rushes and bent to gingerly pick up his captive and place her on the fur. For an instant she opened her eyes, but apparently was so deep in sleep that she didn't waken. Which was just as well, Tedric decided. He didn't want this ornery wench waking everyone with her shouts to be left alone. He'd look foolish if he were found offering her assistance when he'd given strict orders to the contrary.

Placing the other fur on top of her, he pulled it near her chin. His fingers brushed her cool cheek, and he realized how soft her skin felt, almost like velvet. She was so astoundingly beautiful with all that dark hair billowing onto the fur to frame her lovely, perfectly formed face.

He noticed Wick staring at him with a huge grin on his toothless mouth. Tedric quickly pulled his hand away, almost as if her flesh had burned him, and stood up. "I don't want my captive to fall ill before the exchange is made," Tedric lamely explained.

"Aye, my lord." Wick nodded, but the knowing grin never left his wrinkled countenance, even after Tedric had departed.

Chapter Five

"Wake up, you Norman witch. Chores need to be done before the morn is wasted." A toe rudely dug into Amberlie's side, causing her to come awake instantly. For a second, she glanced around, not certain where she was until she noticed Glenna, standing above her. Glenna roughly pulled the warm sheepskin from Amberlie. "There'll be no lying abed for you, my fine lady—not as long as you're in my charge."

Amberlie bristled with rage to be spoken to so harshly. She was so angry that she hardly noticed the furs which had warmed her during the night. How dare this Saxon woman speak to her as if she were a lowly serf! She didn't care if Glenna was Tedric's wife; she wouldn't allow the woman to get away with such ill treatment of her. From the malicious gleam in Glenna's eyes, Amberlie could see how much delight Glenna took in humiliating her, confident that Amberlie would do whatever she was bid, expecting a cowardly response.

Rising to her feet, Amberlie gritted her teeth

and forced a deceptively pleasant smile. "I've not had the honor of an introduction, my lady—if you *are* a lady." From across the cave, Amberlie heard Wick chuckle.

"Why, why—I'm Lady Glenna," Glenna sputtered, her face reddening with the implication.

"I take it you're not Tedric the Barbarian's leman." She was goading this woman too far, but for some perverse reason, Amberlie couldn't help herself. She realized she'd likely suffer for her impudence.

Glenna shook her fair head, malice hardening the blue of her eyes to ice. She raised a hand to strike Amberlie, but the sound of Tedric's voice cut through the cave like a sharply honed ax. "Glenna! See to your duties."

Glenna spun around and pointed to Amberlie. "Didn't you hear what this spawn of Satan said to me, Tedric?"

"Aye, I heard."

"Then she must be punished!"

Tedric towered over both women. From the cruel twist of his mouth, Amberlie could tell that he was less than pleased with what she'd said to his wife. Her surge of bravery dwindled away with his next words. "Lady Amberlie is my prisoner. If there is any sort of punishment to be meted out, I shall be the one to do it. Not you, Glenna. Now, please see to my mother."

"But . . . 'tis my duty to oversee this Norman witch . . . you said last night . . ."

"Enough! I know what I told you. I'm ordering you to see to Mother now!"

Glenna appeared to realize that further argument would be in vain. But before she left them, she shot Amberlie a contemptuous look. Amberlie knew this woman was far from finished with her. And it appeared Tedric wasn't finished either.

He firmly and masterfully grabbed her arm and walked her out of the cave. Fear grew as big as a peach pit in her throat. She could barely speak. "Where . . . are you taking me? What will you do with me?"

He didn't answer, but marched her through the throng of people who were outside, going about their morning chores, breaking their fast, and gawking at her. God, no one will help me, she thought in a panic. No one will aid me if this barbarian beats me — or worse. The image of this large and powerfully muscled man ravishing her was more than Amberlie could bear to dwell upon, even for a second. Henri had been a gentle lover, a sweet youthful lamb. This lion of a man could no doubt crush her with his bare hands, rip her apart with his sex. She'd be dead before he finished with her.

"Please, you must listen to me. I'm sorry for what I said to your lady wife. I'll apologize to her. But . . . 'tis sorry you'll be for harming me . . ."

He pulled her up short, and would have knocked her off balance if his hand had not retained a firm grip on her arm. "You're in no position to threaten me."

Amberlie winced at the growling sound of his voice. At that second, he truly resembled a lion with his wild mane of hair framing a lightly stubbled face. And his eyes were such a clear, penetrating blue that she could see her own terrified reflection within them. She hated showing her fear, but most of her life she'd lived under others' domination, afraid of her own shadow and always doing as she was told. Yet something surfaced within her for the barest second, something akin to defiance and a boldness she'd seldom experienced. This man was quite capable of torturing her and raping her — even killing her. But she'd be damned if she was going to go to her doom like a docile ewe.

She breathed hard, her hands clenching. "You are bigger than I. You may do whatever you will, *monsieur,* but I shall fight you with bared teeth and sharp claws."

"Ah, 'tis a she-cat you would be," he returned.

She nodded, her tongue feeling thick and heavy in her mouth. Suddenly, he threw back his leonine head and gave a deep laugh. Amberlie was more baffled than embarrassed and annoyed when the Saxons began giggling and laughing among themselves, for she realized she was the object of their amusement. "Why does everyone laugh?" she cried.

"Because, Lady Amberlie, even a vicious tigress must eat and wash herself sometimes."

Amberlie was still puzzled, but he pushed her toward a group of his followers, who parted to reveal a campfire from which the scintillating smell of frying pork wafted over her and caused her mouth to water.

"Sit," Tedric ordered, and Amberlie instantly sat upon the ground. Tedric leaned his large frame against the trunk of a spreading oak tree whose leafy limbs offered cover from the early morning sunshine. Instantly, a Saxon woman served up two plates of the pork with freshly scrambled quail eggs to both of them. Someone grudgingly placed a cup of cool goat's milk in Amberlie's hand. "Eat," Tedric commanded, but Amberlie had already started chewing before Tedric had even spoken, so ravenous was she. "You see," he said a few seconds later with a knowing smile, "even a she-cat gets hungry and will eat from the hand of whoever deigns to feed her."

A blush suffused her face. The hateful man had never intended to harm her — only to see that she ate. Then why didn't he just tell her from the beginning instead of trying to frighten her? Or was she the one who'd frightened herself? But she wouldn't allow him to think he'd gotten the best of her. "Barbarian," she hissed under her breath before taking a deep swallow of the milk. Apparently he'd heard her for she noticed that he cocked a wary eyebrow at her, and she suppressed a delighted smile.

When she'd eaten her fill, Tedric motioned to her to rise. Once again, he took her by the arm, and this time he led her away from the others, into a secluded glade of the forest by a small pond. Amberlie glanced wildly around, aware that now they were very much alone. Did he plan to rape her here?

"I'll not stay here! I'll fight you, by God I swear you'll not take me easily! I'd rather die than be raped by a barbarian!" Amberlie's fear caused her to panic and she tried to wrench away from Tedric, but his superior strength kept her arm locked in his hand. Her fear was so great that she didn't realize that Tedric was silently staring at her, watching her flail at him like a startled hen whose chicks were in danger from a fox. She came at him, her hand curled into a claw, ready to rake her nails across his skin and scar his other cheek. But in one lithe gesture, he grabbed her and turned her so that her back was against his chest.

Her breasts heaved, her breathing was labored. Her attack had been like throwing stones at a mountain; Tedric wasn't the least daunted. His breath wafted across the back of her neck, sending odd shivers down her spinal column. He spoke, his voice an angry growl beside her ear. "I'm not an easy target like Wulfgar for your venom, nor am I easily swayed by a pretty face and figure. If I'd wanted you, my lady, then I would have bedded you beneath the furs with me last night. I'd not have had cause to rape you for you'd willingly have stayed."

"You arrogant, conceited—"

"And that snippish Norman tongue of yours would have been put to better use."

Amberlie gasped. As a widowed woman, she understood full well what this barbarian meant and what he'd have made her do to him with her tongue. "I won't . . . pleasure . . . you in that

56

way." She could barely say the words, the thought was so abhorrent.

"Which way is that, my lady?"

"With . . . with . . . my tongue." She felt like she was going to faint.

"I don't understand what you mean, my lady," he answered, all innocence. "I meant only for your tongue to taste the sweet apples which grow wild in the forest. Is there some trick Normans do with their tongues that Saxons do not?"

He was making sport of her, and Amberlie felt her entire body redden. Even the back of her neck felt warm, and when Tedric turned her to face him, there was a definite twinkle within his blue eyes. "I brought you here so you could bathe . . . and take care of personal matters." He gently removed pieces of limp straw from her hair, souvenirs of her night upon the rushes. Amberlie moved back, suddenly very much aware that this was no ordinary man; Tedric was a man whose very touch caused a slow burn to begin in her blood—a condition for which she had no explanation.

"How do I know you won't look whilst I am bathing?"

"You don't, my lady, for I'm a mere man and you're a beautiful woman. But I saw you bathing near Woodrose before I kidnapped you, and 'tis somewhat familiar I am with your loveliness." That remark sent a scarlet flush over the length of her body. Amberlie had forgotten that he'd been spying upon her.

"I trust you will allow me some privacy."

"As you wish, my lady." Tedric bowed deeply and went to sit beneath the spreading branches of an oak tree. He gazed up at the morning sky with such thoughtfulness that Amberlie wondered if he might be praying. She dismissed the notion. Tedric was a barbarian and a pagan, no doubt having partaken in the pagan revelries she'd heard about. Tales abounded among the knights about pagan orgies where the Saxons danced naked in the moonlight, the women mating with the men like wild beasts only to produce bastard children nine months later. Had Tedric danced naked with a willing wench? Had he mated with a woman beneath the wild moon?

She groaned aloud. She had to stop these sinful thoughts. Only God knew the reason for them. As soon as she was returned to Woodrose, she'd seek out Father Ambrose and confess—somehow she'd rid herself of the wanton images of Tedric the Barbarian or go mad in the attempt.

Out of the corner of her eye, Amberlie watched Tedric until she felt certain he wasn't going to accost her. A hedge offered cover while she removed her mantle, bliaut, shoes, and stockings. As she entered the water, she wore only her chemise.

The water felt wonderful and refreshing. She washed away the grime from her night spent upon the dirty rushes and wondered who had kindly covered her with the sheepskin. Perhaps it had been Wick. She'd thank him at a later time. She knew it hadn't been Tedric—the conceited bully!

58

Dipping beneath the slow-moving stream, Amberlie suddenly realized that this must be the same stream that bypassed Woodrose Keep, the very same stream in which the serving women washed the clothes, the same one from which Tedric had snatched her the day before. All she had to do was follow the stream's current and find her way home, an easy enough feat.

But how to escape without Tedric seeing her?

Casting another look in his direction, she saw that he appeared to be dozing. Such a silly trick, she decided. Tedric wasn't dim-witted enough to actually be sleeping while his prized prisoner bathed. He'd taken a great risk in kidnapping her, but he wouldn't regain the keep because of it. The reason behind her kidnapping was unimportant to her. All she wanted was to return home and bring down this renegade Saxon with her own knights. But how?

Wading toward the opposite shore and attempting to run would be a wasted effort. She doubted that she'd get very far before Tedric caught up to her, for apparently he was quite familiar with the woods. Pretending to be involved in her washing, she kept a wary eye upon her captor while her mind revolved like a cart's wheel until she found the answer.

She'd simply have to drown.

Chapter Six

Amberlie noticed a wild tangle of vines to her left, a perfect hiding spot from Tedric. All she had to do was casually wade in that direction, quickly bend down, and never surface again. At least, she wouldn't surface *there*. She'd swim back to where she'd entered the stream while Tedric looked for her. Then while he continued searching for her, she'd swim in the opposite direction until she reached Woodrose Keep. As a child, she'd learned to swim in the treacherous Channel that separated France from England. She was certain she was up to swimming against this lackadaisical current.

Yes, the plan would work. It had to work, but she mustn't seem too eager to escape. She must put him off guard and not allow him to believe that she had a plan in mind. He must think that she was a silly female without a thought in her head. She ceased bathing and called out to him, "You're peeping at me!"

Tedric fully opened his eyes. "Aye, but I wasn't staring at you. There is a difference."

"How smug you are! I see no difference, and I don't like it. I wish for some privacy." The whole time she spoke, she moved towards her left while Tedric remained seated, apparently not realizing what she was doing. Perhaps he was truly dense. She found herself strangely disappointed at the knowledge.

The vines grew thicker. Her figure disappeared behind the wild cluster. Now was her chance!

Amberlie let out a false scream and dove beneath the water. Tedric had already risen to his feet. By the time he'd splashed into the stream, she was already swimming past him underwater like a slippery eel and heading in the opposite direction. For a second, she surfaced below where she'd entered earlier and caught a breath. She knew she mustn't let Tedric see her, but she had to see what he was doing. Just as she'd thought, he dove near the vines, searching for her, frantically calling out to her. For a moment, she felt almost guilty not to be drowning, he appeared so concerned. But she had to prevent him from regaining her home. Woodrose Keep belonged to her!

With a self-satisfied smile, Amberlie took another breath and dove beneath the surface, feeling sorry for Tedric. It seemed he'd been easily duped.

Vines grew even thicker in spots along the shoreline where she swam. Their roots extended beneath the water and made passage somewhat precarious and dangerous. Many of the vines grew quite tall, their branches fanning out like a bear's talons to taunt and snag any debris floating past. It was Amberlie's destiny that her hair snagged on an underwater branch.

She made a vain attempt to pull away, but her effort was useless. A long strand of hair had wrapped around the branch, and she couldn't seem to untangle it. It felt as if her scalp were pulling free each time she tried to extricate herself. She couldn't rise to the surface, trapped as she was under the water. She tried to remain calm, but her lungs started to burn. Only seconds were left. She couldn't hold her breath for much longer. If only she hadn't acted on impulse, but somehow had planned her escape better. If only Tedric would look this way!

Her lungs felt like they would burst, and still she worked feverishly to untangle her hair. She wouldn't give up—she couldn't give up. She wouldn't drown here in less than five feet of water. Though not a boy, she had won her father's hard-earned praise by swimming treacherous currents when she was barely ten years old, had won her father's love by her own daring.

She wouldn't die like this, she didn't want to die now! She was too young for the grave, too much alive to give in to death. More than anything she wanted children, and she would accept any husband whom King William chose for her—even an elderly, toothless man. Gratefully she would marry as long as God allowed her life. Yet she couldn't hold her breath for much longer, and finally she swallowed water.

She stopped struggling. A strange lethargy seized hold of her and she began to drift with the current. Death was but seconds away, and suddenly she no longer feared it but almost welcomed it. Moments before her eyes closed, she was vaguely aware of Tedric, who bumped against her. He grabbed her around the waist with one hand while his other brandished a blade and swiped at the strand of her hair, freeing her from the branch. Then he lifted her high above the water's surface and swiftly waded to shore with her in his arms.

Tedric placed her face down on the soft grass and pushed the water from her lungs. Immediately, Amberlie regained consciousness, nearly choking on the water she'd swallowed as she regurgitated it on the ground. *"Mon . . . Dieu,"* she whispered brokenly, her throat aching with the effort. Never in her life had she felt so horribly numb. Her entire body shook so hard she couldn't control it.

"How are you feeling?" Tedric asked in concern, rolling her onto her back after she'd finished coughing. She nodded weakly, unable to answer him since her teeth chattered so badly. He grabbed her mantle from where she'd left it and wrapped her in its warmth. Held against him, Amberlie heard the wild thump of his heart against her ear and realized he was shaking too.

He stroked her wet hair, pushing it away from her face. Despite her recent brush with death, she felt safe, incredibly protected, and didn't ponder why that should be so.

His hand gently turned her face to his and she saw eyes which were now an angry blue, though they also bore signs of genuine concern. " 'Twas foolhardy of you to try to escape."

"Why?" she croaked, her throat burning. "Because I outwitted you?"

"Because you could have drowned!"

"I've always been an excellent swimmer. If not for that branch—"

"You'd be dead," Tedric said matter-of-factly. She realized that he was right, but she wouldn't admit to it.

"I'd not have been forced to escape if you hadn't kidnapped me," she argued.

Tedric nodded. "Aye, 'tis true. Yet you belong to me until I see you safely returned to your people."

"I belong to no one, especially not such a barbarian as yourself!" Amberlie attempted to sit up, but she fell back against Tedric's strong chest as dizziness overwhelmed her.

"Indeed, you're an ungrateful wench. I saved your life, and you're in my debt until I decree otherwise. Right now, you're weak as a chick and entirely in my power. I can do whatever I choose to you, and you cannot resist."

Despite her weakened physical state, she shook her head in denial. "You're a ruthless man who will stop at nothing to have his own way. I'm not a docile ewe who'll follow after you. I won't do what you want, no matter what it is!"

He considered her a moment, and then before she could protest, he lowered his head and kissed her. His mouth felt warm and alive against her cold, trembling lips. It seemed the kiss instilled life into her, bringing with it a strange, sweet sensation which was more heady than any wine she'd ever drunk. Moaning lowly, she clung shamelessly to his wet tunic, abandoning herself to the reckless and mind-drugging kiss that robbed her of her good sense.

Tedric broke the kiss first, and looked down at her for long moments. Amberlie stared back, her eyes wide and perplexed, an awful fear stealing into her soul that somehow she'd enjoyed that kiss when reason decreed otherwise. This was the man who'd slain her beloved husband, who might have taken all chance of bearing children away from her when he'd coldly murdered Henri. She hated this man and wouldn't allow herself to feel anything for him—even her own disgusting lust.

"I shouldn't have done that, my lady. I apologize," he said coldly just when she thought she'd go mad with the silence between them.

Splotches of color stained her cheeks because he'd been the one to end the kiss, not she. He didn't care about her as anything other than a hostage, and had kissed her only to prove he possessed power over her. Absurdly, she felt that she should apologize to him because she'd enjoyed the kiss—a very great sin in her mind. "Apologize to . . . your wife . . . for kissing me," she whispered brokenly.

"I have no wife."

"But is not Glenna . . ." She broke off at his sardonic smile, detesting herself for even asking about the woman, as if she cared if this vile Saxon was wed or not. Her flush deepened, and she glowered at him for making her respond to him like a whore.

"Glenna is my betrothed," he said without emotion.

"Then I suggest you kiss and embrace her, for I hate your very touch!" she spat out like a hissing kitten.

"Then mayhaps you should release my tunic; otherwise I shall think you prefer a Saxon barbarian over your gentle Norman knights."

Amberlie realized that her hands were still curled around the wet cloth, her fingers brushing against the matted hair on his chest. Hurriedly, she let go, almost as if she'd been burned, and pushed resolutely away from him. Slipping out of Tedric's embrace like an eel, she sat up, grateful that the landscape had ceased spinning. Pulling her gown toward her, Amberlie turned her back and threw off the mantle before placing the dark bliaut over her head.

"May I offer assistance?" she heard Tedric ask behind her, but she ignored him. Finally, when she'd put on her stockings and shoes, she carefully made it to her feet, more than a bit surprised and shocked to find Tedric's hand on her elbow. "I want only to return you safely to your family," he offered in explanation.

"I want only to be returned! Why have you done this to me?" She blinked back tears, wanting only to retreat to the keep, away from the odd sensations this man stirred within her each time he touched her.

Tedric sighed and rubbed his forehead with his hand before looking toward her with a black scowl. "Guy de Bayonne holds my sister. I apologize for any discomfort you've experienced at my hands, but I'm not sorry for kidnapping you. You're my last hope, and I will use you in any way necessary to get her back."

Amberlie had no doubt he would. Tedric was widely reputed to be a conscienceless and formidable foe, as Guy in particular maintained. But he seemed to love his sister very much and be worried about her. He knew nothing of her near ravishment, and Amberlie saw no purpose in telling him. But if she reassured him that his sister was safe and well treated, then he might let her go.

It would be so simple, Amberlie thought, to tell Guy to send Tedric's sister to him. Since she was the lady of the keep, Guy should obey her, but then again, she couldn't remember a time when Guy or Julianne had ever listened to anything she said. Julianne considered herself to be the mistress and Guy the master. Yet she clung to the hope that Tedric would release her if he believed that she could send the girl back to him. "Your sister has come to no harm," she hastily assured him. "She is quite safe. Release me, and I will beseech my kinsman to let her go."

"Nay, my lady."

"But . . . why not? You have my word."

"I trust not a Norman's word. Not even yours. So beg me not to release you."

"I beg nothing of no one, certainly not of you!" she haughtily told him, and threw off his hold of her arm. She marched back to the cave without a second glance at him, but she knew he followed her.

For the rest of the day, Tedric personally guarded Amberlie. He realized that she might attempt an escape again, and could be successful if she wasn't carefully watched. He blamed himself for her aborted escape that morning, acknowledging that he'd underestimated her. Certainly, she wasn't the docile creature he'd first thought, but instead was rather fearless. At least she didn't seem to be frightened of him, only contemptuous, and this bothered Tedric more than he cared to admit.

He'd given her simple chores to do, such as helping the women with the cooking and washing, but he very seldom was far away though he pretended to be absorbed in grooming his horse or training his men for battle. He knew what she was doing every second and to whom she spoke—not that anyone truly spoke to her, of course. The women cast cold stares in her direction, speaking only to each other, which was just as well, Tedric decided. He didn't need Amberlie de Fontaine winning the hearts of his people—or his own heart. And if he wasn't careful, the Norman witch was going to claim it.

Never had he intended to kiss her, or expected her to respond to him. He'd wanted to punish her for her escape attempt, to let her know that he could do what he wished to do since she was his prisoner. But he wouldn't physically harm a woman, even one who was his enemy, and a beautiful enemy at that.

Despite Tedric's vow not to be swayed by Amberlie's loveliness, he found he truly couldn't take his gaze from her for long. In his eyes, she was the most beautiful woman he'd ever seen. There was something exotic about the color of her eyes, the way her dark-winged brows arched haughtily whenever she deigned to glance at him. And her mouth was perfectly shaped and perfectly kissable; her lips had felt like velvet and tasted sweet like spring berries. He'd never forget that first kiss, and he laughed dryly to himself, because there wouldn't be another one. He didn't trust himself to stop kissing her, and knew that just to touch her was dangerous.

But soon, his torment would end; it had to end. That morning he'd sent three of his trusted men to the keep to speak to Guy de Bayonne about the exchange of prisoners. It was highly possible that de Bayonne could hold his men, but Tedric thought it unlikely. The man would have to be mad to place Amberlie de Fontaine in any more danger, and Tedric had heard the rumors that his cruel enemy lusted after his dead nephew's widow. Tedric believed that Edytha would be released, but his heart lurched in his chest as he realized he'd be forced to return Amberlie to de Bayonne. He needed to forget, to feel nothing for his captive. The sooner he parted with her, the better off he'd be, he resolutely decided—and swore under his breath.

"Watch your shoulder!" Tedric shouted in aggravation to one of his men who wielded an ax at an invisible enemy. "If you were in combat with a Norman, you'd have lost your arm by now!"

Amberlie heard Tedric's shout and looked in his direction. He oversaw a group of men who parried and thrust in mock battle, and she realized he had their complete attention. He was their leader, the man whom the displaced Saxons followed and to whom they looked for guidance. Even at a distance, Tedric was a huge man, wild in appearance, but there was something about the way he held his leonine head that reminded her of a king amongst his doting subjects, rivaling even King William himself. Despite her hatred for him, she watched in fascination how the muscles in his upper arms strained, how he stood with legs wide apart, his calves strong and thick, but yet lithe of limb. He was a magnificent-looking man, she decided silently, but felt the sting of her own traitorous thoughts when his cool blue eyes met hers. Hurriedly, she turned her head away and went about stirring a pot filled with barley soup.

" 'Tis time for Lady Mabel to sup," said one of the women, and handed a wooden bowl to Amberlie to fill. "Make yourself useful and bring it to her." No please or thank you was forthcoming, and Amberlie grimaced at the woman's rudeness. But, strangely, she was becoming used to it, realizing that her situation here was little different from her situation in the keep, for the servants there thought more of Julianne than her.

Carrying the evening fare, Amberlie made her way to Lady Mabel's side. Glenna's cold gaze swept over her, and she'd have rudely swiped the bowl from Amberlie's hands if Tedric's mother had not stopped her. "I should like very much if Lady Amberlie would tend to me," Lady Mabel said softly. "You may go now, Glenna."

"But I cannot leave you alone with this Norman witch, my lady," Glenna protested hotly. " 'Tis foolhardy."

Mabel smiled pleasantly but her tone was stern. "I trust the Lady Amberlie shall not harm me or wish me ill. Will you, child?" Mabel asked Amberlie with a probing look.

"I would not harm you, my lady."

Mabel seemed satisfied, and gestured toward Glenna to leave them alone, something Glenna did with little grace, sending a black scowl in Amberlie's direction before she left. "You mustn't mind Glenna, my dear. She's quite possessive of me but is truly harmless."

Amberlie wasn't certain of that, but she warily smiled at the older woman and sat on the rushes beside her to hold the bowl while Mabel daintily sipped the broth. This was the first time she'd met Tedric's mother, and she could see that Tedric resembled her in the strong chin, the probing eyes. But where Tedric's features were angled and chiseled, Mabel's were softly refined. Finally, after a few more sips, Mabel waved the bowl away.

"You've hardly finished, my lady," Amberlie noted.

" 'Tis enough," Mabel said dismissively.

"Is there anything else I may do for you?"

Mabel squeezed Amberlie's hand. "Aye, tell me how is my daughter. Is she well? I fear so for her."

"She is well," Amberlie reassured her. "Old Magda keeps close watch over her."

"Magda, you say? Aye, 'tis good. She is trustworthy." Mabel's features relaxed some but her eyes were guarded. "How do I know you're telling me the truth? Edytha isn't like others . . . and she could have come to great harm in a nest of Norman vipers."

"To my knowledge, my lady, no one has harmed your daughter," Amberlie said more harshly than she'd intended. These Saxons must believe she and her people were some sort of demons straight from hell, without thought for other people. Yet, if she'd lived through what Mabel and the others had apparently lived through, then she'd probably feel much the same.

Mabel's mouth trembled and tears filled her eyes, turning them from a wintry blue to the color of a clear lake. "I'm sorry, but 'tis hard for me. Edytha is my only daughter and . . . different."

Amberlie patted her hand. "Your daughter will be safely with you soon. I know my family will return her unharmed."

" 'Tis hard for you too," Mabel observed, as if seeing Amberlie for a human being with feelings and emotions. "You're a gentlewoman, unused to such a rough existence, as was I until a year ago. Sleeping in caves and moving to Weymouth's cellar when we must flee is no life for a sick woman. I want only for this to end so I may go home—I want to go to Woodrose Keep—but 'tis gone from me. 'Tis gone and won't be reclaimed, but my son doesn't admit this to himself." Mabel smiled sadly and lay upon her pallet. "I shall sleep now. In my dreams, I am home with my husband and children beside me, and I am happy once more."

The poor lady. Despite Amberlie's predicament, brought about by this woman's renegade son, Amberlie felt deeply sorry for her.

Amberlie left her and walked through the damp labyrinth of corridors, but realized she was headed away from the cave's opening. Then she noticed a torch flickering to her left. Deciding this was the direction she'd taken earlier, she headed toward the light, and entering a deeply shadowed rock-hewn room, she bumped into Tedric. He appeared just as surprised to see her as she was to see him. But he recovered more quickly than she. "Do you search for me, my lady?" he asked in a voice that sounded husky and melodious at the same time. He spoke so close to her ear that she felt his breath upon her cheek.

"I . . . am lost," she answered in a breathy voice, alarmed to realize that she was in Tedric's chamber and very much alone. In her hand she carried the soup bowl, but all she noticed was how warm she felt in his presence. In the semi-darkness, she caught his musty male scent, and something inside her responded to this maleness and the intimacy of the situation.

"I am lost too, my lady, lost beyond all reason," he whispered, and his words slid warmly over her like black velvet. She felt his arms go around her waist, pulling her against him, which she didn't protest because suddenly she'd ceased thinking clearly. It seemed the most natural thing in the world to lift her face and encounter Tedric's lips as he claimed hers in a kiss which was sweet and demanding, so passionate that her body willingly melted into his.

Molten heat crawled through her blood, flaring hot and bright like torches in a dark night. His mouth tasted like freshly drunk wine, his tongue sliding sensuously to mate with hers. Tedric's hands came to rest upon her bottom at first, massaging her buttocks until he pulled her up against his rock-hard arousal. Amberlie groaned, her body instinctively pushing into his as she responded to a primitive need. It had been so long since a man touched her and kissed her like this—so long since she'd felt any physical desire—that she moaned like a hungry beggar who'd been served a supper. She would have given into her debauched longings, would have followed Tedric to the furs, if not for the sound of a laughing child from somewhere nearby. The sound instantly broke her trance.

"Non!" she violently exclaimed, and lifted the soup bowl to hit the side of Tedric's face. The broth spilled over his cheek, neck, tunic, and her hand. She didn't stop to think about her action; all she wished was to stop the passion in her veins for this man—this barbarian who'd murdered her husband.

"Teasing witch!" Tedric growled, and held his head before grabbing her wrist when she would have fled. His clasp felt like iron. "I'd throttle you if I were another sort of man."

She didn't tell him that he appeared almost laughable with the soup dribbling down his face. But Amberlie was far from laughing as the import of what she'd done sunk in. He could very well make her suffer now, suffer at the hands which only moments ago had promised great pleasure. But he wouldn't use her as his leman, and she wouldn't allow herself to give in to her

baser instincts with a man who had killed her beloved Henri.

"I—hate—you to touch me! I hate you!" she
shrieked, and attempted to pull away, but he
wouldn't release her. Instead he came up close to
her, so close she felt the thunderous beat of his
heart. His eyes were now a deep furious shade of
blue, so blue they shone almost black in the
torchlight.

" 'Tis obvious, my lady, that you're either over-
starved for affection or used to giving away your
favors. I've yet to discover which, but I do tell
you that you're more trouble than I've bargained
for."

"Free me then, you barbarous knave!"

A cruel smile twisted Tedric's lips. "I do not remember hearing such a plea from your wanton
lips seconds ago."

Amberlie's flush reached her hairline for she
couldn't dispute him. She'd acted like a promis-
cuous washwoman, and glanced away from him
in shame.

"I'll take great delight in turning you over to
your kinsman on the morrow."

The import of his words caused her head to
snap back to his face. Her eyes widened, and her
dark brows shot upwards. "Guy has agreed to release your sister?"

"Aye," he replied with such coldness that Amberlie wondered if this was the same man who'd
kissed her so passionately.

Hope rose within her. Tomorrow she'd be home

again, away from this horrible cave and these swinish Saxons—one in particular, whom she'd be pleased never to see again. "I am to be set free tomorrow," she said, but it sounded more like a question than a statement.

"Guy de Bayonne has agreed to my terms and promises no reprisals."

That didn't sound like Guy, Amberlie thought, but she didn't contradict Tedric. All she dwelled upon was going home. Even life with Guy and Julianne was preferable to being held prisoner. When Tedric dropped her arm and said nothing else, Amberlie made a move to leave. His voice stopped her. "My lady, you've made a mess and will clean it up—beginning with me."

Chapter Seven

"What do you mean?" Amberlie clutched the material of her gown in her perspiring hands, definitely not caring for Tedric's commanding tone.

"You've spilled broth upon my chamber floor," he told her with a curt nod at the earthen floor.

"You're living in a cave," she reminded him.

"Aye, but this is my home until fate deems otherwise, lady. My tunic is soiled and broth covers my face. Come here."

Amberlie hesitated; her heart beat hard against her rib cage. She didn't trust Tedric not to touch her again, but worse, she didn't trust herself to stop him if he did. She shouldn't have hit him with the bowl, and now she would pay for her impetuous action by being forced to touch him again. Damn the man! "I'm not a serf," she countered haughtily.

"Nay, you're my prisoner until I release you," he reminded her. But she wondered if there was a hint of a threat that if she didn't do as he wished, he wouldn't release her. He found a coarsely woven rag and threw it at her. Catching it, she glared at him when he imperiously muttered. "Clean me, my lady."

"You're an ill-bred lout," she mumbled under her breath, not failing to see his jeering smirk as she mustered her courage and attended him. With shaking hands, she wiped the broth from his face, careful not to make direct contact with his skin. Her eyes unswervingly traced the scar on his cheek, following the thin, pale line to where it ended at his jawbone. The cut looked deep enough to have caused great pain when it was first inflicted. Tedric noticed her preoccupation with the scar, and Amberlie, seeing how intently he watched her, clumsily smeared the broth's remains into his tunic.

"Aye, 'tis true you're no serf," he told her with a twinkle in the depths of his ice-blue eyes, as he stilled her wrist with his hand. "I doubt you've ever attended anyone in your life."

"I have," she insisted, hating the feel of his iron hold on her. "I used to attend my husband at his bath before he was murdered." The moment she uttered those words, she wished she'd remained silent. The merry twinkle disappeared from his gaze, and his eyes grew hooded. She wasn't certain why she'd mentioned such a private aspect of her marriage to Henri, unless it was to taunt Tedric with her memories, to make him squirm with the knowledge of all he'd taken from her.

"Leave me," he whispered in such a low, ragged tone of voice that Amberlie strained to hear him. For a few seconds, it seemed she was rooted to the spot, but her legs swiftly carried her away from Tedric when she noticed the cruel twist of his mouth, the cold, unrelenting stare directed at her.

She found herself by her own pallet, and sinking onto the rushes, she pulled the sheepskin around her in an attempt to ward off the sudden chill which threatened to freeze her very heart. Never had anyone looked at her with such contempt.

Somehow she'd forgotten that Tedric was her enemy, a fact she must never forget. Clearly, the man had kissed her for his own amusement, had touched her as a diversion to while away the time until he released her. She meant nothing to him, and she hated herself for responding to him.

Amberlie noticed Wick, who sat a short distance from her. He stared at her, and for the briefest instant, he flashed her a smile. "My thanks to you for providing me with a coverlet from the cold last night," she said, and stroked the soft sheepskin. " 'Twas very kind of you, Wick."

Wick shook his head. " 'Twasn't me, but Lord Tedric. He be the one who covered ye."

"But — he was the one who commanded that I receive no coverlet," she insisted.

"Ah, 'tis a soft heart he has, my lady. He'd not see ya shiver from the cold and catch a chill."

Pulling the sheepskin tightly around her, Amberlie reclined on the rushes. So it was Tedric who'd disobeyed his own orders and covered her. What a perplexing man he was!

She guessed she should be grateful to him, but she wasn't. That simple act of kindness only indebted her to him, and she wanted to owe nothing to Tedric the Barbarian. He'd killed her sweet Henri, forcing her into youthful widowhood. Because of Tedric, she would now be forced to marry a wealthy nobleman, and heaven knows what ill treatment she'd be subjected to at another man's hands. Henri had been gentle and loving with her, which was peculiar given the fact that he'd been Julianne's child. She didn't know what her future held now—and all because Tedric had ended her dear husband's life.

"I vow to find a way to make him pay for taking you from me, Henri," she whispered softly, hoping Henri's spirit heard her. "Some way I'll avenge your death, somehow I'll bring Tedric to Norman justice." She meant each word she said, but she wouldn't admit that her vengeful attitude stemmed not so much from the loss of her husband as from her own alarming response to his murderer's stirring kisses.

Chapter Eight

Amberlie woke the next morning to discover Wulfgar watching her. Quickly, she sat up, suddenly aware that the cave was empty except for the two of them. Not even Wick was nearby, and she found this odd since the old man had been one of the few people apparently designated to stay constantly near her. Hastily, she brushed her tousled hair away from her face. "Where is everyone?" she asked with a wary glance at Wulfgar.

"Gone, my lady, all gone except for us."

"Gone where? How did everyone leave without my hearing them? Why did Tedric not tell . . ." Quickly, she grew quiet, not caring for the sudden eruption of laughter from Wulfgar and the knowing look in his eyes. She chastised herself for even thinking about Tedric. Apparently Wulfgar knew far more about what had passed between her and Tedric than she cared to dwell upon.

"Lord Tedric owes you not an explanation for his actions. He is no longer here, having ordered everyone to take their leave of this place during the night. We've scattered to the four winds as a means of protecting ourselves from Norman vengeance, now that Lady Edytha is safe with her family."

"Edytha has been returned?" Amberlie's shocked statement sounded like a question. When had all of this taken place? she wondered. When would she herself be returned to Woodrose Keep? Or would she be returned? Her eyes contained suspicion. "I can't imagine Guy de Bayonne releasing Tedric's sister before I am returned."

Wulfgar shrugged. " 'Tis little concern of mine what your kinsman thought, but he released Edytha into the company of three of our men last eve. Our own small force was nearby to make certain no Norman followed, though Tedric made it plain that your safety would be jeopardized if de Bayonne attacked. It seems that Guy de Bayonne sets great store by his pretty niece, my lady, to agree not to pursue us before your release." Wulfgar leered, but made no move to touch her, though Amberlie sensed his restraint might wane.

She didn't like his insinuations, but at the moment she didn't care what he thought about her relationship with Guy—or what Tedric might have thought either. She wanted only to go home. "When shall I be set free?"

"Now, my lady, but first I'll blindfold you. We don't trust that you won't reveal our hiding place."

Amberlie started to protest, but she thought

better of it, and allowed Wulfgar to tie the covering over her eyes. He extended a hand to her and led her out of the cave to place her on a horse. Wulfgar didn't mount behind her but walked, leading the horse in the direction of the keep.

The early morning sunshine spilled through the overhead branches, and meadowlarks chirped in the bows of trees. The forest had come to life sweetly and slowly as they progressed toward their destination. For all of Amberlie's relief to be going home, she couldn't help but wonder why Tedric hadn't escorted her—and she swallowed her hurt that she could be so easily discarded by a crude and overbearing barbarian. But her good sense kept telling her that she was well rid of Tedric, the renegade who'd murdered Henri, the hateful man who'd inflamed her with his kisses, only to send her on her way without a word of farewell. But she silently vowed to avenge herself upon him for all he'd done to her. If it took the rest of her life, she'd make him pay for his crimes against her.

So busy was she mulling over her future plan of revenge, that she didn't realize Wulfgar and the horse had ceased walking. "Why have we stopped?" she asked worriedly after Wulfgar removed the blindfold. They were in a particularly dense part of the forest.

"This is as far as I go, my lady. You've only to follow the path to the keep."

"You surely jest," she objected with some force. "I know not the way to the keep from here. You simply can't leave me to fend for myself in this—this wilderness." Amberlie glanced wildly around, fearful that that was exactly what Wulfgar proposed doing.

Wulfgar grabbed Amberlie around the waist and lowered her from the horse to the ground. "Lord Tedric has given me his orders, my lady. I must obey or risk discovery by de Bayonne and his men. 'Tis necessary for me to leave you here. You'll fare well; I fear not for your safe return."

"But I do fear, you crude oaf!" she spat out. "I know nothing of this forest—I've never wandered this far from the keep."

"Stay to the path, my lady," Wulfgar responded without emotion, and handed her a leather pouch filled with water before he hauled himself onto the back of the huge beast and turned away, leaving her standing alone.

"You're a horrid man!" Amberlie cried after him. She waited some minutes, wondering if Wulfgar would have a change of heart and return. He didn't. Apparently, she'd served her purpose and now, with orders from Tedric, Wulfgar had released her to fend for herself. "I shall make you suffer for this," she said aloud through clenched teeth, addressing an invisible Tedric. Common sense dictated that she not stand in one spot all day. The sun was higher in the sky now, an indication that it was nearly noon. She had no idea how far she had to walk, and prayed that the keep was close enough for her to make it by nightfall. She didn't relish spending a night in the forest alone.

Wiping away tears that threatened to fall, she headed down the path, which was overgrown with milkweed. It seemed she'd trudged for almost an hour when she sensed she wasn't alone. She felt the same way she had felt on the day by the pond before Tedric kidnapped her. Halting for a moment, she barely breathed as she glanced around but saw no one. Yet the hair on the back of her neck rose up, and she nearly gave into tears imagining that someone more truly terrifying than Tedric might be stalking her, watching her every move. But she had no alternative but to continue, and with each footstep she prayed that God would guide her safely home.

Before half an hour had passed, Amberlie walked out of the forest into an open meadow and blinked in astonishment. Before her were her Norman knights on horseback, approaching with the gold and red de Fontaine banner held aloft and blowing restlessly in the breeze. Guy de Bayonne sat upon a white destrier, and upon seeing her, he immediately spurred the cantering horse into a full gallop. Before she could gather her wits about her, Guy had stopped and jumped down to enfold her in his arms.

"Amberlie, *cherie,* you're safe," he breathed into her ear as he caressed her hair. "We've been so worried, so concerned about you. Are you safe? Are you well? Has Tedric harmed you in any way?"

Amberlie glanced up at Guy. She'd never cared

for him before now, but at that moment, she was so overcome with joy to be free that all she could do was hold onto the swarthy-faced man before nodding she was all right. "Please take me home," she begged in a small voice.

"Bien, home, *cherie."* Guy scooped her into his arms and placed her on the horse, nimbly climbing behind her. He held onto the reins, locking her body between his arms. Amberlie leaned against him, her body and mind so weary that she wanted all conscious thought to cease. Most of all, she ached to forget the unsettling emotions that Tedric had released within her. But she wouldn't forget Tedric — ever — and before she was finished, he'd not forget her either.

What she didn't know was that Tedric hadn't forgotten her. From a distance, well hidden behind dense thickets, he watched de Bayonne ride away with Amberlie. He'd followed the entire distance from the cave to the meadow, his eyes trained upon Wulfgar and ready to pounce if the man took any liberties with her. However, Wulfgar had followed his orders exactly, a relief for Tedric. Still, he'd wanted to be the one who returned her to her people, all the while wishing he didn't have to give her up. But he knew de Bayonne and his knights would search for him, and he couldn't risk his own safety to return Amberlie to her kinsman.

He hadn't expected to feel such pain when the

return actually occurred. Even now he watched as Amberlie's long hair streamed behind her, her body imprisoned in his enemy's embrace, as de Bayonne carried her away from him. Which was just as well, he decided, and hardened his heart. From the way she'd clutched at de Bayonne and allowed him to seat her so cozily against him, it was clear that she and the man were lovers.

Forget her! his mind screamed. And Tedric knew this was his only alternative. Amberlie de Fontaine was his enemy, and now that Edytha was safe, her usefulness had ended. He would go about organizing more men, training them into competent soldiers, and eventually would rush the keep and win back his home. Until then, he couldn't return to the cave, having ordered it abandoned, for he felt certain that de Bayonne would discover the hideout soon. At the moment, his army was dispersed in several different hiding areas. He would bring his followers together when it was safe. And he would fight against de Bayonne one day. The image of Amberlie clutching at the man sealed their fates, for now he had more reason to hate Guy de Bayonne. He hated him for being the man who'd won her love.

Aware that the knights would soon attempt to ferret him out of the forest, Tedric silently and quickly snuck away to meet his family in the abandoned cellar of a burned-out keep called Weymouth.

* * *

"Such a disobedient girl you are." Julianne peered disapprovingly at Amberlie, who sat tiredly in a chair. "You've caused us no amount of trouble by your sneaking away when I ordered you not—"

"Julianne, please don't badger Amberlie," Guy declared, and patted Amberlie's shoulder. "She has been through enough without having to listen to your sharp rebukes. And I am tired of hearing your voice."

Guy's criticism seemed to take Julianne by surprise. She lifted her head haughtily and squared her shoulders. "You approve of her conduct, my brother? Then perhaps you should explain yourself to King William when he visits in a fortnight and you have to tell him how this wayward girl left the confines of the keep, after I ordered her not to, and was captured by one of King William's most notorious enemies, the Saxon dog who murdered my son. Explain to him how you've let this treacherous dog slip through your fingers—again. I should like to hear such an explanation."

"I've sent troops to search the woods for Tedric," Guy heatedly returned, but he had the sense to flush. Julianne's words struck an unpleasant chord within him because the crafty Tedric hadn't yet been brought to heel.

"Hah! Father Ambrose could have found the man by now," Julianne noted with a sneer.

Such a bitter exchange of words, especially the comments about Tedric, was more than Amberlie could bear at the moment. Weariness bowed her down, and she wanted to sleep and forget the last few days had ever happened. She needed to sleep so she could stop thinking about Tedric and her wanton responses to his kisses. "I should like to retire," Amberlie suddenly announced, interrupting Julianne, who would have gladly continued her full-scale tirade.

"Oui, a good idea," Guy quickly agreed, more than amenable to ending the discussion. He solicitously helped Amberlie to her feet. "We all should retire for the night, eh, Julianne?"

"You may sleep," Julianne sniffed to Guy, "but I shall spend the night on my knees, praying that my son's murderer be found and brought to justice. Perhaps the Lord shall deliver Tedric to me, for most certainly you cannot." She turned her attention to Amberlie, and her dark gaze raked Amberlie from head to toe. "And I have much to discuss with you, once you're well rested, my daughter. Things of a personal nature which could very well endanger your value as a bride, now that you've been captured by a barbarian." Julianne turned and stiffly departed from the solar, her words hanging ominously in the air.

Amberlie caught her breath, knowing full well what Julianne meant to speak to her about at a later time. She'd lost her virginity to Henri on their wedding night, but to lose her honor to a Saxon would be unthinkable as far as Julianne was concerned, and would lower her value in the marriage contract to a Norman nobleman. But

Tedric hadn't violated her, not really. Yet who would believe he hadn't raped her? "Good night, I shall see you on the morrow," she said to Guy, and began to move wearily to the doorway. His hand on her arm stopped her. His countenance no longer expressed concern. His mouth had thinned to a hard, disapproving line, and his eyes sparkled with suspicion.

"Did Tedric ravish you?"

The question needed to be asked. Though she'd cloistered herself with only Julianne and Guy, it was clear from the guarded looks thrown her way by the servants and some of the knights upon her arrival home that everyone speculated about what had happened to her at Tedric's hands. She didn't wish to speak of what had happened to her body beneath Tedric's questing hands, for then she'd be forced to admit how wonderful his touch had felt upon her flesh, how his sinful kisses had burned through her resolve and scorched her soul. She didn't want to speak about Tedric at all, but it was clear that Guy held other ideas. "I'm waiting for your answer, ere I'll believe the worst," she heard him say when she didn't immediately reply.

Shaking her head, Amberlie looked him straight in the eye. "He didn't ravish me."

"Did he touch you then? Did the brute run his hands over your beautiful body, *cherie?* I cannot bear to think of it." Guy pulled Amberlie close against him, and the chain mail from his hauberk ground into her breasts. "I want to be the only man to touch you and bring you pleasure, only

91

me, Amberlie."

Guy's mouth descended upon hers, bringing with the kiss a plea for something she wasn't prepared to give to him. Curling her hands into fists, she pushed against him, offering no response. Finally he ended the assault. "Let me go — at once!" she commanded, much offended but not truly surprised by Guy. For months, she'd endured his heated looks, always watching him and wondering when he'd spring upon her. Why now? she wondered.

"Did Tedric kiss you like that?" he asked, his voice husky and filled with jealousy. "If so, I shall search the forest myself and find him. And when I do, I shall kill him, for no man touches you but me."

Amberlie took advantage of his loosened embrace and jumped away from him. She wiped the back of her hand across her mouth to erase the vestiges of Guy's kiss. "I don't want you to touch me — ever again! You're my kinsman, the uncle of my husband."

"Not for long," he returned with an amused snort, though he made no further move toward her. "King William arrives in a fortnight to see how work on the keep is progressing. I plan to petition him for your hand in marriage. I want you to be my wife."

Amberlie's heart thudded in her chest. As much as she hated the idea of marrying a man chosen by the king, she detested the thought that William might allow a marriage to Guy de

Bayonne. Henri had considered his step-uncle to be conniving and unscrupulous, but Guy was a fine soldier and had fought side by side with Henri in battle. His prowess with a sword had made up for his deficiencies of character. But to marry such a man was unthinkable. She'd sooner marry the Devil. She clutched at the folds of her gown. "If the king grants your petition, I shall refuse you."

"Ah, *mon petite,* you shall do what you are told. Now to bed with you before you fall over from weariness." Their conversation ended when he held the door open for her. She knew it wouldn't do any good to argue further with him, for Guy was the type of person who'd walk away from an argument when it wasn't going his way.

Amberlie walked the short distance to her room, her mind in a fog. Magda joined her and silently helped undress her. Wearing only her shift, Amberlie climbed into the high, wide bed and snuggled beneath the covers, too tired to dwell upon Guy's absurd notion of marrying her. All she wanted was to sleep and forget Guy and a shaggy-haired Saxon who'd started a slow burn in her body with his kisses.

But even that was denied her.

Her dreams contained images of Tedric's face, and in these dreams she waited beside the pond for him to come to her—and when he did, she found herself willingly wrapped in his impassioned embrace, willingly drowning in his fevered kisses. She ached for him, begged for him to love

93

her, and just before Tedric lowered her to the soft grass, she glanced up to find that her lover was no longer Tedric but Henri.

In her dream Henri didn't smile his boyish grin; he didn't hold out his hand to her when she told him how glad she was to see him. Instead, his face was hard, his voice was cold. "You've betrayed me with my murderer," he told her. "You're a weak woman to let him kiss you. Until my death is avenged, you'll know no peace and love shall be denied you."

She woke from the dream in a puddle of perspiration, her heart pounding loudly in her ears. Though Henri was dead, she had no doubt that his spirit had somehow come to her in a dream to heap this curse upon her. Henri knew how she'd betrayed him with his murderer, and he wanted her to avenge his death. But how could she do that?

"Weymouth Keep." She spoke the name aloud, unaware at first that she'd even said it until she remembered that Tedric's mother had carelessly mentioned this as a hiding place. Amberlie realized that Guy's knights wouldn't find Tedric in the forest—he was hiding in the cellar of Weymouth Keep until he could organize and train more men for battle. That was where Guy would find him, and poor Lady Mabel had unwittingly been the instrument of her son's downfall.

A sinking sensation of guilt flooded Amberlie even as she made the decision to tell Guy where to find Tedric. Part of her hated what she must do, but the dream was so real and vivid in her mind, and Henri so alive and contemptuous of her, that she knew only one path was open to her. And if her own guilt for having responded to Tedric's advances was alleviated in the process, then so be it. She owed Henri her loyalty, and she must be the one to bring Tedric to justice. And when she did, these disturbing dreams of being locked in the brawny Saxon's arms would cease.

At least, she trusted this would be so.

Chapter Nine

Amberlie watched the next afternoon as Guy led his knights out of the bailey, riding in the direction of Weymouth Keep. She didn't move away from the tower wall until the red and gold banner was but a speck in the distance. "I've done the right thing," she whispered, and thought about how Henri's life had been cut short. Yet she also thought about Tedric for more than a fleeting moment, and could almost imagine his fierce stance as he fought for his freedom, only to be defeated in the end. She knew Guy would take him alive; Julianne had ordered that Tedric be brought to her upon his capture. Given her uncertainty about seeing Tedric punished, Amberlie shivered to imagine just what Julianne might have in mind for the man, and she suffered pangs of guilt.

She turned and pulled her cloak about her, and found herself facing Father Ambrose. He smiled benignly. "My child, have you anything to confess to me?"

Amberlie shook her head. "Nothing, Father."

"Julianne said you might have something to tell me concerning . . . your ordeal." Ambrose looked almost uncomfortable.

Amberlie's cheeks grew pink with her blush until anger darkened them. How dare her meddling mother-in-law send Father Ambrose to her to get her to confess her sins! She was no child, and she wouldn't confess to Ambrose how she'd fallen under Tedric's spell — she couldn't. The humiliation of responding to Henri's murderer was too much for her to even think about, much less openly confess. "I have done nothing wrong that I must seek forgiveness." A lie, but better to let her sin remain in her heart than to tell Ambrose, who might break his priestly vow of silence and reveal the contents of her confession to Julianne.

"But Julianne said you must unburden yourself," he persisted.

"I care not what Julianne said or what she wants!" Amberlie snapped, her dark eyes shooting fire. "I am mistress here, not Julianne, and I will not be treated as a child." With those words hanging in the chilly air, Amberlie swished past Ambrose and headed for the kitchens.

For the next four days, she busied herself with household duties, taking most satisfaction from ministering to the sick who lived at Woodrose, and in the tiny village surrounding the keep. Gundred, a small, stooped old woman, was Amberlie's mentor. She'd lived at Woodrose all of her eighty years, and was much revered for her knowledge of herbs and healing poultices. Gundred's little cottage was a hodgepodge of dried fruits, berries, and leaves that hung from the rafters and were freely scattered upon a wooden table. She had explained to Amberlie what each of the herbs were and what each herb and fruit could do to help ease the pain, and which ones should never be given since sickness would surely follow, and perhaps death. Assisting Gundred when she ministered to the sick was the highlight of Amberlie's day; though it distressed her to see someone suffering, she felt useful and much needed.

It was on the fifth day as Amberlie helped Gundred prepare a poultice for a sick baby that she heard the horn blow in the distance. "Sir Guy returns," Gundred said matter-of-factly, and continued her ministrations for the crying child. Amberlie's heart began to pound hard, and her mouth grew dry with tense fear. Had Guy captured Tedric?

A serf who'd been working on the castle's fortifications appeared at the cottage door. "My Lady Amberlie, Lady Julianne insists ye wait with her in the bailey. Sir Guy approaches with his captives."

Minutes later, Amberlie stood beside Julianne and watched from the battlements as the conquering knights approached. Three knights on horseback entered the bailey first; each held a woman before him. Instantly Amberlie recognized the figures of Glenna, Lady Mabel, and Edytha. Despite the enmity she knew she should feel for these women, Amberlie felt only pity. Glenna tried to appear indifferent and proud, Lady Mabel looked frail and sick, while Edytha only seemed confused and frightened. But it was the sight of Tedric that caused her heart to lurch painfully in her chest.

Guy, atop his destrier, galloped into the bailey. Behind the horse ran Tedric, whose arms were tethered to the back of the animal by a short rope. His tunic had been stripped away to reveal unevenly placed stripes across his broad and muscular back which were raw and covered with dried blood. His face was puffy and his eyes blackened. Apparently, Tedric had been savagely beaten, and Amberlie had no doubt that Guy had delivered the blows.

"Ah, my son's killer is finally here," Julianne jeeringly proclaimed, and rubbed her hands together in what only could be described as vicious glee. "Now he shall suffer for robbing me of my child, and no one can help him. Come, Amberlie, we should see to our guest — and his discomfort."

Amberlie hesitated, not eager to face Tedric again, not willing to contribute to his further suffering or his family's though she knew she should by all accounts be pleased to have Tedric in her power. After all, this was what she'd planned. Revenge had been uppermost in her mind for months. Yet now that the reality was upon her, she didn't know how to deal with it for cruelty truly wasn't in her nature.

"Why do you dawdle?" Julianne's beady and perceptive gaze fastened upon her. "Are you fainthearted, or perhaps there is another reason you're not eager to face your husband's murderer?"

"Neither," Amberlie lied, and propelled her legs to move down the wooden stairs to the bailey below and away from Julianne's penetrating stare. "I'm as eager as you to see justice done."

The Saxon women were lowered from the horses. Amberlie breathed a relieved sigh to see that they hadn't been mistreated. Glenna immediately went to Lady Mabel, holding the thin, old woman about the waist while Edytha cowered beside her mother. Flaubert, the young knight who'd ridden in with Edytha, watched the young girl with something akin to adoration. He loomed protectively over his charge. When Amberlie approached the group, Flaubert came forward and bowed to her. "My lady, what is to be done with these prisoners?"

Amberlie thought it odd that he addressed her and not Julianne, but perhaps he realized that Julianne's venom against Tedric might extend to these innocent women. Empathy for their plight touched her heart, for she remembered how frightened she'd first been after her own kidnapping. Even Glenna glanced fearfully at her, but it was the blatant fear shimmering in Lady Mabel's eyes which undid Amberlie. No matter how she might detest this woman's son, Lady Mabel and these two other women were blameless.

"Flaubert, I place you in charge of these captives to see that no harm befalls them," Amberlie said, trusting her intuition that Flaubert possessed a kindly disposition. "Take them to the kitchens for nourishment and then to Magda. Under no circumstances are they to be placed in chains, by my order as lady of this keep." That very order would prevent even Julianne and Guy from harming them. She knew that every knight would bow to her authority in this instance for she very seldom issued such a statement.

"*Oui,* my lady." Flaubert bowed to her, and with the help of the other two knights led the women into the keep.

Amberlie glanced around, and saw that Julianne was much more interested in Tedric than in his family. Julianne savagely kicked out at Tedric, who was on all fours like a wounded lion, ready to pounce but unable to move because of the way a strong, able-bodied knight held the tether. Julianne screamed at him in French, all of her hatred unleashed through her feet, hands, and words. Never had Amberlie seen such hatred directed at another human being, and something inside of her churned in disgust. Julianne was totally out of control.

101

Guy, on the contrary, gave Amberlie a large, pleased smile and slid down from his horse to escort her personally toward Tedric. "Because of you, *cherie,* I have captured my dear nephew's slayer. You are the reason he fell into my hands. I am forever grateful." Guy laughingly took her hand and kissed it. Amberlie drew away in repulsion, but not before Tedric had settled his agonized gaze upon her, and she saw unbridled hate flare within his eyes. He fell onto his side just as Julianne directed a painful blow to his back with an ax handle she'd taken from a knight, who stood nearby and jeered along with the rest of the soldiers.

"Stop!" Amberlie screamed, unable to stand any more of this brutality.

Julianne halted, surprise and bafflement giving way to anger that Amberlie had been the one to call out. "Have you a soft spot in your heart for your husband's murderer, Amberlie? Well, I do not! Tell me why I should stop, tell me why I should not derive great joy from hurting this barbarian killer, the killer of my son!" Julianne clenched her teeth and her hands. For an instant, Amberlie thought the woman might attack her. She'd never seen such undisguised hatred on another human being's face, and she felt chilled to her very soul.

"I—I don't believe such punishment is proper for this man." She didn't know why she said such a ludicrous thing. "Tedric is a proud Saxon," she continued lamely. She was not certain what she wished to say, but she knew she couldn't stand seeing Tedric brutalized, no matter that he'd killed Henri.

Guy snorted in disgust. "Death is his destiny, though he is prideful. I shall take delight in killing him."

Julianne's eyes narrowed at Amberlie, and she ignored Guy. "Then what do you suggest as punishment for your husband's murderer? I think he should be thrown into the pit and kept there until he rots, but I want to hear how you think he should be punished."

"It doesn't matter how Amberlie wants him punished," Guy interjected with a nasty glance at Julianne. "I want him dead—at my hand—to pay for the way he lanced me in the side. The pit is not enough to satisfy me."

"The pit is my choice," Julianne insisted, "but since Amberlie is lady of the keep and my son's widow, she must decide what to do with Henri's murderer."

Amberlie thought it was a fine time for Julianne to remember that she was lady of the keep and that, as the mistress, her wishes must be respected. Was Julianne testing her, trying to decide if something had happened between herself and Tedric?

Tedric lay on the ground, apparently in a great deal of pain, but his eyes held nothing but hatred and contempt—and he directed it in Amberlie's direction. She knew Guy wanted this man to die, not to avenge Henri, but to alleviate his own humiliation for not having captured Tedric before now. He wanted Tedric to die for an insignificant wound he'd suffered at Tedric's hands. Julianne wanted Tedric to spend the rest of his life in the pit, a place dug deeply in the earth behind the keep from which no man could escape without help. Tedric would die slowly and painfully for he'd be fed rancid leavings from the table that not even the dogs would touch. Amberlie couldn't stand for such a proud man to be treated like an animal; there had to be another way to punish him.

Amberlie heard herself speaking before she fully realized what she was saying. "Tedric shall be my personal slave, performing all of the duties which only a woman does for her mistress. He shall clean my clothes and fetch my meals, serving at the high table with the women. As a once-proud nobleman, he will suffer the slights of his own people and our knights by serving the widow of the man whom he murdered. He'll never be free but will live in bondage until he draws his last breath. That is what I decree as lady of this castle."

"You're mad!" Guy shouted, and cursed. Taking Amberlie's arm in his hand, he squeezed tightly. "The man deserves death and you decree he live in bondage. What justice is there in that?"

"I've spoken," Amberlie reiterated, and pulled

away from him. "As Henri's widow and the mistress of Woodrose, I have the right to expect my wishes to be fulfilled without interference from you — or anyone." She peered at Julianne, expecting a tirade, but strangely none was forthcoming. Instead Julianne only nodded.

"Such punishment is fair exchange for my son's death. I agree with my daughter-in-law."

"You're both mad!" Guy strode away from them, apparently of the opinion that it would do little good to fight both Amberlie and Julianne.

Julianne looked down at Tedric and made a cackling sound. "Proud Saxon indeed!" Then she entered the keep.

Amberlie watched as Tedric was hauled to his feet by two knights. Before they led him past her, he turned frosty eyes upon her. " T'would have been better had you killed me."

Chapter Ten

The slave collar tightly encased the thickness of Tedric's neck. Ranulf, the blacksmith, closed the lock and said nothing to Tedric, the man who had once been his lord and now was to serve the Lady Amberlie at Woodrose. But Maeda, Ranulf's wife, had a great deal to say, and ceased her sweeping of the floor of the tiny hut.

" 'Tis sinful that Lord Tedric should be treated thus," she whispered, hot tears of anger filled her eyes. "I thought Lady Amberlie was kind, but now I fear she is as evil as the Lady Julianne and that wretched brother of hers. May a pox take the lot of them!"

"Quiet, woman," Ranulf ordered. "Do ye wish for Norman wrath to settle upon us for your loud and vicious tongue?"

"I speak only the truth, my husband."

"And the truth is disturbing to me and to Lord Tedric." Ranulf managed a weak smile at Tedric, who sat before him on a stool. "Forgive my wife, my lord."

"I forgive her willingly, Ranulf, but I'm no longer your lord, but a slave."

"Will you run or fight?" Ranulf inquired.

Tedric shook his head. "Neither, for my actions might harm my family. My mother isn't well, and with winter's sting soon to be upon us, I cannot risk her health by running away — or fighting."

"But when spring comes, my lord, what then?"

Tedric smiled wanly, not about to confide in anyone, even a trusted man like Ranulf. He feared that his words would be taken wrongly and passed along to Guy de Bayonne, who'd no doubt retaliate by harming Edytha, his mother, or Glenna. For now, Tedric would be forced to play the slave — until something happened to turn things to his advantage. But what that might be, he didn't know.

"Quiet, yon comes Lady Amberlie," Maeda warned, and went about her sweeping. She bowed respectfully when Amberlie entered the small house.

"I've come for my slave. Is he ready?" Amberlie asked Ranulf. Tedric sat rigidly still, fists clenched. Apparently someone had given him a blue tunic to cover the welts on his back. Yet his face was still bruised and the skin beneath his eyes was colored a purplish-black. Amberlie tried not to stare at him, but she couldn't help herself.

"Aye, my lady, and here is the key which removes the collar." Ranulf handed Amberlie a small key, which she tightly clutched in her hand.

"Come," she commanded Tedric. "The evening

meal awaits and needs to be served." With an imperious swish of her dark gown, Amberlie turned and left the blacksmith's hut with Tedric following behind her.

"Expect no thanks for saving my life," Tedric said in a voice which didn't sound at all slave-like in tone as they crossed the bailey.

"Should I have stood idly by and watched your execution?" Amberlie retorted with barely a twist of her head in his direction. "I was kinder to you than you were to my husband."

"I remember not killing your husband, my lady. But I shall not beg to be released from bondage either."

"Still prideful," she mumbled, and attempted to harden her heart against him. It would never do to feel anything other than contempt for such a man. He'd taken so much from her. Henri's death must be avenged, and humbling Tedric was the tool.

"You're a heartless woman, my lady, but I beg nothing for myself, only for my family. Please do not be hard on my sister or my mother; and Glenna is a true lady, not a thrall."

Amberlie spun around, nearly colliding with Tedric's broad chest. Her mood veered sharply to rage. "I would not wish your punishment to be visited upon those close to you. Your mother and Edytha are with Magda in the weaving room where they'll be safe. Edytha helps with the sewing and your mother, who is ill, has been given a pallet where she can rest and do needlework when she feels well enough. Your precious Glenna sees to Lady Julianne, which is a most sought-after position among the serfs. I hold no animosity against them."

"Ah, then I am to be thankful for your kindness, my lady? Is that what you wish?"

"A bit of gratitude for saving your wretched life would be sufficient."

"For that, I am not grateful, but I do thank you for extending some generosity to my family."

Amberlie turned, unable to look upon this man whose face was so battered and bruised for much longer. She felt an overwhelming urge to tend to his bruises and to the wounds on his back, which she knew must hurt him still. But she was mistress of Woodrose, and it wouldn't do to extend any kindness to a slave, especially this slave. Already, some of the knights were watching them, openly curious as to the reason their mistress occupied herself with a slave.

Inside the great hall, Amberlie took her place upon the dais beside Guy. On his right sat Julianne. The older woman's mouth curled up into a vindictive smile when Tedric approached with a trencher of freshly cooked venison and rice, placing it grudgingly before Amberlie. He looked distinctly out of place among the serfs, for Tedric was larger in height, his body bronzed and well muscled. His face showed no emotion, resembling a mask.

"Your slave needs to learn the proper way to serve," Julianne told Amberlie from across Guy.

"Also, he must learn humility. I should be most pleased to teach him, my daughter."

Amberlie hid her repulsion from Julianne, knowing just how cruel Julianne could be and how delighted she'd be if Amberlie turned Tedric over to her for punishment. There were too many slaves already at Woodrose who'd suffered beneath Julianne's heavy hands and thin beating rods. "Indeed, this slave has much to learn, and in time, he will," Amberlie said. "But I think his subservience will be sufficient punishment for his crime in the end."

Julianne considered the arrogant stance of Amberlie's new slave with a finger on her lips. *"Oui,* the end is what counts," she said cryptically.

Guy sniffed the air in disdain. "The lout deserves to die, and I agree that the end is what counts for I'll have my way in the end."

Amberlie ignored Guy, her attention on Glenna, who approached the dais and placed trenchers before Julianne and Guy. Amberlie didn't miss her air of arrogance or the way her eyes flickered possessively across Tedric. But her mouth dropped open when she noticed the slave collar. No matter what Amberlie felt about Glenna, the woman truly cared for Tedric, a fact made obvious by the small tear coursing down her cheek. For the entire meal, Tedric stood stone-like, except when Amberlie ordered him forward to refill her cup with mead or clear away her trencher.

After the meal ended, Amberlie went to her

110

chamber. Magda appeared as she did each night to help Amberlie undress. "I've ordered Lord Ted . . ." The old woman broke off with a scowl on her face and began again. "Your new slave is warming the water for your bath, my lady."

" 'Twas kind of you," Amberlie said, and pulled off her headdress so Magda could begin combing her hair. She sat before the mirror, her own dark-clothed figure suddenly very unappealing to her eyes. She was so tired of wearing black, so sick of mourning for Henri, that she felt much older than her twenty years. "How are Lady Mabel and Edytha faring?"

"Fine, my lady."

It seemed that was all the information Magda would willingly volunteer. Amberlie bit down upon her lower lip, for she sensed Magda's animosity, more so than usual. Of all the serfs at Woodrose, Amberlie wanted Magda's respect. "You're upset with me, aren't you?" Amberlie watched Magda's reflection, aware of the thin line of her mouth, and the way she harshly combed Amberlie's hair, pulling at her scalp. "You know I informed Sir Guy as to Tedric's hiding place."

"Aye, my lady."

"I did what needed to be done."

"Aye, my lady."

"For the love of God, Magda, say something else!"

"Would you like a fire lit, my lady?"

Exasperated, Amberlie ordered Magda to get

111

the tub ready for her bath and to light the hearth. Soon, Tedric began carrying in buckets of water and pouring them into the tub. Not once did he look her way, but he diligently performed his task. Amberlie realized how demeaning this must all be for him, and she wondered if she should have allowed Guy to execute him. Why had she saved his life? He deserved to die for killing Henri. Didn't the Bible say an eye for an eye? A life for a life? Who was she to contradict the word of God?

"Your tub is ready, my lady," Tedric said woodenly.

Amberlie rose from her chair by the mirror, and realized that Magda was no longer in the room. "Please find Magda for me. I need more kindling for the fire."

Tedric bowed and disappeared.

Quickly disrobing, Amberlie slipped into the small wooden tub, pulling her legs up to her chest to accommodate her length. The water lapped at her thighs, just barely covering her breasts. How wonderful the water felt upon her body, the tensions of the day receding. She closed her eyes and began to doze. She barely heard the chamber door opening, though she stirred awake as she heard wood being thrown upon the fire, followed by hissing and sizzling sounds. Without opening her eyes, she asked Magda to please wash her back. Amberlie felt her long hair being lifted from her neck. The soft cloth gently stroked along her collarbone to the center of her

112

back, kneading her flesh in the most delightful way. Amberlie moaned under Magda's massaging fingers, never having experienced such a wonderfully refreshing bath before. The muscles in her neck and back relaxed; the tenseness left her body entirely.

"Oh that feels so wonderful," she breathed, and started to doze again, vaguely aware that the cloth traced a path to her lower back and around to her hip, where it skimmed across her abdomen and found its way up to her chest. The cool rag dipped between the valley of her breasts, stopping for a moment to wet each one. Then fiery fingers kneaded each globe until the nipples stood out hard and firm — and Amberlie's eyes flew open, for this was a most unusual washing. "Magda, what are you doing!" she shouted, much flustered, and grabbed at the cloth.

" 'Tisn't Magda, my lady."

It was Tedric.

He lecherously grinned at her, laughing aloud when she bolted to her feet and threw the wet cloth to hit him solidly in the chest. His amusement ceased when Amberlie, who was startled and embarrassed, tripped in her haste to get out of the tub and secure a towel. She tumbled to the floor on her side, completely naked, and so humiliated she wished to die. Tedric picked up the towel and laid it over her. "Are you hurt?" he asked, genuine concern replacing his earlier amusement. He reached out to help her up.

She slapped his hands away. "You lecherous

lout! How dare you sneak into my chambers and—and wash me! Where is Magda?"

"She was called away by a serf who is in childbirth. I volunteered to bring in the wood for her."

"And to wash me!" Amberlie finished, her cheeks burning a bright red.

"Nay, that wasn't on my list of duties, but I didn't mind, my lady, truly I didn't. If I remember correctly, I am your personal slave." He shot her a devastatingly handsome smile, so dazzling that her pulse quickened.

With as much dignity as she could muster, Amberlie wrapped the towel around her and stood up. "Your duties do not extend to such personal matters as tending to my bath. I should have you flogged for your impertinence, your presumption—"

"Mayhap you should have me killed."

Her hands tightened around the towel. "You'd like that, wouldn't you? Then you'd be a martyr to your people and your cause."

"I trust your good judgment, my lady."

"And I trust you'll remember your place here, slave! You're no longer master of Woodrose Keep. For the rest of your days you'll serve me and my kin. I'll see to it that you haven't one moment's rest during the day. If not serving me, you'll be slopping the pigs or cleaning out the stables and foul-smelling dovecote. No chore will be too demeaning by the time I finish with you."

"All of this fury is because you enjoyed my touch. You know that, Amberlie."

"You hateful, arrogant man!"

"Why? Because I deign to tell you the truth? Because you respond to a barbarian like a washwoman each time I touch you?"

"Get out of my chambers," she said through gritted teeth, and turned her back to him. Somehow she knew he hesitated a moment, but then she heard the door close behind him. She changed into her nightclothes and slid beneath the pelts on the bed, remembering his remarks.

Tedric had spoken the truth, and the truth pricked at her heart like a thousand thorns. She'd never thought herself to be a weakling; dependent upon others, yes, but not so weak that her knees felt ready to collapse each time he laid a finger upon her. The brawny man possessed a power over her and had caused her no amount of grief, in the past and the present. How would she deal with her own shameful weakness for him in the future?

She had to stop herself from thinking wanton thoughts about him, from dreaming about his kisses. She'd made a mistake by making him her slave, but if she ordered him to other work, Guy and Julianne would want to know the reason why, and Julianne had sharp eyes and ears. Amberlie couldn't bear for the woman to know that she harbored a secret lust for her son's murderer. It seemed she had no other alternative but to keep to the punishment she'd decreed or look the fool. But at what cost to her self-respect?

As she drifted into sleep, she considered pressing King William about marrying her off to one of his noblemen soon. A husband was what she needed. Surely if she were wed to a Norman nobleman, one of her own kind, she'd no longer be tortured by images of Tedric the Saxon. And perhaps, in time, she'd come to love her husband. As long as she would be treated with respect and not abused, she felt certain she would be happy with whomever William decided upon. Guy might believe he could convince William to make her his bride, but Amberlie doubted the king would marry her off to her late husband's step-uncle. The bonds of kinship were too close for the Church to approve such a match, and William was ever loyal to the Church.

Having decided on the course of her life, she fell asleep, but still she dreamed of a brawny yellow-haired barbarian.

With a bucket in hand, Glenna made her way to the pond. She followed behind some serving women, measuring her steps because she hated to return to the keep. For over a week now, she'd performed an endless round of chores. By nightfall, she fell exhausted onto her pallet in the weaving room, hoping and praying that Lady Julianne, the old crone, didn't waken during the night and summon her. It seemed the woman constantly required something—a cup of water, a footstool, kindling for the fire—and not once had she expressed the simplest gratitude. For the

116

last few days, the woman had been ill with a stomach grippe, and this was the first time all day that Glenna had been able to take some time for herself.

Of all the positions in the castle, Glenna's was the least strenuous. She thanked God each day that she hadn't been placed with the lowborn creatures in the washroom. The knights were a lecherous lot who availed themselves of any washwoman they pleased. And Glenna realized she had Amberlie to thank for ordering her to care for Julianne. But she'd sooner die than thank that haughty bitch for anything.

It was obvious that Tedric found his position as slave to Lady Amberlie de Fontaine to be less than horrible. When Glenna saw him these days, he no longer had that warm look in his eyes for her; his attention was always riveted on the dark-haired witch who treated him little better than a mongrel cur. Glenna was much peeved that he didn't have the inclination to speak at length with her, even on the few times when he'd visited his mother and sister in the weaving room and Glenna had been there. Lady Mabel was always so pleased to see him, and poor Edytha would clasp him around the legs like a small child, crying that he not leave her. He barely spoke to Glenna other than to inquire how she fared. She knew the reason why he no longer seemed to care about her. Tedric was besotted with the Norman witch.

"I hate her!" she muttered under her breath,

fearing she was losing Tedric's adoration to the very woman who'd placed him in bondage.

"Ye said something, Glenna?" a serving woman named Runa asked, turning around to stare at her.

"Nay, I was mumbling to myself."

The women stopped by the pond and dipped their buckets into the water, chattering among themselves. For the most part the serving women ignored Glenna. Autumn's chill was in the air, but after rushing around more than half the day, exerting herself for the dour Lady Julianne, Glenna was glad of a cool breeze.

Runa set her full bucket on the grass and smiled at Glenna, apparently not the least daunted by Glenna's haughty demeanor. Three of the woman's bottom front teeth were missing, and two were blackened on the top. Glenna thought that Runa would be quite pretty if she kept her mouth closed. "I know someone who's taken with ye," she told Glenna.

Glenna smiled wryly. "One of the castle serfs, no doubt." She'd had some unseemly offers from a few of the serfs, and one or two of the men had been quite handsome and well built. But they were serfs and she was a lady who was far above them, no matter how far she'd fallen.

"Nay, not one o' them, but a knight. Sir Christophe, to be sure. He's quite in love with ye."

Sir Christophe. Glenna hid a secret smile. She'd been aware of Christophe from the moment she'd laid eyes upon him. A tall man with raven black hair, he'd helped her carry a heavy bucket up the narrow, stone stairs to Lady Julianne's room only the other day. She'd thanked him coolly, giving him the impression that she didn't care for his Norman good looks and polite manners, though inside, she quivered with a strange excitement. More than once she'd had to remind herself that Tedric was her betrothed and she loved him. But there was something about Christophe . . .

"Don't ye care that one o' the finest knights in Christendom is in love with ye?" Runa inquired curiously when Glenna failed to respond instantly.

Glenna shrugged. "Not particularly." She was more than interested in Christophe, but it would never do to let a common serving wench know the thoughts of a lady.

"Aye, but ye're a cold one. If 'twas me I'd be beside meself with gladness. I'd be on me back in a moment if Sir Christophe wanted me for a bit o' dalliance."

Glenna's face hardened. "I'm not you. I'm Lady Glenna, betrothed of Tedric of Woodrose. I don't dally with Normans."

"Tsk, my fine lady, ye're the same as me now." Runa dismissed her with a snort, and stood up to follow behind the other women, who'd finished filling their buckets and were headed back to the keep.

Glenna started down the path, the last in line. No sooner had she walked six feet than a hand was clasped over her mouth. She struggled and tried to scream, but a voice whispered harshly in her ear, " 'Tis me, Wulfgar."

She ceased struggling and the hand was removed. She faced Wulfgar. "Where have you been?" she asked, and peered down the path to make certain that no one watched them. Quickly, she followed Wulfgar when he motioned for her to join him behind a thicket.

"I've been hiding in the woods since Lord Tedric was taken," he explained. "Old Wick and I have been trying to organize our men again."

"And have you?"

"Nay, my lady. Sad to say that most of the men are scared of being captured by de Bayonne and made into slaves like Lord Tedric. 'Tis better to run wild than be chained."

"Aye, 'tis better."

"Why haven't you run away?" Wulfgar asked her. " 'Twould be easy since no knights guard the women when they come to the pond. I've been watching ye for the last few days."

"I can't run away, Wulfgar. Where would I go? With you? Nay, I must stay and look after Lady Mabel and Edytha for Tedric—now that he's too busy with Lady Amberlie to do so himself." She could barely say Amberlie's name. It tasted vile in her mouth.

"You're jealous of her," Wulfgar said with a gleam in his eyes.

"I hate her! And now that William the Bastard is due for a visit, Tedric is constantly near her, helping her oversee the cleaning since Lady Julianne has been indisposed the last two days. 'Tis a humiliation for him, but still he plays the slave without complaint."

"William the Bastard is coming to Woodrose?" Wulfgar grabbed at her arm and knocked over the bucket, splashing water on the hem of her skirt.

"Now look what you've done, you clumsy knave!"

"Forget your kirtle, Glenna. Stop and think what this visit means to us." Wulfgar's gaze was intense, more bright and fevered than Glenna ever remembered seeing. "The Norman king is coming here, here to Woodrose. God in heaven, Glenna, the vicious cur has fallen into our laps."

"So?"

"God, but you're dense, my lady, pardon me for saying so. But we can help Lord Tedric, we can help all loyal Saxons, by murdering the butcher ourselves."

Glenna's hand flew to her throat. Murder? Was Wulfgar insane to contemplate killing William the Bastard? Surely such a plan wouldn't succeed. But if it did, then Tedric might retrieve Woodrose. Without the Norman king, England would once again belong to the Saxons, and not these accursed foreigners. Lady Amberlie de Fontaine would be an unpleasant memory after she returned to her native Normandy. Tedric would forget her and marry Glenna, the woman who truly loved him. Glenna's mind spun pretty pictures of herself and Tedric, and the beautiful fair-haired children they would have one day—as soon as William the Bastard was dead.

"Do you think we could do it?" she asked in a low, excited voice.

"Aye, we will do it, my lady. I'll be waiting for you here the next time you draw water. Tarry behind the other women and give news to me of what is happening in preparation for the Bastard's arrival. I'll think of a plan."

Glenna had a moment's doubt. Wulfgar wasn't the brightest man. "But . . . but . . . we must think about this . . ."

"I'll do the thinking, my lady. Now you must hurry back or you'll be missed." Wulfgar left her, the forest swallowing him up.

Glenna turned onto the path and started for the keep. Up ahead she saw the daunting dark figure of Sir Christophe coming toward her on a white charger. He stopped before her and smiled a rich smile which set her silly heart to beating. "I noticed you didn't return with the others," he said in his heavily laced accent as he spoke to her in her own language. Despite her hatred of Normans, she found this one to be unaccountably charming.

"I spilled the water. How clumsy I am," she coyly explained, her dimples deepening.

"Oh, no, you're far from that." He got off the horse and gallantly lifted her onto the animal's broad back. His hands lingered at her small waist for a few moments longer than was necessary.

122

But Glenna didn't mind. "I shall ride you home. Night is falling, and a pretty woman shouldn't be abroad in the dark."

Climbing behind her, he urged the horse toward the keep. Without warning, he began to sing softly in French, a song she'd never heard before and didn't understand. The clear tones of his voice echoed seductively in her ear and sounded wonderful. For the first time in a long while, Glenna felt truly beautiful and desired. It had been so long since Tedric wanted her. For just a few moments as she rode along with the cool wind blowing through her hair and the feel of Christophe's broad chest pressed intimately against her back, Glenna forgot all the horrors she'd endured the last year.

For a few minutes, she even forgot Tedric.

Chapter Eleven

The trestle tables in the great hall shone with an uncommon brightness. Tapestries, woven with threads of gold, had been taken down and beaten of dust, and now hung upon the walls again to block out the damp chill of autumn. The floor had been swept clean and new rushes put down. The rest of the keep had undergone similar cleanings. Each chamber had been straightened, the bedclothes washed, and the windows thrown open to air out the moldy smells of moss and leaves in the mattresses. King William was coming and Amberlie wanted all to be in readiness.

Amberlie glanced out of an upstairs window and noticed the diligent actions of the workmen on the east side of the keep. They hurried to complete the walls made of a stone called ashlar that would enlarge the keep by three stories on that side. Since Guy had taken charge after Henri's death, the keep, which had been wood and stone in Tedric's time, had been progressively changed to a motte and bailey castle. Guy was anxious to complete the eastern portion of the castle for William's inspection.

Amberlie saw Guy gesturing frantically to Flaubert, the knight who'd been placed in charge of the construction. His swarthy face even at this distance looked to be a bright shade of red. Flaubert kept shaking his head in disagreement. Apparently, something wasn't going the way Guy wished.

"My Mercy is gone. Where is my Mercy?"

Amberlie swung around, startled to see Edytha standing a few feet away from her. The girl clutched frantically at the material of her bliaut, fear glittering in her blue eyes. "Mercy?" Amberlie answered blankly, wondering how the girl had escaped Magda's vigilance again. Just the day before Julianne had bitterly complained that Edytha was prowling the upstairs rooms and had to be contained.

"My Mercy is gone," she repeated again as if Amberlie were deaf and hadn't heard her the first time.

Suddenly Amberlie remembered Edytha's doll. "I haven't seen Mercy. Let me help you search for her." Amberlie decided the doll must be in the weaving room, and led a distraught Edytha in that direction. Just as they walked into the room, an apologetic Magda rushed toward them.

"I'm sorry, my lady, but Edytha sneaked away from me again. She was sleeping when I went to the kitchen to get broth for her mother." Magda took Edytha's hand and led her toward the pallet where Lady Mabel sat, drinking her broth.

Edytha burst out in tears and placed her hands over her face. "My Mercy is gone!"

"Edytha has misplaced her doll," Amberlie informed Magda, but her gaze was on the less than friendly visage of Lady Mabel. "I thought Mercy might be in here."

"Nay, we've not seen it." Magda seemed extremely flustered and nervous. "Please do not tell Lady Julianne that Edytha sneaked away again. The child doesn't understand she is to stay in this room—"

"I won't tell Julianne anything," Amberlie assured her with a smile.

" 'Twould have been better had you said nothing to Guy de Bayonne. We'd be safe at Weymouth if not for your bitter tongue!" Lady Mabel spat out the words contemptuously, her anger hardening her usually gentle features.

So there it was. Lady Mabel knew she'd been the one to tell Guy where Tedric and his family had been hiding. Amberlie knew it wouldn't do any good to offer an apology. True, she was sorry about Edytha and Lady Mabel, even Glenna. But she didn't regret Tedric's capture. He was an outlaw, and only because he'd saved her life had she saved his. Yet it hurt to be the recipient of Lady Mabel's contempt. "Then your tongue should not have let slip such information to me," Amberlie said softly.

Lady Mabel's eyes gleamed with tears, but she comforted Edytha by stroking her daughter's hair, dismissing Amberlie with that tender gesture. Amberlie left the weaving room and headed toward Julianne's chamber, much shaken by the confrontation with Tedric's mother but determined to hide this emotion from Julianne's sharp eyes.

Julianne sat against a mound of pillows, her gray hair hanging in braids past her shoulders. The white of her gown heightened her paleness. Glenna instantly stopped tending to Julianne's bedcovers when Amberlie entered the room, her expression clouded in intense dislike. "Leave us," Julianne ordered without a glance at Glenna, who obediently left them alone.

Amberlie dutifully bent to kiss Julianne's cheek. "How do you fare today?"

Julianne snorted. "Hah! I should be dead. Never have I been so ill with the grippe, but I have beaten it."

Amberlie couldn't help but smile. As much as she disliked Julianne, she was tougher than old leather. Amberlie believed that having survived Henri's death, the woman could survive anything. "How goes the cleaning?" Julianne asked worriedly. "Everything must be perfect for the king's visit."

"It goes well." Amberlie patted Julianne's hand in reassurance. "The king and his court will be much impressed by Woodrose."

"I should be overseeing things. I am mistress here."

Amberlie drew back her hand, stung that Ju-

127

lianne would say such a thing to her, even in private. But for all intents and purposes, Julianne was the mistress, not she. Tedric's life had been saved not because Amberlie had asserted her authority as mistress of the keep, but only because Julianne had seen fit not to interfere. It wouldn't do any good to debate the point either, Amberlie knew, for Julianne saw her only as someone to marry off to a wealthy nobleman.

"Keep me informed of the progress with the household duties. I must know all that is happening below stairs."

Amberlie bit down upon her lower lip and nodded. *"Oui,* I shall tell you all." She realized that Julianne was finished speaking with her when she closed her eyes. Amberlie started to leave the room, but remembered Edytha's doll and began quietly searching for it.

"What are you looking for?" Julianne was staring suspiciously at her.

"Pardon, but I wondered if Edytha mayhap left her doll in here."

"Edytha? You mean that simpleminded creature whom Magda cannot watch for more than a few minutes without losing?"

"Yes. The girl is very upset."

"Hmph! That child hasn't the sense the Lord gave to her at birth. I told Magda I do not want her roaming the halls and rooms. A knight nearly attacked her once. And if I remember correctly, you came to her rescue, as you're doing now." Julianne settled a penetrating gaze upon her. "If I didn't know any better, I'd think you care more about these Saxons than your own family. Because of you, Tedric the Saxon freely roams the bailey and keep as your slave. I cannot help but wonder what happened between you both when he held you captive."

Julianne's insinuations weren't lost upon Amberlie. She controlled her facial features, and somehow managed to curtail her blush as she remembered the way she'd responded to Tedric's kisses. "Nothing happened, I assure you."

"Have you forgotten my son?"

Even if Amberlie had wished to forget Henri, Julianne wouldn't let her. Not one day went by without Amberlie's attending Mass for Henri's soul in the small chapel. At first, she'd gone for solace; now she went primarily out of duty. Amberlie wondered how Julianne would react when she married someone else. Would she insist she go to her grave as another man's wife but with Henri's name on her lips? Julianne was obsessed with Henri more in death than she'd been in life. "I can never forget Henri," Amberlie softly proclaimed.

"I hope you speak the truth. My son mustn't be forgotten."

"Have you seen Edytha's doll?" Amberlie was growing exasperated.

"Nay, now leave me to my rest," Julianne intoned disagreeably. Amberlie quietly left Julianne's chambers.

Julianne waited until Amberlie had closed the

large oak door before she reached beneath her pillow and pulled out the ragged figure of Edytha's doll. Her grip tightened around the scrawny thing, and she scowled at it as if it were a living creature which had done her great harm. Yesterday she'd awakened to see the Saxon girl standing beside her bed. With vicious curses, Julianne had run off the frightened girl, who had dropped the doll in her haste to escape. Julianne had seized it and hidden the pitiful thing. Evidently the girl didn't recall where she'd dropped it, and Julianne took delight in keeping it from her. Anything which caused a member of Tedric's family dismay brightened Julianne's own dreary existence.

And now the little Saxon girl cried for her cloth doll.

Well, let her cry! Julianne thought viciously. Such trivial tears were nothing in comparison to the ones she'd cried since Henri's death.

On unsteady feet, Julianne rose from her bed and made her way to the hearth. Orange flames danced in abandon like whirling demons, and Julianne felt absolute power as she tossed the cloth creature into the fire to be instantly devoured by the hungry red flames.

The little Saxon girl would never see her cloth baby again. For the first time since Tedric's capture, Julianne smiled. Going back to her bed, Julianne rested peacefully.

The bailey was alive with activity. The knights practiced their skills with sword and ax while workmen carried stone and mortar to the construction site. Amberlie hurried from the kitchen, where she'd overseen the preparing of salted meats for the king's visit. Flaubert halted her, breaking away from his work.

"My lady, I must speak to you about Sir Guy. He has overstepped the bounds of his authority." From the frown lines on Flaubert's forehead it was evident that Guy had annoyed the man. Evidently, what she'd seen from the window earlier had indeed been an exchange of words.

"I don't understand. Whose authority has he overstepped?"

"Yours, my lady." Flaubert licked his lips in indecision, as if at war with himself, but finally he pressed on in a forceful voice. "Did you not order Tedric to be your slave, to answer only to you? As mistress of the keep, you had the right."

"Yes, that is true."

"Sir Guy has decreed that Tedric belongs to him. With King William's approaching visit we need all the hands available to finish the keep. Tedric is now a workman, and Sir Guy has ordered that no one shall decree otherwise — *no one,* my lady."

Amberlie knew that meant Guy didn't want her to interfere. Usually, she wouldn't have cared if a slave had been given heavy tasks, but Tedric was *her* slave, and she realized that Tedric must have been put to work earlier in the day. She'd been so busy that she hadn't missed him. Anger suffused her face to a bright peach at Guy usurping her authority. "I shall take care of this," she told Flaubert, and hurried across the bailey to where the work was progressing.

Just as Flaubert had told her, Tedric was working alongside the masons. He lifted what looked to be a heavy stone, and the muscles in his upper back and arms bulged with the effort. In the clear daylight without his tunic on, the stripes of his earlier whipping were now evident, criss-crossing each other, though they had faded somewhat with time. Sweat covered his skin and plastered his hair to his head to hang wetly to his broad shoulders. She'd thought the workmen were all able-bodied men, but in comparison, Tedric was far brawnier and stronger than any man she'd ever seen. Amberlie swallowed hard as an odd sensation that was pleasantly painful knifed through her from watching the interplay of muscle against muscle on his torso.

"Be easy with that stone, you sorry Saxon!" Guy's shouts at Tedric as he laid the stone in place drew her attention. "I'll beat your hide if it cracks."

"I trust you will not touch one hair upon my slave's head, Uncle," Amberlie ground out after she'd made her way to Guy's side. Her eyes flashed with a warning anger. "Tedric is my slave, not yours. You've no right to order him to perform the work of a mason. As lady of the keep, I instructed what was to be done with him, and I do not take lightly to having my authority usurped, by you or anyone else."

Guy threw back his head and laughed. He chucked her under the chin. *"Cherie,* you have no authority here."

"I'm mistress of Woodrose."

"Who has told you such a lie? Not Julianne. Now be of good cheer and go about your chores. I want the king to be impressed by my changes here."

"I order Tedric to be turned over to me!" Her voice rose much higher than she'd intended, stunning the workmen and Tedric into inactivity. A Norman woman didn't take issue with a man, especially not a kinsman.

Guy roughly took her by the arm and pulled her out of earshot of the men. Flaubert kicked at a pebble, but neither his nor Tedric's gazes wavered from Amberlie and Guy. "I could beat you for such insolence, and no man would dare to stop me." Guy's face was but an inch away from hers, and the burning anger in his eyes wasn't to be dismissed lightly. "I don't know what sort of spirit of defiance has gotten into you, Amberlie, but I will break you of it. My wife shall not openly defy me."

"I am not your wife, nor will I ever be. I'll kill myself first."

"You're as good as mine. The king shall turn you over to me, for I've done a fine job at securing Woodrose from enemy attack. Just ask your favorite slave how well I run Woodrose.

Ask him if he prefers to work for you or me. Go on, Amberlie, ask him."

A breeze ruffled the strands of dark hair about her face, but an ominous silence hung in the air, as if everyone had heard and was waiting to see what she would do. Not about to be undone by Guy, she shrugged loose of him and marched toward where Tedric stood with the other workmen, watching her. She made a grand show of being in control, but her legs felt weak and her stomach churned. She'd saved Tedric's life, but by doing so, she'd humiliated him in front of his own people and the knights. But she couldn't believe he preferred being a slave to Guy de Bayonne.

"I give you a choice, barbarian," she said, her mouth incredibly dry and her heart pounding so hard she could barely hear herself speak. "You may be my slave or slave to Sir Guy."

Tedric drew himself to his full height of over six feet. The sun gilded his hair, encircling the slave collar in a golden haze, and brightened his eyes. Never had she ever seen a more magnificent-looking man; even in his bondage he put other men to shame. "I choose not to be a slave to you, mistress, if the choice is truly mine. Women's work is not to my liking."

"But the work is less strenuous . . ." It was ridiculous that she stand here and try to convince a slave to curry her favor over Guy's. Why was she humiliating herself like this? "I am not a hard taskmaster, as you well know."

Tedric inclined his head in agreement but shrugged his massive shoulders. "I am a man, my lady, not a serving woman."

"Aye, you are a man." Her mouth went completely dry now but silly tears stung her lashes to be turned down by — a slave! Quickly she turned toward Guy. "The slave has made his choice. He belongs to you." Before she could humiliate herself further, she rushed away to seek the solitude of her chamber.

Tedric belonged to him now. Guy crowed his delight by refilling his tankard with mead at the high table. Julianne was still too ill to join him for supper, and Amberlie was much too mortified. Served the wench right, he decided, and quaffed the brew. She'd overstepped her bounds by asserting her right as mistress of the keep when everyone knew that Julianne was truly in charge. No fainthearted mistress was Julianne. And now that Tedric was in his power, Tedric would pay dearly for causing him months of untold misery with his renegade activities, for making him look the fool with the king.

Before Guy finished with the proud Tedric, the Saxon wouldn't be building the keep but would be resting beneath it in eternal slumber — and he'd make certain that King William decreed Tedric's death. Another week before the king's arrival, one more week before Tedric died.

Guy gestured toward three of his knights. The

men immediately rose from their supper and headed out into the bailey. They accosted Tedric in the kitchen just as he'd finished his meal of porridge. Though Tedric protested and nearly succeeded in pulling away to defend himself, he was no match for three well-armed men. "Come peaceably or your family will suffer," one of them threatened.

Tedric could do nothing else but go with them. Soon he found himself thrust into the large, dark pit behind the keep without a blanket to warm him. And he wondered who was behind his punishment — Guy or Amberlie.

Chapter Twelve

The day of the king's arrival dawned with an overcast sky and a blustery wind from the north. Amberlie had risen early, her efforts harnessed into making certain that all was in readiness. Guy had ordered his knights to be more vigilant than normal in case of an outburst among the Saxon serfs. Amberlie, however, doubted that such an outburst would occur now that Tedric had been captured and thrust into slavery. She hadn't seen him for nearly a week. Never, as she strode through the bailey, overseeing odd tasks, had she noticed him at his toil on the building site. But she'd been so busy, besieged by numerous duties, that she hadn't stood idly by in the hope that she might glimpse him. Tedric had made his choice and thrown in his lot with Guy de Bayonne, making her look like a silly fool in the process. And what did she care about Tedric anyway? The man had nearly seduced her into forgetting her dear husband. And no matter her own failings, she'd always remember that Tedric had robbed her of her life with Henri.

Amberlie was with Julianne in her chamber when Magda ventured into the room, her face ashen and her eyes round and flat-looking like two coins. "Your king comes," she informed them. "I've seen his banners from the battlements."

"King William is your king, too," Julianne reminded her, a triumphant smile turning up the edges of her mouth. "It's time you Saxons realized he is your liege."

"Butcher," Magda whispered and turned hurriedly away, but not before Amberlie had read her lips. Luckily, in her haste to get up from the bed Julianne didn't hear the Saxon woman.

"My cloak." Julianne motioned to Glenna, who immediately but grudgingly covered the woman with the ermine-lined cloak.

"Are you up to such activity?" Amberlie worriedly asked her mother-in-law. Julianne's complexion was still peaked, and she hadn't regained her usually hearty appetite.

"*Oui,* I must meet my king, greet him at the door to the keep. 'Tis my duty."

It was really Amberlie's duty as lady of the keep, but Amberlie didn't argue.

As Amberlie stood by to help Julianne in case of weakness, the woman staunchly made it to her feet. "See, I am my old self again." A small smile graced Amberlie's face, belying what she really felt inside. Though she was glad that Julianne had nearly recovered, she hated the thought of

138

being pushed into the background again. During Julianne's illness, she'd overseen the running of the keep, and she'd done an able job of it. But soon, her efforts would be forgotten when Julianne took over. She must petition the king to find her a husband soon. She needed a home of her own where she was the lady of the keep and of her husband's heart.

Julianne's eyes raked over Amberlie's petite figure, encased in a gray wool bliaut over a white chemise with a jeweled belt at the hips. "Where are your mourning clothes?"

"It has been over six months since Henri's death. I felt the king's visit was special enough so that I might wear something other than black." Amberlie hated having to explain herself to Julianne, but there was something about the woman which always unnerved her and caused her to feel like a child caught in some naughtiness.

"I trust you have not forgotten my son—or who murdered him."

"I have not forgotten."

Her answer seemed to mollify Julianne. *"Bien,* then we go to greet our king."

Knights stood at respectful attention on top of the battlements and in the bailey as William and his entourage entered. The clip-clop of their horses' feet on the stones echoed across the courtyard, and then was drowned out by a sudden outpouring of cheers from Guy and his

139

knights. The Saxons who were in attendance cheered as well, but less lustily.

Guy was the first to greet William. He bowed low to the king, who was of average height and whose hair was sprinkled liberally with gray, and waited until William ordered him to rise before greeting him with the customary kiss on both cheeks. Julianne curtsied unsteadily, leaning upon Amberlie's arm for support. Then Amberlie moved forward, curtsying deeply, only to find herself in a huge bear hug upon straightening. "Ah, how is my pretty girl? Has it really been over a year since we've last met?" William appraised her with a fatherly eye. "You've lost weight, *cherie.*"

Amberlie had no course but to agree. *"Oui,* sire."

"During my visit, I shall make certain you are fattened up like a fine French sow."

"I have been most unwell, sire," Julianne interjected as the king's attention was fixed on Amberlie. "Stomach grippe, a most unpleasant business."

"C'est dommage. Then I hope my visit will not wreak havoc upon your health, madam." William directed a weak smile at Julianne and taking Amberlie by the elbow, he escorted her into the keep. Under his breath, he whispered to her, "You're a saint, *cherie,* for putting up with Julianne de Fontaine. Your dear father, who, as you know, was one of my closest friends, never had a kind word for her."

Amberlie grinned mischievously to recall some

of the less then repeatable names her father had called Julianne. "No, sire, he never did. She is a difficult woman, but I trust she means well."

He patted her arm conspiratorially. "You're much too lovely to be sealed away with a woman who'd keep you a nun in memory of her son. I think the time has come to find you a husband."

"If—that is your wish."

"Oui, cherie, I owe it to your father to find a man who is worthy enough of your beauty and kindness."

"And have you found such a worthy man, sire?" she hesitantly asked, almost fearful to hear the answer.

William walked toward the high table, glancing affectionately at her. "You're a special case, because of the affection I hold for you and the friendship I bore for your father. To be honest, I've not yet decided on the man for you, but be of good heart that when I make my choice for you, it will be for the best."

"Oui, sire," she agreed, though she wasn't so certain about that.

The king's men spilled into the great hall, and there was much laughing and joking as they mingled with the knights. Servants hovered inconspicuously near, having neatly laid cloths upon the trestle tables earlier. Under Amberlie's supervision, they'd set the tables with the finest silver spoons and knives. The salt dishes and silver cups had been carefully placed beside each manchet, a thick slice of day-old bread that served as a plate for the roasted meats.

William's personal squire came forward hurriedly, taking immediate control from the servants when each dish was placed before his king to make certain the meats were correctly cut to his lord's preference. The wine flowed freely, and Amberlie sensed that more than one knight began to relax after having lifted his cup for replenishment. She smiled inwardly. She felt rewarded for her hard work — especially when William ordered the knights to rise to their feet and toast her efforts. Basking in the glory, she didn't fail to miss Julianne's mouth pursed like week-old prunes, or the way Guy lecherously lifted his cup to her. She could almost read his thoughts, and would have sworn that he was thinking about how he'd ask the king for her. She made a silent prayer that William would refuse Guy. He must refuse him.

Well past midnight, William rose from a long evening of fine foods and wines. "I must excuse myself for the night," he apologized. Julianne had already long since been allowed to retire because of her health. Amberlie, who was still wide awake, rushed to William's side. "I shall show you to your chamber, sire."

"No, please, you've done enough and must be tired. Sir Guy shall do the honors."

"With the greatest of pleasure, sire." Guy smiled smugly, practically crowing his delight to be the one to escort the king to his specially prepared chamber, which happened to be Guy's own room. Then he would sleep in the great hall on pallets with the rest of William's entourage, Guy

142

didn't mind giving up his bed during the king's stay. Truly, he wished to sleep beside Amberlie's warm body, to devour her with passion. She'd pleased him greatly this night, having been the perfect mistress of the keep and infuriating Julianne in the process. But he must tread carefully—now that he had the king's ear.

"Sire, I should like a word with you." Guy approached William a bit hesitantly after he'd shown him into the room. The squire was busily laying out William's toilet articles and his dressing gown, but seemed oblivious to Guy's presence.

"What is it, de Bayonne? The day has been most long and I am weary."

"Oh, nothing, sire. I withdraw my request, for you need your sleep."

"Out with it!" William snapped, and lifted his arm for the squire to remove his tunic. "You've wanted to speak to me all evening—I could read your face."

"Well, sire, there is a matter of marriage."

William cocked an eyebrow. "Whose marriage? Yours? I thought you were confirmed to bachelorhood."

Guy smiled sheepishly. "Nay, sire, not any longer. I have a wonderful woman in mind and hope my choice meets with your pleasure for you must give permission for us to marry."

"Oh, is she under my wardship?"

"*Oui,* sire. I should like your permission to marry Lady Amberlie de Fontaine."

"Your niece? Are you mad, man!"

"No—no, sire. You forget that Amberlie is my step-niece. I have no blood ties to Amberlie. Her mother-in-law is my stepsister."

"I've not forgotten!" William burst out, causing Guy to scurry to the opposite side of the room. Sweat broke out upon Guy's forehead. "By Church law, you're within the bounds of consanguinity," William reminded him with a frown.

"But—but for special circumstances such laws can be—relaxed." Guy swallowed hard, his expression hopeful but sheepish. "I have fallen in love with the lady, sire, hopelessly and truly in love."

"Then that is reason enough not to allow such a marriage. Love can besot a man's brain and make him untrustworthy on the battlefield."

"Oui, sire, if you say so, but still I love her."

"Eh? I know what you love more, and it is made of stone and mortar."

"True, sire, I will not lie and say I do not value Woodrose Keep as my own. My sweat and blood are poured into these walls; on the morrow you shall observe the remarkable changes I've made here. With Amberlie as my wife and Woodrose Keep in my possession, I can do far more justice to your glory." Guy had the good sense to be quiet for a few seconds, before deciding that now was the time to tell the king about his latest success. "I've also captured the renegade Saxon who has been responsible for uprisings all during the last year. Tedric, formerly of Woodrose."

William sat upon the pelts on the bed and

144

stroked his chin thoughtfully. "So, you've caught this traitor."

Guy proudly puffed out his chest, seeing that he had the king's undivided attention. *"Oui,* sire, he will not do any damage to the keep or your kingdom any longer. All that awaits is your sentence of death."

"Why have you not put him to death on your own?"

"I thought you might wish that privilege for yourself, since he is the one who killed Henri de Fontaine and kidnapped Lady Amberlie — a most heinous crime, my liege."

"Kidnapped Amberlie? I hadn't known that. Did he violate her?" William's lips grew pale.

"No. Amberlie swears that he didn't touch her. She is the one who told me where to search for Tedric." Guy felt Amberlie's assistance in the capture might sway William to his side. If the king believed he and Amberlie were close — perhaps intimate, then he might approve the match.

"I should like this Saxon to be brought before me on the morrow — after I inspect the keep." William pulled the pelts over him.

"As you wish, sire. I trust you'll decide in my favor about Lady Amberlie."

"I shall consider all you've told me. Now I should like to sleep." William dismissed Guy by closing his eyes. Guy bowed and quietly left the room. But still he wasn't satisfied. The king hadn't said aye or nay. Guy hoped that once the king realized how loyal he was, he'd agree to the marriage. And if he must prove his loyalty to personally killing Tedric, he would. In fact, he'd relish it.

Amberlie was just about to blow out her candle when a slight tap sounded at her door. "My lady, 'tis Mabel of Woodrose. I—I should like to speak with you, if you are awake," said the feeble-sounding voice.

Throwing back the covers, Amberlie answered the door in her shift, baffled that Tedric's mother was about and at her door on such a chilly night. The chill seeped into her bones as she stared at Mabel. Mabel's usual pallor had been replaced by slightly rosy cheeks, but still she leaned against the wall for support. "Please come in," Amberlie said, and helped the woman to a chair. Quickly, she covered Mabel with a pelt from her bed, very much aware that Mabel's frail form shook beneath the fur. She wondered if the woman had a fever. "You should be abed," Amberlie said softly.

Mabel shook her head. Her large blue eyes swam with tears. "Nay, I cannot sleep, not when my son is soon to die."

"Tedric is not in harm's way, I assure you. He is a slave to Guy de Bayonne."

"Nay, nay he is not." Mabel grabbed for Amberlie's hand. "Your kinsman has placed my son in the pit, where he will surely die unless someone can save him. If not by starving my boy, de Bayonne shall kill him some other way. Please, my lady, I beg of you, if you have no heart for

146

my boy, and I know you believe him guilty of murder, think of me and my poor Edytha. We've done naught to hurt you. Find it in your heart to entreat Guy de Bayonne to release my son from the pit. A life of slavery is more than enough punishment—I do not want my son to die!"

The pit was a hellish place for it was only a deep hole cut in the ground and covered with wooden slats; in it one could see the sun, but the warming rays never reached those depths. But Tedric had killed her husband. And he'd made his choice to suffer at de Bayonne's hands of his own free will, rather than serve her. Tedric belonged to Guy now, and he could do with him as he pleased.

But never had anyone pleaded with her like Lady Mabel. The woman's pale face was streaked with tears, and the hand clasped around Amberlie's shook so much that Amberlie didn't have the heart to deny her request. She knew that Guy wouldn't willingly release Tedric, but perhaps the knights who guarded the pit would. "I will do what I can," she said lowly, "but I can't promise—"

"Thank you, my lady! Thank you!" Mabel didn't seem interested in hearing the rest of what Amberlie would say; she knew only that Amberlie was willing to help. Mabel rose slowly to her feet, and Amberlie supported her as she walked to the doorway. Magda appeared in the doorway and she immediately took Mabel's arm. "Lady Amberlie will help my son," she whispered to Magda with a jubilant smile.

For the first time since Amberlie had known Magda, Magda smiled back. "Thank you, my lady. I'll keep you in my prayers."

The hood of Amberlie's cloak covered her unbound hair, as on slipper-clad feet she stealthily made her way down the back stairs of the keep. Carefully, she maneuvered a path over the sleeping forms of some of the knights and serving help as she found her way to the wooden back door. The hinges squealed, sounding like a screech owl, and she held her breath. No one stirred except to snore or moan in sleep.

Few stars illuminated the night sky. The entire grounds behind the keep were bathed in darkness, but Amberlie knew the direction well enough to traverse it without a candle. It wasn't so much that she dreaded having to explain herself to her knights as to Guy or Julianne if she were caught. She wasn't certain if she was on a fool's errand or not, but she had to try to free Tedric from the pit—though she knew it wouldn't be easy. However, she was lady of the keep, and her word should mean something. Shouldn't it?

The three guards by the pit noticed her immediately, and raised their lances. " 'Tis Lady Amberlie," she hurriedly explained, recognizing one as Sir Christophe.

Christophe ordered the other two knights to lower their weapons. Moving toward her, he took her arm and propelled her away from the pit. "May I assist you, my lady?" he asked just as if he were used to seeing her walking near the pit in the black of night.

148

"I understand that Tedric the slave is in the pit. I should like him freed to my service again." She spoke evenly and without hesitation, yet Christophe seemed greatly taken aback.

"He belongs to Sir Guy, my lady. I cannot release him to you."

"I'm mistress here and I insist that you do. I've no reason to believe that Sir Guy wishes his death in this way."

Christophe shook his head. "I cannot, my lady."

"I insist!"

"Only the king can release him over Sir Guy. I'm sorry."

She could tell Christophe wasn't going to change his mind easily. "I could have *you* thrown into the pit for disobeying my order." Why she said such a stupid thing she didn't know. She only knew that she was frustrated that no one paid any heed to her, that Julianne and Guy so thoroughly controlled everyone from the knights to the lowliest slave. She had no power. "I demand you release this man to me—"

"I shall deal with Lady Amberlie, Christophe," said Guy's cool and malevolent voice behind her.

She didn't need to turn to see the anger in his eyes; rather she sensed it in the way he roughly grabbed her elbow and steered her toward the keep as if she were a slave herself. And in fact she was, for she had about as much power as Tedric in the pit.

"So, *cherie,* you think to free my slave. Tell me, why does it matter so much to you if Tedric lives or dies? Is there some reason that I should suspect a soft heart on your part for him?"

She tried to shrug loose, but Guy held her fast and so she allowed herself to be led. "I trusted you wouldn't kill him. The Saxons shall rise up if Tedric dies, and I'm sick of violence."

"Ah, *cherie,* if not for violence I'd be out of an occupation, so to speak. Let the Saxons rise up. They'll be dead for I have an excellent group of knights, and the king has brought his own knights. If the Saxons don't know that they're outnumbered, then they're a stupid bunch and deserve to be killed."

"Have you no heart at all?"

Guy halted in his tracks, pulling her up short against him. *"Oui,* my heart belongs to you and you stomp upon it. I've spoken to the king about you. He is giving consideration to our marriage."

Amberlie felt her stomach sink almost to her toes. For the first time since Guy had broached the subject to her, she now felt that perhaps William would order her to marry him. She could protest the alliance, she knew that, but no one had ever listened to her or understood how she felt. Not even her father, who'd ordered her to marry Henri when she was barely fourteen years old. Luckily, the marriage had been a happy one, if not a fruitful one, because Henri had loved her and been kind to her. But she doubted if Guy would be so kind, not when he was filled with such burning hatred for Tedric, when by rights she should be the one eager to see the man dead.

Guy wanted her only for her home and lands.

150

He'd been married to a wealthy lady for a short time years ago, and the bride had died under odd circumstances. Henri confided to her that he wondered if his uncle had killed the woman after the marriage because she no longer served his purpose. If so, what might Guy do to her?

"I won't marry you." She glared at him.

He peered instantly at her, his face turning into a hostile mask to match her own. *"Bien,* that is your answer but the question lies with the king, and he shall decide. But I tell you one thing, *cherie.* I will make certain that Tedric dies, for I don't trust your answer about what didn't happen between the two of you."

"Nothing happened."

"Really? So it won't matter if I kill the heathen, will it? I mean, if nothing happened then his death shouldn't concern you."

"Guy, please don't. Consider his mother and sister." Why was she begging Guy de Bayonne? What did she care about Tedric's family? But she did care and that was the root of the problem, because they *were* Tedric's family, and this sudden knowledge startled her. Did she possess a soft spot for him? Impossible.

Guy considered her and smiled ruthlessly. "If you care so much about saving his life, then I will bargain with you. Marry me and Tedric will live—as my personal slave—but he'll live."

It would be so easy to agree. But she couldn't. Marriage to Guy would be a nightmare and she had no assurance that Tedric wouldn't be killed anyway. She wouldn't bargain away her happiness

151

for the man who had killed her husband. She couldn't, even though an unfamiliar part of her ached to do so, if only she knew for certain she could save him. "I can't," she whispered, and clutched at her cloak as the wind whipped it about her to reveal her thin shift beneath.

Her tempting curves weren't lost on Guy. A lecherous gleam flooded his gaze as he lightly stroked her jawline. "You're a sweet temptation, *cherie,* but soon you'll be my wife. No matter what you want or don't want, you'll marry me, and Tedric shall die." With a hearty laugh, he bowed; they had reached the keep's back door and he held it open for her.

Amberlie hurried upstairs, not looking back. Her heart thumped hard in her chest and her palms perspired, but she felt wretchedly cold. To her misery, Magda appeared in her chamber. "My lady?" Her voice contained hope.

"I cannot save him," Amberlie whispered miserably, and questioned her own emotions as to why she felt so terrible.

"At least you tried. Thank you, my lady." Then Magda left her alone.

All Amberlie could think was that she'd failed — again.

Chapter Thirteen

"Up the ladder, man, we've not got all day. The king is waiting for you." A knight's lance painfully pressed against Tedric's thigh, rousing him from a fitful sleep. The boards above the pit had been removed and for the first time in over a week, sunshine spilled into the slimy, dark area, practically blinding Tedric. On the side of the pit, a long ladder rested.

Tedric recognized the knight with the lance as a man named Baudelaire, a hardened-looking man with a long chin and deceitful eyes. The climb up the ladder was difficult. Tedric grew dizzy but fought the overwhelming urge to fall back down. He wouldn't humiliate himself in front of his enemies. By sheer will, he made it up, with much prodding in the rump from Baudelaire's lance, to stand finally on his own two feet when he reached flat ground.

Another knight, whom Tedric recalled as Christophe, smiled almost apologetically when he grabbed Tedric by the arm. Tedric felt weak-kneed, and his stomach growled loudly like a forest animal. He'd lost count of how long it had been since he'd stopped eating the slop which had been thrown into the pit, food not fit for human consumption. Evidently, Guy de Bayonne had intended to starve him to death. But now, William the Bastard wanted to see him, and Tedric immediately understood that the plans had changed. He was to die in front of the king.

"No use trying to fight us," Christophe advised with a warning shake of his head at the sudden way Tedric thrust out his chin and clenched his fists. "You're much too weak to challenge us." That was true, and Tedric also lacked the strength really to care what happened to him. He'd spent over a week in near darkness with barely enough water to drink, much less bathe. He was dirty and chilled, having not been allowed even his tunic. Seven days' growth of beard stubbled his face, and tawny hair hung to his shoulders in stringy waves. He accepted what had happened to him, and what soon would happen, but he worried about his mother and sister. As his eyes adjusted to the sunlight, two more knights appeared and attached heavy chains to each arm. Like a weak, wounded lion, Tedric was pulled into the keep.

He heard Guy de Bayonne's triumphant laugh before he saw him. His hated enemy sat upon the dais, smirking at him. The Norman king sat in the center, flanked on both sides by Julianne de Fontaine and Amberlie. Tedric couldn't help but notice Amberlie, dressed in a gray gown with a white linen headdress on her head. If he'd felt better, he'd have turned his eyes away from her to prove that she affected him not at all, but she was so lovely to gaze upon that he couldn't stop staring at her. He hated himself for his weakness where this Norman wench was concerned. The woman had betrayed him and reduced him to a wretched creature, being led before her in chains. Still, he longed to touch her soft cheek, to brush his lips against her sweet mouth. He'd have continued staring at her, but then he saw that her eyes had widened, and her hand clutched her throat in what he took to be pity. He didn't want her pity. So he scowled at her, preferring her repulsion instead, and turned his attention to the king.

"Our prisoner has arrived, sire." Guy de Bayonne gestured a well-manicured hand toward Tedric while addressing the king. "Tedric, the renegade, awaits your pleasure."

William leaned back in his chair, forming his fingers into a tent, and studied the prisoner, his expression guarded and emotionless. He took in every aspect of Tedric's appearance, from his dirty, mud-filled hair to his filthy torn hose. He noted bruises on Tedric's massive torso, even the whip marks on his back that were healing over with scar tissue. The man could barely stand from weakness, but there was an arrogance about him, a cockiness which not even the whip had dispelled. "So, you're the Saxon who has bested my most able-bodied knights for so long."

Tedric didn't know how to respond to the king's statement, so he said nothing, but he didn't miss de Bayonne's sheepish expression at the humiliating remark. "You're a traitor to your king," William continued. "I have it within my power to execute you. What say you on this?"

"Nothing, for you shall do what you wish."

"Oui, I shall."

"Sire, how shall he die?" Julianne asked much too eagerly, her lips curled upward into a pleased grin. "I can offer several suggestions to bring about his end, something painful to offer me suitable vengeance."

William shifted in his chair. "I'm certain you've thought of many innovative ways to kill this Saxon traitor. But I would like to hear what sort of tortures the Widow de Fontaine has in mind for her husband's murderer." William's voice was calm, his gaze steady. All eyes from the king to the lowliest slave in the great hall turned toward Amberlie. Tedric ignored her; instead he concentrated on the rush-covered floor beneath his mud-caked feet.

"I . . . I do not know, sire," Tedric heard her say in a soft, silky whisper after what seemed to be a long time. "Torture is not to my liking."

"Ah, then you wish the slave to die quickly."

"I do not wish him to die at all."

Both Guy and Julianne gasped in unison. William quietly assessed Amberlie's pale face and Tedric's rock-hard demeanor. The prisoner's eyes

156

stared straight ahead. "Don't you want this man punished for his crime against your husband?"

Amberlie earnestly inclined her head in the king's direction. "I believe sparing his life and forcing him to live as a slave would be just punishment for Henri's death. He . . . is a proud man who is unafraid to die. By killing him, you'd be doing him a favor."

William stroked his chin. "Really? That is most interesting."

"Sire," Guy hastily broke in, his voice sounding shrill, "Lady Amberlie has a tender heart. You mustn't seriously consider what she says for she is only a woman."

"*Oui,* sire," Julianne put in. "My daughter-in-law hasn't been coached in the art of meting out justice."

William nodded and said to Tedric, "It seems your mode of death is undecided, Saxon. What say you?"

In a low, tired voice, Tedric answered. "I won't beg for my life. To exist as a slave is to live as an animal, and I am not an animal to be kicked and beaten, humiliated at every turn. I ask nothing for myself but I beg mercy for my family. My mother is ill, and my sister is frail of mind. The woman to whom I am betrothed has done nothing to warrant punishment. You are a mighty king, and I hope a just one. Take not your wrath out upon my family. I beg mercy for them, only for them . . . sire." He could barely force out that last word.

157

Not a sound could be heard in the great hall. Everyone seemed to be captivated by Tedric's plea. Some of the Saxon serving women who'd served Tedric's family before the invasion wiped at their eyes. A lump formed in more than a few Norman throats at Tedric's concern for his family. Though they were the conquerors, the Normans too had families they loved with as much fervor.

William aptly read the situation. This man was no ordinary renegade but a noble man, a man who inspired allegiance among his own people and who had also softened the hearts of his enemies. Might such a man be valuable to him? Killing him would serve no real purpose but to prove how mighty a king he was, and he'd already done that hundreds of times over the last year. Something warned William that Tedric could be put to better use by keeping him alive.

A slight sound on his left drew his attention to Amberlie. Her wide, frightened eyes had fastened upon the captive and not once strayed. The woman was enthralled by the Saxon, though she didn't know it—not enough reason to suspend the death sentence, but something he'd dwell upon at a later time. However, the remembrance of Guy de Bayonne's request, his hunger for Amberlie, and his desire for Tedric of Woodrose's demise gave William pause. He didn't care for Guy, who was a good knight but too crafty and clever—and perhaps guilty of the murder of his wife. Guy's wife had been a kind, sweet woman, not unlike Amberlie de Fontaine. Was it possible that the same fate might befall Amberlie, the child of William's best friend? He also didn't care for Guy's lust for power, which he considered more dangerous than lust for a woman. And Guy had taken over the keep's operations on his own initiative. Perhaps it was time to put Guy in his place.

"A noble spirit resides within you, Saxon," William responded, choosing his words with care. "I trust you're aware of my power, that not only might I order you slain but your family as well."

Tedric swallowed hard, his face ashen. He could barely speak from fear for his loved ones. "Aye, sire."

"Then be of good cheer that I do not order their deaths — or yours at the moment." As he leaned forward, William's hands clenched the edge of the table. "You are familiar with this area, the woods and the animal life within it. I have been led to believe that stags abound in the forests. Is that true?" Tedric could only nod. *"Bien,* then on the morrow I will hunt and you shall be my guide." He turned to Amberlie. "And you, madam, shall accompany me and my party." Amberlie too could only nod, apparently more than amazed by this turn of events. "Please see that Tedric is bathed and given adequate nourishment, my lady, for I wish him to be well and hearty on the morrow."

"Oui, sire, as you wish," Amberlie responded with a grateful smile.

William then ordered the two knights who'd dragged Tedric into the hall to remove his chains. The king was very much aware of the horrified expressions on Guy's and Julianne's faces. Both said nothing, having the good sense not to interfere. Before Tedric was led away, William warned him. "Remember, Saxon, that you shall be watched—and your family's safety rests with you."

Tedric inclined his head in agreement, realizing William was testing him. Then the king told Amberlie she could deal with her charge, and she left the great hall to see to Tedric's needs.

Glenna had seen and heard all that transpired between Tedric and the king. As she carried her bucket to the pond with the other women, she listened as they spoke of William's sudden generosity. They were very much impressed; Glenna, however, wasn't. This was the sort of information which Wulfgar needed to kill the bastard king, and she would act upon it.

After the women filled their buckets and turned hurriedly back to the keep, Glenna dawdled behind and watched for Wulfgar, who didn't disappoint her. Quickly she told him of the king's hunt on the morrow. "Good, good. Tomorrow I strike," Wulfgar told her, and hurried away to blend into the forest.

Glenna started back, and stopped short to notice Sir Christophe, standing on the path some distance away. She doubted he'd seen Wulfgar, and then knew he hadn't by the huge smile he bestowed upon her. Without words, he held out his hand and took her bucket, as he'd done each day for a week now. He hadn't tried to steal a kiss yet, and Glenna was disappointed. She wanted him to kiss her, but wouldn't admit such a traitorous thought when it was Tedric whom she loved. At least, she thought she loved Tedric. Such a long time had passed since they'd lain together that she wasn't certain anymore. Her dreams now centered upon Christophe. Though she found the knight handsome, she worried that she was being unfaithful to Tedric, disloyal to her own people.

"You needn't wait to help me," she snapped at Christophe, hiding her happiness at seeing him. "I can manage to carry a bucket on my own."

"I know," he said softly, his dark eyes softening like melted butter when he looked at her. "You can do anything you want, *cherie,* but I wish you wanted me as much as you long for your Saxon."

This man could adequately read her thoughts. Did he discern her traitorous sentiments? Glenna narrowed her eyes at Christophe. It would never do to fall in love with this man. Never. He was her enemy.

"Just stop waiting for me and helping me! I hate you!" Rudely, she grabbed the bucket and quickly trudged down the path back to the keep, not turning around to see if Christophe followed.

She knew he didn't. She found herself blinded by her own tears because she'd hurt him.

The kitchen help buzzed around Tedric, who sat in a small wooden tub. The serving women giggled and hovered in groups at the doorway to watch the large man at his bath. There was very little privacy for a slave, and since the kitchen was the nearest place to bathe, the buckets were hauled there. "Stop your gaping, you silly wenches," a disgruntled male serf shouted at the tittering group. "Lord Tedric would like to bathe in peace."

Glenna, being the boldest of the women, and recognized as Tedric's betrothed, walked past them. With a flash of warning in her blue eyes, she ordered all of them to leave their lord alone. Quickly, they dispersed and someone shut the door. Lifting her bucket, she rained some water upon Tedric's hair, and went about lathering it with a scented soap she'd taken from Amberlie's chambers. "I have news, my lord," she whispered softly, making a grand show of cleaning his long mane in case someone watched from the window. "Wulfgar plans to kill the Bastard on the morrow, during the hunt."

Tedric grabbed Glenna's wrist and stopped her. "He mustn't. You must get word to him. My family is in danger — as are you — no he cannot do this. I forbid it!"

"But — but, Tedric — I cannot find him. I know

162

not where he is." Glenna glanced to make certain no one was in earshot. "The king shall be slain by a stray arrow—who shall be able to prove—"

"Norman knights know their own arrows. By Christ's blood, Glenna, is Wulfgar so dense?"

Tears choked Glenna's throat. "He—we—didn't think. I know not what to do! We only wanted to help."

Sheer terror showed on Tedric's countenance. "Get away from me," he ordered none too softly. "Don't help me again, for I need not your type of help." Glenna left him in tears.

For a long while he sat in the tub, staring moodily at the far wall. What was he going to do now? The Norman king had given him a bit of freedom as a test of his loyalty with his loved ones' lives as the prize. William could still execute him, but if he were obedient and caused no trouble, then his family would most likely live. And now Wulfgar and Glenna were jeopardizing everyone's futures.

Rising from the tub, he heard the door opening. Assuming it was Glenna again, he turned around to face her. "I told you to leave me alone," he began, but instantly bit off his words at seeing Amberlie, who stood just a few feet away from him. In her arms, she carried men's clothing.

"Oh! I am sorry," she said, and swiftly turned her back to hurry toward the door.

"Wait!" Tedric pulled a towel around his waist. "I am covered, my lady. What do you want?"

Turning around, Amberlie saw that Tedric had indeed covered himself. Shyly, she inched toward a chair and laid the garments upon it. "Sir Christophe was kind enough to give you a tunic and hose. Sir Flaubert has volunteered his mantle and boots. I hope the clothes fit, for you are exceedingly large." Amberlie flushed a deep crimson, and her gaze unwittingly strayed to his covered groin area and then to his face. "I mean you're much taller than they and large of chest."

"Thank you, my lady," he said simply, holding the ends of the rough linen towel about his waist. "I shall thank Flaubert and Christophe when I see them."

"They wanted you to look your best for the hunt tomorrow."

"I appreciate their kindness."

"Have you eaten yet?"

"Nay."

"I shall have Runa prepare you a dish."

"That is most kind of you, my lady."

Amberlie hesitated a moment longer than was customary in such a situation. She couldn't stop staring at the powerfully built man before her. Rivulets of water dripped down his slick, muscled chest like oils. One of his thighs was visible, the taut muscles bulging with his straddled stance. She swallowed hard, willing herself to look at his face—a face which was more than handsome with all that wet tawny hair slicked back and hanging to his shoulders. She couldn't help but remember what she'd seen of his lower body when he'd turned to face her. And never in her life had she been so captivated and embarrassed. Indeed, Glenna was a fortunate woman. With a strength of will, Amberlie composed her features and managed to look and sound haughty, the perfect lady of the castle. "King William has advised me that he shall break his fast before dawn on the morrow and wishes for you to sleep in the great hall tonight with his retinue. I've ordered a pallet and blanket for you to be placed on the floor. You shall be under Sir Christophe's protection. Consider yourself fortunate that you are still alive."

Tedric gave a tiny bow. "I do, my lady." Amberlie made a move to turn away, but Tedric said, "Why don't you want me dead?"

"You know why. Having you live as a slave will be punishment enough for Henri."

"But what about you? Why don't *you* want me dead?"

Backing away, Amberlie shook her head. Tiny wisps of hair escaped from her headdress as she reached for the door handle. "I know not why," she said, only knowing she must escape from Tedric's spell over her, from the way she couldn't stop staring at him.

"I think you know why, my lady, but are frightened to admit your own desires."

Like a frightened sparrow, Amberlie took wing and hurried out of the room, slamming the door soundly behind her. She practically ran to the fortress-like protection of the keep and threw her-

165

self into her chores. There was much to do while the king and his knights were in residence, but despite all of the work and activity, Amberlie couldn't stop thinking about Tedric and remembering how he looked as he stood naked and wet in the tub.

She doubted she'd ever forget.

Chapter Fourteen

Amberlie descended the stairs of the keep, dressed in a green bliaut with a rusty-brown mantle thrown over her head to blend in with the autumnal colors of the woods. Light had not yet broken when she entered the great hall to find the knights already breaking their fasts. William had finished eating minutes earlier, and already taken his leave to tend to his horse in the courtyard. She covertly glanced around for Tedric, but didn't see him or Sir Christophe, which was just as well for she wasn't eager to face Tedric this morning after having viewed him the day before. Even now just thinking about the incident caused her blood to warm her cheeks.

Sitting down to break her fast, Amberlie was met by Guy, who practically snarled at her. "Hurry and eat, the king awaits."

Amberlie helped herself to a pear from a large bowl on the table which contained apples as well. "You're rather grumpy and tense this morn. What ails you, Uncle?"

He shot her a withering look. "You know very well what is wrong with me, you traitor!"

"I, a traitor?" she asked in all innocence. "Kindly explain."

"Tedric was to have died. The king would have ordered his death, if not for you. I wanted the man dead and you interfered, busy wench that you are."

"You're a sorry loser, I think."

Guy leaned close to her; the fetid smell of last night's ale hung heavily on his breath. "Listen to me, *Cherie* Amberlie, and understand my words. You shall marry me—I will make certain that William turns you and your lands over to me. You may have won the skirmish, but I shall win the battle, if it's games you want to play." Viciously, he pulled on his hunting gloves, just as the olifant sounded for all to mount. "Come along, the king is ready." Guy stood and strode out of the keep. Amberlie followed along after him, wondering if the king would indeed turn her over to Guy as a bride. A chill enveloped her just to think about such an unspeakable union. She must speak to William about her marriage, and speak to him soon. There was no telling what Guy might talk the king into doing.

Tedric knelt down on his haunches and measured the deer tracks in the soft, wet earth with his fingers. He'd earlier examined a number of scratches on a mulberry bush and the droppings made by their quarry. Clearly they were hunting a large stag, and Tedric had no doubt it was one he'd hunted only two seasons earlier, though it seemed like two centuries ago, when this land had belonged to him. Rising to his feet, he addressed William, who was on horseback. "Your prey is nearby, sire."

William slid from the large destrier and motioned to his squire to bring his bow and arrow. "The animal, he is large?"

"Aye, I remember him. A most handsome and clever beast."

"Ah, *bien*. But it is not the kill, eh, but the hunt which warms the blood."

Tedric agreed, having always been an ardent huntsman, not so much for the kill as for the stalk. Yet it had always been important to provide food for the table. Still, he'd never had the heart to kill this large stag they now hunted for he was a majestic and noble animal. The knights gathered in a group behind the king, each with a bow and arrows, but Tedric guessed that not one would shoot at the animal for fear of hitting it and offending the king.

Not only did Tedric search for the stag, but also for any sign of Wulfgar. Somehow he'd have to signal to him to cease this mad plan of his to kill the king. He surveyed the woods for any sign of Wulfgar's footprints or presence. So far, he'd seen nothing out of the ordinary. Each time he glanced around, he cursed inwardly to notice Amberlie, with Guy hovering at her side.

Why must he care so much about this woman who wanted to see him shackled for life in slave chains? He should leave her to Guy de Bayonne and forget her. But he couldn't, and he worried that if he wasn't careful, Amberlie de Fontaine would cause his ruination.

"The stag, he is there." William pointed a long finger toward a heavily wooded portion of forest. Not more than two hundred feet away stood the large animal, apparently oblivious to the group of people who watched it dine on the leaves of a low shrub plant. Making ready his bow, William began to move stealthily forward, his gaze never wavering from his prey.

Though part of the hunting party, Amberlie was there only as a courtesy to the king and was quite bored with the whole affair. She got off her horse when a tiny chipmunk on the low branch of a huge, spreading oak tree caught her fancy. Drawn to the tiny creature, she quietly meandered toward the tree to get a better look at it.

Having centered his attention upon the king, Tedric caught a flash of movement out of the corner of his eye. To his left, he discerned an arrow, pointed directly at the king from behind a giant oak tree. Wulfgar!

The blood pounded through Tedric's temples, nearly deafening him. It sounded as if thousands of trampling feet ran through his head. Glancing wildly about, he saw that the others intently watched the king, waiting for the man to land the telling shot. No one saw the long arrow but himself—and Wulfgar had a clear view. His arrow wouldn't miss its mark, and the king would fall dead at their feet.

Wasn't this what Tedric wanted? No matter what happened to himself, whether he'd be run instantly through by William's knights or hung, William would be dead and England would be free. Wild hope surged hotly through him as he watched Wulfgar's arrow follow the king's movements. Yet what other repercussions would such a death herald for England? What of his family? Could he just stand idly by and see the man mowed down before him? Only seconds were left before Wulfgar would loose his arrow upon the king, and Tedric was still undecided.

Tedric caught sight of Amberlie's mantle, fluttering in the breeze. Nonchalantly, she strolled into his line of vision, innocently positioning herself between the arrow and the king. If Wulfgar pulled the bowstring now, she'd be the one killed, not William! Tedric wouldn't—he couldn't allow this to happen, not to Amberlie—"

"Amberlie, no!"

Before he was even aware of moving, Tedric dashed toward the startled woman, pushing her roughly aside to sprawl upon the grass like a baby sparrow who'd fallen from the nest. In his desire and haste to save Amberlie, Tedric had forgotten about his own safety. A sudden burning sensation streaked mercilessly through his side, and he knew Wulfgar's arrow had found its mark in his own flesh.

Dropping to his knees, he heard Amberlie scream. The raised voice of the king shouted to the knights. Pandemonium broke loose in the forest. The knights ran hither and yon, swords drawn and ready to do battle against one lone man, but Tedric no longer cared. Somehow his head rested on Amberlie's lap, and she actually cried tears over him, all the while praying to the Holy Virgin to spare his life. And he knew that even if he died at that moment, he had already found paradise.

Old Gundred finished sewing the gaping wound, and then applied a smelly poultice to the raw and viciously red area. Tedric had lost a great deal of blood by the time he'd been brought from the forest to be placed in Amberlie's chambers at the keep, much to Guy's disapproval. But the king had ordered Amberlie to care for Tedric herself, and no one disobeyed the king.

Under Gundred's watchful eye, she'd mixed a concoction of herbs and leaves that Gundred had brought with her. She followed the directions exactly for too much of the brew could kill instead of cure, and carefully lifted his head to force the liquid down his throat.

She finished wringing out a blood-streaked rag, one of many that had been used to cleanse the wound and stem the bleeding. The man had lost much blood and looked deathly pale.

"Shall he live?" Amberlie asked the old woman, gazing worriedly down at Tedric, who lay upon her bed. A large wolf pelt covered him, but already the man shook from chills.

"Only the mother goddess who gives life knows for certain. 'Tis she who brings forth life each spring to burst anew upon the earth. Perhaps if my Lord Tedric has pleased her, she will let him live. I've done all I can for him." Gundred shook her head, her mass of gray hair reaching to her waist like strands of moss. "He is a strong man, or was until his imprisonment in the pit. Ye could have prevented his capture, my lady. Ye are responsible for his downfall."

"How dare you berate me. Tedric is a renegade, a murderer and a kidnapper. I did only what was expected of me." But Amberlie held back tears of self-recrimination because Gundred spoke the truth. Never would she openly admit that she'd made a mistake in telling Guy where Tedric had been hiding. The man had been a hunted criminal, and she'd done her duty to her family and the king. But this was the second time that Tedric had saved her life. How much longer could she continue hating this man?

"Aye, my lady, but why do ye care to save his life now? If ye wish only to see him dead, then cease your ministrations and leave him to death. Mayhaps some tender affection lies within your bosom for him."

Amberlie shook her head. "I care not for him, other than I would for any other person who is sick or injured. I don't like to see someone suffer, that is all."

"I see through ye, my lady. I know what ye feel."

"You know nothing. Now get out, Gundred. I can care for him by myself." Amberlie busied herself with tearing strips of cloth to bind

Tedric's wound at a later time and ignored the old woman, who wasn't so easily put off.

"I can make ye a love charm, my lady. Something that will set Lord Tedric's heart to pounding each time he sees ye. He'll want no other but ye—if he lives, that is," Gundred whispered into Amberlie's ear, and gave a small cackle.

Amberlie had had enough. Her nerves were frayed from the day's terrible events, and now here was an old woman giving vent to her heathen beliefs. It was all too much to endure. "Gundred, I want no part of your pagan beliefs, and I'm in no need of a love charm. Now please leave."

"As ye wish, my lady, but I can help ye win any man ye want, be he knave, knight—or lord." Her clear-eyed gaze turned to Tedric on the bed.

"Get out!"

Gundred shrugged her shoulders and shuffled to the door. "Silly, old hag," Amberlie groused under her breath when she was alone with her patient. Love charms. How ridiculous! As if she'd seriously consider indulging in such a superstitious heathen belief. Aside from Gundred's ability to cure, Amberlie doubted the woman served any useful purpose at all.

Completing her task, Amberlie placed her hand on Tedric's forehead and found he burned with a fever, which was to be expected. His wound was deep, and probably he was in a great deal of pain, so it was better that he slept to regain his strength. But to look at him now no one would recognize him as the golden Saxon, a barbarian known for his strength and obstinacy. He was weak and helpless, tossing and turning as the fever rose, and Amberlie could only feel pity and concern.

Every few hours, she applied a fresh poultice and bathed his fevered brow with a wet cloth. That was all she could do for him, other than force the nasty-tasting brew she and Gundred had concocted down his throat. His fate was up to God and she prayed—but just to insure he'd be all right, she also said a prayer to the mother goddess.

Magda and Lady Mabel, with Edytha following, visited the sick room later that day. Lady Mabel still didn't look well enough to be walking around, but she insisted that she be allowed to see her son and Amberlie wouldn't refuse her. Her eyes filled with tears as she reached for her son's hand. "He runs a high fever. What have you done for him?" she asked Amberlie. When Amberlie explained, she nodded and asked if she could sit with him for a while. Amberlie agreed, and settled the old woman in a comfortable chair beside the bed, where Mabel took over stroking his burning brow with wet cloths. Edytha sat in mute silence on the floor near her mother, tears streaming freely down her face. "Will Tedric go to heaven, Mother?" she finally asked.

"I pray not, child."

"Then do you pray for him to go to hell?" she asked, misunderstanding her mother's response.

"I pray that the Lord takes him not away from us."

"Does she pray too?" Edytha pointed to Amberlie.

"I know not, for she is a Norman and thinks not like us," Mabel softly whispered to her daughter, but Amberlie heard her and tensed. No matter that she was caring for their kinsman, these people still saw her as the enemy.

When the strain became too great for Mabel, Madga led the woman back to her pallet in the weaving room. Edytha stayed behind for a little while longer and intently watched while Amberlie tended to Tedric. "You helped me too," the girl said, with just the hint of a smile on her lips, before she practically ran from the room to join her mother.

Amberlie realized Edytha must be remembering how she'd helped fend off Baudelaire, the knight who had tried to attack her. She wondered just how much Edytha discerned of events, everyday activities. It was becoming clear to Amberlie that Lady Mabel sheltered the girl, perhaps too much.

King William appeared at the chamber door, alone, shortly after sunset. He entered the room and stood by the bottom of the bed, contemplating the restless and fevered Tedric after inquiring about his health. "For a Saxon, he is brave, *cherie*. I believe we both owe him our lives."

Guy and Julianne didn't appear, but Amberlie knew that Guy prowled the hallway, for she'd seen him and his disapproving scowls a number of times when she'd opened the door to Magda, who brought pitchers of fresh water.

Toward midnight a knock sounded on the door, and Amberlie wearily answered it to discover a pale-faced Glenna. "May I see him, my lady?" she asked on the verge of tears, and her gaze flew past Amberlie to Tedric's prone figure on the bed.

Amberlie longed to refuse Glenna's request for she didn't like the woman. However, Tedric loved Glenna and the woman was his betrothed. Reluctantly, Amberlie waved her inside.

Glenna's hands reached out to stroke Tedric's face. The tears started to flow and slid down her cheeks. "His skin is so hot to the touch. I fear he might die."

"He won't die. I won't let him," Amberlie said forcefully, suddenly deciding that she would somehow pull him through this crisis and definitely not liking the way Glenna possessively touched her charge.

Jealously congealed upon Glenna's face. "Oh, my lady, I doubt you shall have anything to do with his recovery. Tedric is strong of body and heart. He'd not expire in a Norman woman's bed!"

Amberlie held the door open to Glenna. "You'd best leave now. I'm certain Lady Julianne must have need of you."

"I should be the one tending to Tedric, not you!" Glenna objected. She stole one last look at Tedric before leaving.

Fatigued and worried, Amberlie sat beside the

177

bed and peered at the man, who shivered in his delirium like the leaves on a tree during a violent windstorm. Glenna was right, Amberlie decided. Tedric's betrothed should be the one who cared for him, who performed the intimate services of nurse. Why had the king insisted she be the one to look after the man? Yes, he'd saved her life, and she realized she was indebted to him, but there were others who were more qualified to nurse an extremely ill man back to health.

The room grew stuffy but she hesitated to throw open the windows when Tedric shivered from chills, his teeth chattering uncontrollably though he burned with a high fever. The fire in the hearth made the room hot and uncomfortable. Pulling off her bliaut to cool herself, Amberlie wore only her shift as she sat upon the wolf pelt to place a wet cloth upon Tedric's forehead. Tiredness seeped into her bones, and she closed her eyes. Without warning, she found her wrist locked in Tedric's surprisingly strong clasp. She opened her eyes to find herself staring into his brightly fevered blue eyes. "Warm me," he begged, "please, in the name of God."

Three heavy pelts covered him already, and there were no more in the keep that weren't being put to use on what was an especially chilly night. She didn't know how to answer him for the man's entire body shook with cold, and she wasn't certain he even knew who she was. "Mayhaps I can find one more pelt for you." She started to move away, but Tedric wouldn't let her go.

"Nay, nay," he mumbled. "Please—please." And then in an instinct of self-preservation, Tedric pulled her toward him until she lay atop him. Amberlie squirmed to free herself, but Tedric didn't heed her pleas to release her. In fact, he didn't seem to hear her. At first, she was shocked by his brazenness, until she understood that he was delirious and reaching out for some physical comfort and contact.

The man had saved her life. She owed him something, she knew that, yet she hadn't forgotten he had slain Henri. But the king had commissioned her to care for Tedric, and one didn't disobey a royal command. Yet Tedric held her atop him, pinned to his shivering body, and she couldn't move. She doubted this was what the king had had in mind. Perhaps if she lay quietly, Tedric would free her.

The day's ordeal had taken a toll upon her, and she felt unbearably tired, now that she was in a reclining position. Her lids grew heavy, and she found herself dozing, only to be wakened by Tedric's shivers. What harm could be done by crawling beneath the pelts and offering bodily warmth to a dangerously ill man? she asked herself when sleep became too hard to resist. No one would enter the room without her permission, and the hour was late. No one would see her burrowed beneath the pelts with Tedric. Not only would she be getting much-needed sleep but she would also be helping Tedric.

Easing her body out of Tedric's embrace, Amberlie crawled beneath the pelts, careful of

Tedric's wound. In his delirium, he moved and ensnared her in his arms so she was forced to wrap one of her arms around his chest, almost as if she belonged in that intimate position. Amberlie knew she should be embarrassed, but she was too tired to care. And anyway, no one would ever see them. She'd take just a short nap, she told herself.

With a wild wind whipping through the turrets and Tedric's uneven breathing in her ear, Amberlie fell into a deep sleep.

Chapter Fifteen

Julianne's shrill scream woke Amberlie, shortly after dawn. Amberlie reacted to the sound as if twenty hungry dogs were upon her, ready to devour her with bared fangs, by instinctively bounding from the bed to stare in sleepy-eyed befuddlement at the horrified face of her mother-in-law and the calmer face of the king.

"Le bon Dieu! What have you done, what have you done?" Julianne cried, and positioned both of her hands over her heart, almost as if she were suffering some sort of an attack. "My son must be turning over in his grave at this repulsive sight. You've dishonored my son! For this, I shall never forgive you. Never!" Her face became an effigy of hatred as she stomped from the room, without first asking leave of the king.

Amberlie, still in the grasp of sleep, was more than puzzled, wondering what had precipitated such a violent response. Only when King William cast a disparaging glance toward the bed did Amberlie suddenly remember that she hadn't slept alone last night.

"Oh, no!" she muttered, and placed a trembling hand over her mouth to see the brawny man who lay in her bed. During the night, the covers had slipped from Tedric's body and now rested heedlessly below his waist. His muscular upper torso was bare, the morning sunshine highlighting the slave collar around his neck. Thick light-colored hair covered his chest and formed a V below his waist before disappearing beneath the pelts. Despite the unseemly situation, Amberlie couldn't help thinking that he seemed very much at home, as did she, standing with bare feet in only her shift before the king of England. Nervously, she pushed back the tousled, dark curls from her face and wondered what King William must think of her.

She swallowed deeply, her hands shaking. "Sire, please, I can explain. This is not what it seems. You know this man has been very ill."

"Oui, but he doesn't look so sick to me now, *cherie."* William moved past Amberlie and placed his hand upon Tedric's forehead. "His fever, it has broken."

"It has!" Amberlie exclaimed in disbelief after feeling Tedric's cheeks. Sometime during the night Tedric had passed the crisis, and now felt cool to the touch. His breathing too was regular, and his coloring no longer deathly pale. Glancing up at the king, she smiled in relief, but was immediately chastised by the quelling look he gave her. Turning up the covers over Tedric, she then slipped into her green velvet dressing robe and waited in the center of the room.

"Lady Julianne is very upset," he reminded her.

"I know, but I've done nothing wrong."

"Bien, I am sure you are innocent of any—indelicacy—where this man is concerned. But Julianne has spoken to me already about your kidnapping. Her fears are great that something happened between you and this Saxon, that your value as a bride has diminished. And now, to be found in bed with him—well, *cherie,* you can see the problem here. I might not be able to find you a suitable husband—at least, not one whom you would prefer."

Amberlie's fingers clutched at the top of her robe. Slivers of fear curled inside of her stomach like tiny worms. Her worst nightmare was about to come true, she knew it. The king was going to force her to wed anyone who would have her. "If that is the case," she said through stiff, pale lips, "then I shall remain unmarried."

William sadly shook his head. "No, *cherie,* you will marry again. I've already been approached by someone for your hand."

This was worse than she'd first feared. Only one man had asked for her, and she already knew who that was. "I would rather enter a nunnery than wed Henri's step-uncle." Taking a huge gulp of air, she approached the king with hesitant steps and lifted her hands imploringly. "Sire, I beg of you as a good and gracious sovereign, as the childhood friend of my father, please recon-

183

sider. I could never care for Guy as a husband, I could never respect him enough to give him due as my lord. I don't expect to find love in another marriage, but yes, I should like to love again. Yet, if there will be no true affection, then I should want to be a good wife and proud of my husband. Guy de Bayonne repulses me."

"But you need a strong man to care for you. Your father would have wished for a man who can protect you—and Guy de Bayonne can offer you protection here at Woodrose."

Tears swam in her eyes to even be considered as a bride for Guy. "I beg of you, sire, on my dear Henri's grave, I beg of you not to give me as bride to Guy de Bayonne. Shall I get on my knees, shall I crawl to you?"

William pulled her up by the arms just as she began to do that very thing. "Let me think on this some more, *cherie*. I would not have you beg to me. Out of respect for your father I would not wish to see you unhappy."

"*Merci,* sire. You are a great king." Amberlie clutched at William's hands and humbly kissed each one.

"And you are a blatant flatterer, still using your little girl tricks on me. Now see to your charge," he ordered with a gentle smile before kissing her cheek and then departing the room, softly closing the door behind him.

She didn't know how long she stood there, staring at the wooden panels on the door in a trance, worrying and wondering what her future held. Had William truly understood how much she dreaded a marriage to Guy? And if he did understand, would he insist she marry him anyway? Never had she known of any Norman woman who'd married for love. Though her own parents had loved one another very deeply, their marriage had been arranged, as had her own to Henri. Just once, she'd like someone to listen to her and respect her opinion—especially when it involved turning over her person to a man whom she detested, making her wed such a man.

A moan from the bed interrupted her reverie. Tedric stirred and turned his face toward her upon waking. He watched her from shining blue eyes. "Water—please, my lady—water," he whispered hoarsely. After pouring a cup of water, Amberlie went to the bed and held it to Tedric's lips while he drank greedily. Her hand brushed against his mouth when she took the cup away.

"Your fever has broken," she told him, disturbed by the warmth that flowed through her at touching him. An absurd reaction, she decided, since she'd slept quietly with her arm around him during the night. After such an intimacy, being near Tedric and touching him shouldn't bother her at all. But it did, and the difference was that now he was wide awake and lucid. She even found she couldn't look at him now without blushing to recall how she'd fallen blissfully asleep in his arms. Thank God that the man had no memory of the past night. Leaving his side, she sat on the window seat at the opposite end of the room. "I think you'll be well. Gundred's potion is most effective."

He watched her, his expression serious. "Are you well, my lady?"

"Certainly."

"You weren't hurt when I pushed you to the ground, I mean."

"Nay, I'm fine. You saved my life. I am forever grateful to you."

"Then why do you sit so far away? I promise that I shall not touch you again."

"What do you mean—again?" A slow flush rose from her toes to her hairline for she knew exactly what he meant when he smiled lecherously at her, a unique accomplishment for a man who had been deathly ill only hours earlier.

"I held you in my arms while you slept. Your presence was most comforting to me, your body most warm while I sweated out the fever."

Amberlie rose to her feet, unaware of how becoming she appeared to Tedric with her hair a mass of curls about her face and shoulders. "I know not what you mean," she lied, unable to admit she'd been so weak with fatigue, and some emotion which she wouldn't dare name, that she'd crawled beneath the pelts with him like a whore. No matter that Julianne and the king might spread the truth throughout the whole castle, throughout the kingdom, she couldn't admit anything of a personal nature to this man. "You are wrong, and must have been delirious, for I know not what you mean."

"Once again, my lady, you avoid the issue, but I am too tired to argue. I should like to rest some more."

"Then by all means do. I'll send for Magda to tend to you."

Tedric lifted an eyebrow. "So you shall not care for me any longer?"

"You've passed the crisis now, but I shall see you're well taken care of—and moved out of my chambers as soon as you're stronger. This arrangement is—unseemly."

"Ah, my lady, if I must gain strength and lose your sweet presence, then I trust I shall remain as weak as a baby sparrow."

Amberlie glanced out the window, not wanting him to see the way her face flamed with his words. What was there about this man that could always reduce her to one immense blush?

For the next three days, Amberlie tended to Tedric herself. She was the one who changed the linens on his wound and who fed him with her own hand until he was strong enough to take the spoon himself. However, Magda stayed in the room at night while Amberlie slept in Julianne's room to appease Julianne's strict sensibilities. Still, Julianne regarded her with hate-filled eyes. On the fourth day after the attack, William visited Tedric and seated himself in a nearby chair. He ominously fingered the ruby-hilted dagger at his side and ordered Amberlie out of the room.

"I trust I make no mistake by visiting without guards," William began in all seriousness. " 'Twould be a pity to run you through after Lady Amberlie has nursed you back to health."

Tedric shifted his position in the bed, wincing

slightly at the stiff pain in his side but facing the king with a gaze that was strong and earnest. "I have no thoughts of harming you, sire, for I must think of my family."

"Ah, *oui,* they are very important to you, this mother and sister—and betrothed. The woman who tends to Lady Julianne, she is the one you plan to marry?"

"Her name is Glenna."

William nodded. *"Trés jolie,* quite lovely." William was strangely silent for some moments, and Tedric doubted that the man had come to see him about Glenna. Suddenly a tiny smile crossed the king's face. "You don't trust me, do you? Be honest, for I appreciate honesty, though it does have its sting."

"I admit I don't know what your business is with me, unless it is to order my death."

"Ah, you're a suspicious man, but I'd be less than easy too, if I were you. I assume you know who is responsible for your wound, because I doubt you were the target, or Lady Amberlie, *n'est-ce pas?"*

"I know nothing, sire."

William wagged a finger in Tedric's face as if he were a naughty youngster. "You're lying, but I'm not here to pull the truth out of you—at least not about who tried to murder me. I'm here to offer you a proposition, Tedric, one which only a fool or a madman would refuse, and I think you are neither." Relinquishing his hold on the dagger, William leaned back in his chair, apparently content with the knowledge that he now had engaged Tedric's curiosity and not his contempt. "Your cause will eventually fail," the king began. "Except for Saxon resistance in the north, all of England has fallen to me. I told you that I didn't believe you were a fool, and I don't. Only a fool would continue to wage a losing battle, and Tedric, you've lost already, and I think you realize this. So" — and here William stretched out his legs, as if he prepared himself for a lengthy visit — "we have a great deal to discuss. I assume that I have your permission to stay."

Tedric hated the man, but something about the king's confident demeanor struck his curiosity. Whatever William was planning might have grave repercussions for him and his family, and since he was in no position to do anything other than listen, Tedric gave the king his full attention. "Please continue, sire."

The king's voice dropped in volume, so Tedric strained to hear him. "Guy de Bayonne believes himself to be master of Woodrose, but I admit that, though Guy is a brave knight, he is less than an able administrator. He has yet to gain the good will of your people while you, Tedric, possess it already. I've seen the way the Saxons cluster outside in the bailey for word of your health these last few days. I saw how overcome they were in the great hall on the morning when you were brought before me in chains. Even my own knights' hearts were touched by your concern for your mother and sister." William's gaze traveled across Tedric's person. "You're a natural leader, a man to be reckoned with, and I don't

189

say this lightly for I know about your battles to win back the keep. And I believe that if your mind was at rest about the keep, your energies could be put to better use in defending England for me."

Tedric could barely breathe. What was William saying to him?

"Tedric, I want the good will of the Saxons. I ache to put an end to the violence which has thrown this land into chaos. If I had a man, a Saxon like yourself, in charge of Woodrose Keep, then I'd have one less area of the country to worry over. But I can only turn over Woodrose and the surrounding land to a man whom I can trust, a man who will pledge his allegiance to me. If you agree to throw down your weapons against me, I shall turn over Woodrose to you."

"You jest, sire."

"*Non,* I do not take lightly this proposition." William looked almost affronted. "Because you saved my life, and because you're needed to restore peace here, I trust that you are the right man for such an undertaking. Do you not want control of Woodrose again?"

Tedric nodded, his mouth suddenly dry. "Of course."

William smiled in smug satisfaction. "Then you cannot deny me."

"All I must do is pledge my loyalty."

"Yes, and mean it. Otherwise, I should be forced to come down very hard upon you and your family," William warned.

Tedric gripped the wolf pelt tightly in his

hands. "And that is all I am obliged to do?"

William grinned sheepishly. "Well, not quite."

"Hah! I thought as much." Tedric gave a derisive snort, not the least bit concerned that he might have offended the king. He hadn't.

"You're right to be suspicious, for only a foolish man would accept without thinking there might be another condition. And now I know you're the right man for this undertaking."

"What else must I do to reclaim my home? Must I wed Lady Julianne?" Tedric was joking, but suddenly a shiver slid like ice down his backbone for the king wasn't laughing.

"You must wed but not the Lady Julianne," William responded. "I order you to marry Lady Amberlie."

"The woman hates me," he ground out in disbelief and regret.

"Maybe, maybe not, but would you turn down my proposition because of a woman's feelings? Not only would you reclaim your birthright, but you'd wed a beautiful young woman. Why care if she hates you? Amberlie shall make you a dutiful wife."

"I can't be certain she won't knife me whilst I am sleeping, sire."

William let out a huge guffaw. "Then your life shall not be dull!" The king quieted. "What say you, Tedric? Have I your allegiance?"

Tedric's head swam with the implications of William's proposition. If not for the imposed marriage to Amberlie de Fontaine, the arrangement would be near to heaven. But Amberlie was the main reason he hesitated. Could he live with the Norman wench, could he sleep with a woman who despised him, no matter how attracted he might be to her? If he agreed to William's plan, Amberlie would go from being his enemy to being his wife. What would she think about all of this? he wondered. But William didn't intend for her to have any say at all in the matter, so Tedric guessed that her own feelings were unimportant.

And what about Glenna? How would he explain things to her? Yet Glenna was a Saxon and she knew how precious Woodrose Keep was to him. He persuaded himself that Glenna would understand. As for Guy de Bayonne and Julianne, he didn't even consider their feelings, because Tedric doubted that the villainous twosome ever felt true human emotions at all.

"Have I your word on this?" Tedric heard William softly ask him.

The moment was at hand. "Aye, sire, I pledge my allegiance. And I shall take Amberlie de Fontaine to wife."

Chapter Sixteen

"Sire, please, you cannot be serious about this marriage. I hoped to marry but not . . . Tedric." To even say Tedric's name left a bitter taste in her mouth. What could the king be thinking? Was this a cruel hoax? Was he suffering from madness? Apparently not, for he seemed perfectly sane and wasn't laughing as if in jest.

Amberlie stood beside William on the battlements. A brisk, cool breeze blew Amberlie's mantle about her figure and ruffled her dark curls. She placed her hands upon the stone wall, and her troubled gaze swept the countryside that was carpeted before them in jewel shades of orange and yellow, interlaced with splashes of green. At the moment she couldn't appreciate nature's beauty. Never had she felt so forlorn and bereft, having no one to turn to, no person in whom to confide her fears about this strange alliance which the king wished her to make. He seemed not disturbed at all by her reaction. In fact, if she looked closely, she discerned a mischievous twinkle in his eyes.

"Would you rather I released you to Guy de Bayonne as a bride?" William asked, the ruby brooch on his red mantle sparkling in the sunshine. "Either way, Tedric shall regain Woodrose."

It wasn't Woodrose she worried over, but the horrible sin which would fall upon her soul to wed Henri's murderer, to be the man's wife. "Tedric is a barbarian, sire. His people's customs are strange to me, their beliefs are heathenish. I remind you that he is responsible for my husband's death. The man has agreed to marry me only to reclaim his lands, not because he burns for love of me. Surely, you recognize all of the reasons why I cannot marry him."

"Then you choose de Bayonne as your husband?"

"I choose neither, sire."

William held up his hands in supplication, a sad smile on his lips. "I'm sorry, *cherie,* but you will marry one of these men. I could force you to marry Tedric, but I think you should come to this decision on your own. He has agreed to marry you and protect you, as your father would have wished."

"My father wouldn't have wished for me to marry a barbarian!"

The king seriously contemplated her before speaking in the same tone of voice which her father had used with her many times when he was exasperated with her as a child. "Hmmm, but you're wrong, Amberlie. This Tedric isn't a barbarian, nor is he a heathen. True, his customs and upbringing are different from yours, but I trust you can train him to be a proper husband. After all, Henri was a perfect mate for you."

"Henri was docile and sweet, not arrogant and filled with manly pride like Tedric."

The king laughed shortly. *"Cherie,* it is his manly pride which is the attraction for you, I think. And you are captivated by the brute, are you not?"

"No, I am not—"

"Don't lie to me, Amberlie, for you do it so poorly. I am your sovereign and demand your honesty. At least look into your heart and be honest with yourself. Admit that you're attracted to Tedric. I can see too that he's taken with you. So, what is wrong with such a match, eh?"

"He is my enemy, sire."

William vehemently shook his head. "If I didn't believe that Tedric would be loyal to me, I wouldn't have offered him Woodrose and you as his wife. In your heart you know that he will be a far better husband and protector for you than Guy de Bayonne. But alas, you must choose. I cannot sway you further one way or the other."

Amberlie thought he was doing a very poor job of trying not to sway her. The king wanted her to wed Tedric; in fact, he'd already promised her to the man as his wife, and the king didn't make promises lightly. William fully expected her to marry Tedric, whether she wished to or not. And the king's word was law.

"When is this marriage to take place?" she asked without feeling.

"Three days hence. I've already ordered the kitchen help to begin preparing for the wedding banquet. Of course, I didn't know who the bridegroom would be." William looked awkward and had the grace to blush. "So, *cherie,* whom will you choose?"

"Tedric of course, sire." Amberlie sighed in defeat, wondering if the man even possessed a last name.

"The king has humiliated me!" Guy shouted to Julianne when they were alone in her chambers. "Even now the preparations for this wedding banquet progress, and he has yet to tell me that he has turned over Amberlie to this—this pagan!" He held his head in his hands, his body trembling with rage. "Is the man mad, Julianne?"

Julianne impatiently tapped her fingertips upon the arm of the chair where she sat, swathed in black like a mother abbess. "Mad, no, but crafty is our king. Always he has resented your taking control of the knights after Henri's death without his authority. And now, my silly brother, the king has struck at the heart of you with invisible arrows. Never did he intend to offer Amberlie to you as a bride. You've disgraced me and my son with your ridiculous request."

"Henri is dead, deader than that damnable chair you're sitting in! When are you ever going to forget that milksop of a boy you weaned?"

Clearly, that was the worst thing Guy could say to Julianne. She rose from her chair in a threatening cloud of black. "My son was a noble knight, more noble of spirit and pure of heart than you or any of your knights. He isn't dead to me for he lives in my soul, my mind is filled with his face. Henri is more alive to me than are you. And as of this moment, you are dead to me."

"Come now, Julianne, you don't frighten me with your contempt, your disdain. The moment Amberlie marries Tedric you're reduced to taking the Saxon's charity. Amberlie will be mistress of Woodrose, and you'll be nothing but a cast-off relation. You'll have no value here."

Julianne was irked by Guy's accurate assessment of the situation, but she stilled her fears by glaring at him. "It appears you have less value than I, dear brother. After all, you asked the king for my son's wife and were not given the courtesy of his reply. If our king thinks so little of you, then imagine how your enemy shall treat you when the king is no longer in residence at Woodrose."

"Ah, Julianne, but you are a cold-hearted woman."

"And you are an unprincipled conniver, but you are the only confidant I have. Never forget that we're family, united by our common heritage."

Guy's voice was hoarse with frustration. "What will you do?"

"Nothing for now," Julianne said, and sat back down. "But I will somehow, some way, avenge myself upon Tedric of Woodrose for my son's death. And my son's treacherous widow shall not escape my wrath unscathed."

On the morning of the wedding, the castle household stirred from sleep before daybreak. Servants sleepily left their pallets and lighted the huge hearths in the kitchen and the great hall in preparation for the marriage feast. Dawn had just broke when Amberlie heard a cock crow in the bailey, rousing her from a fitful sleep.

She gazed around her chambers with unseeing eyes. All she could think about was the wedding that would take place within a matter of hours. On top of the large cedar chest at the foot of her bed lay her wedding attire. Even in the dawn's misty light she discerned the vivid blue color of the bliaut and the girdle, which was fashioned from soft dyed wool and inset with pearls and tiny sapphire stones, much valued since it was a wedding gift from the king. Beneath the bliaut she'd don a white chemise made from the finest silk, and she'd cover her hair with a white silk headdress. Upon her feet she'd wear blue slippers, and she remembered that the last time she'd worn them was before she'd left Normandy, over a year ago.

"What am I doing?" she asked herself, and couldn't dispel the misery she felt within her soul. She hadn't seen Tedric to speak to him since the day she agreed to marry him. The king had moved him out of Amberlie's room and into the smaller room beside his own. She wasn't allowed to tend to him any longer, Magda having permanently replaced her. Though she hadn't seen him, she'd heard his booming voice sometimes in the hallway, and she knew that with each passing day, he had grown more vigorous in body. No doubt, he'd sufficiently recovered from his injury for he took his meals in the great hall now, while the king had ordered that she dine in her room. It was a most lonely activity, but he didn't wish her to be seen until the day of the wedding. Amberlie guessed it had something to do with her being found beside Tedric in bed, and William wanted to quell any rumors throughout the keep about her honor—or lack of it.

And what of her honor? she asked herself. Apparently, it meant little to the king to force a marriage between herself and a slave. And what of the wedding night to come? Amberlie shivered just to imagine the scene, and prayed that Tedric would still be too weak physically to possess her. Just the very thought of his touching her turned her legs to liquid. She hated Tedric and resented his intrusion into her life, but her body responded differently than her mind did. Whenever Tedric touched her she behaved wantonly, and she couldn't bear for the man to know his effect upon her for it gave him a power over her, leaving her too weak to resist him. She knew she would surrender herself to him when the time came, but she vowed to harden her heart against him. Tedric would marry her to inherit the keep and land he so desperately loved, but the union would be a loveless one. Tedric might possess her body, but never would she give him her heart and her soul.

Amberlie rose and gazed out of the window at the busy scene below as serfs raced hither and yon in the bailey, carrying huge silver platters of foods from the kitchen to the keep. Just then Magda entered the room with a tray. "I thought you'd be hungry and would be ready to break your fast, my lady, before I help you dress for your marriage." Smiling benignly, Magda placed the tray upon a small table. Freshly picked plums from the keep's orchard and a cup of wine beckoned from the tray. Amberlie decided the wine was more sorely needed than the fruit on such a morning, but felt unable to eat or drink anything for her stomach fluttered with nervousness. "Lord Tedric breaks his fast with the king," Magda told her.

"Really, such an odd conspiracy."

"Aye, I admit 'tis an odd turn of events, but we're well pleased, especially Lady Mabel. Did you know that Lady Julianne has turned over her chamber to Lady Mabel and Edytha as she's taken up residence in the east wing of the keep? Sir Guy too."

Amberlie didn't know that Julianne and Guy had moved out of their rooms into the newly constructed east wing. She almost felt guilty and responsible for what was surely Julianne's decision to vacate her chamber, for she doubted anyone, even the king, had ordered her out. Yet she felt relieved too, for she'd no longer have to be aware of Julianne's presence nearby, now that Tedric would be her husband and would sleep in the same bed in which Henri had slept. She wasn't bothered by Guy's decision to move.

When Amberlie was dressed and Magda had finished arranging the headdress in place, the woman stood back and appraised her. "You're truly lovely, my lady," Magda said simply. This was high praise from the usually quiet woman. "Lord Tedric is indeed fortunate and will be pleased with you. On the morrow, you'll be pleased too with your morning gift."

Amberlie barely heard her as tiny butterflies took wing in her stomach. "What do you mean?" she asked absently, taking a deep breath to steady her nerves as the time drew near for the wedding.

"Your morning gift, my lady. On the morning after the wedding, the groom gives his bride a gift to prove that she has — pleased him — beneath the furs. 'Tis our custom and much valued by the bride, for it means that the bride not only has won her husband's heart but is true mistress of the keep and its people."

Amberlie gazed at the woman in stunned silence, immediately understanding the significance of the gift and feeling outrage and embarrassment. "And what sort of a gift am I to receive for pleasing Lord Tedric?"

"The circlet, my lady," Magda patiently explained. "It has been passed down to every mistress of Woodrose by her lord and husband. Lady Mabel has already given it to Lord Tedric. 'Twas the one thing of value she was able to save when she fled the keep. And now it will be passed to you, and should be worn on the morn after your marriage night."

"So all should know that Lord Tedric is pleased with me."

"Aye, my lady."

" 'Tis a silly and barbaric custom."

Magda looked much affronted and hurt, thereafter going about her chores in sullen silence. Dismissing the woman from her room, Amberlie realized that she'd offended the old woman with her remark. Her nerves were on edge, and the very thought of her wedding night caused her no end of distress. But clearly, the custom of the morning gift probably meant a great deal to the Saxon people. Amberlie thought it was a strange way to gain acceptance from a people, by physically pleasing their lord. Yet her mind wove erotic images of herself in Tedric's arms, lying beneath the furs with him. Would she please him enough to earn the circlet? She couldn't help but be intrigued by the custom, though she thought it was strange.

An authoritative knock sounded on the door,

and she opened it to King William. He wore a red tunic with a gold-colored mantle and looked quite handsome. Holding out his arm to her, he smiled. "Your bridegroom waits nervously below stairs, *cherie.*"

Amberlie doubted that Tedric was more nervous than she as she took the king's arm and made her way down the stairs to the great hall. After all, he was getting his heart's desire, while she was simply marrying a man who was the lesser of two evils. This arrangement seemed less than fair to her, but she entered the hall with her head held high. No matter her own qualms, she wouldn't allow others to know her heart was heavy with dread.

Never had she seen so many people squeezed into one place. The knights and serfs all craned their necks to get a good view as the king of England led her to stand beside Tedric on the dais. For the first few moments, she didn't deign to glance at him, her attention diverted by the glowering glances thrown her way by Guy and Julianne. But slowly, she focused on the man she was soon to marry, and noticed that he wore a mantle and tunic which were fashioned from a rich burgundy velvet. His shoulders seemed incredibly broad and strong, muscular enough to rip apart the material with a jerk of his arms. Never had she seen a more handsome man. It was quite different to imagine the slave any longer, though the golden slave collar still encircled his neck.

As Amberlie studied him, her breath died in her throat. No longer did Tedric wear the long hair of his people. Instead, his hair was now cut short, in the bowl shape of William and his knights. This was a very telling change, Amberlie thought, because she guessed he'd cut it to prove his loyalty to William. But more than that, he'd cut his hair because his love for Woodrose was greater than anything else in the world. He loved Woodrose more than he would ever love her or any woman. However, when he smiled at her, her insides warmed and tumbled like hot coals. She wouldn't let him know how his very presence always affected her, so she quelled her own weakness by turning her attention to the king.

William purposely placed her hand within Tedric's large one and stood in front of Father Ambrose, who patiently waited to perform the ceremony. The king trained his eyes on the crowd of people. From his tunic, he withdrew a key and held it up for everyone's inspection. "This is the key which unlocks Tedric of Woodrose's slave collar. When I remove it, he shall truly be your master and my servant. Respect his authority, for if anyone does not, he disrespects his king." With much solemnity, William placed the key into the small lock of Tedric's collar and unhinged it. Mutters of approval and happy weeping echoed throughout the hall as the king drew it from Tedric's neck. Then Father Ambrose stepped forward and performed the ceremony.

The day had been one of the most trying of Amberlie's life. Happy congratulations were bestowed upon her; Lady Mabel and Edytha dutifully kissed her cheeks. Everyone enjoyed themselves at the wedding feast as they partook of the wines and cheeses, the partridge, venison, and fish. Sauces made from the herbs in the keep's garden, and honey, thick and rich from the beekeeper's hives, were placed upon the tables to be used at will. Woodrose's bounty was evident, and everyone helped themselves to liberal portions. Joviality reigned within the great hall, but Amberlie sat upon the dais with only Guy for company, as Julianne had earlier taken to her bed. King William sat at the far end of the table in a lengthy conversation with one of his knights, while Tedric had joined in the festivities, leaving her alone for a few minutes when she declined to join him.

"You're a foolish woman, Amberlie," Guy solemnly intoned, and refilled his cup with wine. "Now your life will be filled with Tedric's swinish relations, and you'll always know your husband married you only to reclaim his lands."

Amberlie made no pretense of hiding her contempt. "Far better to marry a man who'd reclaim his lands than one who'd marry me only to gain power over me, as you were wont to do."

"Such cruel words from such a pretty face, *cherie*. But I trust you not to become too attached to your husband. Unforeseen circumstances could arise to destroy your union."

Amberlie clenched her fingers together. "Is that a threat of some sort? I trust you spoke not in earnest."

Guy exhaled in what Amberlie discerned as smugness. His eyes glowed, and she followed his gaze to where Tedric and Glenna stood together in rapt attention of a minstrel's song. "Love can be destroyed before the seeds are sown by reasons other than death, *cherie.* When you grow weary of your Saxon's roving eye, I shall always be nearby to offer you—comfort. For I sense your husband is still besotted with another."

Seeing Tedric with Glenna tore at her insides, but she wouldn't give Guy the satisfaction of knowing that his words had hit their mark. Instead she smiled at him, as if she didn't really care that her husband stood so closely beside the woman he'd have married, if not for the king's command. It was her own wedding day, not Glenna's. Why wasn't Tedric sitting beside her, taking delight in the minstrel's song?

Glenna no longer wore her old bliaut but a green velvet one, which caused her blond hair to look lighter and her skin to glow like sunlight. Each time the woman smiled up at Tedric, Amberlie could tell that Glenna still loved him. Perhaps she should have married Guy de Bayonne instead—at least he wouldn't have forced her to sit through this humiliation.

After a few moments, Tedric sensed his bride's gaze upon him, and politely withdrew from

Glenna to come sit beside Amberlie. She crowed inwardly in triumph because Glenna's face fell at his departure. For the next two hours, Tedric sat beside her, his attention not once diverted from her. He offered her choice pieces of meat from his trencher and refilled her cup with wine himself. If not for the fact that Amberlie had trained herself to hate this man, she would have willingly drowned in his attention. Yet she treated him coldly, barely answering him when he spoke. Still, he sat near her and pretended an affection for her, which she guessed he didn't feel.

When the sun had set, Tedric turned to her and whispered in her ear, "The hour grows late, my lady. 'Tis time to be abed. Go to your chamber, and send your serving woman to me when you are ready for my company."

"What if I am never ready for you, my lord?" she dared to ask as panic overwhelmed her.

Tedric's brow rose warningly. "Then I suggest you pretend, for you'll not escape your wifely duty so easily."

"Have I become the slave? Will you taunt me with your strange Saxon ways beneath the furs?"

To her amazement, he laughed. Amusement and something that resembled sheer lust glittered in his sky-blue eyes. His face moved toward hers, his mouth nearly touching hers. The sweet scent of wine clung to his breath. "When I taunt you, my lady wife, 'twill be with pleasure, but if you desire surprises, I shall willingly oblige."

His words shook her to her very soul. Twin

blushes coated her cheeks as she withdrew from the great hall, unable to reply to him. Before she mounted the stairs, Amberlie felt a hand on her arm and turning, she encountered Glenna. "So, my fine Norman lady, you think you've won."

Amberlie shrugged loose. "I've won nothing."

"Hah! You married the man who was promised to me more than ten summers ago, when I was but a child. Though Tedric may bed you until he gets you with child, I am the woman who has his heart. Perchance one night you'll waken and find your bed empty. Wonder not where he'll be, for he'll be with me, in my bed."

"No doubt in the weaving room with the other women servants. Lord Tedric would never humble himself so."

Glenna's eyes gleamed maliciously. "Nay, my lady, but in my own chambers which Lord Tedric has given me, above stairs from yours." With that bit of information hanging in the air, Glenna turned on her heels and left Amberlie standing on the bottom step with her mouth agape.

So Tedric had seen that Glenna was given a room away from everyone else's, a place of complete privacy. She should have expected this from Tedric, but somehow she hadn't. She knew, now that Tedric was lord of the keep once more, she should expect him to treat his family well — even Glenna, who'd been loyal to him and kind to his mother. Glenna might only be indulging in wishful thinking where Tedric was concerned. Yet, as Amberlie climbed the stairs to her bridal chamber, she didn't know what to think about the man she'd just married. Somehow she'd have to submit to him, but she vowed that she'd find no joy in the coupling.

When Amberlie entered her chamber, she was more than surprised to discover Tedric's few belongings had been placed in a chest by the wall. An extra tunic and mantle with woolen hose lay in the bottom, and beneath them was a silver dagger, its heavy handle carved in an intricate swirled design. Apparently, this was a gift from William for the king's initials were scratched into the hilt. Amberlie could only marvel at how Tedric had cast a spell over the king and the Norman knights. Such a conquest was unheard of, though Amberlie was well aware that many Saxon nobles had sworn allegiance to William in other areas of the country long before now.

She laid the clothes over the dagger, and spied a coarsely woven cloth in the corner of the chest. Though she didn't know why, she was drawn to the cloth, which was Saxon in design. Gingerly picking it up, she unwrapped the folds and uncovered a small golden circlet with a number of twinkling garnets embedded in it, interspersed at equal intervals along the crown. It was the morning gift, the bride's gift which had been passed down from each lord of Woodrose Keep to his wife for generations. And Amberlie thought it was the most beautiful and delicate piece of jewelry she'd ever set eyes upon.

In the candlelight, she lifted it out of the cloth

and went to the small mirror on her dressing table. She pulled off the white headdress and placed the circlet upon her dark hair. "How lovely," she breathed, as if in a dream to see her own reflection gazing back at her and looking like a princess. Her eyes sparkled more brightly than the garnets. Never had she felt so beautiful. She sensed the love and devotion behind this gift. No wonder Lady Mabel had saved it. This circlet was special and more precious than any jewel Amberlie had ever owned.

But she didn't own it. Not yet. Not until Tedric gave it to her. Not until she pleased him.

From down the hall, she heard Magda's voice as the woman headed toward Amberlie's room. Swiftly, Amberlie recovered the circlet and placed it in the bottom of the chest, where it would wait until Tedric presented it to her on the morrow.

The pelts were pulled to her neckline when Tedric entered the room sometime later. Magda had already prepared Amberlie for bed by helping her change into a lavender-colored shift whose bodice threadings were a creamy white. This was the same gown which she'd worn on the night of her wedding to Henri, some five years earlier when she'd been no more than an ignorant girl. She'd placed it away for the material was too fine, the shift too lovely for everyday wear. Now, she was a woman, no longer an untried girl, and her full breasts were a testament to that change, having outgrown the shift; they strained against the thin silk like ripe melons. Beneath the covers, though, she felt cold, and her hands perspired in anticipation. Now she knew what was expected of a wife, but this was so different from her wedding night with Henri. Barely older than she, Henri had been fumbling, but so sweet and careful of her. She doubted Tedric would be a fumbling bridegroom.

Tedric stood confidently before the bed, his clear blue eyes watching her with an intentness that set her heart to beating in rapid thumps. "I didn't expect to find my bride already abed with the covers to her neck," he said with a crooked grin.

"I'm sorry if I've displeased you." She sounded as cold as she felt, despite the pelts and heat from the hearth.

He cocked a wary eyebrow. "Are you? I think not, my lady, for I believe you take great delight in doing your best to displease me. But never mind. I enjoy a challenge. 'Tis the chase that makes the hunt worthwhile."

"My lord, I am not a hare or deer to be cornered by a hound. I am a woman."

"Aye, I know." His voice sounded so husky and seductive that shivers ran the course of her body. Coming round to her side of the bed, he clutched the pelts in his huge hand and in one swipe, he pulled them from her.

"Tedric! How dare you . . ." She began reaching for the pelts, only to have him stay her

211

hands. "I should like my covers. The room is chilled."

"You have no need of covers, for I shall warm you."

Intense heat flowed through her body when he moved his hands away, flinging the pelts to the floor. From above her, resembling a huge, blond giant, he looked at her, truly looked at her as he examined each inch of her perfectly made figure from her dark, sable locks to the tips of her toes. Never had anyone in her life, not even Henri, looked at her like this. Though she knew she should resent his inspection, she found she didn't mind, for something liquid and hot, and not unpleasant, began to stir and flow within her—especially when his lustful gaze settled upon her breasts and he licked his lips.

Unexpectedly, he turned away and started shedding his clothes. Flickering hearth flames bathed the room in golden splotches of light, gilding Tedric's broad back. Amberlie watched in fascinated silence; she couldn't help herself. It seemed that she hadn't the strength or inclination—or perhaps it was her own weakness—to stop staring. She'd known that Tedric was a powerfully built man, but now, in her chambers with him as her husband, she felt overwhelmed and lightheaded at the forced intimacy.

He dropped his tunic, then underclothing, before he removed his hose. Rippling firelight played over the planes of his bronzed back and buttocks, which Amberlie noticed were pale and

212

tight. When he turned to her and started for the bed, Amberlie quickly averted her eyes, suddenly embarrassed and humiliated that he should believe she was curious about his physical attributes. She couldn't avert her eyes for long when Tedric came to stand directly beside the bed, not the least modest about his nudity, and waiting for her inspection.

Her eyes swept across his expanse of chest and down, almost as if a magnet pulled her gaze, past his tapered waist and taut abdomen, down, down to that part of him which intrigued and frightened her. His shaft was already aroused, springing forth from its nest to taunt her. Amberlie couldn't swallow, could hardly breathe, and couldn't look away. The thought entered her mind that Tedric was more of a man than she could accommodate. She'd always believed that Henri had been well endowed, but now she realized that there was no contest between the two men. Tedric easily won.

"Is all to your liking, my lady?" he asked in a voice which sounded thick and heavy in her ears.

Suddenly Amberlie felt very warm, and glancing up, she managed to make her own voice sound as normal as possible. "If all were to my liking, my lord, I'd not be here with you now."

Gently, so gently that Amberlie at first didn't feel the pressure of his hand, he stroked the side of her head, before wrapping a dark strand of hair around his fingers. "So soft your hair feels, as soft as a doe's forelock. And 'tis the same hue."

A shiver slid through her, disturbing her composure. Bending low, Tedric placed a feather-light kiss upon her lips but didn't draw away. And Amberlie didn't either. From somewhere in the recesses of her brain, she told herself not to submit to him, not to be disloyal to Henri. But when his mouth touched hers, she felt a strange quiver of pleasure dart through her stomach like a huntsman's arrow, and the pleasure won out. No matter what had gone before, Amberlie couldn't stop herself from returning his kiss. A power greater than her disdain for him allowed her no self-control.

Blue eyes locked with brown ones. Tedric deepened the kiss, sending Amberlie into a maelstrom of passion, which until that moment had been kept in check. Now, with just a kiss, unbridled desire swept over her. She moaned against his mouth, not realizing that his arms had clasped her around the waist and had pulled her hard against his chest when he joined her on the bed.

Her arms wrapped around his neck of their own volition, a silent signal to both of them that she was finally giving in to the attraction which had bound them together from the first. She loved the way his hands expertly roamed over her buttocks, bringing her to rest against his rock-hard erection. Through the thin shift, she felt him nudging between her thighs, and Amberlie didn't draw away, but pushed closer into him, eager to feel his thickness.

Tedric groaned and broke their kiss to gaze deeply into her eyes. "Is that truly what you desire, Amberlie?" he asked, and rubbed suggestively against her. "For once we've begun, I will lose control, and you'll be at my mercy."

She was at his mercy now, for already she'd lost control of her emotions, her own body. Speech was lost to her, and she nodded, too trapped by the fierce desire in his eyes to resist. With a leisurely movement, Tedric undid the laces on her shift until her breasts spilled free of the material. He lowered the shift to her waist, his fingers caressing her nipples into taut dusky peaks. And then he bent low to taste each one, to tease and lick until a fire swirled inside of her.

She found herself kneeling on the bed while he suckled her. Her hands grasped his broad shoulders, her fingers sunk into his flesh. Nothing like this melting, hot yearning had ever happened to her, not even when she'd been Henri's wife. What was there about this man that could seduce her senses, could transform her into a quivering mass of lust? No longer did her eyes behold Tedric the barbarian, the man who'd killed her husband. In the foggy haze of passion, Amberlie saw with her heart.

She cried out softly when he pushed the shift past her waist to puddle at her thighs. Tedric then laid her down upon the bed to remove it entirely from her while he pulled her lower body up to the edge of the mattress, allowing her legs to wrap around his thighs of her own accord. "Ah,

215

Amberlie, Amberlie, you are so beautiful." He praised her with words, but better expressed how lovely he found her with his hands and lips.

A heated and wet warmth met his finger when he parted her legs to slip inside her, to tease and taunt her. Amberlie felt herself opening more to him with each gentle thrust as he readied her for him. It had been such a long time since she'd lain with Henri that she'd feared she would detest lovemaking with another man. But Tedric was no ordinary man, not ordinary at all, she quickly realized as he expertly spread open the petals of her flesh with his fingers, as he magically swept away the image of Henri from her mind. Suddenly, there was no other man but Tedric, and it seemed as if until this moment, she'd never been with a man before.

But she had, and her body quickly reawakened to long-dormant pleasure.

Desire curled within her abdomen like a fiery whirlpool. Every nerve in her body ached for Tedric to quell the heated core of her womanhood by filling her. She rode upon his finger, her passion at a fevered pitch, as she thrashed her head from side to side and arched her back. There was no denying that she wanted this man, and when he suddenly withdrew from her, she stared at him in wide-eyed distress. He placed his arms on each side of her body, imprisoning her between them, and gazed down at her in what she could only read as pure lust. "Don't stop— please," she whimpered, forgetting that she shouldn't beg this man for anything.

"Will you beg me to pleasure you?" he asked, and captured a nipple between his sensuous lips.

Amberlie writhed beneath him. Her body was in torment to belong to him. *Oui,* I'll beg if you want, I'll get on my knees and beg."

He ceased his teasing assault. "I'd rather see you on your back, fair wife. Never will I allow you to beg, Amberlie, never do I want you to beg for something that brings us both pleasure." And before she was aware, Tedric rose above her on the mattress and slid his thick length into her, bringing a shattering moan from between her lips.

Her hands clasped the bed sheets as he thrust within her. His movements were at first leisurely and slow, but then she arched against him and Tedric was lost. Powerful arms enveloped her, holding her tightly against his chest as she clamped her legs around his waist, bringing him into her so deeply that they were closely melded. With a wild and primitive abandon, Tedric filled her until Amberlie felt the core of her womanhood contract and expand in pulsating waves of pure bliss.

"I can wait no longer, sweet love," he whispered hoarsely against her ear, and purposely stilled his motions. "Soon, I will explode."

Without words, Amberlie knew the moment was at hand. Grasping his shoulders, she pushed into him, and her mouth sought his in a kiss which sent her over the edge into a whirling starburst of shattering fulfillment. At the very instant that pleasure claimed her, Tedric thrust and spilled himself into her with a lusty growl of completion.

He lay atop her for long moments until their breathing steadied. Then he moved her toward the center of the bed, and went to retrieve a pelt from the floor before he lay beside her, covering them. His hand rested intimately upon her breast, his fingers gently stroking the nipple until it was hard as a pearl. "I love touching your breasts." Tedric turned her face to his and kissed her. "I love touching all of you."

Amberlie's senses returned despite the delicious sensations which darted through her each time he stroked her. A blush spotted each cheek as she relived in her mind what had just happened between them. A wanton, that's what she'd been, a sinful wanton who'd willingly enjoyed coupling with Henri's killer—what else could she think of herself? Tedric had seduced her, but how she'd wanted to be seduced, how she would have begged him to love her if he'd decided to torment her by stopping! Though he was her husband, she was no better than a whore in her response to him. She'd never respond to him again, she vowed to herself. Granted he would make love to her, but she didn't have to enjoy it.

"Amberlie, what is wrong?"

She heard him, and his breath caressed her cheek, but she didn't want him to know how his very presence undid her. Tedric was her husband now, but still, he was the enemy. "I—I am fatigued," she said.

He chuckled. "Your body tells me that you're wide awake."

"Then my body lies."

"Your lips lie, but not your beautiful body. Never your body." He nibbled on her breasts, and Amberlie was lost once more as she realized that Tedric was ready again for her—but worse, she was ready for him too.

Opening her legs to him, she reveled in her own wantonness when his sheath impaled her. This time their mating was more hungry and savage, quicker to reach the pinnacle. Tedric spent himself inside her, and her own body exploded with an intensity that left her weak and shaking later when he held her in his arms. Her earlier vow not to respond to him had fallen by the wayside, and Amberlie knew Tedric possessed a wanton, wicked power over her—a delicious, dastardly power that she craved with her entire being.

If only he weren't her enemy.

Before she drifted into sleep, she stirred and found her new husband watching her with a possessive gleam in his eyes, but a gentleness too that somehow touched her. "I like looking at you," he said, almost shyly.

She enjoyed looking at his body too, but she'd never openly admit such a thing to him. Instead, she said, "Do you have a surname? For if you do, I know it not."

"Eriksen."

It had a heathenish, savage sound to it, Amberlie thought. Not soft and lyrical as a French name. "I see," she stated without emotion.

"Do you like it?"

She shrugged. "A name, that is all. What significance is there in a name?"

"None, unless you're the bearer of that name."

Turning onto her side, she presented her back to him. She was more than startled when Tedric drew her to his chest, his arm extending over her waist and pulling her against him so that her buttocks met his shaft. But she quickly discerned it was limp, and breathed a tired sigh of relief. She doubted she could stand being loved again, though the thought of Tedric's possession caused a slow burn to flame within her.

She knew when Tedric fell asleep by the rhythmic sound of his breathing. "Amberlie Eriksen," she whispered into the darkness, and somehow it didn't sound as horrible as she'd thought it would.

Chapter Seventeen

She is so beautiful, thought Tedric as he gazed upon the sleeping face of his wife. How privileged he felt to be her husband, how lucky was he to be alive and allowed to spend this morning beside her warm body in bed rather than in a hastily dug grave. He owed his good fortune to the king, and though he was still wary of William, Tedric knew he would willingly obey the man, for William had given him a gift far more precious than Woodrose and the surrounding lands. He'd given him Amberlie as his wife.

Amberlie stirred in her sleep and flung her arm across the pillow, nearly hitting Tedric in the eye, but he dodged her unintended assault. A small smile split his lips to see that she nestled so near to him. He liked having her next to him, so close beside him that their hearts echoed as one beat. He feared, however, that once she wakened, she'd again regard him with suspicion and hostility. Or perhaps, after their night together, she might look favorably upon him . . . No matter that she didn't love him; passion and mutual attraction bound them together. And for the moment, that was more than enough as far as Tedric was concerned.

Never in his wildest imaginings had he expected Amberlie to be such a receptive and passionate lover. Her desire for him pleased him beyond measure. During the night he'd wakened and had skillfully roused her from sleep to take her again, and she'd more than eagerly responded to him. No matter what she felt for him outside of bed, in bed she was a bewitching wanton, totally unlike the demure and passive woman she led others to believe she was. And if he weren't careful, he could easily fall in love with such a woman.

"Guard your heart," he told himself, worried that she'd eventually hurt him if he allowed himself to feel anything other than physical desire for her. True, he was besotted with her peach-tinted beauty, her long lashes that lay upon her cheeks like dark half-moons. And her body, her absolutely lush body, which was soft as velvet and so responsive to his lovemaking that Tedric wondered indeed if last night hadn't been part of his imagination—but it was real, very real, and the proof lay contentedly beside him, looking so voluptuous in sleep that he felt himself hardening with desire.

Noise in the bailey distracted him, and his gaze wandered to the window where dawn's pink streaks stained the sky. Already he'd been abed for too long. He was lord of Woodrose again, and there was much to oversee, especially now that William, king of England, was his guest. Only last week he'd been considered an enemy of the crown; now he was the king's liege man. The irony of the situation caused him to chuckle quietly.

So as not to waken Amberlie, he carefully rose from the bed. He glanced down at her, and realized that he'd be forced to battle his basic instincts not to touch her during the day. He already looked forward to nightfall, to the moment when Amberlie would belong exclusively to him again without the distractions of the daily routine. For now, however, William awaited him downstairs to discuss further fortifications for the keep, and he must school himself to keep desire at bay.

In the semi-darkness, Tedric dressed in silence. When he was finished, he reached into the chest for the cloth which contained the circlet. Removing the material, he reverently placed the gleaming golden and garnet object atop the pillow he'd just vacated. Tradition decreed that he personally present the morning gift to his bride. And there was nothing he'd have preferred more, but he wasn't married to a typical Saxon woman, or to a woman who even cared about him. But the woman would know she had pleased him mightily, he'd see that she did. Yet he, a brave warrior of his people, was too shy to present the morning gift to his own wife.

Stepping away from the bed, he could almost imagine how the circlet would gleam like the sun atop Amberlie's dark hair. He knew she'd be radiantly beautiful. Filling his eyes with her loveliness, Tedric then left the chamber to speak with the king.

Where was Mercy?

Edytha had thoroughly searched the room she shared with her mother, upsetting Lady Mabel by her endless hunts for the lost cloth doll. But nowhere was her baby to be found. Each night, before she fell asleep, Edytha clutched a small wolf's pelt in her arms that the kind Sir Flaubert had given to her, but the fur didn't take the place of Mercy. She wanted her baby and wouldn't rest until she found her!

When Magda came into the room to help her mother dress, Edytha sneaked away. She was dressed only in her shift and barefoot, but she didn't mind the drafty hallway. Her mission was far too important to feel the early morning's chill.

She'd spotted Tedric coming out of his room, and quickly hid within an alcove. Tedric didn't like her to roam the hallways without Magda or Glenna. She knew that if he saw her, he'd bring her back to her room, and she'd be unable to look for her baby. Waiting until he disappeared down the winding, narrow stairs, Edytha then moved silently along the hallway until she came to Tedric's room and discovered the large, thick oak door was ajar. Perhaps Mercy was inside.

She went directly into the room. A hazy purplish-pink light from outside illuminated the furnishings and the sleeping figure of Amberlie on the bed. Edytha stopped cold in her steps on seeing the dark-haired woman. She hadn't expected to see her, and didn't quite understand why this lady slept in her brother's bed. During her stay in the cave, she'd seen Glenna asleep beneath the furs with Tedric once and had accepted it. Seeing Amberlie lying in the bed was a bit confusing to Edytha, but she guessed it had something to do with the marriage ceremony she'd attended the previous day. Her mother hadn't explained what marriage meant when she'd asked her, but now it slowly dawned upon Edytha that Amberlie was sharing her brother's bed—something Glenna had told her with disgust on her face, and something Edytha didn't think Glenna liked at all.

But she was here to search for Mercy, and she didn't care to think about anything other than her baby.

On silent feet, Edytha looked behind the chair, the small table, and a large chest. She got on her hands and knees by the bed and looked beneath it. No Mercy. Finally, she looked toward the top of the bed, thinking that she should search there, and her gaze fell upon the golden circlet beside Amberlie on the pillow.

She recognized the circlet as belonging to her mother and wondered how it had gotten here.

Many times she'd asked her mother if she could play with it, but always her mother told her that the circlet was much too valuable for her to touch. Once, her mother had placed it on her head for a short time and let her look at her image in the mirror, but had quickly taken it from her to put away for safekeeping. But that had been when Edytha was very young, and she hadn't seen it in a long time.

And now it was right before her, and Edytha so wished to try it on her head again that she forgot about Mercy. Reaching out for the circlet, Edytha took it from the pillow and clutched it to her bosom, practically flying out of the room. Finally she had something that she could hold and admire, something the dark-haired lady must have wanted very much to keep in her bed.

Amberlie jerked awake with a start. Sitting up, she sensed that someone was in the room, but she saw she was alone. Very much alone, for Tedric wasn't there.

An all-consuming blush warmed her. How wantonly she'd behaved last night! Had that insatiable love-starved creature been herself? Never in her years as Henri's wife had she responded in such a fashion. What sort of a spell had Tedric woven over her to make her forget her scruples so completely? But even as she worried over her own lusty actions, she wondered if she'd pleased him and knew she had. A man didn't make love

226

over and over to a woman he didn't desire, and certainly if she hadn't satisfied him, she'd have known. After all, a woman sensed these things.

Her gaze rested on the chest by the bed. The circlet. Was it still there? She looked, and saw the woven cloth. But it was no longer wrapped about anything. Evidently, Tedric had carried the gift with him, and he'd give it to her later. And with her whole heart, she knew she'd earned it, but more, she wanted it.

Glenna woke in not the best of moods. She'd passed a sleepless night, her thoughts centered below stairs upon Tedric making love to his new wife. Her body had burned for the man, and she'd risen from her bed to ease her ache, only to literally bump into Sir Christophe in the dark bailey. Christophe had been on watch and asked her why she was abroad on such a cold night. Glenna had been so overcome by her own agitation about Tedric that she'd allowed herself the tainted pleasure of seducing another man. Well, not seducing actually, for Christophe hadn't been tempted to leave his watch. He'd told her in no uncertain terms that he knew what she was about and refused to be second best. But he wanted her, she knew he did. And though she'd originally kissed him to somehow spite Tedric, she had found great delight in his lips.

That delight had caused her no end of consternation, for afterwards she'd forgotten about

Tedric as her mind dwelled on Sir Christophe's noble form and handsome face. But this morning, things were different. Tedric and how he'd spent his night were uppermost in her thoughts.

Dressing in a blue woolen girdle which matched her eyes, Glenna left her small room and made it down the extremely narrow wooden stairs to the lower floor. As she did each morning, she went to check on Lady Mabel, who'd taken the place of her own dear mother. Opening the door, she called to her but found the bed was empty. She quickly decided that the woman must be in the great hall to break her fast, a fact which pleased Glenna for it meant that Tedric's mother was gaining strength again. She made a move to leave, but stopped when she heard a sound behind the oak-planked door.

Peering around the door, Glenna noticed Edytha, whose large, blue eyes stood out starkly against her pale complexion. "Edytha, are you playing a hiding game?"

"N — n — ay."

"Then why are you behind the door, hiding like a thief?"

" 'Tis Mother I am hiding from."

"For the love of heaven, why?"

"So she'll not take my play toy from me." Glenna noticed Edytha kept one hand behind her back.

"Well, you can show it to me. I won't take it away from you."

"It is mine! I won't give it back!"

"I promise I won't take it, you can show it to me," Glenna sweetly cajoled, fearful that whatever Edytha was hiding might be harmful to her. "Please, you can trust me."

Edytha thought for a long moment, her eyes wary, but she was by nature a trusting soul, especially with Glenna, who was always kind to her. The girl's hand moved from her back, and she showed Glenna the golden and garnet circlet.

All color faded from Glenna's face. Her breath caught in her throat for she instantly recognized the circlet as Lady Mabel's morning gift. Lady Mabel had shown it to her in the cave. It was the woman's most precious possession, the one thing Mabel had saved when the Normans invaded the keep. "This shall be your morning gift when you wed my son," Mabel had told her with a soft smile. She'd held it out for Glenna to touch, and she'd placed it upon Glenna's head. "A perfect fit, child," Mabel had proclaimed with tears brimming in her eyes. Glenna had cherished it from the start, eager for the morning when Tedric would hand it to her. But now that morning would never come.

"Where did you find this?" Glenna asked, a bit confused, for Tedric's bride should now be the owner.

"On the Norman witch's pillow," Edytha answered.

Glenna knew whom Edytha was speaking about since she had parroted Glenna's cruel name for Amberlie. "Did she see you take it?"

Edytha shook her fluffy golden head. "Nay, she was asleep."

"And you took the circlet off the pillow, but she didn't waken?"

"Nay, I told you, she was asleep." Clutching the circlet in her small hands, Edytha went to the mirror and placed the object upon her head. "So pretty," she breathed at her reflection.

True, the circlet was pretty, more than pretty. Glenna felt as if a sharp-honed ax dug into her heart. How often she'd dreamed of owning the circlet, of being the next one to wear it. But Tedric had given it to Amberlie, which meant only one thing—Amberlie had pleased him greatly. And he was more than willing to express his gratitude with the gift. Everyone from serf to knight would know the new mistress had won her husband's heart and was also entitled to their loyalty. When Amberlie entered the great hall to break her fast on the morning after the wedding night, all would see the circlet atop her head and know what it signified.

But Edytha had the circlet. Glenna wondered if Amberlie knew it had ever lain upon the pillow. Had she seen it before the girl took it? Somehow, Glenna doubted it. Apparently, Tedric had placed it on the pillow for Amberlie to find when she woke. But Edytha had snatched it while Amberlie was still asleep. Glenna doubted that Amberlie would truly realize the gift's significance, even if she'd seen the circlet. The woman considered the Saxons and their customs to be barbaric, so why should receiving a morning gift mean anything to her? Since Tedric had placed it on the pillow, he'd intended that Amberlie wear it. However, if Amberlie appeared in the great hall without the circlet, Tedric might, in his pride, refuse to question her. The Saxons would immediately think that the absence of the circlet meant Lady Amberlie hadn't pleased their lord. They'd be contemptuous of her. Tedric would be so humiliated by what he'd consider *her* contempt for his customs that he'd quickly seek solace in Glenna's arms. But only if he knew for certain that Amberlie had seen the circlet and turned down the gift.

And this was where Edytha would unknowingly help her.

"Would you like to play a game with the circlet?" Glenna asked sweetly, and just as she'd planned, Edytha eagerly nodded in agreement.

"Find your brother in the great hall and show him the circlet. Say to him that Lady Amberlie wishes not to receive it," Glenna told the innocent girl. "Tell him that Lady Amberlie said the custom is not to her liking. Do you understand what to say?"

Edytha nodded slowly but seemed confused. "Aye."

" 'Tis a game, that is all."

"I will remember."

"Make certain you tell Tedric that Lady Amberlie refuses his gift. Make no mention of me in your game, but I shall be listening."

231

"Will my mother be angry because I have the circlet?" Edytha gazed with fear at Glenna.

"Oh, no, she will be pleased," Glenna insisted, and hugged Edytha around the shoulders. "Now let us get you dressed in your kirtle and you can find Tedric."

Minutes later, Glenna watched from the back of the great hall as Edytha approached Tedric and her mother, who sat upon the dais. Luckily, Magda was the only other person nearby, the king being absent. Glenna was pleased that Tedric wouldn't be totally humiliated. With all of the talk from the knights and the scraping of bowls as the serfs served up porridge, Glenna inched forward to overhear Edytha, who spoke exactly as Glenna had instructed her.

"Oh, what a horrid woman!" Lady Mabel exclaimed, and clutched at her son's hand in support. " 'Tis a black heart she has to refuse."

"Edytha, are you certain you heard correctly?" Tedric asked, his face an ashen color.

"Aye."

"Perhaps Amberlie doesn't understand the custom."

"Hmph! Pardon me for saying so," Magda hastily chimed in, "but Edytha is speaking true, my lord. Just yesterday morn I mentioned the custom to Lady Amberlie, and she said 'twas silly and barbaric. She knew what the circlet meant."

Mabel's eyes filled with tears. " 'Tis a shame upon us, a terrible humiliation."

"More so upon her than on us," Tedric ground

232

out through his teeth. Looking at Edytha, he managed a gentle smile. "Would you mind bringing the circlet to your room and placing it in Mother's chest? Magda will go with you."

Edytha seemed to realize that the game was ending, and somehow she'd lost her obsession with the circlet, now that she'd viewed her mother's misery. Giving a tiny nod, Edytha started to follow Magda out of the hall but spied Glenna. " 'Twas a sad game," she mumbled to her.

"I'll think of a better one next time," Glenna assured her, and smiled brilliantly. "But you played this one very well."

Very well indeed, Glenna crowed silently to herself. An indignant red stained Tedric's usually bronzed face. He resembled a volcano, ready to explode with fury and fire. But Glenna knew that he'd keep himself in check, and he'd never mention the circlet to Amberlie. His pride would prevent him.

Amberlie swung around at Tedric's sudden appearance in their chamber, not having heard him enter. She'd recently finished placing her headdress upon her head, a sheer piece of blue material that she felt would show off the circlet to advantage. She smiled shyly at him, her palms perspiring from nervousness.

Tedric stood in the doorway, assessing her with what she could only discern as an aloof coolness.

He extended his arm to her. "The king is in the great hall to break his fast. I trust you are ready to join us."

"I am ready." She hesitated, her gaze wandering to his hands in search of the circlet. Where was it?

Tedric's eyebrows rose a fraction of an inch. "My lady, is something wrong?"

She shook her head in puzzlement at not being given her morning gift, but decided he might bestow it upon her after he broke his fast. She moved toward him and resting her hand upon his arm, she allowed him to escort her below stairs. When they entered the great hall, all eyes turned upon them from the king's to those of the lowliest Saxon serf. William rose to greet them and gestured politely to the spot next to him, which Amberlie immediately took. Tedric sat beside her. Down at the opposite end of the long table sat Guy and Julianne, near Lady Mabel, Edytha, and Glenna. She'd expected a stony reception from her relatives, and the hatred in Glenna's face, but there was something odd about Mabel. The woman had seemed pleased just the day before, or as pleased as one could be expected to be when one's son was forced to marry his enemy. Mabel had kissed her and smiled warmly upon her marriage to Tedric. Now she didn't acknowledge Amberlie's friendly nod or return the smile.

Something was very wrong, and Amberlie sensed it also in the great hall. As she nibbled on a ripe plum, she peered at the scene before her.

234

The knights ate with gusto, the long trestle tables covered with their bowls of porridge, their tankards slopping over with fresh milk. Nothing unusual there, she decided. But it was the chilly looks sent her way by the Saxon serfs who waited upon the knights, the disapproval in their attitude, the way many of the serving women watched her from under lowered lashes that gave her pause.

What had she done?

During the course of the meal, only King William spoke to her. Tedric seemed more concerned with his food than with her, and she felt amazement that this man could one night love her until she was so satiated that she was spent, and the next morning treat her as if she carried the fever.

William cleared his throat, interrupting Amberlie's thoughts. "I extend an invitation to you, Tedric, to visit my royal household in London with your bride before the harsher weather sets in. What say you?"

Amberlie knew Tedric couldn't refuse. No one refused William, but she tensed anyway, waiting for Tedric's response. "We should be delighted, sire," Tedric politely returned without a glance at her.

"*Bien,* I am pleased. My Matilda shall enjoy having Amberlie for company."

"It has been a long time since I've seen Her Majesty." Amberlie smiled, but the smile didn't reach her eyes. She worried her lower lip as the tension in the great hall thickened. Was it to do with the knights, she wondered, for she was aware that they were loyal to Guy de Bayonne and not her husband. It would take more than the king's gifts to Tedric to win them over. Yet the knights treated her no differently. Again, she was aware of the undercurrent of condemnation which crept into the faces of the Saxons each time they openly regarded her. She couldn't very well order them flogged for looking askance at her, since cruelty wasn't a way to win loyalty.

But Tedric must notice, she thought, wildly uncomfortable. Surely, he could see something was wrong. However, each time she cast a glance at him, if he happened to be staring in her direction and caught her eye, he purposely turned away, ignoring her. What had she done to deserve this shabby treatment?

" 'Twas my pear you just wolfed down, woman! If you had but asked, I would have told you 'twas mine." Julianne's high-pitched voice resounded throughout the great hall. Everyone turned their attention upon the woman who stood with arms akimbo over the frail Lady Mabel. "I gave you my chamber, but I'll not give the food from my trencher to you."

"I begged your pardon," Mabel retorted, her usually pale face now alight with red splotches of anger. "I'd no idea 'twas your pear, for it must have rolled toward my side of the table. I wouldn't purposely take food from your mouth, woman."

"What is happening down there?" Tedric inquired, and heaved his broad frame from the bench to see to the disturbance.

His mother waved toward Julianne. "This woman accuses me of thievery over a small pear. As if I would purposely steal such a thing from my son's table." She glared at Julianne, getting her point across by stressing the word "son."

Julianne threw an imploring look at Guy, who only grinned and said nothing, and then at the king, who left the hall, leaving the disturbance for Tedric to decide. "There are other pears in the fruit bowl, Lady Julianne," Tedric kindly reminded her.

"But I wanted that one!"

"Should I heave it up and present it to you?" Mabel cried, and looked toward her son. "The woman is irrational."

"How dare you criticize me, you loathsome woman. I see I shall find no justice in this house. I see very well what I can expect now that a Saxon rules Woodrose." Julianne made a sweeping turn and left the dais.

"A Saxon has always ruled Woodrose, but for your Norman brutality!" Mabel called after her. "The woman is mad," she said to Tedric, her voice lowering in her anger. "Truly and hopelessly mad."

"We're all a bit mad in our own way," Guy interjected, and turned to Tedric. "But I shall speak to Julianne about her unbecoming behavior. The last few days have been filled with changes. By your leave, my lord, I should like to see to my sister."

Tedric inclined his head in dismissal, not the least upset to see Guy go. He heaved a sigh. What a morning, he thought dismally. He existed in a nest of Norman vipers. Julianne detested him and his family and made no bones about her feelings. Guy was still in charge of the knights, but soon that situation would change. Already Sir Christophe seemed wont to obey Tedric without question, and Christophe was a man with many friends who'd follow his lead, now that the king backed Tedric as lord of Woodrose. Tedric fully intended to place Christophe in charge of the knights, and if Guy de Bayonne didn't like it, he could take himself and his mean-spirited sister back to Normandy, for the king had already approved Tedric's decision.

And then there was Amberlie, the one Norman whom he couldn't send back—and wouldn't send back, though her refusal of the morning gift ate away at his insides like a disease. He'd never tell her how much pain she'd caused him by rejecting the circlet, nor how a part of him now disdained her for what she had done. Last night had proved to him without a doubt that, in bed, they were evenly matched. No other woman had ever made him feel more alive. He'd been so eager to pleasure her in return—and had succeeded.

Why must she be so stubborn, so condemning of his people and their customs? She was now officially the mistress of Woodrose; all would bow

238

to her out of respect for him but not for her. In their eyes, she'd still be the enemy.

Turning around, he found Amberlie's doe-brown eyes upon him. "I apologize for Julianne," she said.

"Apologize for no one but yourself and your own actions, my lady. Now I have things to oversee. I trust you do too." He curtly bowed, and without another word, Tedric strode out of the great hall and into the bailey.

Color stained her cheeks for she realized he had coldly dismissed her and chastised her at the same time, but what she'd done, she didn't know. Glancing toward her new family as if for answers, she noticed that Mabel and Edytha were withdrawing from the hall, without so much as a polite word to her. Glenna held Lady Mabel by the elbow to guide the older woman's steps, but she looked back over her shoulder at Amberlie. There was so much malice upon her face that Amberlie shivered.

Something was wrong, horribly wrong.

For half of the day, Amberlie took over the duties inside the keep which Julianne had performed. There was a heady feeling about having the servants instantly obey her, now that she was mistress. However, these very same servants, people who had at least smiled at her on occasion, now stonily regarded her and went about their work with grim countenances.

Near midday, she decided to visit Gundred, who, though a bit peculiar, always seemed pleased to see her. The old woman was placing a poultice on the chest of the serving woman called Runa, who coughed nastily.

Amberlie didn't immediately enter the cottage, but waited outside while Gundred dealt with her patient. " 'Tis cold in the chest," Gundred observed sagely, and advised the serving woman how to care for herself.

Runa sneezed and wiped her nose with the back of her hand. "I'll do all ye say, but I must ask Lady Amberlie if I can take a leave of the kitchen for the day. I feel ungodly terrible."

"I'm certain Lady Amberlie will allow ye a day to rest. She has a kind heart, though I hear she has no heart for Lord Tedric." Gundred made a small clucking sound.

Amberlie stiffened outside the doorway; her ears perked up at Tedric's name. "Oh, aye, 'tis true, Gundred, 'tis true," Runa sniffed in agreement. "I was in the great hall this morn when he led her to the dais. No matter that she is a Norman, we all expected Lord Tedric to have given her the morning gift. But she wore no circlet atop her head. 'Tis shameful for him to have married a woman who gives no pleasure to her lord."

"She is the one brought low, not Lord Tedric."

"Aye. Not to receive a morning gift from her husband is the greatest of humiliations. Poor man," Runa lamented, "how terrible it is to be

240

wed to a cold woman, and Lord Tedric is such a fine strapping man. Lady Amberlie will lose him for certain. Glenna will see he doesn't lack for warmth."

Gundred mumbled something which Amberlie couldn't hear. In fact, the blood pounded so hard in her ears that she was temporarily deaf as she quickly retreated from Gundred's small cottage. Pain and humiliation flushed her cheeks. Tedric had never intended to give her the circlet, she realized that now. But to cause her such embarrassment with Woodrose's own people was unforgivable. Did he hate her so much that he delighted in humiliating her?

Apparently, he did. She now knew without a doubt that Tedric had married her only as a means to an end, and had quickly consummated the marriage as a way of retaining the lands. He'd done the king's bidding—and made a fool of her in the bargain.

She found a small wooded path, away from the keep, and found sanctuary beneath a sheltering oak tree. Tears formed in her eyes and spilled freely down her cheeks. She didn't bother to wipe them away.

Never had she expected such treachery from Tedric, not after the night they'd spent together. She'd freely given of her body, had taken more than her share of pleasure and given him pleasure in return. Maybe she'd originally thought the morning custom was silly, but no longer. She'd wanted the circlet as proof that she'd pleased

Tedric as only a dutiful wife could. But he'd betrayed her with her own weakness for him, using that weakness to gain vengeance upon her family for what they'd taken from his.

She'd never forgive him, never.

He'd suffer for her humiliation. When he came to her again, as she knew he would, she'd treat him with coldness and would find no pleasure in their mating. He had used her strange, ungovernable attraction for him to gain power over her, reducing her to a mewling, writhing plaything. But no longer. Her flesh was weak, but her spirit was not, and to punish him, she'd not respond to him, even if it meant her own physical needs wouldn't be satisfied.

It was the only way to make him suffer.

Chapter Eighteen

With a heavy heart, Amberlie wiped away her tears. The sun rode high in the sky, and she realized it was well past midday and time she returned to the keep. The day had grown warmer, and she was glad she'd removed her headdress at the keep and now went bareheaded. A slight breeze ruffled her dark curls as she entered the meadow which served as a buffer between the forest and Woodrose Keep. She glanced toward the stone structure, and her heart leapt in her chest for Tedric was fast approaching on a large, black gelding.

The sun gilded his blond hair, and highlighted the ruby brooch on his mantle which twinkled like rosefire. Tedric looked quite impressive and very large as he reined in the horse. But she kept walking, not about to stop, and forced him to canter alongside her.

"Sir Christophe told me he saw you leave the keep some time ago. 'Tisn't safe to be abroad, my lady."

"Oh? Perhaps that was true some weeks past

when a renegade Saxon prowled the area, but no more, my lord, as you well know. I've nothing to fear in the woods."

Tedric laughed down at her, instantly understanding. "Mayhaps you should still be fearful since you gaze upon the renegade leader."

"I fear no one, especially not you, my lord." Amberlie stalled in her steps and shot him a frosty look, which caused Tedric to frown.

"I've never wanted you to fear me, Amberlie."

There was something in the way he said her name which sent a frisson of heat down her legs. He bent down, grasped her around the waist with one strong arm, and pulled her up beside him. "Come, I've had food prepared and we will eat in the meadow."

"Is that an order, my lord? I've duties which must be performed."

"Hmm, so cold you sound for such a warm-blooded wench, but aye, this is an order. And if it's a duty you wish to perform, well, I can think of one that needs doing." He grinned at her, and positioned her so that her backside contacted the spot between his legs to feel his arousal. Her heart lurched madly, the magnetism of him so potent that she felt herself weakening, even as she determined not to respond to him.

"I'm mistress of the keep now. I cannot be away for long."

Tedric's lips touched her earlobe in a whisper-soft kiss that sent delightful shivers down her spine. "You'll be gone for as long as I wish, my love."

Her every sense was on the alert, knowing full well what he meant. She took a deep breath, fortifying herself for the battle of wills to come.

Stopping near an ancient elm tree at the edge of the meadow, Tedric slid from the horse to help her down, careful to place her body close against his when he lowered her to the ground. A lecherous but devastatingly handsome smile curled up the corners of his mouth, immediately turning her legs to liquid. For a moment longer than necessary she held onto his broad shoulders to steady herself. "I'm really not hungry," she said inanely, unable to think of anything else to say as a telltale blush consumed her cheeks.

"But I am. Please indulge me, my lady."

Tedric unhooked his mantle and gallantly laid it upon the grass for her to sit upon beneath the shade of the leafy bowers, which hadn't yet succumbed to the autumn chill. He retrieved a woolen bag from the horse's neck, and opened it to bring forth a wedge of cheese, a hunk of bread, an apple and a pear, plus a leather pouch containing mead. "I trust this is to your liking," he said, and waited until she'd chosen first before making his decision.

Suddenly she was quite hungry, and she broke a piece of bread and waited while he cut into the cheese with his hunting knife and offered a thick slice to her. It tasted delicious, more so as she dined outside beneath the vibrantly blue sky with the sparrows winging from the tree to the grass, where they feasted upon the crumbs of bread which Tedric threw to them. Even a shy squirrel advanced near to clasp an offering within its tiny grasp.

Amberlie giggled at the adorable creature and tried to coax it closer, but the little animal would have none of her and soon scampered up the tree with its booty. Her laughter died in her throat when she discovered that Tedric was no longer smiling but watching her in all seriousness. "You shall be a kind mother," he told her. "Our children shall be much loved."

Children! She'd barely contemplated having a child, but her face blazed with the memory of the previous night as she realized she could already be carrying Tedric's child. If she wasn't already with child, it wasn't from a lack of trying. But she'd been married for nearly five years when Henri died, and she hadn't conceived. Tedric might have made a bad bargain by marrying her after all. "I . . . I may very well be . . . barren," she forthrightly told him. "Henri and I were unable . . ."

"My seed shall take," he declared softly.

" 'Tis confident you are, my lord."

He smiled smugly. "Aye, for I know you shall bear me sons and daughters who will do me proud."

"Is there reason for your belief in this matter, my lord? Have many women born your bastards?"

"Ouch, there's a thorn within your softness, my lady, but I take no offense at your question. No, I have no bastards."

"None that you know of."

"None to speak of."

"How know you this? How is it that Lady Glenna never conceived your bastard? Were you not man enough to get her with child?" She was going too far, she knew it, but she couldn't help herself. Something drove her to probe him mercilessly, to wound him for his humiliation of her.

With a quick and agile movement, Tedric pulled her toward him and pinned her to the ground. His face was scant inches from hers, his body pressed intimately against her heaving bosom. "Your pretty mouth asks too many questions, sweet, and I refuse to be baited. 'Tis only by God's power that I have no child to claim as my own—and certain twists of lovemaking which do not require the spilling of seed within the woman, but give pleasure as well." He lifted the hem of her deep blue kirtle and found the spot between her legs. "Mayhap you'd like that now."

"Nooo," she moaned, and would have pushed away except Tedric was heavy upon her and she was no match for him physically.

"Aye, my heart, you're more than ready for a bit of pleasuring." His fingers traced the folds of her flesh, parting them and easily slipping inside to torment and delight her at the same time. "How warm and wet you are."

"Oh, stop, please, please, no," she begged in a breathless voice which sounded nothing like her own.

"Admit that you don't want me to stop, Amberlie, tell me you want my fingers inside you." His lips settled upon hers in a warm, moist kiss

247

before he parted them with his tongue to invade the recesses of her sweet mouth.

She moaned against his lips, she couldn't help herself. No matter her resolve, Tedric always undid her with but a touch. "Surrender to me, give all to me," he hotly whispered against her mouth, "and I will give you paradise."

"Nay, nay," she protested, but her voice was low and trembling as she was already losing herself to his skillful manipulation of her weak flesh.

"Part your legs wider, sweet," he gently urged, and as in a dream, she did. Tedric groaned, his hand leaving her only to wrap with the other one around the voluptuous curve of her buttocks. His head moved lower upon her body until his mouth found its mark, and he tasted her with low, leisurely flicks of his tongue until Amberlie thought she would die from the intense sensations. A fire burned within her, singeing her very core, lapping at her resolve until nothing remained but her own primitive yearnings.

Her hands tangled within his hair, drawing him nearer to her molten center. She imagined she heard Tedric give a small sound of triumph as he pushed her nearer and nearer to the edge of madness, the fiery bliss she craved. Her body arched instinctively to meet each tongue thrust, and soon she moaned in wanton abandon, not caring that they were in a meadow beneath the golden sun.

And then it seemed as if the very sky above her exploded into a million suns as did her body.

Her lusty moans of completion echoed back to her, the exquisitive throbbing so wonderful that she clasped him to her to keep it from ending. But eventually it did, and Amberlie lay spent and dazed.

Her gaze focused upon Tedric when his face came into view. He dropped beside her to cradle her in his arms, then took her hand and planted a tender kiss upon it. "You're more woman than I dared to dream, sweet Amberlie."

She didn't know how to respond to that statement for if it were true, wouldn't he have given her the circlet? But the circlet made no difference now. Once again, she'd surrendered herself to him and detested herself for doing so—and in the middle of the day and outside too. Why must he bring out her wanton nature? Why did she let him?

"I—I must return to the keep. My chores await," she insisted and managed to break away from his embrace.

"So, you've had your pleasure and now you're through with me. How fickle you are, but I, on the other hand, am still very much aroused." Tedric moved to nibble upon her neck, and she noticed the large bulge between his legs which his tunic barely concealed. She swallowed hard and looked away, but perversely she wanted to touch him and have him bury his length inside of her—right here, right now, in the middle of the day. Heaven help her, but she was a wanton creature!

"The king is still in residence," she said shakily,

grabbing at any straw to put distance between them. "He might have need of me."

"His need isn't as great as mine, my love, but for the moment, I will set you free. Tonight, however, you belong only to me—and no chore or king shall take you from me."

He let her go, and she scampered away like a frightened field mouse, very much aware of the lust shining in his eyes. She must get away from him, she must stop the desire which soared through her each time the infernal man as much as looked at her.

Amberlie straightened her clothes, her embarrassment more than obvious when Tedric stood and plucked a tiny wild rose and placed it behind her ear. His warm fingers brushed against her lobe and entangled in her hair. "A remembrance of our afternoon together, my lady, so you never forget your pleasure."

"Oh, why must you remind me!" she cried, and turned away to run back to the keep.

"Wait, I shall take you!" he called after her, but Amberlie didn't stop to look back.

When she arrived home, disheveled and out of breath, she found Runa waiting for her to plead illness. Amberlie didn't wait to hear her entire tale of woe, but quickly sent her to bed. Magda immediately informed her that Julianne and Lady Mabel had had another nasty altercation, this one over who had suffered the most during childbirth. A serf had been caught pilfering precious sugar from the larder.

Amberlie dealt with the minor problems, but constantly she was distracted by what had happened in the meadow. What made her discomfort greater was that as she supervised the serfs in the great hall who were readying the evening meal, she was conscious of Tedric, hovering near with the king.

Each time she caught his eye, she blushed with embarrassment and felt a deep sense of despair. Her body had defeated her mind again, and Tedric didn't seem the least bit disturbed. But the next time he came to her, she'd be less responsive and would wipe that smug smile off his face for good!

After partaking of the evening meal, Amberlie rushed away from the table and went to her chamber. She considered locking the door, but decided against it. She knew Tedric, and he'd probably just break it down if she attempted to keep him at bay. Throughout the supper he'd watched her, and the desire in his hot blue gaze had been unmistakable. No doubt he'd assert his husbandly rights, and as his dutiful wife, she'd give him access to her body. "But I won't enjoy it," she mumbled.

"Pardon, my lady?" Magda asked, and picked up Amberlie's discarded bliaut to lay in the chest. "Did you say something?"

"Nothing, I said nothing."

Magda went about her chores, barely glancing at Amberlie. Amberlie thought the woman was acting oddly. She knew Magda didn't entirely trust her yet, but the woman had seemed to be

251

warming toward her. Now, however, she perfunctorily performed her duties, all semblance of warmth having dissipated — and Amberlie knew this change had occurred that morning. Magda was cold because Tedric hadn't presented his wife with her morning gift.

Tedric arrived, his face wreathed in a sensual smile as he shooed Magda from the room. Amberlie stood beside the bed, wearing an older shift which was thin in spots and had seen better days. Tedric critically examined her. "I think you need new clothes. Mayhaps in London, we shall find a weaver who deals in silk and the finest of velvets. Winter will be upon us soon, and from what I've seen of your wardrobe, you need warmer things, as do I. I'm ungodly tired of wearing other men's leavings." Tedric stretched and nearly ripped apart the tunic, which had belonged to Sir Christophe, who was a big man, but not as large as Tedric. "Would you like that?" he asked, and placed his arms around her waist and drew her to him.

"Whatever you prefer, my lord."

Tedric lifted a brow. "Icy cold are you? Well, my love, I have just the medicine for chill." He kissed the beating pulse at the base of her throat, then laved the spot with the tip of his tongue. His hands moved from her waist to her buttocks and he pulled her up against him, and as on that afternoon, she again felt his arousal, but this time his shaft was harder and there was more urgency in the way his fingers moved over her body.

"Nothing will be mended by — by — this," she breathlessly whispered, and stiffened beneath his assault.

"What do you mean?" he asked, and nibbled upon her lips.

Her hands settled between them as a barrier. His heart beat just below her fingertips as she turned her head to end his seductive assault of her lips. "Making love will not change how we feel about one another."

"And how is that?"

Amberlie locked her dark gaze upon him. "You are my enemy, and I am yours. This changes nothing. I fail to see the point of our lovemaking when we distrust one another."

A warning cloud darkened his features. An imperceptible twitch at the corner of his mouth was the only indication that she might have angered him. Instead of releasing her as she'd thought he would do, Tedric lifted her into his arms and carried her to the bed. He placed her against the pillows, her long hair spilling like a dark fan across it. Looking down at her, he seemed to trace each line of her face. "Do you enjoy what I do to you, Amberlie? Do you like when I pleasure you? Be honest for I will know if you lie," he warned.

There was no way out of it. Tedric knew already how much she loved him to touch her. "I like it," she admitted, and hated herself for the truth.

"Then there is no problem."

"But we hate one another," she persisted. "You know how I feel about you, and yet you'd come to me anyway when I can't forgive you for what you did to my husband—" She caught herself, breaking off for a moment, and then said, "What you did to Henri."

A light of understanding flared within his eyes. "Ah, so that is it. You still believe I killed Henri, and this is what eats away at you. What if I told you that I never touched Henri de Fontaine, that I have no memory of murdering him? What would you say then?"

"I'd say you are a liar."

He heaved a gigantic sigh of irritation. "I'm not lying, Amberlie. Am I to be made to suffer the rest of my days for a crime which I deny? Your king has forgiven me my deeds. Why can't you believe me?"

Why couldn't she believe him? That was the heart of the matter. Tedric denied Henri's death, but Henri was dead, killed by a Saxon's hand while defending the keep. And everyone knew Tedric had had few scruples about reclaiming it. She was proof of that. Yet there was something about him, an earnest appeal in his voice, in his face, which caused her to doubt Tedric's hand in Henri's death. If only she could believe him.

"You are my enemy," was all she could say.

"I am your husband!" he proclaimed, and kissed her with such outrageous passion that Amberlie clung to him to keep from drowning in her own tormented desire. He broke away from her and whispered huskily, "Remove your shift while I blow out the candles. In the dark you can pretend I'm your Henri, pretend I'm anyone at all, but I will gain your response, Amberlie. You will respond to me, or I will die in the doing."

Rising from the bed, he blew out the candles. In the darkness, she heard his clothes landing on the floor beside the bed. Then he was beside her, and he took her in his arms. "You haven't removed your shift."

A tiny tremor rushed through her. "I see no reason to bow to your commands. You may take me clothed or unclothed, but the end will be the same. I shall not respond to you—ever. Perhaps you should seek out Glenna for a warm and willing response." Where her courage, or foolishness, came from, she couldn't guess. She only knew that Tedric had an overwhelming effect upon her body, one she intended to break. There was no love lost between them. Each mistrusted the other, so there was no point in pretending—especially not now, not when he'd humiliated her by not giving her the morning gift. But she'd be damned if she asked for it, damned if she responded to his experienced lovemaking.

She felt his roughened hand as he cupped her chin and turned her to face him. Even in the darkness, she discerned pinpoints of blue fire within the depths of his eyes. "Take the thing off, or I shall rip it off."

She knew he meant it.

Moving out of his embrace, she kneeled upon the bed and pulled the garment over her head. Tedric, to her surprise, grabbed for it and threw it upon the floor. "Come here," he gruffly ordered, and without a word, she lay back into his arms.

"Amberlie, you must understand something," he said in a strange and seductively husky voice after a few strained minutes of silence. "Our marriage isn't one of love, but that isn't unusual. Many marriages aren't based on love, or physical attraction either. However, that is where our union differs. We are drawn together by our passion for one another, by the very thing which you deny." To prove his point, he touched her breast and began massaging the nipple, nearly wringing a moan from her, but she kept her response in check. Still, he seemed to know he pleased her and continued playing with her.

"I enjoy touching you," he continued, "and I believe you enjoy pleasing me. Pleasure isn't wrong, nor is it anything to be thought sinful. Didn't you like what I did to you in the meadow today?"

She had loved it, and the conceited man knew it! "I liked it," she finally admitted in a small, tight voice.

"Do you think it was sinful?"

If that was sin, then hell must be filled with people like herself. But the pleasure she'd experienced was close to heaven. "I . . . I don't know."

"Well, it wasn't," he firmly stated. "Married people should find enjoyment in each other's bodies, it is only right." His hand moved lazily from her breast and lightly skimmed across her rib cage and abdomen, to finally find its home within the dark nest which hid her femininity.

She smothered a small gasp when two of his fingers slid inside her wet warmth without warning. She could hear the triumph in his voice to find her already primed for him, and she silently cursed her own wanton response. "No doubt, Amberlie, you enjoy how I make you feel." He kissed her softly upon the mouth. "What say we call a truce?"

"I . . . I don't know what you mean." Now her own voice sounded thick and husky. The man was breaking down her resistance!

Tedric sat on his elbow and continued to kiss her with tiny kisses which skirted across her lips and nose, up to her eyelids, down to her cheeks, and home again to her mouth. She felt his lusty smile upon her. "In the bedchamber, we will put our differences aside. When we come together, we shall forget we are enemies. Our passion, our desire for each other, will be most important when we're alone. You'll accept my lovemaking and will find pleasure in it. Our bodies shall have absolute rule over us. There will be no holding back, no coldness. Many marriages have survived on less than this, my heart. No matter how much you hate me, you can't deny that what you feel for me is more overpowering than your own hatred. And I will be a husband to you, finding as much pleasure in your body as you'll find in mine. No one need ever know our weakness, for in here, we're powerful." He kissed her lightly. "And wanton." He kissed her again, and his breath sent waves of shivers down her spine. "And wild."

It was all too much for her. From the seductive kisses to the way his voice moved over her, and the expert manipulation of his fingers as they worked upon her pulsating bud, Amberlie knew she was lost. Her own primitive yearnings and desires won out. In a blinding haze of passion, she threw her arms about his neck and kissed him with wanton abandon. "I agree," she mumbled against his mouth. "I'll do anything you say—anything you want—"

"Let me love you now, my heart, let me pleasure your beautiful body."

"Oh, anything, anything." He stilled her words with a fevered kiss which banished all thought. His hands moved across her flesh, but always they came back to pleasure the tiny ridge between her thighs, to make her so flushed with lust that she arched against his fingers, aching for fulfillment.

"Not so fast, slowly, my lady wife. We have all night. We have all our lives." But even as he spoke, Tedric continued to arouse her, first by taking each nipple into his mouth and suckling until she thought she'd go mad with want, then by thrusting his fingers inside until she knew she was going to burst. "Please, please," she begged in a haze, "I cannot wait—I must—please, Tedric—"

"If I give you pleasure now, sweet love, will you pleasure me in turn? My body still burns from this afternoon, and I would have some relief." His teeth nibbled her earlobe. "I ache to be inside you, but I shall give you what you want.

Do we have a bargain, like for like?"

She'd have promised anything at that moment. "Aye, I will pleasure you, my lover, I will do whatever—" But she didn't finish her statement for Tedric masterly controlled her body and her senses. With skill and a wild hunger to match her own, Tedric's fingers brought her to ecstasy. His mouth smothered her moans in a kiss which promised a great deal more to come.

Amberlie lay trembling, her body throbbing with its release. His wonderful hand had stilled as he gazed down at her flushed face, her satiated body. A sliver of moonbeam allowed her to see his eyes, and within their depths she saw a man who yearned for her hand upon him, waiting to see if she lived up to her promise to him.

She thrust her breasts against his chest, rubbing instinctively against him, glorying in the feel of his hard body against her soft one. Her hands stroked his broad-planed shoulders, the powerful muscles of his upper arms. She ached to touch all of him, to know every inch of him. Without thinking, with only passion as her guide, she slithered her hand down his taut abdomen to seek the muscle between his groin, which tormented and fascinated her. She enfolded it within her palm, feeling its power, the strength and hardness of Tedric's desire for her. Her fingers moved over it, teasing and taunting, purposely making it harder. She heard Tedric's sharp intake of breath, and he lay rigid beneath her exquisite torture.

"Does this please you, my lord?" she whispered.

"Aye, my lady, aye, it does."

"Is there more you would have me do?" Vaguely, she wondered who this woman was who tempted this man beyond redemption. Was it herself? But there was something so freeing about being able to accept and give pleasure that Amberlie gave herself permission to behave wantonly, finding the only real joy she'd known in her life. Henri had been a considerate lover, but not like Tedric, nothing like Tedric. And if she'd have willingly enjoyed her husband's body, she knew Henri wouldn't have approved. But Tedric was different. He expected her to enjoy him. And what was so odd was that she did.

Tedric swallowed convulsively. "Aye, there is more."

Amberlie grinned. "Whatever you prefer, my lord."

And then she did the most preferable thing in Tedric's mind by moving lower upon his body and tasting him. His groan of pleasure echoed in her ears. She'd have continued on, except Tedric urged her to stop. "No more, my lady, no more, for you've gone too far."

Pulling her up to him, he then laid her on her back and rose over her. "Such sweet teasing must be rewarded," he whispered raggedly.

Somehow, pleasuring him had aroused her again. Amberlie opened her legs to wrap them around his waist. The tip of his shaft penetrated her ever so slightly, almost teasingly, until she arched toward him, and he slid inside of her. She took all of him, every pulsing inch of him. His thrusts impaled her, bringing her to new heights of ecstasy, and with each one, Amberlie put the past further behind her. There was nothing but Tedric, had never been anyone but him, or so it seemed.

The moment she strained for was at hand, and she knew Tedric had reached his limit. The zenith of passion was but a heartbeat away, a second in time. And then when it happened, she pushed into him at the same moment that he spilled inside of her.

Their moans of completion mingled.

Chapter Nineteen

A slave, that's what she was, a slave to her own base desires. Amberlie stared at the ceiling as dawn's pale light stole into the room. In the dark of night, she'd felt safe to act out her desires, to become a woman whom she didn't recognize. But now that light was breaking, and she could see Tedric's face as he slept, an unwelcome blush crept into her cheeks. Never in her entire married life to Henri had she behaved in such a wanton fashion. She'd been happy with Henri but lukewarm about lovemaking. Sometimes she'd found pleasure in it, but most times she hadn't, and she hadn't minded.

But all Tedric had to do was barely touch her and she went wild with desire, acting like an insatiable pagan. What made her situation worse was that Tedric knew how he affected her — and he loved baiting her, seemed to truly enjoy watching her cry out in ecstasy. And how she had cried out, many times, as he loved her during the night. She pressed a hand to her face to cool her burning cheeks as she remembered. How would she continue living with this bull of a man, a man who never seemed to get enough of her? Was it natural to be taken so many times and so many ways in one night? she wondered. Yet she couldn't deny herself, for Tedric was more than a wonderful lover. He was magnificent.

Truly magnificent, she decided as she gingerly picked up the pelt to stare at his bare body. Tedric was the most handsome man she'd ever laid eyes upon. He belonged to her now — all of him. And they'd made a bargain, a strange bargain; even to contemplate it sent odd tingles down her stomach to her toes. Physical attraction, not love, was the main ingredient. She'd learned an important truth last night — it wasn't necessary to love with the heart to enjoy one's self in bed.

"I hope you like what you see, my lady," said Tedric's deep voice next to her ear.

Like a little girl caught in some naughty mischief, Amberlie hastily dropped the pelt. "I — uh — was pulling up — the cover," she told him, but the blush upon her cheeks told the tale. Dropping back upon the pillows, she couldn't even look at Tedric she was so embarrassed. Instead she turned her attention to the brightening sky outside the window. "I must rise soon. Today is the last day the king will be at Woodrose. There is much to do before our departure to London on the morrow."

"Aye, but that can wait, and I'm certain the

king will understand if you aren't immediately present at table this morning. After all, we've been married but two days." Gently, he turned her face to his, and she gazed into twin sapphires, hot and glowing flames of desire. He couldn't want her again; he couldn't mean to take her to dizzying heights of ecstasy again. But he could and he did — exquisitely.

Over an hour later, Tedric left the bed and dressed. Amberlie dozed, waking when she felt his warm kiss upon her forehead. He stood over her, bestowing a tender smile upon her. A wild thought blazed through her mind. If she didn't know better, she'd swear he might love her. Quickly, she shook the absurd thought away. Such a thing was impossible.

" 'Tis time to stir," he said.

Nodding, she sat up and would have gotten out of bed, but Tedric didn't leave the room. She pushed her long dark hair out of her eyes. "Why do you dawdle?"

"I like looking at you. I can wait for you to dress, and we can go below stairs together."

Amberlie was horrified. He couldn't mean to stand there and watch her while she completed her morning toilette, while she dressed. It was indecent, it was pagan — it was exciting. Tingles of anticipation raced through her as she contemplated rising from the bed, naked and flushed from his lovemaking, to preen before him in the daylight. "Magda must help me dress," she demurred.

"I will help you," he quickly volunteered, and bent down to pull the cover from her, but Amberlie's modesty overrode her own desires, and she clutched tightly at the pelt.

"Please, I'd rather you didn't. There are personal things . . ." Her voice broke off, her gaze moving toward the chamber pot.

Tedric seemed to understand immediately. "So there are. Forgive me, my lady, I didn't think. I was but swayed by your beauty this morn and wished to bask in your loveliness for as long as possible. Night is a long way off," he reminded her, and kissed the tip of her nose.

Amberlie giggled and blushed anew. "You're a horrid man."

"Nay, my lady, just one who is besotted with his bride." He turned away and left the room, leaving her sitting in the bed with her hair tumbling past her shoulders in tousled curls and a satisfied smile on her lips. She couldn't help wondering who was besotted with whom.

When Amberlie finally entered the great hall, no one was present but Runa. "How is your cold today?" Amberlie politely inquired. She bit into a ripe pear.

"Better, my lady," Runa insisted, but wiped her runny nose on the back of her hand. Luckily the woman was cleaning the tables and not handling food.

"Where is the king?"

"Out hawking, my lady. He left shortly after

light."

"Lord Tedric went with him?"

"Nay, I saw him with Lady Glenna a few minutes ago near her room." Runa immediately stopped speaking. Her complexion turned unusually white, then reddened. The dishes in her hands shook. " 'Tis sorry I am, my lady. I mean I'm not certain where he might be. May I go now?"

Amberlie nodded, unable to speak for the moment. So Tedric had left her bed only to seek out the woman who'd have been his wife if not for the king's decree. Had the man no conscience, no morals? How could he make love all night long to her and then rush to Glenna in the morning? Was he that insatiable, or did Glenna truly own his black and wayward heart?

Once more he'd made a fool of her. To remember all she'd done with him and to him, the wonderfully strange things he'd done to her—well, she couldn't bear thinking on them. Was he at this very moment pleasuring Glenna in such a way?

Acute feelings of jealousy bit at her insides and twisted her heart. She must discover the truth for herself.

Climbing the flight of stairs that led to the third floor, Amberlie didn't know what she'd do when she found them together. Nothing had prepared her for such treachery. Though she had expected Tedric might seek out Glenna eventually, she hadn't believed it would happen so soon.

He'd humiliated her by not giving her the morning gift, and now to dally with another woman when the spell of his kisses still lingered on her lips . . . The idea upset her more than she cared to admit.

The door to Glenna's room was ajar. With her hand on her throat, Amberlie peered in and found no one was there.

"Searching for someone?"

Guy's voice startled her. Spinning around, she nearly collided with him. "Don't sneak up behind me!" she harshly cried to hide her own embarrassment of being caught outside Glenna's door.

"I beg pardon, *cherie,* but you were so involved in looking in Glenna's room that you didn't hear me. Now why are you here at all? My understanding is that you and Glenna despise one another, so I trust your visit wasn't a friendly one." He crossed his arms over his chest, a knowing gleam in his eyes.

"I wasn't looking for Glenna."

"Ah, then Tedric."

"No!" she quickly retorted, biting down upon her lower lip at the hot denial in her own voice. She couldn't admit the truth to Guy, though he might have his suspicions. "I was searching for Edytha—she has wandered away again," she lied, and hurriedly fled down the passageway.

"Probably looking for her cloth baby," he observed, following after her. Suddenly he stopped beside the window in the hall, which opened onto the bailey. Guy snickered and grabbed her hand to bring her to stand beside him. He leaned closer to the sill. "Look, there's your beloved spouse now, *cherie*."

Gazing down upon the scene below, Amberlie felt her heart flutter like a torn banner in the breeze to see Tedric with his arm wrapped tightly around Glenna's shoulders. Amberlie set her mouth in a thin line. So she'd been right to be worried that he was with Glenna. Evidently he still cared for the woman if he sought her out so soon after the night he'd just spent with his own wife. The cruel knowledge left her legs incredibly weak. She shouldn't be surprised at Tedric's actions, but strangely, she was quite shaken.

Amberlie couldn't face Guy, expecting his knowing smirk.

"It seems your husband has betrayed both of us."

"What do you mean?" She drew her face into a blank mask and turned her attention to Guy.

Anger deepened his voice. "No longer am I in charge of the soldiers, by order of the king. I suspect Tedric had a hand in appointing Sir Christophe to my position." Guy's mouth twisted into an ugly scowl. "I won't overlook this humiliation easily."

Amberlie suspected that Guy meant to cause trouble, but when or what she couldn't fathom. "What will you do?"

He wagged a finger at her. "That, *cherie,* is something only God and I know, for I don't tell my secrets to the enemy."

"I'm not your enemy but a Norman like you."

Guy grinned in amusement and fingered his dagger at his side. "If you insist. Now don't worry about my plans, or Woodrose either, for the keep will be in competent hands while you are away on your sojourn to London with our king—and your most noble husband."

"Whose hands?"

"Sir Christophe's, of course," he replied in all innocence. "Now I shall leave you so you can spy on your husband and his lover without my interference." With a nasty smirk, Guy bowed to her and left her standing beside the open window.

She wouldn't look, she wouldn't, but despite her resolve, Amberlie couldn't help herself. Peering into the bailey, she saw that Tedric and Glenna were still huddled in the same position. Tedric appeared to be tenderly wiping a tear from her cheek.

Swift and fierce jealousy writhed inside her. She didn't know how long she watched them, frozen as she was by their shared intimacy. Only when Glenna turned her head and happened to see Amberlie at the window did Amberlie discern the naked triumph on the woman's face and draw back.

Brazen whore! she cried inwardly, and stilled her shaking hands by clasping them together. Though she willed herself not to care, she couldn't chase away her own insecurity. Tedric had married her, but he hadn't promised her that he'd never dally in another woman's bed, just that when alone together, they'd succumb to their own lust and would freely enjoy lovemaking. He'd lived up to his end of the bargain, and heaven help her, so had she.

But so soon to be betrayed?

"Mother and Edytha will be fine with you watching over them. I know you'll make certain no harm comes to them whilst I am gone." Tedric wiped a lone tear from Glenna's cheek. "Now don't cry, you must be brave."

Glenna nodded, and her hand clung to his arm. "Aye, but I fear being with these Normans."

" 'Tis nothing to fear. Sir Christophe has volunteered to safeguard you. He shall make certain no harm comes to Mother, and my sister also." Tedric hugged her around the shoulders. Her head tilted up at him, but somehow he didn't think she was looking at him but at something else. Her fear appeared to have vanished when she again riveted her attention upon his face. He thought she looked odd, almost as if she'd won a small battle. "Is something wrong?" he queried.

"Nay, all is well, Tedric, all is well."

Tedric didn't understand Amberlie's icy attitude. He'd come up behind her as she worked in the great hall and placed his arms around her waist and kissed her neck. She'd jumped as if he

270

intended to do her harm, and shrugged out of his embrace, telling him that such behavior was unseemly and set a bad example for the serfs.

" 'Tis wrong to show affection for one's wife?" he'd asked, and shook his head in a semblance of disbelief. "Norman customs are not to my liking, if indeed this is a Norman custom." Suspicion coated his voice.

She answered him without looking at him as she went about checking the silver spoons for tarnish. "Misplaced affection is wrong, especially if it is displayed at the wrong time. We made a bargain, you and I, to only touch within our chamber. You aren't living up to your word."

What was the matter with her? he wondered, sorely vexed. That morning she'd been so passionate and giving, and now she was as cold as a frozen stream. He guessed that if he truly turned his energies in her direction, he'd be able to thaw her like the sun in springtime. But he decided not to press her—that, for whatever reason, she wanted no part of him then.

But later, that would be a different story. When they were alone, he'd make it different.

The trek to London lasted six days. By the time the king and his retinue reached the royal hall in Westminster, the same one that had been built by Edward the Confessor and which was outside the smelly city itself, night had fallen.

A servant quietly led Amberlie and Tedric to

their chamber by torchlight. A large canopied bed beckoned to the tired duo, and Amberlie fell upon it, her weariness dulling the hunger pangs which plagued her. "His Majesty has ordered a bath and food to be sent," the woman informed them in French after lighting a torch in the wall sconce.

Tedric didn't quite understand her, so Amberlie acted as interpreter. He nodded eagerly, and shot Amberlie a lustful look which she had come to know full well. "Don't you ever get enough?" she asked after the woman had departed the room. "We've been traveling for days and are dirty, tired, and hungry, and all you can think about is bedding me."

"Not quite true," he said, and began pulling off his tunic. "Perhaps I think about making love to you because traveling has prevented it. Thinking about it and doing it are two very different things."

"I'm really very tired," Amberlie protested weakly, but she didn't ward him off when he sat beside her and ensnared her in his arms. Already, her eyes were closing, and she was only vaguely aware that Tedric kissed her gently before settling her back upon the bed.

Servants with buckets of warm water arrived to fill the large tub. Others brought in two trays of tempting food. Delicious aromas of freshly cooked venison, vegetables, and wine filled the room, but Amberlie was already asleep and quite unaware of the activity surrounding her.

"Would ye care for a wash, my lord?" a pretty young woman with hair the color of spun gold asked Tedric, pointing to the tub. She shyly cast her gaze toward the bed where Amberlie slept, before her eyes wandered appreciatively over Tedric's imposing body and brazenly appraised the bulging spot within his hose. "I promise to be very quiet and not waken yon lady. I can do anything ye'd wish."

Tedric imagined she could, and she was an appealing wench, clean too, from the look of her. But he shook his head. There was only one woman whose touch he craved, and at the moment she was in the realm of dreams.

Minutes later, after dismissing all of the servants, Tedric sat naked in the warm tub and sipped from a cup of mead. He watched Amberlie the whole time, seeing the beauty of her face, which was framed beneath an abundance of thick black hair. Her full breasts beneath her bliaut rose gently with the rise and fall of her breathing. Despite the fact that he too was fatigued from the days of traveling, just looking at her stirred a fire in his loins. He'd never responded to a woman in such a way before, so that all he had to do was gaze upon her to be filled with lust.

What was there about Amberlie that spurred such savage flames within him, that set her apart from every lover he had ever known? Many women had aroused him, even Glenna, who'd been no virgin when he'd first taken her and had known exactly how to please a man. But no woman had so totally bewitched him, besotted him, until he salivated with sheer lust and grew drunk with the very act of possession, an act which should have freed him of the spell she'd woven over him. Each time he made love to her only heightened his desire to love her again.

And each time he loved her, gentle feelings rose to the fore—feelings he buried to keep him from falling under her magic spell. He didn't want to weaken and fall in love with his own wife.

Tedric shook his head to drive the powerful feelings of affection away. He mustn't feel anything for Amberlie but passion and respect as his wife. She was his enemy, and though he fully anticipated she'd bear him healthy children, Tedric didn't trust her. Never could he forget that she was a Norman noblewoman, a woman who hated him and felt she had good cause for that hatred. She thought he had taken Henri de Fontaine's life; and no matter how passionately she responded to his lovemaking, Tedric suspected that if she got the chance, she'd somehow destroy him.

Amberlie sighed in her sleep and rolled onto her stomach. There was something so stirring about the image of her perfectly shaped buttocks that Tedric decided six days of celibacy was long enough.

Like a moth drawn to a flickering flame, Tedric got out of the tub and padded toward Amberlie, unmindful of being dripping wet. Placing his cup on a small table, he gazed down at his wife.

Tedric knew he must make love to her. Every aspect of her body held him in thrall and filled him with such desire that he couldn't help himself, didn't want to resist touching her.

Bending down, he lifted the hem of Amberlie's gown and ever so gently skimmed the silk fabric past her flawlessly shaped calves, over her thighs, to finally crest the curve of her bare buttocks, before settling the material around her waist like a blue cloud. Never had he known such a perfectly formed woman. Even her derriere was tinted a golden shade of peach. He lightly stroked the rounded mounds with the palms of his hands. Amberlie stirred and lifted her head to turn and look at him with sleepy eyes. "Tedric, what are you doing?"

His hands stilled. "Don't you like what I'm doing?" he asked with a grin on his face that Amberlie could only describe as devilish.

She knew very well what his intentions were. A quick glance at his jutting manhood was proof enough. Her heartbeat quickened, and she flushed, much too aware of her response to Tedric. Why must she feel all quivery whenever this man so much as touched her? Her response was indecent, it was wrong to feel passion for Henri's killer. She must school her responses to Tedric, her enemy. "I told you that I'm tired," she said irritably. "Besides I'm dirty and in no mood for—"

"Then I shall wash you," he insisted. Leaving the bed, he went to the tub, retrieved the wet washcloth, and wrung it out before returning to sit beside her on the mattress. Bending over her, he started to wash her face.

Amberlie pushed his hand away. "I'm not a child! I can wash myself!"

"Aye, but will you be able to wash well behind your ears, between the folds and crevices you can't see? I think not, my lady. I can help you with your bath."

"I know what sort of help you'd be, and exactly what you'd help yourself to," she grumbled, and rolled onto her back.

" 'Tis a husband's duty to see to his wife's comfort," he huskily whispered into her ear, bending low, "and pleasure."

Amberlie shivered from the tingling sensation which darted up her spine. She recalled the time he'd entered her room as her slave and had washed her breasts. How wonderful that had felt!

"You'd rest more pleasantly after a wash. My bath has refreshed me." To prove his point, Tedric gently skimmed the cool cloth across the tops of her breasts. "I think only of your comfort, my lady. I recall one time when you didn't complain about my skill with a washcloth."

Amberlie blushed to her hair roots, embarrassed for Tedric to have read her thoughts. But she remembered the image of Tedric embracing Glenna before the journey and couldn't forget the sight. She wanted to fight her attraction for Tedric, but all the horrid man had to do was touch her and she was lost. Leave me alone! she

276

longed to cry, but with each stroke of the cloth across her heated flesh, Amberlie lost her resistance. Even the image of Glenna in Tedric's arms vanished. Now she was Tedric's slave, controlled by her own lust for a man whom she hated.

One of his hands found her breast, and he massaged the nipple through her gown until it rose hard and stiff. "Do you like this, my lady?" he whispered thickly into her ear.

"I—I thought you wanted to wash me," she replied in a voice just as husky.

"Oh, then all you want is a bath, nothing more?" He looked so smug that Amberlie would gladly have grabbed the washcloth and thrown it in his face. But she couldn't still the ache between her legs, the way her body responded to his gentle handling of her.

"I won't beg—I won't—"

He broke off her words, pulling her toward him with lust smoldering in his blue eyes. His lips claimed hers in a burning kiss which left her clinging to his broad shoulders as passion overwhelmed her. If she hadn't already been reclining on the bed, she would have fallen. His lips broke away from her mouth and nibbled upon the soft flesh of her neck. "Your clothes are in the way, my sweet. Shall I remove them?" At her nod, Tedric smiled. "But these clothes are old, and soon we shall buy cloth for new ones. Do you mind if I strip them from you?"

Amberlie sucked in her breath; her eyes grew large at such an outrageous but heart-stopping suggestion. But she nodded, too in thrall to him to refuse. "I—do—not mind."

His hands worked at the neckline of her bliaut. "Are you certain?"

"Aye, Tedric, aye."

He pulled at the material and wrenched it away from her, leaving only her chemise to cover her nipples, which strained toward him, two hardened peaks which he bent to suck until she moaned in tormented delight. His hands ran the length of her thighs before one settled between her legs and stroked the moist warmth of her woman's core with the wet cloth. " 'Twould be a good idea to remove your shift so I could wash you properly, wouldn't it?" he asked.

Amberlie swallowed convulsively. Liquid heat gathered and spread like molten gold through her lower body. She could barely speak. " 'Twould be a . . . good idea."

His mouth was but an inch from hers, his breath hot upon her lips, when he said, "Tell me what you want me to do. Tell me."

She licked her lips. Her breath came in tiny gasps. "I want you to . . . to . . ."

"Say it," he ordered, and purposely taunted her with the washcloth.

"Uncover me. I want you—to uncover me."

"With pleasure, my love, with pleasure." Grabbing hold of the well-worn shift with one hand, Tedric yanked it from her, tearing it easily. He threw it atop the bliaut, which lay upon the floor. His eyes fastened upon her nakedness, and he drank in the beauty of her face and form like a man quenching a great thirst. "God, but you're perfectly lovely," he said in praise, and began a slow exploration of her breasts. His hands cupped each one; his fingers tenderly followed the soft contours and laved the nipples into hardened peaks with his lips. Then his fingers searched and found the pulsing bud between her legs once more, but this time there was no cloth. He stroked her, primed her with his fingertips until Amberlie couldn't stand his wicked teasing.

"Tedric, please — please — "

He knew what she wanted. He wanted it too. Tedric pulled her up against him so that they met breast to chest, eyes to eyes. She arched against him, lifting and opening her legs to him. He slid into her, the beauty of her face inflaming his desire. A hollow moan escaped from between her lips. "Do you like this, my lady? Tell me that you like how I love you."

"Oh, Tedric — Tedric, I like this so — so much." She was practically whimpering as he thrust into her slowly, giving her some of him, but retreating, only to slide slowly inside again, yet not filling her to the hilt as he longed to do.

"I love that you like this, I want you to feel pleasure, my sweet Amberlie."

Her fingers dug into his shoulders, and he heard the pleading in her voice. "Fill me, fill me, please."

He lunged into her, impaling her on his pulsating shaft, and didn't withdraw. She cried out

279

loud, not from pain but from such pleasure that he felt all powerful, all knowing, all protective. Amberlie squirmed against his length, which buried deeply inside her with each thrust. Finally, he ceased thrusting, sensing that Amberlie had taken control. She arched and pushed into him, squeezing and taunting until his body threatened to explode. "I cannot wait," he insisted, and groaned into her hair.

"Not yet," she whispered, and slowed her movements. Tedric hovered, poised on the brink of madness while his body dictated his will, but somehow he held himself in check. She set the pace for their lovemaking, flexing her muscles around his shaft to gain the greater pleasure. Like one trained to the art, Amberlie somehow knew how to excite him but keep him from spilling into her before she was ready.

He watched her, fascinated by how the torchlight illuminated her face. She looked wild and wanton with all the dark hair spilling across the pillow, her lips moist and parted, more than bewitching in the way her eyes glazed over with ecstasy as she neared the pinnacle. Nothing was more beautiful to him than this woman, this dark-eyed goddess. He couldn't wait any longer, and he ceased thrusting. "When, Amberlie, when?" he cried, almost in pain for his pleasure was so great.

She gazed up at him, almost as if she didn't see him. It was then he felt the spasms begin inside her body. Her time had come. "Now! Oh, now!" She arched upward, welcoming his last lusty thrust, which threw both of them over the edge into an explosive whirl of such intense ecstasy that when it was over, they lay spent in each other's arms.

"Would you care to finish your bath, my lady?" Tedric asked with a grin some minutes later.

Amberlie pushed her hair away from her shoulder and sat up. "I suppose you'll want to wash me."

"Aye, but only if you insist."

She laughed, knowing she wouldn't refuse him. He derived as much pleasure from touching her as she enjoyed being touched. She was no longer shocked by Tedric's lusty behavior, or her own, for that matter. Tedric had this all-consuming power over her body which she was slowly coming to accept. For Tedric, lovemaking was a necessary and expected part of life, and he took full enjoyment in it. And under his expert tutoring, she was beginning to feel the same way.

Settling into the tub, Amberlie turned over her bathing to him. Tedric was tender in his ministrations and constantly praised her body. Never had she felt more beautiful than when she allowed Tedric to have his way with her. But on the morrow, when light broke, she knew that his heart would belong to Glenna and not to her. Though Glenna was miles away, Amberlie felt the woman's presence most acutely during the day.

But at night, she lived up to their bargain and enjoyed her husband's lovemaking. She simply couldn't resist the man. As long as they remained in London, Glenna was nowhere around to tempt him. And Tedric belonged only to her.

Chapter Twenty

"Amberlie, *cherie,* how pleased I am to see you again." Matilda, Queen of England, hastened to embrace Amberlie the next morning when she joined the queen in her chamber. Amberlie sat next to her on the red velvet cushions of the window seat. The River Thames flowed swiftly past in the distance, and on this particular morning, a slight mist hung in the air. They spoke for a number of minutes about Amberlie's father, who had been a favorite of Matilda's and a dear friend to the king. Both reminisced fondly about Normandy, their eyes wistful, growing silent in their memories. Finally, Matilda cleared her throat. "I have spoken to the king about your situation," Matilda began, a slight smile hovering on her lips. "Are you pleased with William's choice of husband for you?"

Amberlie knew better than to complain to the queen about the king's decision, but truly she had nothing to complain about for Tedric was a devoted husband — at night. *"Oui,* Your Majesty, I am well pleased."

"I hear this Tedric is a handsome man. I look forward to greeting him. In fact, he is hawking with the king. What say we join them?"

"If that is your wish, Your Majesty."

"We shall take my ladies with us." Matilda rose, and her thin figure elegantly moved across the room to an outer chamber, where she ordered her ladies to join them.

Half an hour later, the women walked the distance from the royal hall to the open field. To protect themselves from the misty weather, each wore a mantle and hood. They stopped a short distance from where William, with three of his own men and Tedric, was in conversation with the falconer. Tedric turned and happened to see Amberlie among the women. He bowed politely, and this elicited a giggle from a pretty auburn-haired young woman. "Such a handsome devil!" she exclaimed. "See how broad of shoulder he is, how thick of calf. *Il est magnifique!"*

"Oui," an even comelier brunette agreed. "I should like to meet him."

"Yvette! Denise!" said Matilda in sharp reprimand. She was aware that Amberlie might be uncomfortable with other women eyeing her husband. "Return to the palace at once."

Blushes immediately suffused both women's faces, and they looked confused, wondering what they'd done to deserve such harsh treatment from the queen. But both curtsied deferentially and hurried away. "Please forgive them, *cherie,* they are very young," said the queen.

"And very beautiful," Amberlie said, disliking the sudden jab of insecurity she experienced. She'd worried about Glenna, but now Tedric would be surrounded by many beautiful women while at court—women who would no doubt praise his every action and each syllable he uttered. She might be his wife and share his bed, but Tedric didn't love her and never would for they were enemies.

They watched William and Tedric, involved in the sport, for quite a long time. Some others of Matilda's ladies politely withdrew with the queen's permission. Finally, the gentlemen headed in their direction, and William introduced Tedric to Matilda before they retired to the great hall for the midday meal.

Amberlie sat next to Matilda during the meal, and Matilda smiled knowingly at her. "My husband was right to order your marriage to the Saxon. This Tedric is a good man and will protect our kingdom. I can tell these things."

"I am pleased you approve, Your Majesty." Amberlie stole a glance at Tedric at the same time as he looked at her from the other end of the long table. She glanced away, instantly warming beneath the fire she saw in Tedric's eyes.

Matilda laughed, the tiny lines around her eyes crinkling in amusement. *"Oui,* William chose well. He is responsible for a marriage of love, is he not?"

Amberlie was startled. "You are mistaken, Your Majesty. Our marriage is based upon enmity, not love."

"Cherie, you are a fool if you believe such a thing." Matilda brushed some bread crumbs from her skirt and peered intently at Amberlie. "Tedric is in love with you. I see love on his face each time he looks at you. The man adores you, *cherie.* Open your eyes."

"I hasten to disagree. He loves someone else."

"Pooh! He loves you, and I won't hear to the contrary. You're in love with him too."

Amberlie shook her head in denial. "Oh, no, Your Majesty, I do not—"

"So, you dare to disagree with your queen. I thought your dear father taught you well."

"I'm sorry, forgive me, I didn't mean to contradict you."

"Don't look so affronted," Matilda said kindly, patting Amberlie's hand. "I was but teasing you. Still, I speak the truth. Not only must you open your eyes but your heart as well. Then you shall see the obvious. *N'cest-ce pas?"*

The obvious. Matilda was evidently of a fanciful nature.

Amberlie glanced at Tedric again, and still she found that he watched her. More and more, it seemed, she noticed his gaze following her. She couldn't stop staring at him either, watching him whenever he thought she was occupied with something else or even sleeping. Sometimes she feigned sleep just to peer at him when he rose naked from their bed, to drink her fill of his handsomeness without his awareness. She was conscious of his every movement and took unwilling delight in it. Was this lust—or love?

When Amberlie returned to her chamber that afternoon, she discovered one of Matilda's ladies waiting for her, an elderly woman whom she recalled as Isabelle. The woman proudly pointed to the bed, where lay a jeweled headdress and a red bliaut, fashioned from the softest velvet, accompanied by an embroidered wool girdle which was scarlet in hue. "A gift from Her Majesty to keep the flames high in a man's eyes," Isabelle informed her with an impish smile. "There will be much merriment at court tonight, and Her Majesty expressly wishes you to wear her gift."

Amberlie stroked the soft material and blushed all the way to her hairline. Evidently the servant who'd tidied her room that morning had discovered the torn bliaut and chemise from the night before and brought them to the queen. "Tell Her Majesty that I am very grateful." She was more than grateful, for the gown was one of the most beautiful she'd ever seen.

Minutes later, Tedric entered, and Isabelle discreetly left them alone. Beneath his arm, he carried a leather pouch of medium size. He frowned upon seeing the clothes upon the bed. "Have I a rival?"

Amberlie laughed, feeling suddenly light-hearted. "A gift from the queen."

"Better the queen than the king." The whiteness of his sudden smile dazzled her. "Now, I have something for you." He offered her the pouch.

"What is it?" she asked.

"Something you need and want very much," he said with a wink, being purposely mysterious.

Her heart thumped hard and her mouth grew dry in anticipation. Her fingers shook. Perhaps, just perhaps, it was the morning gift. In childlike eagerness, she opened the pouch, her hand rushing within its depths to come in contact with thin, gauzy material. Taking it out, she discovered a delicately sewn chemise of such pale yellow that it was almost white. She bit down upon her lower lip to hide her disappointment.

"Do you like it?" he asked, and came behind her and placed his arms around her waist.

"It—is very lovely."

"I wanted to replace the one I ripped from you last night. I found a seamstress in Londontown who sold it to me for a fair price."

Tedric kissed the nape of her neck, and at any other time Amberlie would have wildly responded to him, but now she felt like crying. She'd been silly to expect the morning gift, and she knew she shouldn't be disappointed but she was. All over again. Nothing was going to change between them—ever. The queen was wrong to say Tedric loved her, and Amberlie had been foolish to question her own judgment about his feelings for her, and hers for him. There was only one gift she wanted, one gift she'd have cherished. Tedric might give her pretty clothes, but she wanted something from him that he didn't intend to give to her. She wanted the circlet as proof that she'd pleased him and was truly his wife. This chemise meant nothing, and she suddenly wanted to wound his pride as he'd wounded hers.

Turning around, she threw the chemise at him. He grabbed it in one of his large hands before it hit the floor. "I prefer to wear one of my own."

"Your clothes are worn," he protested, clearly perplexed.

"But they are mine. I choose to take nothing from you. Give the chemise to Glenna for I'm certain she'd be more grateful than I."

He stocd stook still, a hurt look on his face, which he quickly masked by a sardonic twist of his lips. "I apologize, my lady. I forgot that you've never taken anything from me—but your own pleasure in bed."

Raising her hand, she slapped his face. Even as she did this, she knew it was a mistake, but she was unable to control herself. No sooner had she inflicted the blow than Tedric's hand grabbed hers in a hold so tight that she felt her fingers go numb.

"Never, ever do that again, my lady," he

warned in a chillingly cold voice. "I am your husband now, whether you care for me or not. I am your master and will have your respect. I know not what has happened to cause this change in your attitude, this rift between us, but you shall not embarrass either yourself or me when in the presence of others. For the king's and queen's eyes, you will play the docile and contented wife. At Woodrose, you'll bow to my wishes in bed and out."

"And what will you do if I disobey you? Shall you have me flogged? Shall you put me from your bed?" She was being foolhardy and she knew it, but she couldn't help herself.

"Tempt me not, Amberlie. For your own sake, obey me in all things. But I promise you one thing—I shall not put you from my bed. You will bear me children, my lady, half-Norman children to insure that Woodrose remains in my possession."

"I hate you!" she spat out, feeling horribly used and humiliated to be wanted only for the children she would bear him.

"Your feelings cannot be helped," he said almost sadly, "but I do promise you that in my bed, you will enjoy each moment. You know in your heart that you will. Your body belongs to me, only to me."

"My heart never shall."

"That I know well." He dropped her hand. "Dress now for Their Majesties await." He threw the chemise upon the bed and left the room, slamming the huge door behind him.

Amberlie rubbed her wrist to relieve the numbness. Tears shimmered in her eyes, not from any physical pain but from the terrible pain in her heart. Somehow she knew that wearing the red gown that night would gain her nothing. The gown would spark no flames in Tedric's eyes, and later that night, her premonition was proved true. Tedric lay beside her in the dark; he made no move to touch her. And though she should have been gladdened at the fact, her traitorous body ached for him.

Over two weeks later, Amberlie and Tedric traveled the roads back toward Woodrose, escorted by four of William's most capable knights. At first, Tedric had objected to the entourage, still not trusting Normans in general, but the king had insisted. William wanted Amberlie safely returned to her home, and with news of violent uprisings in the north, William feared the spread of them in other areas. As night fell on the last day of their travel, they made camp.

Three of the knights discreetly found spots nearby to rest while the fourth leaned against a tree to watch. Tedric found a warm, dry spot for Amberlie. Placing a blanket before the low-burning campfire, he extended his hand to her, but she sank to the ground of her own accord, barely glancing at him. It had been thus since he'd presented her with the yellow chemise. Tedric didn't know what he'd done wrong, and at this point, after being treated with icy disdain for so long, he didn't care if she ever spoke to him again. Actually, this wasn't true, but he'd grown exhausted—and perplexed, and frustrated—trying to discover what he'd done to cause this breach between them.

Aye, frustrated, he thought, and cracked a twig in two as he sat staring into the flickering flames. His body screamed for release. He hadn't attempted to touch Amberlie in days. Though he'd intended to make love to her each night when he got into bed, he couldn't get up the courage to approach her. There was something in her attitude which led him to believe that she'd no longer be receptive to him. More than anything he craved her willing response in his arms. He couldn't make love to a woman who lay in his bed like a corpse.

He sighed fretfully and lay down upon the blanket he'd placed near Amberlie. As always, she didn't face him, but had turned in the opposite direction, away from him, so he couldn't tell if she were awake or asleep. Tomorrow night, they'd be at Woodrose in their own bed. Perhaps then things might change, once they were home again. In time they'd establish a normal routine, and maybe a normal life together. Tedric closed his eyes after long moments of gazing at the stars, and hope filled him as he drifted into sleep.

"Filthy swine!"

Tedric immediately wakened, his senses alerted to the startled cry of one of William's knights. Two men, unknown to him, were locked in combat with the four knights. Leaping to his feet, he grabbed for his sword at the same moment Amberlie sat up, befuddled and frightened. "What's happened?" she cried.

"Intruders!" he shouted at her at the exact moment Amberlie screamed in terror, her gaze riveted on a spot behind him. She pointed in nameless fear, warning Tedric. Pivoting about, he saw a large, shabbily dressed man rushing toward him with raised dagger. There was a murderous glint in his eyes as he jabbed at Tedric with the knife, but Tedric was faster and sidestepped the blow. The man wasn't as lucky. He fell forward, but quickly flipped onto his back again and hurled the knife at Tedric, nearly hitting him. Tedric ducked and with lightning swiftness, he struck at the man's heart with his sword. Blood gurgled from the man's mouth and, with a dazed expression on his face, he expired. Similar fates awaited his two companions at the knights' hands.

The knight named Etienne had suffered a scratch during the scuffle, and Amberlie tended to him. "Who do you think they were?" Tedric asked the knight known as Maurice as they searched the bodies for clues. But the dead men's clothes were barely more than rags, and they looked to be a villainous lot.

"Cutthroats, I imagine," Maurice said, and bent down to examine the large man who had attacked Tedric. Nodding, he withdrew a small bag of coins from the side of the large man's ragged hose. *"Oui,* my Lord Tedric, a thief and murderer, no doubt. He must have killed some weary traveler for such money, and would have murdered all of us, with the help of his comrades. It is fortunate that Etienne was alerted to their presence."

"Aye," agreed Tedric, now grateful for William's protection. Without these knights, he and Amberlie would be dead.

Later, after the knights had removed the bodies from view, Amberlie sat upon her blanket and trembled. Tedric broke away from a conversation with Maurice and came to sit beside her. Without waiting for an invitation, he placed his arms protectively around her. "Rest now, all is well," he assured her.

Amberlie gazed up at him with huge, dark eyes. "Suppose there are others."

"There are no more," he assured her with a confident smile, and placed her head on his shoulder. "Sleep. I'll protect you."

"I doubt I'll fall asleep."

"Then close your eyes and think about returning to Woodrose. We'll be there by mid-morning."

Amberlie sighed. "I truly can't wait to get home."

Tedric couldn't wait either, for now hope blossomed within his heart that he might eventually win Amberlie's affections. Fear had driven her to take comfort from him, and she seemed not about to part from him now, for her long, slim fingers clutched at his arm. It felt wonderful to hold her again.

And, once they were home, she'd get over whatever had bothered her in London. She must, because he doubted he could live without her avid response to his caresses.

Chapter Twenty-one

From her vantage point in the east tower, Julianne watched as the small traveling party rode into the bailey. William's knights protectively halted their steeds alongside Amberlie and Tedric. Rage puffed out Julianne's cheeks, and she clenched her fists as she spotted Tedric's fair head.

Her son's murderer still lived!

"Is there no justice in this accursed world?" she cried aloud. Why was Tedric still alive? Had the brutes she'd hired to murder him even found him on the road, or had they run away with the money she'd paid them without seeking out their prey? She'd paid the bastards a hefty sum to be waiting and watching for Tedric's return. That accursed Baudelaire was to blame, she decided. Evidently she shouldn't have trusted the knight to plan anything of this magnitude. It was obvious she'd be forced to take matters into her own hands, for Baudelaire was a bungler and Guy, her precious stepbrother, was too fainthearted to do anything other than speak against Tedric. Where actions counted, Julianne could trust only herself.

There were other ways to murder someone.

She was contemplating her next move when an impatient knock sounded on the door. Opening it, she encountered Baudelaire, who hurriedly brushed past her to enter the room. "Our plan has failed, my lady. I've just discovered from one of the king's knights that they killed the three men you hired. Tedric escaped unharmed."

"I know that, you imbecile. I have eyes in my head to see the man is fit and hearty. I shouldn't have trusted you. I won't again."

"My lady, I assure you that my tongue is mute. Never shall I ever tell another living soul what we've done."

Julianne appraised the long-faced man, not trusting him, but at least he'd tried to get rid of Tedric—not like Guy, who preferred to wait for what she didn't know. "I paid you well for your silence, Baudelaire. For such a sum you should also be blind, but I need your sharp eyes as well. I'm just not certain you can be trusted."

"I will do anything you wish, my lady. Henri de Fontaine was my lord, and I honor his memory."

"Hah! You honor my purse, but never mind." Julianne settled herself on the window bench. Her stomach bothered her suddenly, a large aching pain consumed her, and she feared the grippe again. Gritting her teeth, she attempted to will away the pain. "Are you familiar with the woodlands here about?"

"A bit, my lady. I've done a lot of hunting."

"I've heard tell about a climbing plant with berries that grows wild in the woods. In late summer the blossoms are greenish-yellow. Have you seen such a thing?"

"Mayhaps, but the blossoms are dust now."

"Fine, but I don't want the blossoms. I want the plant and berries. Search and bring me what you find. But make certain no one knows what you are about. Tell not even my brother."

Baudelaire grinned maliciously. "The plant is poisonous, my lady?"

Julianne shrugged and pursed her lips in thought. "We shall see."

Glenna eased her sweaty body from beneath Christophe's and settled onto her side. Her fingers lightly traced the line of darkly matted hair which extended from his navel to his groin. Christophe groaned and pulled her toward him, kissing her with passion despite the passionate morning he'd spent in bed with her.

"You truly know how to arouse a man, *cherie.*"

"I like touching you," Glenna candidly admitted. "You have a wonderful body."

"And yours is perfection."

"I know." She wrinkled her nose at him.

"Ah, such modesty overwhelms me."

She laughed huskily. "Christophe, I am far from modest."

"Bien, for I like a lusty woman."

"I like how you speak. Would you say something to me in your language?"

"Je t'aime."

Glenna giggled. "That sounds pretty. What did you say?"

"I told you that I love you."

"Oh!" She sat up, moving toward the bottom of her bed, and reached for her kirtle. Her long blond hair flowed around her like a veil.

"Will you not tell me the same, *cherie?"* Christophe sat up and pulled her up against his chest. "I should like to hear you say it."

"I prefer to show what I feel, rather than say empty words."

"There is nothing wrong with saying how you feel, Glenna. I have waited to hear these words from your lips for over a week now, since the first night I came to you. I am tired of sneaking into your room. I want to marry you."

"Christophe nay!"

He tilted her face up so he could look into her eyes. *"Oui,* I've decided to ask Lord Tedric for you upon his return."

"You will not!" Glenna pushed away from him and practically jumped from the bed, clutching her kirtle to her breasts. "I won't marry you. Tedric will never allow our marriage."

"Why not?" Christophe inquired with a raised eyebrow. "Because you think he still loves you?"

"He does love me. Tedric has always loved me. We are betrothed."

"Lord Tedric is married now, and his heart lies with his bride, not with you. *Mon Dieu,* Glenna, face the truth. I'm the man who loves you! I'm the man you'll marry!"

"Nay! Tedric married that Norman witch only to keep Woodrose and his lands. He could never love her."

"But he does love her," Christophe softly told her, and rose from the bed to dress. "He won't come to you any longer."

She shook her head in denial, hot tears glimmering in her eyes. How dare Christophe tell her such a lie, how dare he dash her hopes of bringing Tedric to her bed again! "If you ask Tedric for me, I will refuse."

"Ah, such a child you are." Standing before her, he kissed her. "If you refuse me, *cherie,* then you refuse a life of happiness. Why wait to become another man's leman when you can be my wife? But I tell you one thing, so you will know. I am not a second choice to Tedric. When you marry me, it will be because your heart overflows with love for me and no other reason. The time has come to bury your childish dreams."

"Leave me, Christophe. Just go." She didn't believe she could speak further, for something about Christophe always touched her heart and made her feel vulnerable and weak. He closed the door behind him, and Glenna heard noise in the bailey. She saw that Tedric was back and speak-

300

ing to the knights, but strangely she felt no gladness at his return.

"Avenge me, avenge me."

Amberlie woke to the low voice in her ear. The room was dark, except for the bright glow from the hearth. Tedric snored deeply beside her, the trip home having wearied him. She closed her eyes again and began to drift off to sleep, but once more, she heard the voice.

"Avenge me, avenge me."

This time she bolted upright in bed, her hands clutching the pelt in rigid fear. With her heart beating loudly in her ears, she gazed about the room, believing that someone was there and hiding. She saw no one, nothing out of the ordinary, but clearly she'd heard a voice. A log fell in the hearth and she jumped, instantly berating herself for being afraid.

But afraid of what?

Lying back down, she pulled the pelt to her chin and moved close to Tedric. Once more, she started to doze. Once more, the voice whispered in her ear, startling her awake. Then she saw him, standing only three feet from her bedside.

Henri gazed down at her, a look of utter sadness on his face, but he possessed no substance, only a shadowy form. Stark fear seized hold of her, Tedric's name dying on her tongue for she suddenly couldn't utter a sound. And then he disappeared, melting away into the darkness.

301

She blinked and stared in disbelief at the wall. This time it was no dream.

Amberlie followed behind Gundred in the forest as the old woman searched for herbs and plant roots to be used for medicinal purposes. Wild ferns, growing in profusion upon the forest floor, silenced their unhurried footsteps. Many times Gundred bent down to point to a particular plant and advised Amberlie as to its efficacy, or whether it was friend or foe to humans.

Each time Gundred dug up roots or pulled pieces of climbing vines from trees, she placed them in a straw basket which Amberlie carried. " 'Tis important to have knowledge of such wildlife," Gundred explained to her. "For they can make well or do ill. Here, my lady, look closely at this mushroom." Gundred moved aside a fern and Amberlie noticed a yellowish-colored mushroom that seemed harmless enough. " 'Tis deadly and 'twill kill the one who eats it within a matter of hours. Mark its shape and color well."

It always amazed Amberlie how much Gundred knew about such things. Amberlie needed to learn from the woman, as Gundred was quite adept at making poultices, at knowing how many berries of a certain plant would kill rather than cure. For a number of months, Amberlie had been helping to tend the sick at Woodrose, following Gundred's instructions in the medicinal arts, whereas Julianne had lost interest in such things a long time ago. Amberlie knew that Gundred welcomed her help and her interest. The old woman knew she wouldn't live forever, and she was eager to pass on her knowledge of healing.

They'd gone a bit further into the woods when suddenly Sir Baudelaire appeared on the tiny footpath in front of them, startling both of the women. A leather pouch was slung over his shoulder. "You gave us a fright!" Amberlie cried, her eyes raking over the man. She didn't like Baudelaire or trust him, as he was the knight who'd attacked Edytha.

"Pardon, my lady." He bowed respectfully, but Amberlie sensed no respect in his attitude. Clearly, he didn't like her, most probably because she'd been the one to hit him on the head with the heavy candlestick. She still could see the tiny scar on his right temple where she'd hit him. "I was but taking a walk."

More like dallying with a woman, Amberlie thought disdainfully. "I suggest you walk back to the keep, for I'm certain you are needed there."

"*Oui,* my lady, but I shall be most pleased to act as your escort home. The woods can be a dangerous place."

"I appreciate your offer, but we haven't finished our gathering."

With another respectful bow, he headed past them. Amberlie bent down to pluck some wild mint from the ground when she heard Gundred snort. "That one is up to mischief, my lady."

"No doubt, but there's very little harm he can

303

do here." They continued their work, and when they completed their gathering, they started down the path to the keep, but Gundred halted. Her ears perked up.

"Someone is moaning. Do ye hear, my lady?"

Amberlie listened for a few seconds, at first hearing only the chirping birds and crickets. But then she heard what Gundred had heard. She nodded at the old woman, and they moved in the sound's direction, which emanated from some twenty feet off the path. The moaning grew louder as they stealthily approached, on guard. Within a nest of ferns, Amberlie discerned the blue of a tunic before she saw the man who wore it.

"Why, it's Wick!"

The old man heard her and raised sick eyes to her, too weak to lift his head. "Lady Amberlie?"

"Aye, and Gundred too." She felt his forehead and found he burned with a fever. "How long have you been here?"

"I—I know not. A day perhaps."

Amberlie looked at Gundred. "We must get him to the keep. Wait here with him while I get help."

Wick grabbed her hand. "Thank ye, my lady, ye're kind to help an enemy."

Tedric personally brought Wick to the keep, placing the small, sick man before him on the large gelding. He laid him on a pallet in the sick

304

room, next to the storeroom, where a supply of herbs, ground to a find powder, was kept in pouches to be used as medicine. Amberlie offered Wick a cool cup of water, which the old man greedily quaffed. She left her husband with Wick, silently closing the door behind her.

"I never thought to see you again," Tedric told him with a worried frown. "Where have you been these last weeks?"

The water seemed to restore Wick's strength some. "In the woods, my lord, living from hand to mouth."

"And Wulfgar? What of him?"

"I know not where he is. I've not seen him for some days." A warm smile enveloped Wick's mouth. "I'm pleased to find ye alive, my lord. These Normans have been good to ye?"

"Aye, in their way."

"And ye're married to Lady Amberlie?"

Tedric nodded.

"Good, good, that's how it should be."

Tedric could tell that Wick was growing tired. Just at that moment, Amberlie entered the room with Gundred and Tedric started to withdraw, knowing the women needed to tend their patient. But he touched Amberlie's hand as she stood next to him in the tiny room. This was the first time he'd touched her since the night of the attack on the way to Woodrose. "Gundred shall sit the night with Wick," he told her, and gently squeezed her fingers. "You have other duties which need your attention."

Immediately, he noticed her blush, but there was a look of desperation, even fear, on her face which he didn't understand and had never seen before. What was wrong with her? he wondered. Why did she no longer welcome his kisses and caresses? What had happened to turn her away from him so entirely? The woman was an endless mystery to him.

Later, Amberlie waited in her chamber for Tedric to appear. She stood with outstretched hands before the hearth, trying to dispel the chill in the room. No matter that she wore an emerald velvet dressing robe for warmth, it did little to relieve the cold which had settled upon her. She knew why she was chilled to her very marrow, why her heart thumped hard within her chest. Tedric intended to assert his husbandly rights.

They hadn't given in to their passion for weeks, not since their first night at the royal palace. That night would be forever etched in her memory; she would never forget it, no matter how she might try.

She shivered, a horrible feeling of dread rushing over her. Even now, she glanced around the room, half expecting to see Henri's spirit again. Henri had been very real; she knew what he wanted of her. How could she avenge Henri's death when she was married to the very man who had killed him? How could she harm the man who gave her such pleasure? She couldn't tell anyone what she'd seen, not even Tedric. People would believe she was mad.

Lost deeply in her whirling thoughts, she didn't hear Tedric enter the room, and had no idea he was there until he came up behind her and placed his arms around her waist. "You look so beautiful with the fireglow on your face," he said. "Your skin is golden and so smooth." His hand lightly traced her jawline, and he turned her in his arms.

His eyes were dark and molten. She felt herself being pulled into his gaze, drawn by his passion. When Tedric's hand cupped her breast to toy with the nipple through the velvet, she moaned in pleasure. It had been so long since he'd touched her like this, so long that she'd almost forgotten how wonderful it felt. As if this was the signal he sought, Tedric lifted her in his arms and carried her to the bed. His mouth moved over her lips in a kiss that left her weak and clinging to his shoulders.

"I want you, Amberlie, I want you so much," he whispered in her ear, and removed her robe. His fingers played lightly over her breasts, his lips finding a nipple and taking it deeply into his mouth, eliciting another moan from her. How wonderful it felt as he suckled, how weak-willed she was to enjoy it!

"Avenge me, avenge me." She heard Henri's voice so clearly that she stiffened beneath Tedric's questing hands and mind-drugging mouth.

"No, no, stop!" she cried, and wasn't certain if she meant for the voice to cease or for Tedric to leave her alone.

Tedric lifted his head from her breast. "Am I hurting you?"

He had never hurt her, but maybe it would have been better if he had. Things would have been so much simpler if she could hate him. Shivers coursed through her, and she imagined that Henri watched and condemned her for reveling in his killer's touch. She had never believed in spirits, but now she did, for she'd seen and heard one. And he wasn't pleased. "I—I can't do this—I mustn't—"

"What in the name of heaven is wrong with you?" Tedric asked as a question, but it was really a shout of utter frustration. "You're my wife. I want to make love to you."

She lay there with her breasts bared to him, fear in her eyes, not only because of Henri, but because she knew now why Henri was so adamant that he be avenged. She was falling in love with her own husband, and she feared this worse than Henri's ghost. To save him, she must make him hate her. "I don't want you to touch me—ever again," she desperately proclaimed.

He looked at her as if she were mad. One moment she'd been writhing in pleasure, and now she regarded him with loathing on her face. Tedric hadn't a clue as to what was wrong with her, but she was pushing him beyond endurance. "I could take you by force if I wanted. As your husband, I have the right."

She knew he'd never force her, and she also knew how to stop him from wanting her. Opening her legs wide, she gave him a bitter smile. "Go on then. I shall not fight you, but neither will I respond. I pray you, just get it over with quickly."

There was something in her face, a coldness in her voice which settled the matter for him. He knew she didn't want him. Somehow things had changed between them, but when he didn't know. Or had things always been this way? A lance-like pain twisted inside him because he knew now that he'd lost her. But had he ever truly possessed anything other than her body? Right now he doubted if she even had a heart.

"I will spare you a fate worse than death, my lady." Slowly, he rose from the bed and stood looking down at her. Slivers of ice replaced the heat in his eyes. "May you pass a good night in your lonely, cold bed." He reached for his mantle from the chest and twirled it about him, striding toward the door. Without turning once to see the tears sliding down her cheeks, he slammed the door behind him.

Chapter Twenty-two

Tedric didn't return to their bed that night or the next. For two miserable days Amberlie pretended an indifference to the man which she was far from feeling. But every time she saw him, her heart speeded up and her palms perspired. Was this love? she wondered, and realized yes, it was. She knew now that she loved Tedric, the knowledge having come to her on the night he made love to her in the royal palace. Or had she loved him all along and simply not known it? Either way, her feelings didn't matter now. She'd succeeded in driving Tedric away, in getting him to believe she truly hated him.

She'd avenged herself upon him for Henri's death by her hateful words and lack of physical response. But where was the sweet taste of vengeance? All she felt was its sting.

Lady Mabel was coldly polite, speaking to her only when Amberlie asked her a question. No doubt the woman already knew Tedric had left their bed, and was more than disapproving of her. In fact, Amberlie realized everyone in the keep knew she slept alone. She'd overheard two women speaking in the storeroom as she tended Wick in the next room. "Well, of course it would come to this. Lord Tedric didn't give her a morning gift, so Lady Amberlie is a poor wife," one of the women said as if she had firsthand knowledge of their private moments.

"Aye," agreed the other one. "And a man puts aside a cold woman for a warm one. And we both know who she be." They both laughed. Amberlie colored fiercely as she spooned broth into Wick's mouth for she knew very well who they meant.

"My lady, may I speak?" Wick asked with a solemn expression on his face.

"Of course. What is it?" She held the spoon aloft.

"Lord Tedric don't love any lady but ye, no matter what tales ye hear."

If only she could believe that, but she didn't. No matter, nothing would change their situation. They were from different lands, their customs strange to each other. Tedric didn't love her for he'd humiliated her by not giving her the morning gift, and she could never truly love a man who was capable of murder—at least, she'd thought that until recently. But always Henri would be between them, preventing her from giving her heart to Tedric. No, too much stood between them, and Glenna was the least of it.

"Open, Wick, and swallow," she said, ignoring

the man, though she knew he meant only to comfort her. "We must get you well again."

Julianne clutched the tiny pouch within her hand, her palm perspiring with her eagerness. The time had arrived to avenge herself upon Tedric, to make him pay for the crime he'd committed. Before this day was over, the barbarian would be dead. The very thought of Tedric's death caused a bright smile to light up her usually solemn face.

Baudelaire had done well. He'd brought her the plant and berries she'd wanted. She'd spent half of the previous night in her chambers using a small pestle to grind the berries, adding pieces of the leaves for good measure, into a fine powder. The substance possessed an unpleasant smell, but she hoped that once it dissolved into wine, the smell would disappear. Now to dispense it into Tedric's wine — and wait.

She made it to the great hall, earlier than usual for the evening meal. Just as always, the wine goblets were already filled and waiting beside each person's trencher on the dais. Since he was lord of the keep, Tedric's goblet was the largest and most elaborate in design. And the hall was empty, as her luck would have it. A sure sign that heaven was on her side, Julianne decided, and brazenly walked toward the spot where Tedric would soon sit. Carefully, she opened the pouch and emptied the reddish contents into the scarlet liquid, dissolving the powder with her index finger. Jubilation engulfed her. As she turned toward her own seat, a huge grin split her lips in two, but she faltered for a moment to see Guy watching her. He stood just inside the arched doorway with his arms folded casually across his chest. A knowing smirk lifted the edges of his mouth.

"What are you doing, dear sister?"

Seeing him took Julianne aback. But Julianne knew that Guy hated Tedric almost as much as she. Instead of sheepishly backing down, or pretending that she was doing nothing out of the ordinary, Julianne proudly squared her shoulders. "I'm doing what you should have done long ago."

"Taking care of our common problem, I trust."

"Someone must."

"But I have a plan already in motion," he cryptically informed her. "However, yours is more swift."

"And more deadly, I assure you."

"You've always been more craven than I, Julianne."

She took that as a compliment, and took her place on the dais, content to watch and wait.

The meal progressed with the usual bounty. Amberlie, however, found she was unable to eat more than a few mouthfuls, though the roasted goose was delicious. Over the last few days her appetite had dwindled, and she hoped she wasn't coming down with the stomach upset that had plagued some of the serfs that week.

A strange silence hung heavily over the great hall, almost as if a thick curtain had descended to block out all sound. Everyone knew there was a tenseness between herself and Tedric. No one spoke on the dais unless it was to order a cup or trencher refilled. Neither did the knights tell ribald jokes, or jostle one another good-naturedly, and as soon as they finished their meals, they quickly left the hall. The serfs went about their tasks on silent feet, careful not to make noise even when they cleared the trestle tables.

Amberlie cast a glance in Glenna's direction, believing the woman's face would beam with smug satisfaction now that Tedric no longer shared his wife's bed. To Amberlie's surprise, Glenna looked as downcast as everyone else.

Well, not everyone, Amberlie realized. Julianne didn't resemble her usual glowering self. The woman actually smiled a number of times, though no one had spoken to her. Guy seemed nearly as complacent as he lounged on the bench and directed a friendly nod to Amberlie.

Tedric was the most ill-humored, grunting instead of answering whenever a serf asked if he needed his wine goblet refilled, wolfing down his food so he wouldn't be forced to suffer Amberlie's presence for longer than was necessary. He'd behaved this way since the night he'd left their chamber. His time was spent among the knights, especially with Sir Flaubert, with whom he discussed the rebuilding of the keep. Though Tedric was Saxon by birth, an instant friendship had been formed between himself and many of the Norman knights, once they'd begun to get over their mutual distrust. Some of the knights were still uncertain, still mistrusting of him, but for the most part they obeyed him. Even Guy, or so it seemed.

But that day there had been some unrest among a handful of knights who'd questioned Tedric's ability to lead them, causing a further darkening of Tedric's mood. Baudelaire had questioned his loyalty to their king. Ever honest, Tedric had answered that he was as loyal to William as any Saxon in a similar position could be. The answer had appeased most, but not all. Tedric now wondered if he should have lied and proclaimed his undying devotion and loyalty to William. All he'd need now would be an uprising among the knights when his private life was unraveling.

He clutched his goblet with one hand and downed his second helping of wine. The first had tasted bitter, but this one was much sweeter and more aromatic. He'd have refilled the goblet again, but for some reason his stomach felt queasy and his mouth burned.

"Tedric, my lord, are you all right?" Amberlie looked at him in concern, the first words she'd spoken to him in days.

"Aye, woman, I am fine!" He sounded abrupt and icy, and was pleased to see her wince from

315

the chill in his voice.

"You don't look well. Perhaps you should lie down."

"And where should I lay my weary head, my lady? In your bed? If I recall, I received only cold company there." He noticed that she flushed, her eyes downcast. Good, he thought, she regretted what she'd done, but he wouldn't crawl back to her. First, she'd have to beg him, though he was literally aching to know that she wanted him again. He hated himself for still desiring this cold-hearted wench who detested him.

He realized what a truly unhappy man he was. Though William had spared his life and returned his lands to him, nothing was more important than love. Oh, not that he was in love with Amberlie; he quickly put that thought from his mind, for to love such a woman would mean his destruction. But he lusted after her. There were other women who'd share his bed but strangely, he didn't want any woman but Amberlie.

God, but his stomach hurt! His insides burned painfully, and he felt horribly nauseated. He needed air. Lurching to his feet, he accidentally knocked Amberlie aside on the bench, but was in too much of a hurry to see to her well-being as he left the hall in great physical distress.

"The man is a beast!" Guy proclaimed, and rushed to Amberlie's aid.

Amberlie righted herself, but her concern was for Tedric. "Something is wrong with my husband. I have to see to him." Guy clamped down upon her hand when she rose to her feet.

"Stay inside. Tedric can care for himself. I doubt anything's wrong with him." His eyes pleaded with her, but Amberlie loosened his hold and immediately fled the hall for the bailey.

The chilly evening breezes enveloped her in a rush of air. At first, she didn't see Tedric as she searched the empty courtyard. A noise behind her drew her attention, and she turned to see Glenna, instantly begrudging the woman's presence. "Lady Mabel wished me to see if Tedric might be ill," she offered by way of explanation, and Amberlie wondered why she felt she needed to tell her anything. Such a courtesy from Glenna was unusual.

Calling Tedric's name, Amberlie began to search in earnest. Glenna followed behind her. It was when they neared the stables that Amberlie saw him, huddled over on the ground, his hands clenching his stomach. "Tedric! Whatever is wrong with you?" She touched his brow but found it cool. However, his face was pasty white.

"My body—I am on fire inside."

"I'll get help," Glenna offered, and immediately she ran into the stables to see if someone might aid them. Luckily, Christophe was the one she found. Christophe carefully lifted Tedric to his feet. But Tedric was a large man and Christophe doubted he could move him without more help.

"I need others to help lift you," Christophe told him, but Tedric shook his head.

"Nay, 'twill be a sign of weakness . . . to get help. I will . . . walk into the keep . . . will walk."

"Tedric, please," Amberlie pleaded. "No one will think any less of you—"

"I . . . will . . . walk," he ground out from between his teeth, and somehow made it into the keep on Christophe's guiding arm with Amberlie leading the way. Amazingly, he managed to get up the stairs, though the pain was excruciating. Amberlie threw open the door to their chamber, and flung back the pelt on their bed seconds before Christophe helped ease Tedric onto the mattress.

Amberlie loosened his tunic and removed it with Christophe's help, while Glenna provided a wet cloth for Tedric's face. Never had Amberlie seen anyone look so ghostly pale or writhe in such torturous pain. Instinctively she knew Tedric's ailment was much more serious than a stomach grippe. In her mind she recalled the leather pouches in the medicine room, and she knew she had nothing to cure such a strange malady. "Fetch Gundred," she told Glenna. "Get her now."

Glenna nodded, her eyes wide, and did as Amberlie bid her. Christophe remained, and removed Tedric's boots. "My lady?" he hesitantly asked. "Do you think Lord Tedric suffers from the fever?"

"I don't know." Amberlie worriedly bit down upon her lower lip, fearful that an outbreak of fever, or even a rumor of fever, could be tragic for all of them. "Say nothing to anyone about this, please, not until we know for certain. But I don't believe Tedric has fever — 'tis something else."

When Magda appeared with Lady Mabel, Amberlie allowed them into the room. Mabel sat upon the bed beside Tedric and held a bowl in front of his face when Tedric started to vomit. " 'Tis a good sign," Mabel contended. "A very good sign."

Amberlie wiped Tedric's face with the cloth. " 'Tis sick I am, my lady," Tedric whispered, and she knew he was humiliated for her to see him so helpless.

"You'll be better soon. Just try to rest."

"Nay, nay, cannot. Insides are aflame." He drew his knees to his chest and moaned deeply.

Gundred ambled into the room and peered at Tedric. Touching his brow, she then made him open his mouth and took a whiff of his breath. "Magda, run to the kitchen and get Lord Tedric milk and bread; aye, get plenty of it. We may have to force it down his throat, but 'tis all that can be done for him."

" 'Tis such a simple cure. How can milk and bread aid him?" Amberlie asked, wondering if Gundred knew what she was talking about.

" 'Twill ease the vicious burning inside from the devil's turnip. The foul stench yet hangs on his breath."

Glenna and Mabel gasped in unison. "Nay,

how did Tedric get hold of such? 'Twas not passed around at the meal. No one else is ill," Mabel noted.

Suddenly Amberlie remembered something which Gundred had told her about the climbing plant known as devil's turnip. The berries could be poisonous. But the kitchen serfs knew the area well, and surely if devil's turnip had been served, more persons than Tedric would have fallen ill. Where had he gotten it?

Gundred answered Amberlie's thought for her. " 'Tis evident that Lord Tedric was purposely poisoned. Someone hated him enough to slip it in his food or drink."

Mabel and Glenna glanced at each other, and then at Amberlie. Though they said nothing to her, she felt she stood accused.

With Gundred's help, Amberlie got Tedric to drink the milk and eat the bread, though he moaned and groaned the whole time, writhing in absolute agony. She took Lady Mabel's place later when Tedric began vomiting. For the rest of the night, no one was even certain that Tedric would survive his ordeal. Father Ambrose appeared to administer the last sacraments, but Amberlie ran him away, insisting that Tedric would live. By morning, though Tedric looked excessively weak and wan, he was still alive, and that in itself was a promising sign.

Amberlie stayed with him constantly, not leaving even when Sir Christophe appeared to insist she take a fresh breath of air, a respite from the foul-smelling sick room. Gundred too remained, and Magda poked her head in the door almost every five minutes to check on Tedric for Lady Mabel. But Amberlie had the oddest impression that Magda was checking on her also, for the woman's suspicious gaze barely left Amberlie for a second.

No one came right out and said so, but Amberlie suspected that Tedric's family thought she'd poisoned him. And their silent accusation stung her more than she could express, the hurt at being thought capable of such a crime more than unbearable.

Toward the afternoon of the next day, Tedric drifted into a peaceful sleep, and Amberlie knew he was going to recover. Sir Christophe dozed in a chair outside the room late that evening, the door ajar in case there was anything Tedric might need. When Tedric finally woke, he looked lucid and a dash of color had crept into his face. Amberlie smiled at him, genuinely pleased that he looked a bit better. She'd prayed the whole time during his illness, prayed for his recovery, prayed that he wouldn't die and be taken from her. If Tedric died, she knew part of herself would die with him. For now, in her heart, she admitted that she loved him.

If only there was some way they could put aside their differences, if only she could believe he was innocent of Henri's death and that no spirit would again come calling for vengeance.

"Are you feeling better?" she asked softly, her

eyes alight with pleasure to know he'd truly passed the crisis. She fluffed his pillow, helping him lean back. "Would you like a cup of water? You must be thirsty."

"Nay, nay, nothing—from you." He sounded harsh, his voice stronger than she'd expected. His eyes settled upon her, hard and accusing. " 'Tis a shame that you didn't choose a more reliable method of murder than poison, my lady wife, for I still live."

The floor seemed to sway beneath her feet. She clung to the large bedpost to support her weight as the blood drained from her. She must be hearing him wrongly, she thought wildly. She must somehow be delirious from all of the time she'd spent caring for him without a breath of air. He couldn't mean his words, he couldn't! "Tedric, you speak wrongly," she responded through pale, trembling lips. "How can you think such a thing of me?"

"What a besotted fool I was!" he cried from his pillow. "To place my faith in you, a Norman, who is as treacherous as all your kind. I knew you hated me, Amberlie, I knew you detested all things Saxon, but I never thought you'd try to kill me. Never!" He took a deep breath, his eyes flashing with anger and pain, such pain that she felt his torment deep within her soul.

"I am innocent!" she proclaimed. "How can you believe me guilty of such a vile and vicious crime, how?"

"Because you believe I killed your husband!"

he shot back. "You wished to avenge yourself upon me. You're adept at the art of healing for Gundred has taught you; you have pouches of herbs in the sick room and were caring for Wick. But never did I believe you'd use the power of healing for ill. Why, Amberlie, when I'd have given you the world if just once you'd have been kind to me?"

"How little you know me," she whispered, her body quivering with the injustice of his accusation. "I freely gave myself to you, but you humiliated me time and again. Still, I said nothing to you. And though I knew I should hate you, I—I found I couldn't hate you as I wished. Something else was happening inside me, and you saw it not."

"Don't tell me that you love me," he scoffed, yet there was something like despair and hope at once in his face.

"I won't say those words to you for I would not have them thrown back in my face by a man who believes me capable of cold-blooded murder." She took a deep breath. "What will you do with me?"

"God in heaven, I don't know!"

"Am I free to leave the keep?"

"Not without an escort."

"Then I am a prisoner."

"I have not yet thought what to do," he said tiredly. "But I will soon depart these chambers and never return."

"As you wish, my lord. May I leave for some

323

air?" she asked stiffly, holding her tears at bay and feeling incredibly sick.

"Only if Christophe accompanies you."

Inclining her head, she left the room to find Christophe on his feet. Apparently he'd heard all that was said. Her face flamed with the humiliation, the unfairness of it all. She didn't wait for Christophe to take her arm, but went flying down the stairs and into the bailey, knowing the knight hurried behind her. She found a deserted spot next to the dovecote and fell to her knees, retching and crying at the same time.

"My Lady Amberlie, are you all right?" Christophe asked gently after she'd finished.

She rose to her feet, the bottom of her bliaut covered in mud. Her face was streaked with tears, her stomach still twisted in knots. Couldn't the man see she wasn't all right? But she held her tongue, for Christophe wasn't to blame for her problem, an unkind fate was. "It seems we're probably going to spend a great deal of time together from now on, Sir Christophe, for I am a dangerous woman."

Christophe let loose a foul curse, then apologized. "You're innocent, my lady. You couldn't hurt any living thing. Lord Tedric will see the truth. He must."

Amberlie doubted that would ever happen. Someone wished Tedric dead, any number of people could have poisoned his food or drink, but he suspected her—the one person who had never hesitated to proclaim her hatred of him—

as, of course, he would. But the unfairness of the situation struck her as ironic. She, who had scorned and thought she hated him, had discovered she loved him too late.

When she returned to her chamber, she found Tedric was gone from her bed, and she knew he wouldn't return.

Chapter Twenty-three

Construction on the keep progressed under the guidance of Tedric and Sir Flaubert. Work on the east tower was completed and attention was turned to the other three corners of the keep. It was hoped that by the end of the coming year all three towers would be finished, and the keep would be completely fortified inside and outside from enemy attack. But who was the enemy? Tedric wondered distractedly. Was it himself, a Saxon, or the Normans? He no longer knew, the distinctions having already blurred in his mind.

And Amberlie. What was she really? His enemy, or lover? Since his poisoning he'd been tormented by the thought that she might not have been responsible, that he'd accused her of a vile deed when she was innocent. He had no way of knowing Amberlie's true thoughts about anything, for she guarded her emotions well behind a passive exterior. Even now that he'd left their bed and accused her of a horrendous deed, he watched her out of the corner of his eye, and saw only a bland mask for a face. But sometimes, there was something in the way she looked at him, something so heart-wrenchingly sad that he wondered if he'd made a terrible mistake by believing the worst of her. But if not Amberlie, then who?

"My lord, may I have a word with you?" Magda approached him as he supervised the placing of the stones by the west tower. Her step was halting, and her face composed, but there was an urgent light in her eyes. He drew her aside, believing she had something to tell him about his mother or Edytha—or perhaps Amberlie. "I've just seen Wulfgar near Gundred's cottage," she whispered softly. "He says he needs to speak to you and will wait for you."

This was shocking and unpleasant news. Why had William's would-be assassin come out of hiding after all of these weeks? As a servant of the king, Tedric would be duty-bound to capture Wulfgar and execute him, but Wulfgar had been his friend and no more of a renegade than himself. The man was foolhardy to place both of them in jeopardy. Tedric kindly thanked Magda and told her not to mention Wulfgar's reappearance to anyone.

When the knights practiced their mock battle strategies that afternoon, Tedric stole away from the bailey and headed for Gundred's cottage. Gundred was Wulfgar's grandmother, and no doubt she was hiding him and feeding him. Perhaps he'd been hiding near there all the time.

Gundred opened the door at Tedric's knock.

With a finger on her lips, she pointed to the thick rafters above them. "Is it safe for him to come down, my lord?" she asked in just above a whisper.

"Aye, 'tis safe."

Gundred called softly to her grandson, and seconds later, Tedric heard rustling noises overhead and then saw Wulfgar peering down at him. The dark-haired man grabbed onto a rafter with both hands and swung down, to drop silently at Tedric's feet.

" 'Tis good to see you again, my lord."

Tedric wished he could say the same. An uneasy sensation reached into his stomach to see the disheveled and dirty young man. Wulfgar's very presence was dangerous, for if anyone learned he'd been the one who'd shot at William—well, Tedric hated to dwell upon what might happen to all of them.

"What is it you want?" Tedric asked without hesitation. The sooner Wulfgar was gone from Woodrose, the better it would be for his family and his own position as lord of the keep.

"Just a talk with King William's noblest knight, my lord," Wulfgar sneered, his beady eyes taking in Tedric's fine tunic and hose. " 'Tis easy to see why you betrayed our people for the Norman king. With your lands returned and a pretty Norman wife to warm your bed, you've sold your soul to the devil. You've become one of them."

"Nay, I am not—"

"Aye, but you are. You took an arrow meant for William the Bastard to save your Norman lady's life."

"Amberlie was innocent. 'Twas no reason for her to be slain too."

"Hah! Truly, you still defend her. Tell me, Tedric, do you think she's innocent now? I hear you've left her bed, fearful that she'll poison you again."

Gundred cackled nearby, but at Tedric's pointed look in her direction, the old woman left the cottage.

"What is it you want with me?" Tedric bit out, managing to intimidate Wulfgar with his scowl of displeasure.

For a few seconds, Wulfgar hesitated to speak. "There is fighting still in the north," he informed Tedric. "Our people hold out against the Normans. I pray you, consider coming with me."

"To fight William's army?"

"Aye. With you along, we'll be able to gather our people and gain strength against the invaders." Wulfgar's face was bright, his dark eyes sparkled. "What say you, Tedric?"

Tedric sighed and placed his hands on his hips. "I say you are daft. The cause is a just one but doomed to failure. Normans overrun the entire country, except for the northern borders, and soon too those parts will fall to the conqueror. I entreat you not to follow this foolish path."

Wulfgar reared back, and then he seemed about to attack Tedric, but Tedric grabbed at the dagger on his side. Seeing Tedric's defensive action, Wulfgar moved away, but he scowled blackly. " 'Tis a traitor you've become, Tedric, a cowardly traitor to your people."

"Nay, I am only realistic." Tedric said boldly, but Wulfgar's stinging retort had hurt because he spoke the truth.

"You've become one of them, man! You're a Norman now, more Norman than one of the Bastard's own knights." Wulfgar settled down and caught his breath. He eyed Tedric suspiciously. "I head north today. May I leave without fear that you'll set your knights upon me?"

"I give you my word, no one knows you are here. I shall tell no one. You're free to go."

Wulfgar nodded, and Tedric solemnly left the cottage to return to the keep. The knights were still practicing in the bailey; no one had seen him leave. Or so he thought.

No one spoke to her. Word had filtered through Woodrose that Amberlie had tried to poison her husband. The serfs reluctantly took orders from her, but no one looked her in the eye. Tedric's family was scornful of her, ignoring her at table. Glenna ignored her entirely. However, she didn't ignore Tedric, having grown incredibly brazen since Tedric began to sleep elsewhere. The woman leaned close to him during meals, and his deep laugh filled the great hall at her remarks, which, of course, she whispered in his ear. It seemed that Amberlie saw them together more and more, and she didn't have to wonder in whose bed Tedric slept. Why did she care so?

A cold wind whipped around the keep, but Amberlie felt very warm on that cloudy afternoon as she sat in the bathing tub in her chamber. A fire roared in the hearth, chasing away the chill as she washed away the grime from her fingernails. She'd been in the woods for a short time with Gundred and Sir Christophe, searching for a particular kind of autumnal bloom to be made into a love charm. Gundred declared that even the most inattentive of men would fall prey to the woman who wore such a potent charm. Before she'd left Gundred's cottage, the old woman had placed one of the white blooms behind Amberlie's ear. When Amberlie protested she didn't believe in such nonsense and started to remove it, Gundred had grabbed her hand and solemnly nodded. " 'Tis a lucky charm, as well. Ye must wear it and not remove it for the rest of the day. What harm is there in indulging an old lady, eh?"

So, here she sat in her bathing tub with a ridiculous bloom behind her ear because she'd promised Gundred. The smell from the blossom was pleasant, and soon it seemed as if the whole room was bathed in the sweet, aromatic scent.

When Amberlie rose from the tub and reached for the linen towel on the floor, the chamber door opened. A gust of wind caused the fire to flicker and crackle in excitement. Air rushed over her naked flesh to dispel the earlier warmth. But Amberlie suddenly felt hot, very hot, for Tedric stood watching her inside the doorway.

It seemed that he looked at her forever. Those blue eyes of his, so icy of late, brimmed over with summer heat. Her heart thumped hard against her rib cage. It had been so long since he'd looked at her like that. Finally, he cleared his throat, seeming somewhat embarrassed. "I'm sorry for walking in. Magda told me you'd gone down to settle Wick to work in the kitchen. I didn't know you'd be here."

"I did that earlier today. Wick is helping the cook, an easy job of filling the goblets and helping to bake bread." Calmly, she wrapped the towel around her, just as if she were perfectly used to Tedric's walking in and finding her naked. Things had been like that once between them, but no longer. An unexpected shiver slid down her backside, and Tedric noticed and shut the door. "What are you doing here?" she asked him when he started to walk toward her.

"I'd forgotten my sword." He inclined his head to where the silver sword leaned against the wall, but his gaze never wavered from her face. Finally his eyes moved lower and took in her full breasts, straining against the towel, before drinking in each temptingly lush curve of her body.

"I should have had Magda bring it to you," Amberlie said, feeling the blush start at her hairline and meander to the tips of her toes. His gaze retraced its path and rested again upon her face.

"There is a great deal I've forgotten," he whispered huskily, and to Amberlie's surprise, he reached for a strand of her hair and inhaled its fragrance. "So sweet, so soft."

She trembled, and for just a second she thought he was going to kiss her. Their lips were

332

but scant inches apart. For seconds, she gazed into his eyes, and it seemed as if the world had ceased to exist, as if no one existed in the universe but them. She knew that he wanted her, that in some dark place of his mind he'd forgotten his accusations. Like one held in a spell, he brought her to him and gently grazed her lips with his in a whisper-soft kiss that he would have deepened except for a loud pounding at the chamber door.

"My lord! Are you in there?" It was Christophe.

Tedric drew back, the sound of Christophe's voice startling him back to the present. "Aye, I'm here," he called, but those blue eyes of his still held Amberlie's, still warm and passion-drenched.

"Come quickly into the bailey. Sir Guy has killed a renegade."

Immediately, Tedric paled. "Damn!" he cursed under his breath, and moved away from Amberlie.

"Tedric—what?" She didn't truly know what to ask him or what she wanted to say. Amberlie only knew that he'd held her in his arms again, that he'd wanted her, and now he was leaving her with no words spoken between them, with nothing resolved.

Retrieving his sword, he took one last look at her, his eyes drinking in every aspect of her body. "My lady, I wish you weren't so hauntingly beautiful. 'Twould make things so much easier." And then he turned away. With his departure, the room felt much colder.

Fingering the white blossom behind her ear, Amberlie wondered if indeed it was a love charm, as Gundred had told her. Had Tedric kissed her because of the blossom or because of a more potent magic?

When Tedric strode into the bailey, he'd already determined whose body he would find. Wulfgar, who he'd seen alive just two days ago, now lay upon the ground, dried blood covering his tunic, and immediately Tedric realized that the man had been lanced a number of times, many times more than was necessary to kill him. Guy's destrier stood nearby, and Guy, with an arrogant, pleased expression upon his face, rudely nudged the dead man with the toe of his boot. "One less Saxon swine to wreak havoc upon us," he remarked upon seeing Tedric.

Tedric felt a sickening, clawing sensation in the pit of his stomach. Poor Wulfgar, he thought, though he kept his face implacable. The man hadn't had a chance from the look of things — not against a knight so cunning and dangerous as Guy de Bayonne. How had de Bayonne come across Wulfgar, a man who knew the forest well and had managed to survive on his own for the last few weeks without detection? Tedric himself hadn't known where he was; the last time he'd seen him had been in Gundred's cottage some two days past.

"I trust you remember that I am a Saxon by birth," Tedric coldly reminded Guy.

"I know, my lord, but your loyalty is to our Norman king, not to such an outlaw as this criminal. The man attacked me in the forest, and to save my life, I was forced to kill him."

"And brutally too, from the look of him."

Guy shrugged, as if the manner of death was of no consequence. He flashed a pompous grin at Tedric and the knights who clustered around them to examine the body. " 'Twas a matter of survival, my lord. I'm certain you'd have acted similarly."

Tedric didn't answer, but his eyes coldly settled upon Guy; Tedric meant to let him know by his chilly reserve that he'd enjoy impaling *him* upon his sword in a similar manner.

Baudelaire stepped from the group. "Do you know who this criminal might be?" he inquired of Tedric.

"Aye, I know him."

"Are you aware that this man was seen near Woodrose just this very week?"

"Nay, I didn't know he was seen," Tedric said truthfully. He'd seen him, but hadn't known anyone else had.

"Mayhaps you let him escape," Baudelaire's grim accusation was immediately repeated in French to the other knights as they turned worried eyes upon Tedric.

"Mayhaps you should spend your time in more productive efforts rather than in loose talk," Tedric shot back, and rose to his commanding height in a purposeful attempt to intimidate the crafty-eyed Baudelaire.

"Lord Tedric is a loyal knight of King William," Flaubert pronounced, and took a step in Baudelaire's direction. "I'll not stand here and allow Lord Tedric to be maligned by one of your ilk. You're a cruel and callous fellow and would like nothing better than to form an alliance against Tedric."

The knights mumbled amongst themselves, and then Guy intervened with an ingratiating smile. "No one is attempting to overthrow Lord Tedric. Baudelaire only questioned why a Saxon renegade was prowling the area. The man is dead because he attacked me. Does anyone wish I had done otherwise? Do you, my lord?" He cast an inquisitive brow at Tedric.

Tedric would have liked to have proclaimed that Wulfgar could have been handled some other way, but he knew that Wulfgar would have viciously fought if cornered. Yet the man was on his way north. The only possible way for Guy to have discovered him was if Guy had followed Wulfgar when he left Woodrose and tracked him down. Even bringing back Wulfgar's body to Woodrose was odd; the only reason for Guy to have done this was to show Tedric that he knew Tedric had allowed Wulfgar his freedom. So what was Guy's plan? "You did only that which you had to do," Tedric admitted, "but I disapprove of your brutal method." He ordered two knights to remove Wulfgar's body and, turning to Flaubert, he ordered him to dig a grave.

When the knights began drifting away, Tedric kept his eyes on Baudelaire, and just as he'd thought, the man immediately began conversing with Guy. "I think some of the knights might attempt an uprising," Tedric said to Christophe.

"Never fear, my lord. Few men will follow Guy de Bayonne. He led the knights at one time, but he was a cruel taskmaster. Besides, the king hasn't approved him, but you he declared our master. The men know that to disobey you is to go against the king."

Tedric hoped that Christophe was correct, but still he felt the undercurrents of dissension and knew it boded ill for Woodrose.

Another morning and Amberlie felt ill. She never felt bad upon waking, but after she'd been up and started dressing a nagging sickness would roil within her stomach. That she was carrying Tedric's child now seemed a clear possibility, and though she attempted to hide her condition from Magda, the old woman had sharp eyes—and ears.

On this particular morning, Amberlie was retching into the chamber pot when she heard Magda's knock. "My lady, are you ill again this morn?"

Shout it for the whole of Woodrose to hear, Amberlie thought in aggravation as she finished and wiped her mouth with a cloth. "Aye, but 'tis nothing," she called weakly, and was more than mortified when Magda entered the room without permission.

The woman eyed the chamber pot. "More like

'tis something that will be born next year."

"Hush! Keep your voice down. I don't want anyone to know about this—this child."

"And how will you keep it a secret? Lord Tedric is bound to know when you start showing . . ." Magda's voice trailed away, and she eyed Amberlie in acute suspicion. "You'd not make yourself a potion to lose your babe, would you, my lady?"

Such a thought had never crossed her mind, and Amberlie was horrified that Magda would think such a terrible thing of her. But the woman thought she'd poisoned Tedric, so she probably thought Amberlie would want to be rid of this child too. "I want this baby very much. I'd do nothing to endanger its existence."

Magda sighed her relief. "Aye, 'tis glad I am to hear it."

"I also didn't poison my husband. No matter what Lord Tedric believes, I couldn't harm him."

"I'm not the one to convince, my lady."

Magda was right. Somehow she must convince Tedric of her innocence before the baby was born. But how, when the answer came down to simple trust? As she glanced down at the bailey, Amberlie's heart thumped hard in her chest for she saw Tedric, and as always, or so it seemed, Glenna was beside him.

They walked together, speaking quietly, and Amberlie's heart stopped when Tedric laughed at something which Glenna said. Dark despair settled within Amberlie. No matter the passion that had bound them together, she and Tedric were two very different people. Their backgrounds and customs were so dissimilar. No wonder Tedric laughed heartily at the things Glenna said, for they understood one another. It was obvious to anyone who had eyes in their heads that Glenna and Tedric were well suited.

But here she stood with Tedric's child growing in her belly. And if he knew about the baby, Amberlie had no doubt that he'd rejoice, for she was giving him an heir, perhaps a male child to make certain he retained Woodrose. But what about her? Didn't she count for anything other than as a breeder? He hadn't come to her; she hadn't seen him since he'd come to their room for his sword. Perhaps she should see Gundred and get another love charm. Perhaps she didn't have the allure to bring Tedric to her without it.

But she didn't want a love charm to bring Tedric to her. When he came for her, she wanted to know it was because he loved her, not for physical pleasure. It seemed that what she wanted was a very small matter in the scheme of things. Yet for Tedric to fall in love with her, to admit he was wrong about her, would take a miracle.

And Amberlie had stopped believing in miracles long ago.

Chapter Twenty-four

"My lady, Lady Julianne is in great pain this morn. She asks for you to tend to her." Amberlie turned from her needlework at Magda's voice. "She truly looks unwell, very pale and doubled over with cramping," Magda added, and shook her head.

"I'll see to her immediately." Amberlie rose from her window bench and went to the east wing of the keep, where she found Julianne in her bed. Her legs were drawn up to her chest, and her face was contorted in agony.

Julianne clutched Amberlie's hand, and her grip tightened around Amberlie's fingers. "I am dying," she moaned through pale, thin lips. " 'Tis something more than grippe."

Amberlie silently agreed with Julianne's assessment. This was no ordinary stomach upset. Never had Julianne looked so pale or her skin felt so clammy. "I can fix you something for the pain," Amberlie said.

"Nay . . . nay. Gundred was already here . . .

and . . . I drank her horrible brew . . . but nothing helps ease my ache. I beg you to care for me, and not these Saxons, for I trust them not."

"But Magda has cared for you for nearly a year. Surely you trust her—"

"Magda is one of them!" Julianne hissed. "She hates me and would take delight in seeing me suffer. I'd rather you, my son's wife, tended to me."

Amberlie saw it would do little good to remind Julianne that she was now Tedric's wife. The woman believed harm would befall her if she was left in Saxon hands. "All right, I'll see to your wants," Amberlie reassured her, and Julianne's features relaxed.

That afternoon Amberlie decided to head into the woods and seek out a plant which might alleviate Julianne's pain. Gundred had pointed it out to her once before, and she recalled that it grew wild near the stream. As she entered the bailey, she saw Tedric, who was overseeing the construction of the west tower. His eyes moved over her face in a familiar fashion that set her heart to pounding. His gaze settled upon the basket she used for gathering, and he frowned. She walked over to him, the wind ruffling the strands of her dark hair about her face, and stopped in front of him.

"I assure you that I'm not up to mischief, my lord. I only go to gather in the woods to make a potion that might help Julianne's discomfort, not to find a poisonous weed for your supper." She'd adequately read his thoughts, and Tedric flushed guiltily. "Since I am a prisoner and at your whim, I request Sir Christophe to accompany me."

"As you will, my lady." Tedric looked around him, but seeing that Sir Christophe was engaged in mock battle with a squire, he bowed deeply. "I shall be pleased to act as your escort."

"Are you certain you want to take me into the woods, my lord? I would then have you at my mercy and might plunge a dagger through your heart."

"I fear you've done my heart harm already, but not with a dagger," he solemnly said.

The day's chill had been somewhat dispelled by the timid sun as the large gelding carried them into the sweetly scented woods, but within the sheltering branches, the air was cooler. Amberlie's hands felt extremely cold, but her face was pink as she flushed to be so close to Tedric again. She sat within the circle of his arms as he guided the horse along the small woodland path. He finally stopped when they neared the stream. The silence was broken by the laughter and chatter of the women from the keep and the delighted cries of their children as they filled their buckets or washed clothing in the cold stream.

Tedric slipped from the horse and helped her down, her body sliding naturally down his length to contact with his lower body. She smothered a tiny gasp to realize that Tedric was aroused, very aroused from the feel of him. He let her go, and then he glanced sheepishly away to take an inordinate interest in a sparrow on the branch above them. "You may go about your gathering," he mumbled quietly.

Clutching her skirts, Amberlie began to make a pretense of searching for the elusive plant that Gundred had shown to her once before. She parted ferns and peered beneath thickets as her wandering took her closer to the stream. But she truly wasn't concentrating on anything, barely saw the wildlife about her, for Tedric occupied her thoughts, Tedric and the immense bulge in his hose. He wanted her, she wanted him. Things could be so incredibly simple, except for the very fact that they didn't trust one another, and Amberlie didn't expect that would change between them.

She found herself beside the stream. From where she stood she could see the women at their washing, and the children, who ran happily along the bank and splashed into the cold water only to dash merrily back to their mothers. One little boy of about three ran further away from his mother than the other children. "Come back, Tim!" the mother called, and Amberlie noticed the child turned and lazily ambled toward her.

How adorable he is, Amberlie thought. She stared at the child as his chubby legs carried him along. Her hand touched her abdomen, and once again she was amazed that she carried a child. For so long she'd tried to conceive with Henri, so many months had she cried each time her flux had started, dissolving her hopes of ever having a child. And now, with Tedric, she'd conceived a child within a matter of weeks. Tedric had promised her that his seed would take, and he'd been right. She wanted this baby, and wanted to shout to the world that she was going to be a mother. But her happiness was tempered by everything that had happened between Tedric and herself. Though Tedric's body wanted her, he wanted Glenna. Never would he give his heart to a woman whom he couldn't trust. And he'd convinced himself that he couldn't trust his wife, the woman who would bear him a child sometime next summer.

Amberlie sighed, and had bent down to examine a small plant that grew by the base of an oak tree when she heard the woman scream. "Tim! My God, Tim!" Amberlie saw the woman was running toward the stream, absolute terror on her face. And then Amberlie saw the reason for it. The little boy had somehow fallen into the stream and was flailing wildly and crying, but the current pushed against him and buffeted him toward the opposite shore. By this time the screams had alerted the other women. Some shouted and clutched their throats in horror. Two women ran into the water, but the current was too swift and knocked them down.

The child's mother rushed headlong into the stream and held out her arms to the boy, but the child couldn't reach her. Though the woman tried valiantly to get to the boy, it was evident that she was a poor swimmer and lacked strength, for the current kept her from him. Finally, she grabbed onto a rock by the shore and screeched her prayer to the heavens to save her child.

Amberlie dropped her basket, and without thinking, she plunged into the stream and immediately began swimming toward little Tim, who miraculously kept his head above the surface. The water was colder than she'd anticipated, but heedless of her own discomfort and safety, she concentrated on reaching the squalling, frightened child. The current too was stronger than normal, but she swam toward the child, and grabbed hold of his arm just as his face went under. She pulled him up, the boy sputtering, coughing, and crying, and wrapped her arm protectively around his tiny body. Instinctively, she began to paddle to shore, having swum a long distance. The muscles in her legs and arms ached, her teeth chattered, but her worry was directed toward the shivering and frightened child. "You'll be fine," she consoled him through shivering lips, but Tim wouldn't be comforted. A gigantic splash drew her attention to she shore and, looking up, she saw Tedric swimming furiously toward them.

In an instant, or so it seemed, he was beside her and took the boy from her. They swam to the stream bank. The child's mother and the other women had run the length of it, and immediately Tim was handed over into his weeping mother's arms by Tedric. Tedric held out his hand to Amberlie, and she gratefully took it as she waded to shore.

"Oh, me lady, thank ye, thank ye with all me

heart!" cried Tim's mother, who Amberlie then recognized as a washwoman named Moll. She instantly wrapped her shivering son in her cloak. "I was afeared me boy was as good as drowned, but ye saved him, saved him for me. Thank ye so much!" Moll, with the crying child in her arms, got on her knees and kissed the hem of Amberlie's drenched skirt.

"She's a true angel," one of the women said, and the others agreed, all clustering around to soothe the child and mother, and to express their gratitude to Amberlie. Such devotion and attention from the Saxons was unusual, but Amberlie barely heard it as her knees buckled, and she'd have literally sunk to the ground in a shivering mass of drenched clothes and hair if Tedric hadn't noticed her sudden weakness and in one mighty swoop caught her in his arms. Picking her up, he proceeded to carry her back to the horse, but Amberlie protested.

"I can walk, put me down," she insisted through numb lips.

"Nay, you're chilled to the very bone, and the sooner I get you back to the keep and out of these wet clothes, the better off you'll be."

"You're wet too," she reminded him.

"Aye, but I didn't swim as far as you. Now be quiet and let's get you home."

By the time they reached the keep and the fire had been lit in the hearth, the story of Amberlie's heroism had spread throughout Woodrose like a raging fever. Those who had regarded her scornfully and insisted she was guilty of Tedric's poisoning now thought she was an angel come to earth. That evening, after she'd changed into dry clothes and ascended the dais for the evening meal, the attitude in the great hall had changed. The serfs met her eyes, their happiness and gratitude evident in the way all of them came before her and bowed or curtsied. Even Lady Mabel had a soft smile for her, while Edytha giggled happily. But from Glenna, Amberlie received only a cold expression.

Tedric was different. The very second she'd entered the hall, he'd risen from the bench and graciously extended his arm to her and led her to her seat beside him. "That was a very brave deed you did today, Amberlie." He spoke softly to her so only she could hear. "I wanted you to know how much my people appreciate your saving little Tim's life."

"Anyone else would have done the same thing," she said, feeling glad to be the object of Tedric's praise.

"You're wrong. Any other Norman woman would not have risked her life to save a Saxon child. I doubt Julianne would."

Amberlie couldn't argue with his logic, for she knew very well what Julianne thought about Saxons. Yet she wondered what he'd do if he knew that she could very well have risked their own child's life to save Tim's. He regarded her in silence; then he stroked her hand with his fingertips and warmly regarded her through those vivid

347

blue eyes of his. "Magda told me today how you helped save my sister from Baudelaire's crude advances after her capture. I thank you for that as well."

"Baudelaire isn't a noble person. He deserved much worse than a knock on the head."

Tedric laughed lightheartedly, drawing everyone's attention to him and his lady upon the dais. For the first time in days, he felt truly happy and relaxed. He knew now that Amberlie wasn't responsible for his poisoning. She'd risked her life to save a child's and this, in Tedric's estimation, absolved her of guilt. A woman so brave wouldn't kill a man in such a cowardly fashion as poison. But if not Amberlie, then who? He couldn't dwell upon who wished him dead, for at the moment Amberlie totally captivated him in the red velvet bliaut that Queen Matilda had given her. He wished with his whole soul to be able to remove the gown slowly, to caress each temptingly beautiful inch of her body. But one obstacle remained—and only one, as far as Tedric could see—how to convince her that he hadn't murdered Henri de Fontaine.

He wanted her to come to him willingly and wantonly, with nothing between them but passion.

"My lord," Glenna said, breaking into their conversation, a malicious twinkle in her eyes. "I found your dagger in my room this morn. Whenever you have need of it I shall bring it to you, or you may fetch it at your leisure."

"Thank you," he ground out, and cast a warning glance at Glenna. Too late, the damage had been done, the happy mood between himself and Amberlie dispelled by Glenna. Amberlie sipped her wine, a strained expression on her face as she gazed straight ahead. Damn Glenna! he thought, and wished the woman would learn to keep her mouth closed. Nothing had happened between them, as Glenna well knew. He'd simply escorted her to her room one night and had gone inside to check for a mouse, which Glenna insisted she'd seen that day. She was afraid she'd said, to sleep in her bed with the tiny creature running loose. He'd searched the room and found nothing, apparently leaving his dagger. And now the wench made it appear that something had happened between them, and from the way Amberlie wouldn't look at him, she believed it too. Soon, very soon, he'd have to marry off Glenna, and he had the perfect mate in mind for her.

The meal continued in awkward silence. Amberlie noticed Magda in the doorway, and the woman gestured frantically to her. Amberlie excused herself from the table. Magda grabbed her arm. " 'Tis Lady Julianne," she whispered, "Father Ambrose has seen her already and given her the sacraments, and now Sir Guy is with her. I fear she is dying, my lady."

Amberlie quietly entered Julianne's room. Evening shadows cloaked the walls in darkness. Julianne lay upon the bed, so pale and wan, so weak that she could barely speak. Guy moved aside for Amberlie to stand beside Julianne's bed. She clasped the dying woman's hand and found it chilled. "Is there anything I can do for you?" Amberlie asked, bending over Julianne.

Julianne barely shook her head. Already her eyes were glazed, and there was no strength in her hand. Her breathing was labored, but strangely, she seemed to be in no pain. "Hen—ri, will see him," she finally spoke, each syllable seemingly wrung from her.

"Her son is all she can think about," Guy informed Amberlie. "She's obsessed with seeing him again."

Amberlie smiled sadly. "I trust she will."

The room's shadows deepened. Magda lit the candles on the table, and just as night fell outside, Julianne breathed her last breath. A lump formed in Amberlie's throat, and her eyes grew misty. She hadn't liked Julianne, but she hoped the woman had at last found happiness; she prayed that she was with her son, whom she'd loved more than life. Amberlie started to leave the room, knowing that Magda and some of the women would soon come to prepare Julianne's body for burial. "Aren't you coming?" she asked Guy.

"Not yet. There are some things I should like to say to my sister—in private."

"Of course. I'll tell Magda to wait until you're finished."

Guy inclined his head and waited until Amberlie had closed the door behind her before he approached the head of the bed. Gazing down at his sister, he chuckled. "So, you're at last with your milksop son. Such a stupid woman you were, dear sister, to believe that Tedric had killed Henri. But then you always believed what I told you, because I am a good liar." He bent near his sister's face and whispered in her ear. "Tedric didn't kill Henri. I killed him. I killed him for Woodrose, but more for his wife. Amberlie is a fire in my blood, a woman whom I desire above all else. Henri couldn't have kept such a woman happy. The little bastard couldn't even get her with child. He didn't deserve such a beautiful woman. When I ran him through with my sword, I saw the disbelief on his face because I, his beloved uncle, was the one who'd ended his life." Guy snickered quietly. "So your venom against Tedric, your efforts to kill him were all in vain, since it was I who took your precious Henri from you."

Guy straightened up, his mouth curled in a cruel smile. "And I'll finish the deed you started. I'll use poison to finish off Tedric, but it will be a poison of the mind. Before this week is through, I'll control Woodrose and Amberlie."

He left the room and found Amberlie in the hallway, and feigned a calm yet strained demeanor. But inside, he felt stirrings of desire for the barbarian's wife, and knew he would finally possess her. Once Tedric was dead, all that should have come to him at Henri de Fontaine's death would finally be his.

* * *

Soon after Amberlie had departed the dais, Christophe approached Tedric with a worried frown on his face. " 'Tis as we thought, my lord," he whispered grimly. "Sir Guy plots rebellion among the knights."

"This is a fact?" Tedric asked, but he knew the answer already.

Christophe nodded. "Sir Antoine informed me that he meets secretly with de Bayonne and some others, not enough men to overthrow you but enough to cause dissension. Most of the knights are undecided, their allegiance is to the king, and they hesitate to rise up. But de Bayonne has planted seeds of doubt in their minds against you. De Bayonne is obsessed with rebellion."

"When does Sir Antoine believe this attempted uprising will take place?"

"Soon, my lord, very soon."

"Then we shall take action and rid ourselves of Guy de Bayonne, but we must catch him before any uprising."

"I shall keep you apprised of the day, my lord."

Tedric poured a hefty serving of wine into his goblet, more than eager for that day to come.

Chapter Twenty-five

Julianne was laid to rest the following day. Tedric stood beside Amberlie as the hurriedly crafted coffin was lowered into the ground. Amberlie knew she should feel grief for this woman who had been her mother-in-law, but strangely, she felt only relief. In fact, the mood within the keep lightened considerably within the next few days. Somehow it seemed that a dark period had passed. But though Amberlie no longer worried about Julianne's dour moods, she couldn't shake a heaviness of spirit each time she thought about Tedric and Glenna.

There were times she'd catch Tedric watching her, as if he wished to speak to her, but she managed to turn away from him. He still slept away from her, and she spent much of her time in the household activities, so exhausted thereby that by the time night had fallen, she crawled gratefully into bed. Many times she accompanied Gundred into the Saxons' cottages to minister to the sick at Woodrose, purposely busying herself so she

353

wouldn't have to think about Tedric. But always, his image was in the back of her mind, vivid and alive, warm and all-consuming.

Amberlie likewise was on Tedric's mind a great deal of the time. Though he spent his days helping to train the knights, and with Flaubert overseeing the construction of the west tower, Amberlie's face was always with him. He wanted her, truly desired her, and no amount of physical work could dispel his need. He would have liked to have returned to their chamber and seduced her into wanting him again, but now, he knew something else must bind them together, an emotion so powerful that it would transcend all mistrust. He wouldn't give a name to what he felt for Amberlie; he couldn't. If he did, he'd be irretrievably lost.

One afternoon, as Tedric directed some of the knights in mock battle, Father Ambrose quietly came to stand beside him. "My lord, may I have a word with you in private?" the priest asked him, his demeanor serious.

Tedric nodded, breaking away. He and the priest went to stand beside a small rose bush that grew wild in the bailey. Ambrose glanced around, making certain they wouldn't be overheard. "I must tell you something that will make you see things differently about your wife, my lord."

"What do you wish to tell me?" Tedric felt cold suddenly, wondering if Ambrose was going to inform him that Amberlie was breaking her marriage vows—perhaps even with the treacherous Guy de Bayonne.

Ambrose hesitated for a moment, then rushed

on. "Your wife is innocent of poisoning you. As a man of God, I can say without hesitation that Lady Amberlie didn't harm you, but I cannot divulge who did the deed. But you needn't worry, for this unfortunate soul is no longer among the living."

Tedric immediately understood what Ambrose was indirectly telling him. Someone had privately confessed to the priest about his poisoning and was now dead. The only person who'd recently died within the household was Julianne de Fontaine. Tedric let out a huge sigh, and closed his eyes for a second. Of course. Julianne. She'd thought he had killed her son, and she'd hated him enough to poison him. For the last few weeks he'd sensed Amberlie was innocent. In fact, he'd known it deep within his soul. And now, there was no doubt. He opened his eyes and spoke to Ambrose. "Thank you, Father. You've set my mind at rest."

Ambrose smiled gently. "My hope is that you and Lady Amberlie will have a happy life."

With all of his heart, Tedric hoped that very same thing. Tonight. He'd speak to her this very night and profusely apologize for doubting her. Maybe she'd forgive him. If only he could convince her that he hadn't killed Henri, then they would be able to share a life. If only a merciful God, if there was a God, would hear his prayer and help him—for this was one problem he couldn't resolve on his own. But for the moment, another more pressing problem claimed his attention when the knight known as Antoine came to speak to him. Antoine was working with Christophe on Tedric's behalf. The time for action against de Bayonne was at hand.

A small group of knights clustered together in the stable. Their attention was riveted upon Guy de Bayonne, who looked particularly commanding as he stood before them, dressed as he was in a blood-red tunic, his hand clasping the jeweled hilt of his sword. They'd met thus for the last few days, conspiring against Tedric of Woodrose. And now the time for their uprising was at hand, but Guy felt a great sense of unease, despite his confident stance. He'd thought these men were with him, but now he wondered if he could count upon any of them save Baudelaire. "We must act soon and swiftly," Guy advised them. "Otherwise Tedric shall become too deeply entrenched here."

"But the man was chosen by our king," a young knight insisted. "As much as I don't trust the Saxon, he has King William's blessing. To go against Tedric is to go against our liege."

"Oui," an older and more experienced knight agreed. "Our plan hasn't been thought out. We're but a small number in comparison to the others who are influenced by Christophe and Flaubert. They follow Tedric and claim he is an able leader, a knight who shall fight for our king. Such assertions cannot be disregarded by any of us."

Baudelaire quickly jumped in. "Bah! You've always been much too careful, François. Tedric knew the Saxon whom Guy killed. I saw the man sneaking near the keep."

"And don't forget that I followed Tedric to the

old hag's cottage, where he spoke to this Saxon," Guy said. "He had the chance to capture him, but he let him go. Tell me now, is this man a servant of our king? Is he loyal? His very actions placed all of us in jeopardy by protecting his renegade cohort." Guy's face turned a blustery red in outrage. He wasn't so angry over Tedric's handling of Wulfgar as over the fact that he needed these men's aid in rebellion, and they didn't seem eager to help him any longer.

"True," another knight agreed, "but this man was only one, and you slew him. He wasn't a threat, and I doubt he ever was. I wonder if you champion rebellion because of your love of King William or your love of power. I don't wish to rise up and then find William's own knights on our flanks."

"Cowards, the lot of you are cowards," Guy harshly told them, drawing black scowls from the assemblage.

Antoine vehemently shook his head. "Not cowards, but careful conspirators. Except for Tedric's Saxon blood, I find no fault in his handling of affairs. He is an able leader and experienced warrior, a fine knight and a fair man. I well understand why our king placed him in charge."

Baudelaire snorted. "Are you saying that Guy de Bayonne was not a good leader? Lest you forget, he ruled Woodrose after Henri's death."

"I remember well, but Guy isn't infallible and made many mistakes."

Guy didn't care for Antoine's assessment of him. The man had always been too cautious for his own good. For weeks, Guy had attempted to stir rebellion in the knights, but always Christophe had intervened to calm them. Now, Antoine was using logic on the small number of men Guy had recruited — or thought he'd recruited. No longer was Guy certain that these men would follow him and overthrow Tedric as master. "Are you with me or against me? I demand your answers now!"

The men turned toward one another, and one by one they silently shook their heads. No doubt they would have left Guy to his own machinations. But like a strong sudden wind from the north, the door to the stable was thrown open, and Tedric and Christophe entered with swords drawn and twenty knights in their wake.

"Here is the nest of traitors, my lord," Christophe solemnly intoned, "and their leader is Guy de Bayonne."

"Arrest them!" Tedric ordered, and the knights immediately circled the small group without even a sword drawn from their sheaths. "All except Antoine, who is loyal. We shall have the truth out of the rest of them, but de Bayonne shall be placed in the pit, and Baudelaire with him, for his treachery and what he tried to do to my sister."

"But, my lord, please have mercy . . ."

Tedric turned a deaf ear to Baudelaire as he trained his gaze upon Guy. "Now you shall learn firsthand about the pit's horrors."

"You truly relish my downfall, Saxon."

"Aye, I admit that I do." Tedric rubbed the scar on his cheek, inflicted by de Bayonne's hand. He remembered clearly how his father had begged the man for his life, only to be cut down like an animal. Two of the knights led Guy out of the stable after they'd taken his sword from him. Two others did the same with Baudelaire.

"You've done well, Antoine," Tedric told the knight.

"Merci, my lord. My loyalty lies with my king and now with you. The men gathered here all decided not to follow de Bayonne, except for Baudelaire. Your keep is now safe from rebellion."

Moments later, as Tedric was leaving the stable, a knight rushed forward, his shoulder bleeding from a large gash. Tedric recognized him as one of the knights who'd led Guy and Baudelaire to the pit. "Lord Tedric, they've escaped!" The knight was out of breath and panting so hard that at first Tedric wasn't certain what he'd said. "Sir Guy and Baudelaire wrestled us to the ground. Sir Guy pulled a dagger from inside his tunic and killed Herbert and stabbed Michel and me. I'm sorry, my lord, so sorry, that they got away."

"But they're on foot, man, we'll find them!"

"No, no, on horseback. Sir Guy's destrier was nearby. They've taken off for the forest!"

Tedric commanded his knights to mount immediately and begin the search for Guy and Baudelaire. It seemed everyone in the keep and bailey was outside, everyone but Amberlie, and he wanted to see her before he mounted up. He saw Magda, and asked her where Amberlie was. At first, Magda didn't look him in the eye, but finally she admitted, "Lady Amberlie rebelled against your orders that she not leave the keep without escort. She required an herb for a poultice for the blacksmith's sick child, my lord. She—she went into the forest—alone. I promised I wouldn't tell you that she'd left the keep, but I fear for her, now that night has fallen and she hasn't returned. I promised that I would not tell you about her condition, but I—must tell you." Magda wrung her hands in agitation, her face clothed in misery. "Lady Amberlie is carrying your babe, Lord Tedric. She shouldn't be abroad now, not with Guy de Bayonne loose."

This was worse than anything Tedric had feared. He could barely speak, but finally he uttered a foul curse as he took his place before his army of knights. "Lady Amberlie hasn't returned to the keep! She must be found—and soon, before de Bayonne finds her and takes her hostage!"

With red and gold banners flying in the chilly evening wind, Tedric and his men rode forth as one.

Amberlie felt entirely justified in leaving the keep without escort. She wasn't a prisoner, but mistress of Woodrose, and needed her herbs and plants for her people. Long ago she'd stopped thinking of them as Saxons and Normans. Now, they were simply people who needed her. The blacksmith's baby girl was ill with the croup. Gundred didn't have the required herb, but the forest did, and Amberlie had left without escort or Tedric's permission to find it.

Dusk was descending. A cool wind blew through

360

the treetops by the time Amberlie found the required herb and was ready to leave the deep woodlands. She trod down the forest path and into the open meadow, hurrying her steps for she wanted to be safely inside Woodrose before dark. Also, she hoped that Tedric hadn't learned from Magda that she'd left the keep. She didn't want to have to argue about her disobedience, her flagrant violation of his command. But she'd done nothing wrong, and refused to suffer for it. Still, she didn't relish another altercation with the man who flaunted his lover before her, humiliating her by his lack of respect for her feelings. Too much had already been said to be readily forgotten, so Amberlie had decided to say as little as possible to Tedric about anything. But soon she'd be forced to tell him about the coming child. Though she'd done her duty by him, she doubted she'd receive the proper respect.

Glancing toward the keep, she noticed a rider approaching, but with the deepening darkness, she couldn't tell who it was. The horse furiously rode in her direction, patches of earth sputtering upwards beneath the horse's hooves. When the rider drew closer, she recognized Guy atop his white destrier, with Baudelaire clinging on behind him. Amberlie wondered why the two men shared the same horse, why they rode so furiously, why they were leaving the keep's protection at sunset. Most probably they'd have ridden past her, but the dying sunlight reflected off the sapphire brooch on her mantle like blue fire and caught Guy's eye. Instead of skirting past her, Guy turned the horse in her direction and halted the animal before her. With a vicious curse, he ordered Baudelaire off the horse, nearly pushing him to the ground in his haste.

"Hand her to me!" he cried to Baudelaire, who captured Amberlie about the waist and hauled her up to Guy before she was aware of their intentions.

"What in the name of heaven are you doing?" Amberlie cried, and dropped her gathering basket onto the grass.

Guy wrapped his arms around her, pinning her within his embrace as he grabbed the reins in his hands. "Doing what I should have done long ago, *cherie*. I've waited much too long for this moment, and now fate has brought you to me."

Baudelaire made a move to climb onto the horse behind Guy, but Guy kicked at him, hitting him in the mouth with the toe of his boot. Instantly, Baudelaire's lips began to bleed. "Have you gone mad! Let me up behind you!" cried the distressed and harried man.

"No! I'm not taking you with me. You can fend for yourself."

"But — but Tedric will kill me!"

"I don't care if you spend the rest of your wretched life in the pit. I've got what I want!" Laughing viciously, Guy painfully jabbed the horse in the side, urging him forward. Resembling a white bolt of lightning, the animal rushed headlong into the woods.

Amberlie had decided that Guy had gone mad. Whenever she demanded that he return her to the keep and insisted he tell her what was happening, he only chuckled gleefully and refused to answer her. His dark-eyed gaze was trained on the gloom ahead of them. He seemed unmoved by Amberlie's trembling, caused by the cold and her own fear. What had happened? she wondered. What was Guy running from? And where did he hope to go? And why take her with him? There were so many questions whirling in her mind, but one was uppermost—would Tedric search for her?

She felt as she had on the night when Tedric had kidnapped her. The burgeoning fear bubbled in her throat, and she thought she'd go mad with her desire to scream, to tear herself out of Guy's arms. They'd ridden for over an hour. She was tired, hungry, and so angry that she'd have gladly scratched Guy's face if she thought it would make him release her. She had no idea where they rode. The wind whipped past them; her white headdress long ago had loosened and blown away. The cold seeped into her very bones until her teeth chattered violently, but still they rode, and still Guy told her nothing.

Finally, they neared the cave which Tedric and the Saxons had inhabited for so many months, the same cave where Tedric had brought her. Guy stopped the horse and without a word, he pulled her down to the ground with him. Amberlie resented his hold on her arm and attempted to break loose, but Guy pulled her, resisting and clawing at him, into the pitch-black cave.

"You're mad!" she cried when he roughly pushed her to the ground.

"I'm far from mad." He pulled the horse inside with them. "Don't think you can try to escape, for

I am all eyes and ears."

"We're going to freeze in here," she protested.

"Then we freeze — together."

Guy sat beside her, wrapping his arms around her. Amberlie pushed at him, but he tightened his hold. "I shall warm you." He laughed and nuzzled her ear.

"Stop it! Stop! What has happened? I have a right to know what I'm doing here."

Guy gave a sigh. "Ah, but you're a tiresome wench, Amberlie, yet still I find you desirable, though you ask too many questions. *Bien,* I will tell you." His lips skirted her lips for a second, but he didn't force himself upon her. It seemed to Amberlie that he took great delight in tormenting her with small physical displays of affection, which he knew she detested. He whispered into her ear, "Your husband wants to kill me. If things had worked out differently this afternoon, he'd be dead and I would be in control of Woodrose. But alas, 'twas not meant to be. I should have slain him like I slew Henri. Then my troubles would be over, and there'd be no need to run."

A shudder rushed through Amberlie, her eyes widened in shock. "You . . . killed . . . Henri?"

"Oui, cherie. Who else?" Guy shrugged. "Ah, you thought your Tedric had murdered him. That's what I wanted everyone to believe. 'Twas better than the truth at the time. How could I admit that I wanted Woodrose and you as my own? Things would have been perfect if only you'd relented and accepted my proposal. Because of you, I'm now an outlaw. But the fates have smiled upon me by plac-

ing you in my path." He claimed her lips in a punishing kiss, laughing when Amberlie pushed hard against him, then wiped her mouth with the back of her hand. "You'll get used to my lovemaking in time."

"I hate you! I'll never give into you! I'd just as soon be dead!"

"Such brave and untrue words. Anything is preferable to death, even me." He smiled a cold, calculating smile. "Now let's rest. We've a long ride ahead of us on the morrow."

"Tedric will search for us. He'll find us," she bravely asserted, but she wasn't certain Tedric would even care if she disappeared from his life.

"I'm not afraid of your barbarian husband," Guy declared as he took out his dagger and went about sharpening it on a rock. "Still, he won't think of looking in the very hiding place he once used. He'll assume I took off for the coast and will somehow return to Normandy. And maybe I shall, but not until Tedric ceases his search." In the murky darkness, Amberlie felt his gaze upon her. "Don't you want to go home to Normandy, *ma petite?* Our times were happy there."

"I want to return to Woodrose and my husband, you murdering cur!"

Guy's eyes flared with anger. "Quiet! You'll still your tongue or I'll knock you senseless. I detest a woman who doesn't know when to keep silent. My late wife opened her mouth one too many times, and I was forced to silence her forever. Don't make me have to resort to such a dreadful deed again."

Amberlie cringed and drew away, wishing she

could melt into the stone wall. She didn't doubt that Guy would do what he threatened. She realized she must mind her tongue or perhaps risk an injury to her child. Because of the child she carried, she wouldn't try an escape at night. But in the morning, if she survived the cold, somehow she'd think of a way to free herself of Guy, though she didn't know how. She knew only that she loathed Guy, hated him more now than she'd ever hated another human being in her life. All of this time she'd thought Tedric had killed Henri, when it had been Guy who'd murdered him. What a foolish woman she'd been!

Tears spiked her lashes, but she refused to shed them and have Guy believe her weak. Inside, she cried for Henri, who'd suffered death at his uncle's hands, and she cried for Tedric and for what could have been—if only she'd listened to her heart instead of her head.

Tedric and his mounted knights halted in the forest. The ceaseless chirping of crickets broke the stillness. "Lord Tedric, we can't go any further tonight. Perhaps in the morning . . ." Christophe began, but Tedric broke him off with an angry shake of his head.

"Nay, 'twill be too late by then. De Bayonne probably believes we'll not continue because of the dark. If only Baudelaire knew where Guy was headed."

"You questioned him at length, my lord. He knew not what Sir Guy had in mind."

Tedric nodded, relieved that they'd captured Baudelaire soon after riding into the forest. The man had been quite agitated over having been abandoned by Guy de Bayonne, but he'd admitted that Guy had taken Amberlie captive and pointed in the direction Guy had ridden. Where was Guy truly headed—to the coast or deeper into the woodlands? And Amberlie, was she all right? He dreaded thinking about the harm that could befall her. Above all else, even if it meant allowing de Bayonne to escape, he wanted Amberlie safely back. She carried his baby. His child was now growing within her. If only she was returned to him, there were so many things he would say to her. Really one thing he'd say to her, the one thing he'd wanted to tell her from the very beginning and was too prideful to admit.

He loved her.

The very knowledge set his heart to thumping hard within his chest. If there was a merciful God, then God would see that his wife was returned unharmed to him so he could get on his knees before her. He'd beg her to forgive him for the wrongs he'd done to her, even for things he hadn't done, if only she was safely returned.

"Lord Tedric, I've found something!" Flaubert, acting as a scout, had ridden ahead of the others. The man reined in next to Tedric and solemnly presented him with a white linen headdress. It belonged to Amberlie.

Tedric clasped the material in his hand and surveyed the darkened landscape. He knew the forest well and the landmarks within it. Now he knew that de Bayonne hadn't headed for the coast at all; the headdress was proof of Guy's direction. "I know where de Bayonne has taken my wife," he told Christophe. "And I will hunt down the man and kill him . . . alone."

"But, my lord, you cannot. De Bayonne is dangerous," Christophe protested, much concerned about Tedric's safety.

"He is no more dangerous than a cornered fox. I can make better time alone, rather than having all of you trampling with me through the forest at night. Most of you are unfamiliar with the surroundings, but I know the woods well." Tedric positioned the sword at his side and gazed resolutely ahead. "The time has come for old grievances to be paid, and I'll make certain that de Bayonne pays his due to me." Without a further word to Christophe, Tedric kicked at the black gelding's flanks, and within seconds, his figure was lost in the dark recesses of the woods.

It was the destrier who sensed Tedric's presence first. The large animal lifted its white head and whinnied softly.

Amberlie, who had been dozing, came suddenly awake. She noticed Guy's shadowy form, standing in the cave's opening, illuminated somewhat by a small fire which Guy had started to warm them. "The beast senses something," he told her when he turned to find her staring at him. He clenched his dagger in his hand. "We're not alone."

Tedric! Amberlie somehow knew Tedric had

found them, but she knew better than to say this to Guy. She swallowed hard, her pulse pounding. And then she saw her husband's looming figure behind Guy's and gave an involuntary gasp that alerted Guy to Tedric's presence. Tedric lifted his sword, the silver flashing like moonfire as his voice filled the cave. "De Bayonne!" Guy, with a mocking grin on his face, didn't turn at the harsh summons. Instead he took Tedric completely by surprise when he fell to his knees and swiftly rolled into the shadows, out of Tedric's vision, and behind the horse.

Guy's jeweled dagger flew through the air, finding its mark in Tedric's right shoulder. Amberlie's screams rent the air as a rush of red stained Tedric's tunic. She heard Tedric give a muffled groan, and saw him lower his right arm to his side, almost as if he'd lost all sensation. With his other hand, he pulled the blade from his flesh, ill prepared to deflect the punishing blow which Guy delivered to Tedric's stomach with his fist. The wind rushed from him, and Tedric fell to his knees and dropped the dagger. Guy took the sword from Tedric's hand.

Standing over Tedric's prostrate form, Guy sneered. "Saxon, your end is much too tame for a warrior of barbarians. I thought you'd present more of a challenge. See, Amberlie, how your fearsome Saxon cowers upon the ground. If only King William could see his brave knight now."

In the firelight, Amberlie saw the dagger, but realized it was too far from Tedric's hand. If only she could reach it . . .

Stealthily, she rose from her position by the wall. Guy seemed totally unaware of her movements as he delighted in seeing Tedric upon the ground. Tedric noticed her, and for only an instant she thought he was silently warning her to keep away, but his eyes then riveted on de Bayonne. "I ask that you release Amberlie, send her back to Woodrose," Tedric said.

"Ah, how noble of you, wanting to save your wife's life, but Amberlie is perfectly safe with me. I plan many uses for her lovely body. Sending her away isn't in my plans."

Just a few more feet and she'd have the dagger. If only Tedric could keep Guy's attention diverted . . .

"Amberlie, touch the dagger and I'll run the Saxon through now!" Guy didn't move his eyes from Tedric or from the sword that he placed by Tedric's throat. With a long swipe of his arm, he grabbed Amberlie's wrist and jerked her roughly beside him. An arrogant, pleased grin turned up his lips. "See, Saxon, I have her and she belongs to me. I do wish you'd have made our little battle more interesting. I hate running through a man who puts up no resistance, but then it was that way with your father too, if I recall."

"He begged for his life!" Tedric savagely reminded him.

"*Oui,* he did. Will you beg for yours?"

"I beg only that you see reason and release my wife unharmed. You can't escape. My men will hunt you down."

"Oh, your men, is it?" Guy scoffed in disbelief,

his eyes filled with bitter hatred. "I trained them, they obeyed me, until the king took a fancy to you. I should have killed you when I captured you instead of returning you to Woodrose."

"But you did return me," Tedric said with equal bitterness, "so you could impress the king, but it didn't work, did it?"

The tip of the blade grazed Tedric's throat, and Amberlie had no doubt that Guy would have ended Tedric's life at that moment. But a howling wind rushed through the cave at that second, and she heard a voice. "Avenge me, Avenge me!" She knew it was Henri, and she wasn't the only one to hear it.

"Who's there!" Guy rasped, and drew back the sword to fight the faceless intruder.

" 'Tis Henri," she whispered, realizing now exactly whom Henri wished vengeance upon.

"What sort of trick is this?" Guy's hand tightened painfully on her wrist as his gaze met hers. She saw his face was ashen, the voice having frightened him more than Guy would admit. But she knew what Henri wanted, and she didn't hesitate to tell him so.

" 'Tis no trick. Henri wants your death." She saw that Guy was about to contradict her through pale lips, but suddenly Tedric made it to his knees and pushed at Guy. She found herself falling to the ground and Guy with her. Tedric now possessed the dagger, but Guy still held the sword. During the fall, Guy's hold on her wrist had loosened, and she scuttled from the fray just as Guy lifted the sword to land a fatal blow upon Tedric.

But Tedric blocked him with the dagger, using his right arm, which somehow had miraculously regained strength.

Guy clung with both hands to the sword, but Tedric's tenacious assault with one arm was so powerful that Guy eventually dropped the weapon. "Go on, kill me, you bastard," Guy hissed, "if you're man enough to take me down."

Tedric dragged Guy to his feet by the neck of his tunic. "I think you should end your days in the pit, just as you planned for my end."

"Never! I am a knight. The pit is for lowly Saxons. I'd rather a swift end to my life, but you haven't the nerve. You're as spineless as Henri, the little toad."

At that moment, a very odd thing happened. In later years Tedric would be unable to explain it, admitting that he hadn't intended to end de Bayonne's life in such a way but had meant to make him suffer for his father's death. But Amberlie knew and as she watched, she knew Henri was about to have his revenge.

The fire began to flicker and die as a cold, rough wind whipped through the cave, pushed Tedric into Guy. The dagger in Tedric's hand lurched forward of its own volition, impaling itself in Guy's rib cage and instantly finding his heart. Guy fell with a horrified expression on his face, his gaze somewhere beyond Tedric, almost as if he'd seen something so terrible that death would be only the beginning of his sufferings. He slumped to his knees, and Tedric released him to fall at his feet.

Strangely, the fire began to glow again. "I didn't mean . . . I don't know how that happened." Tedric looked down at the bloody dagger in his hand, bafflement on his face. Then he opened his arms to her. The bleeding on his shoulder had stopped and she ran to him, to revel in his protective caress. Tedric stroked her hair. "Did he hurt you? Are you all right?" he asked with such concern that tears sprang to Amberlie's eyes.

"I'm fine — fine. But I didn't think you'd come for me when Glenna has your heart."

"I don't care for Glenna, she means nothing to me any longer. I feared only that I'd never see you again," he admitted.

"I worried the very same thing." She was greatly relieved that he didn't love Glenna, but he hadn't said he loved her either and she had to hide her hurt. "Forgive me for believing you'd murdered Henri. I know now that Guy killed him. I can never make up for the things I've said to you, the way I've treated you. I beg only that you can understand."

" 'Tis nothing to forgive for you didn't know me. You thought I was a barbarian. I beg your forgiveness for I know you didn't poison me. My fault was the greater for I knew all along you were incapable of harming me."

"Oh, Tedric, I think we were both at fault."

He kissed her sweetly, and there were tears in his eyes.

Then he held her about the waist, dropping the dagger beside Guy's lifeless body. "He should be buried with it," he said.

" 'Tis most fitting," she agreed, but not for the reason Tedric thought. She'd recognized the dagger when Guy had handled it hours earlier, remembering full well the small jewels on the hilt, for she'd been the one who'd chosen them five years before in Normandy, as part of her wedding gift to Henri. It was appropriate that Guy de Bayonne should be buried with Henri's weapon, a weapon which had been wielded by an unseen force.

As Tedric led her and Guy's horse outside the cave, the moon's bright glow cast a lovely silver patina over the forest. Settling herself into a comfortable position before Tedric on the black gelding, Amberlie sighed her relief, for she knew that she'd no longer be plagued by Henri's ghost.

"Let's ride home, my lady." Tedric's voice sent shivers of desire down her spine. She gazed up at him with soft, dark eyes.

"With pleasure, my lord."

Chapter Twenty-six

Tedric let Amberlie sleep. Though dawn had broken hours earlier, she'd been so exhausted when they returned to the keep that he felt it best she not expend her energy seeing to the household that day. Besides, she carried his child and needed her rest.

He'd long since sent some of the knights back to the cave to retrieve de Bayonne's body and bury it beside Julianne's in holy ground. Father Ambrose had said a quick prayer over it, and now all that remained of Guy de Bayonne and his treachery was a mound of earth.

As Tedric sat upon the dais, he flexed his shoulder. Gundred had placed a cooling salve upon it earlier and bound it with linen cloth. Strangely, the pain which had burned like a brand when the dagger struck was absent. He was a bit stiff, but it was nothing that he couldn't deal with. He sipped a goblet containing mead and smiled to himself. Just that morning Flaubert had hesitantly approached him and asked to wed Edytha. Tedric had agreed, knowing that Edytha must be given the chance to lead a normal life. He had no doubt that Flaubert would take excellent care of her, for it was obvious that the man loved her. He'd already asked Edytha what she wanted, and his sister had shyly agreed to the marriage, taking Flaubert's hand in hers. Aye, thought Tedric, Edytha was more sound of mind then he or his mother had realized.

He was more than a bit startled when Christophe came tearing into the great hall with Glenna in tow. Clearly she'd been crying, for her eyes were red-rimmed and puffy.

"My lord, Lady Glenna has a confession to make," Christophe revealed, and pulled her up beside him.

"Shouldn't she confess to Father Ambrose?"

Christophe pushed her toward Tedric on the dais. "Go on, tell him."

Glenna looked imploringly at Christophe, but she saw only his rock-hard demeanor. She wiped at her tear-stained cheek. "I—I have done you an injustice, Tedric. I, uh . . ." She faltered, but was driven on by the light twist Christophe gave to her wrist and lowered her gaze to the floor. "I made Edytha lie and tell you that Amberlie didn't want the circlet for her morning gift." She looked up at him. " 'Tis only because I see that you love this Norman woman that I tell you this." Glenna swallowed hard. "Edytha found the circlet on the pillow—I saw her with it. I realized that Amberlie hadn't seen it, and I . . . knew

376

she'd be humiliated before everyone if she didn't wear it on the morn after the wedding. And you'd be too proud to ask her why she refused it. 'Tis all I could think of to make you hate her — but you didn't turn away from her."

"And what has brought about this sudden change of heart?" Tedric asked, feeling extremely light-headed and lighthearted.

"I know now what it means to love truly," Glenna said.

Christophe tenderly placed his arm around Glenna's waist and beseeched Tedric in a restrained voice. "If you could forgive her, my lord, I promise that Glenna will wreak no more havoc in your life. I ask for your permission to marry her that I may take her in hand."

"You'll have your hands full, Christophe, but aye, I grant permission. I always thought you should wed her."

"Then you forgive me?" Glenna asked breathlessly.

Tedric laughed heartily, and left the dais to sweep Glenna off of her feet and swing her about the great hall. "Aye, I forgive you, I forgive everyone this day!" Tedric handed her over to Christophe and sped from the hall.

Glenna giggled, pleased that she'd escaped Tedric's wrath so easily, and burrowed into Christophe's embrace, the place where she knew she truly belonged. " 'Tis strange how he behaves."

" 'Tis *amour, cherie,*" was Christophe's assessment, and he smiled down at the woman whom he loved with his whole heart.

"Mother, the circlet! Where is it?" Tedric bounded into Lady Mabel's room, looking much younger than his years, almost like an eager child.

A worried frown creased her brow as she pointed to the chest. "You don't mean to give it to your wife, do you? She rejected it . . . how can you . . ."

Tedric kissed her cheek, breaking off her protests. He smiled down at his mother, who, well-fed and safe in her own home at last, had regained her health. "She never rejected it in the first place. 'Twas Glenna's spiteful doing, and she used Edytha in her plan, but I hold no grudge. I also know Amberlie didn't poison me."

"To think of the way I've treated the poor child!" Mabel cried. "I will beg her forgiveness immediately!"

"Wait until later, Mother. I've plans for my bride." Opening the chest, Tedric took the circlet from it and removed the cloth. Sunshine reflected off the garnets and bathed the room in a rosy glow. The morning gift, and such a perfect morning to bestow it upon his wife.

Amberlie woke slowly from sleep, snuggling into the mattress like a kitten, feeling protected and wanted. At the light kiss placed on the tip of her nose, she wakened to see Tedric in bed next to her. And from the way her legs were wrapped around his, she knew he was naked beneath the pelts.

"Good morning, sleepyhead," he whispered.

"Have I overslept? 'Tis much to do." Amberlie made a move to get up, but Tedric stopped her with his hand.

"Nay, all you must do is see to me this day." His forefinger traced her lips. "But when you do rise, I should like you to wear this." Tedric reached beneath the pillow and withdrew the circlet, presenting it to her with such love, adoration, and desire on his face that Amberlie shivered.

The circlet. Her throat choked with some inexplicable emotion, and it took some minutes for her to speak. "Why do you give it to me now, my lord? 'Twas due me on the morn after our wedding night."

Tedric kissed her brow and then explained about Glenna's manipulation of his sister. Amberlie listened quietly, realizing that Tedric had always intended to give her the gift, that he *had* given it to her. Strangely, she didn't hold a grudge against Glenna — she was just so happy to know that Tedric had truly been pleased with her, had cared enough about her to bestow this gift upon her.

He placed the circlet on her head. Amberlie smiled a brilliant smile that rivaled the bright day outside. "Thank you, Tedric. I'll cherish this for the rest of my life until I give it to our son's wife." Suddenly a happy tear filled the corner of her eye. "I'm carrying your child."

"Oh, Amberlie, I'm so glad." He drew her

against him, not admitting that he'd known since Magda had told him. "I knew my seed would take."

"Oh, you're a conceited and arrogant Saxon!" she cried good-naturedly, and pushed playfully at him. "You knew no such thing."

He grabbed her hand and kissed it. "I know one thing, my lady."

"And what is that?"

"I'm in love with you."

The breath stilled in her throat. Never had she expected Tedric to fall in love with her. The gift of the circlet paled in comparison to this startling news. Her voice was honey-smooth, warm, and filled with desire when she said, "I'm in love with you too, Tedric. I love you beyond all else in this world."

"Amberlie, love!" He reached for her, pulling her against his hard chest. His lips touched hers in a deep kiss that stirred the banked fires within her. She moaned, swept away by the scorching passion that only Tedric could fan within her by his touch, his kiss. With eager fingers, Tedric removed her shift. Naked and aching for his possession, Amberlie linked her arms around his neck.

He broke the kiss and set her atop him. Then he reclaimed her mouth, unleashing all of the love he felt for her. His hands adoringly stroked the lush curves of her breasts before his lips broke away from hers to claim the pearled peaks. Gently he tugged, then laved each nipple with his tongue. Amberlie arched against his mouth, needing to lose herself in his tender warmth. When Tedric's questing fingers trailed the length of her silken thighs to find the pulsing bud between her legs, Amberlie gasped in pleasure. "Open for me, my sweet lady," he softly urged. Amberlie willingly and wantonly obeyed.

Slowly he inserted his forefinger into her, finding her already primed and wet for him. Amberlie softly inhaled, and began a heated exploration of his shoulders and chest with her fingers. And then she slightly shifted her position, her perfectly rounded bottom contacting with his hard and pulsating shaft as she settled more comfortably upon him. Tedric quivered with his own need, his body taut like a bowstring. "You taunt me beyond redemption, my love," he whispered huskily. "Another move and I shall claim you body and soul."

Amberlie's eyes glowed brighter than flames. "Then do so, Tedric. I—I need you so much! I want to belong to you forever." She purposely arched upwards, opening herself to him like rose petals seeking the sun's warmth. Tedric groaned, lost, lost to the passion and love he felt for her, knowing that having claimed her love, he possessed a treasure far greater than precious jewels.

Tedric slowly slid into her, filling her body with his need, his adoration, his love. Amberlie welcomed him, delighting in the power of his possession, whispering how much she loved him with each rapturous thrust. And then in a starburst of mutual ecstasy, they reached the pinnacle before gently tumbling back to earth.

Later, Tedric held her in his arms, and he smiled. Never had he seen Amberlie more beautiful than in that blissful moment when she'd reached the summit, and the circlet caught the sunlight and haloed her face. He knew their passion would never falter, that in years to come, she'd be as receptive to his touch, and he'd be as lusty for her. He loved this woman and would love her forever. He felt Amberlie's dark gaze upon him. "What is it, my heart? Didn't I please you?"

"Very much, but I have one request of you."

He cocked a wary brow, then smiled. "I shall do my best to make you happy."

Her fingers ran through his short hair. " 'Tis your hair. I know the fashion is what the king wears, but I thought you might let it grow to please me."

"You liked it long?"

She nodded. "You looked wild and untamed."

"Ah, so you want me to look the beast, you want me to devour you."

Amberlie blushed. "You've done that many times."

"I'll do anything you want, my lady, anything at all. I love you so that words fail me."

"Then show me not with words, my lord."

Wrapped in her knight's caress, she exulted as he showed her—magnificently.

DANA RANSOM'S RED-HOT HEARTFIRES!

ALEXANDRA'S ECSTASY   (2773, $3.75)
Alexandra had known Tucker for all her seventeen years,
but all at once she realized her childhood friend was the
man capable of tempting her to leave innocence behind!

LIAR'S PROMISE   (2881, $4.25)
Kathryn Mallory's sincere questions about her father's
ship to the disreputable Captain Brady Rogan were met
with mocking indifference. Then he noticed her trim waist,
angelic face and Kathryn won the wrong kind of attention!

LOVE'S GLORIOUS GAMBLE   (2497, $3.75)
Nothing could match the true thrill that coursed through
Gloria Daniels when she first spotted the gambler, Sterling
Caulder. Experiencing his embrace, feeling his lips against
hers would be a risk, but she was willing to chance it all!

WILD, SAVAGE LOVE   (3055, $4.25)
Evangeline, set free from Indians, discovered liberty had
its price to pay when her uncle sold her into marriage to
Royce Tanner. Dreaming of her return to the people she
loved, she vowed never to submit to her husband's caress.

WILD WYOMING LOVE   (3427, $4.25)
Lucille Blessing had no time for the new marshal Sam
Zachary. His mocking and arrogant manner grated her
nerves, yet she longed to ease the tension she knew he held
inside. She knew that if he wanted her, she could never say
no!

*Available wherever paperbacks are sold, or order direct from the
Publisher. Send cover price plus 50¢ per copy for mailing and
handling to Zebra Books, Dept. 4045, 475 Park Avenue South,
New York, N.Y. 10016. Residents of New York and Tennessee
must include sales tax. DO NOT SEND CASH. For a free Zebra/
Pinnacle catalog please write to the above address.*

LET ARCHER AND CLEARY
AWAKEN AND CAPTURE YOUR HEART!

CAPTIVE DESIRE (2612, $3.75)
by Jane Archer

Victoria Malone fancied herself a great adventuress and student of life, but being kidnapped by handsome Cord Cordova was too much excitement for even her! Convincing her kidnapper that she had been an innocent bystander when the stagecoach was robbed was futile when he was kissing her until she was senseless!

REBEL SEDUCTION (3249, $4.25)
by Jane Archer

"Stop that train!" came Lacey Whitmore's terrified warning as she rushed toward the locomotive that carried wounded Confederates and her own beloved father. But no one paid heed, least of all the Union spy Clint McCullough, who pinned her to the ground as the train suddenly exploded into flames.

DREAM'S DESIRE (3093, $4.50)
by Gwen Cleary

Desperate to escape an arranged marriage, Antonia Winston y Ortega fled her father's hacienda to the arms of the arrogant Captain Domino. She would spend the night with him and would be free for no gentleman wants a ruined bride. And ruined she would be, for Tonia would never forget his searing kisses!

VICTORIA'S ECSTASY (2906, $4.25)
by Gwen Cleary

Proud Victoria Torrington was short of cash to run her shipping empire, so she traveled to America to meet her partner for the first time. Expecting a withered, ancient cowhand, Victoria didn't know what to do when she met virile, muscular Judge Colston and her body budded with desire.

Available wherever paperbacks are sold, or order direct from the Publisher. Send cover price plus 50¢ per copy for mailing and handling to Zebra Books, Dept. 4045, 475 Park Avenue South, New York, N.Y. 10016. Residents of New York and Tennessee must include sales tax. DO NOT SEND CASH. For a free Zebra/ Pinnacle catalog please write to the above address.